BOOKS BY TAMMARA WEBBER

CONTOURS OF THE HEART® series:

Easy

Breakable

Sweet

Brave

BETWEEN THE LINES series:

Between the Lines

Where You Are

Good For You

Here Without You

tammara webber

Sweet

a Contours of the Heart novel

SWEET

Cover Design by Damonza

To Hannah

A smart, tough, logical girl
with a mushy center

chapter *One*

BOYCE

Bud Wynn died this morning. According to the attending physician, time of death was 5:23 a.m. He died of liver disease, of cirrhosis, of complications from ascites that caused heart failure—any and all of these would be true enough, I reckon.

I say he died of booze, because that's truer than anything else.

Under the fluorescent lights of the hallway, everybody in that hospital looked a step closer to death than they probably were. I'm sure I was no exception—but I didn't intend to die anytime soon. It might have made me a cold-blooded bastard, but the reason I didn't intend to die was because I was finally free. Free of that gutless, mean old man. Free of the asshole who'd chased off my mother and brother—one to disappear into the dark like a weightless shadow, the other into a grave in Arlington National Cemetery. Free of the charge I took of his final days because nobody else wanted charge of them.

Two minutes after the doctor gave me time alone with the body to say my good-byes, I emerged dry-eyed and signed the papers authorizing the crematory to take him. They would slide him into a refrigerated box in the wall, and there he'd wait out the necessary forty-eight hours until he could be returned to dust. It's what he'd wanted.

"No fucking funeral," he'd wheezed from his piece-of-shit recliner when I came in one night about six months ago, like we'd been in the middle of a conversation. I paused in the doorway but didn't answer. "No goddamned casket. And for chrissake, no crap-ass service. Just toss my ashes in the gulf." Something in my face must have told him I wouldn't be toting his remains to the water at sunset in some sham memorial. "Or the john. Makes me no nevermind."

That was our only conversation about his looming death.

As the sun rose over the gulf, I came home to a place that was somehow different from the shitty single-wide I'd left hours before, because this time he would never return. I'd been claiming it a bit at a time for years now—hard-won territory, every inch—the trailer and the small brick building it leaned into: Wynn's Garage. But neither had belonged to me. Not until today.

Leaving the front door open, I walked straight up to the stained recliner, deep-sea blue in a former life, now faded and held together with duct tape and loose bolts. Dragging it from its corner, I pulled it across the soiled carpet and rammed it through the front door, down the cracked concrete steps, and into the yard. I stared where it sat harmless and ugly on the dead grass.

I picked it up and moved it to the middle of the asphalt driveway the trailer shared with the garage. Pulling my lighter and smokes from my front pocket, I stared at that chair, memories of my father rushing over me one after another until they all blended into one where I entered the room and he said, "Get me a beer before you go out that door, you worthless dumbass" from that chair. I'd fetch a can from the twenty-four-pack in the fridge and hand it to him, stretching out my arm so he'd be less able to grab my wrist and twist it, or yank me closer and punch a fist into my shoulder, my side, my stomach.

Most of the time, he'd just take the beer, his eyes glued to the flickering screen. One time in five, he'd try to get hold of me. My heart rate sped, remembering. I never knew when he'd lunge and when he'd just snatch the can from my hand and ignore me.

I lit the end of a Camel Crush and sucked in smoke and nicotine-aided calm.

Once, when I was seventeen, he'd punched me so hard I couldn't breathe for nearly a minute. I thought I was going to die. Stumbling and knocking over the coffee table as I fell just pissed him off more. He lunged and swung again, but I ducked and he missed. A first. That made him furious, and he came at me just as I hit the floor and my lungs decided to unlock and let me live. He kicked me once before I rolled to my feet and realized I'd grown as tall as him in the past few months. He still outweighed me then, but that thought didn't enter my mind. I was desperate and enraged and scared as hell.

I threw a fist straight into his face, and his nose crunched just like anybody else's. Why that fact surprised me, I don't know. But in that moment, he'd reached the end of his godlike reign over me. I saw the realization of it in his eyes as he staggered and swung, missing again. For the first time, I stepped forward instead of falling back. I lashed out instead of cowering. I hit instead of got hit.

He was bloodied and gasping when I backed toward the door—laboring to breathe, inhaling and exhaling and *alive* and unhurt but for my bloodied fists. I pointed like the grim reaper. "Don't. Ever. Fucking. Hit me. Again."

"Get the fuck out of my house!" he'd hollered, the weak squawk of an old man.

"You won't live forever," I'd said, but he hadn't heard me.

I flicked the still-burning butt onto the seat of that chair, where it smoldered and sank like a crab burrowing down into the sand, leaving only a black-ringed hole. I'd gone to pull my lighter from my pocket again when there was a sudden, gratifying *whoosh* as the seat went up in flames.

I took a step back and pulled out another cigarette, lit and started it, watching that chair turn into a squarish pillar of fire that would soon be reduced to ashes.

"Good-bye, Dad," I said.

Pearl

My hands gripped the wheel, and I took a slow breath as if I were psyching myself to lift a heavy weight or dive off a cliff. Southbound 181 remained a familiar blur of scrubby grass, gnarled mesquites, and mile after mile of weathered wire and post fencing. The monotonous view usually comforted me, every mile marker bringing me closer to home. Today, the closer I got the more aware I was of the confrontation I'd been avoiding for months and the fact that I couldn't dodge it any longer.

A lifetime of camouflage fell away, and I was left with nothing but the truth of who I was and the fact that soon everyone else would know. I swallowed hard, reality tightening its fist around my windpipe.

"Mama, I'm not going to medical school." I forced the words out, testing their impact on my own ears.

I knew my mother well, and while I'd certainly disappointed her before—my shy approach to social situations manifesting in an inevitable lack of leadership qualities, for example—this was disappointment at an unprecedented level. Medical school had been her goal for me my entire life. *Our* goal for me. Until I realized—with crushing clarity, in the middle of a Harvard interview last fall—that joining the medical profession wasn't what I wanted to do with the rest of my life.

I'd ended up waitlisted at Harvard. My near-4.0 undergrad GPA and above-average MCAT scores weren't the reason I'd failed to receive unconditional admittance. The premed associations I'd joined, the internships I'd completed, my sorority membership and exemplary letters of reference—these things weren't at fault.

The determining factor had been my mouth, opening and closing in fishlike absurdity instead of giving a coherent answer to a perfectly standard question from the faculty member leading the interview.

"Ms. Frank," she'd begun, raising her eyes from the paperwork on the table in front of her and pinning me with a focused smile, "tell us, please—what reservations might you have about joining the medical profession?"

There was nothing accusatory in her tone. She'd undoubtedly posed this question before and expected a competent, thoughtful answer in return. Here was the chance to affirm my desire to study medicine at a university that produces highly skilled physicians (*such as Harvard*). A nervous applicant might offer a chuckled comment about paying back formidable med-school loans. A self-confident candidate like my boyfriend, Mitchell, might declare: *I have no reservations; I've always wanted to be a doctor.*

Instead, all I could think was, *I don't want to.* My mouth worked in desperation, trying to find other, more appropriate words to say, but they wouldn't come.

I eventually blurted something inane, and after an awkward pause, the Q&A progressed to other interrogations. I made no further blunders as we discussed my premed preparations, methods of handling personal and educational challenges, and the ways I imagined the healthcare profession might change in the near future.

But in the taxi back to my hotel, all I could recall was that one question and the host of suitable answers I *hadn't* given. Once in my room, I'd called Mitchell and answered his post-interview debriefing with a vague, "It was fine. I'm just sort of beat." I couldn't put my newfound self-awareness into words over the phone. When he didn't press for performance specifics, I wasn't sure if he believed I was too tired to elaborate or if he was merely preoccupied with his own interview schedule. He'd just returned from Durham and would be in Cambridge in two weeks. He'd want to dissect every aspect of Harvard's interview process before he arrived.

I went to sleep hoping the whole thing was just passing insanity, but by the time Mitchell picked me up at the airport the next afternoon, I'd only grown more certain—I didn't want to go to medical school. We'd planned our corresponding futures like we each planned everything else in our lives: every detail strategically premeditated, every probability accounted for. Except for the one where he went on to medical school and I... didn't.

That night, over short ribs at Péché, I confided the truth to him.

Brows drawn, he finished chewing, wiped his fingers, and sipped his pisco sour before answering. "What do you mean, you don't see yourself going to medical school? It sure sounds like you flubbed that interview—with *Harvard* too, Jesus—but you've got several others lined up. You'll get in somewhere. Duke. Vanderbilt. UT Southwestern, if it comes to that. Stop being so defeatist."

I'd been dating Mitchell for over a year, but I'd never been able to get used to his fallback insistence that I maintain a "positive attitude" whenever I raised a concern or wanted to discuss some apprehension. Optimism is all fine and good, but it has squat to do with solving problems. You'd think as a future doctor, he would know that. But then, sometimes it also seemed that the need for compulsory enthusiasm only applied to *me*.

"I'm not being defeatist, Mitchell. I'm trying to tell you that I don't want to be a doctor—not a medical doctor, anyway. So it doesn't matter whether I can get in or where." I knew he was disappointed and probably shocked, so I gave him time to absorb the blow I'd just dealt our future together.

He was quiet for a full two minutes, and then—"Are you fucking kidding me?"

His set jaw and rigid gaze were all too familiar. Months before, we were alone in his dorm room, studying for an exam in organic chemistry, when I got a text from a guy in my technical-writing class. "Why are you getting a text from that guy?" he'd said.

"We're friends. And he was texting me about an assignment, Mitchell."

"Do I look stupid?" His face warmed to a livid red, spittle at the corner of his mouth, and his fingers dug into my upper arms, immobilizing me. He glared at the phone in my hand. "Why won't you fucking tell me what's really going on?"

I gasped, my mouth hanging open. "*Nothing* is going on." I jerked loose from his grip and stood, backing away, only to trip over his roommate's shoes, fall backward, and collide with a desk chair on the way down.

Minutes later, while pressing an ice pack to the goose egg on the back of my skull, Mitchell apologized repeatedly. "I'm sorry—God, I'm so sorry—of course I trust you. These are my insecurities, leftovers from what Darla did to me, you know?" Darla—his freshman-year girlfriend who'd cheated on him with his best friend and broken his heart. "Please, Pearl. You know I didn't mean for you to get hurt. I'll never talk to you like that again, I swear." His blue eyes were glassy with tears.

I'd forgiven him in the end, accepting his sworn promises.

"Are you. Fucking. Kidding me?" he repeated from across the table, snapping those months-old vows like they'd never been given.

Despite the music pumping through the packed restaurant and the voices raised in conversation all around us, the two women at an adjoining table heard him. Both went silent, sliding looks between each other and the developing scene at our table. Mortified, I sensed them deliberating whether or not to intervene. I hated being a spectacle almost as much as I hated what he'd said, and he knew it.

I leaned in, face on fire, voice low. "Mitchell, not here."

"*Not here*?" He angled his head as if he was offended. "You decided to drop this on me here. Maybe you should have considered where you wanted to have this absurd discussion instead of trying to tell me how to react to the fact that my girlfriend is tossing her future away—and *mine*, by the way—like it's no big deal."

His words snuck under my arguments, igniting guilt that what I decided could alter the course of both our futures, not just mine.

"I'm not trying to tell you what to do. I thought we could discuss this—"

"Sure, sure. Let's discuss it. So what are you planning to do instead with your degree in premed biology? Teach high school? Work in some mind-numbing lab for the rest of your life? Oh, wait—I know." He sat back, mouth settling into a hostile smile. "Slink back to your sheltered small-town existence, away from the big bad world, and collect shells or diagnose fish allergies or whatever the hell you did last summer. Is that your brilliant plan?"

Indignant, I sat back and crossed my arms, refusing to answer. I hated when he ridiculed my hometown—a habit that had worsened instead of improving after he'd visited for a week the previous summer. Though he'd seemed impressed with my parents' bayfront property and had spent as much time discussing his surgical aspirations and opinions about the medical profession with my stepdad as he spent with me, he still insisted my homesickness was juvenile. Something to be outgrown.

He dipped his face into my field of vision and peered at me. "Oh Jesus—*seriously*? Have you lost your mind, Pearl? You must be certifiable, because no sensible person would sacrifice the chance to attend one of the top medical schools in the world to work with *fish*."

We'd almost broken up that night, but once back in my room, he convinced me that he was only concerned I was acting rashly.

He begged me to reconsider. "You just have cold feet," he said. "You'll see."

So I agreed to continue the med-school interviews, consider the offers of admission, and even accept one of them: Vanderbilt, in Tennessee—one of two that had also accepted him.

Meanwhile, I took the GRE and applied—on the final date to submit an application—to one graduate program in marine biology, located, as Mitchell predicted, in my hometown. I told myself that if I didn't get in, I would go to medical school like everyone expected me to and no one would ever know I'd applied.

In December, I got the acceptance e-mail. Fellowships had been allocated months before, but I was offered a small stipend—just enough to cover tuition, fees, and equipment—in exchange for working in the lab or collecting marine samples in the gulf. I was welcome to begin in summer, but the student apartments—weatherworn but beachfront—were full. Unlike other students, however, my parents owned a four-thousand-square-foot home minutes from campus. I wouldn't need housing.

There'd be no high-paid position awaiting me when I earned my degree, and most people would never quite understand what I did for a living or why. A lifetime spent studying the ocean and the life in it wasn't something people did for money or social prestige. It was something they were drawn to, like people are drawn to the sea itself. I would discover my research niche in grad school—something environmental in scope—and spend my career building a body of work to support it.

Instead of going to medical school and becoming the surgeon I'd always planned to be.

I'd stared at that screen while rational arguments for bowing out, alternating between the voices of my boyfriend and my mother, played on a loop through my mind. But the mounting elation in the pit of my soul obliterated them. Growing up on the coast, I'd been witness to the devastation, aquatic and human, caused by oil leaks and spills. But there was more to it than seagulls slicked with oil and globs of tar polluting the beach, and marine scientists were the ones who explored those far-reaching consequences. I wanted to be part of that research.

It had taken me a month to tell Mitchell. The first weekend back after winter break, we were watching a movie in my room—rather, he was watching while I was being consumed by guilt for letting him believe we would be going to Tennessee together in six months.

Finally, I sat forward and knotted my fingers in my lap. *Say it, say it, say it.* "So, about Vanderbilt…"

"I had an idea," he interrupted, hitting the Mute button. "Let's go to Nashville over spring break and look for an apartment. If we find something, we can put down a deposit and know we have a place waiting for us in July."

"Mitchell, I'm not going to Vanderbilt." The words rang in the silence following them.

A dark storm brewed in his eyes, but he made no reply at all—just stared at me. While I couldn't blame him for being stunned, his unrelenting muteness unnerved me.

"I'm not breaking up with you," I continued. "I'm just choosing a different graduate studies route. We can make this work—lots of couples maintain long-distance relationships successfully. We should both be able to choose to do what we want with our lives and careers, you at Vanderbilt and me—"

"This is all or nothing." The words seemed to come from some unseen source. The muscles in his face had hardened into a mask of anger. His lips hadn't moved. "All or nothing, Pearl."

I'd expected frustration—resentment even, that I was canceling our plans, but I hadn't anticipated an ultimatum. His threat made no sense. Success in medical school required a solid commitment. We both knew this. And I knew I didn't feel it. "Then I guess it's nothing," I said, throat clogged with unshed tears.

"You *bitch*!"

I flinched, mouth falling open, certain everyone in the sorority house had heard him—and bonus, since it was one a.m., nearly everyone was home.

He jumped up, roaring, "You selfish *bitch*!"

I wanted to yell back, to tell him to get out, get out *now*, but I was immobilized except for the tremors hurtling down my arms and legs. I'd never been genuinely afraid of Mitchell before. Right then, I was terrified.

He twisted, lurching a step back.

Foolishly, I thought he was leaving and recognized his intention too late. "Mitchell, no!" I cried as he grabbed my foot-long lightning whelk shell and slammed it against my bedroom wall, cracking it at the base of the spire.

He was reaching for the pieces as my sorority president and her boyfriend burst into the room. D.J., wearing nothing but boxers, wrenched Mitchell's arms up behind his back and escorted him out of the house forcibly, repeating, "Chill the fuck out, Upstone, or I'll do it for you."

As my sisters gathered in the hallway, wide-eyed and murmuring, Katie handed me the shell halves. "You okay?"

I nodded, fitting the two halves together like puzzle pieces. I'd brought that whelk to school in tenth grade, during a marine-science unit in biology. While classmates admired the treasure in my hands, stretching fingers to trace the pale stripes on its surface as I walked around the room with it, Mr. Quinn told us that its previous sea snail inhabitant must have lived at least twenty years to grow a home that size. Longer than I'd been alive.

"Pearl, he didn't—hit you or anything, right?"

I shook my head, a tear trailing down my cheek. Mitchell's choice of the one item in my room most representing home to me hadn't been an accident. Despite my useless exclamation, I'd known the minute he'd stretched toward the top of my bookcase that I was too late to prevent his retaliation, too late to wish I'd initiated the conversation somewhere else. His tantrum had dispelled any remorse I'd felt for abandoning our plans.

When he texted an apology, I didn't reply. His calls went to voice mail, and I deleted them without listening. My sisters wouldn't let him through the door of our house, and rumor had it that his fraternity president had threatened to revoke his membership if he didn't leave me alone. There'd been an incident the previous fall with a sophomore in their frat who'd stalked one girl and raped another—a freshman in my sorority who transferred away at the end of the semester. After a damage control meeting with their chapter advisor and an alumni mentor, the frat leaders weren't taking any chances.

"D.J. says he and Dean are going *zero tolerance* until they graduate in May." Katie squeezed my shoulder. "Four months and we're outta here, girl. God knows I don't want another drop of drama, but I'd swear on a stack of Bibles autographed by Jesus himself—I'll kick Mitchell's ass all the way down the street if he so much as steps on the goddamned lawn."

Mitchell and I avoided each other for the remainder of our last semester—including ninety-minute lectures in animal virology every Tuesday and Thursday, and eight awkward hours of experimental physiology lab every Wednesday. Graduation, three days ago, had been a relief—though I spent two guilt-ridden days trying and failing to ignore Mama's bliss about my impending ascension to med school. I couldn't ruin graduation weekend for either of us by dumping the truth on her, but my time had run out.

College was done. Mitchell and I had gone our separate ways. I'd informed Vanderbilt that I wouldn't be attending, hopefully making some waitlisted applicant's dream come true. Now there was only one thing left to do.

Tell my mother.

chapter *Two*

BOYCE

I'm not a hero.

That description fit my brother, Brent, all his life, but not me. As a kid, I wanted to be like him—thought I could be, even, if I aped everything he did. By the time he was fourteen, he was close to earning his Eagle Scout rank, so I joined Cub Scouts. Dad wouldn't pay for the fees and uniform, so Brent let me bag grass on the lawns he mowed so I could earn the money for it myself. Years later, I worked out that he'd removed the grass catcher from the mower so he could pay me out of his own earnings to rake and bag that grass.

In second grade, I got damned intense about earning merit badges, but Mom was done sewing the patches on. When I brought home the first one, she lifted her water-crinkled hands from a sink of soapy dishes and told me, "I've got a crap-ton of stretch marks and a bigger ass thanks to you boys. I'm not scarring my fingers up just to sew all those freakin' patches on. Do it yourself like your brother does."

"Look here," Brent said, pushing a big needle through the edge of a patch, over the border, and back down through the fabric. He stitched the one-inch circle to my blue shirt with clear thread that looked like fishing line and then left me to do the others.

I stabbed a few dozen holes in my fingers with that needle, and I'm sure there was a fair amount of blood on that shirt when I was done. The first few patches dangled a little cockeyed but stayed put.

That spring my pack joined the town's annual beach cleanup. I was first to sign up, because I wanted that conservation badge *bad*—even if I did have to stitch it on. My interest wore thin after a couple of hours of unseasonable heat and typical gulf humidity. The plastic gloves they gave us protected against everything but hypodermics—though I didn't have to be told twice not to touch one of those. Needles and I had a mutual hatred for each other. But the gloves stuck to my sweaty hands, and bits of sand snuck in around my wrists and settled, gritty and irritating, between my fingers.

Eager to quit and claim the Capri Sun and hot dogs we'd been promised, I handed a bag full of bottle caps, food wrappers, and one rotting fish head to my den leader.

"Good job," he said, and I could almost taste that hot dog, dripping with yellow mustard and relish. "Plenty of time to fill up another one or two bags before lunch. Deposit that in the big trash can and grab a new one. Don't worry, Mrs. Thompson will blow the whistle when those wieners are ready."

I turned to hide my scowl and muttered a cuss word, determined to fill that bag in record time and then park my butt on the other side of somebody's beach umbrella until I heard my den mother's signal—the same piercing whistle she used to call her sons back home at suppertime. All of a sudden a bunch of little girls wearing matching pink T-shirts and blue vests covered in girly-looking patches appeared between me and the water. Of all the rotten luck—*baby Girl Scouts*. They squealed and raced around, pretending their trash bags were parachutes.

"Crap," I said, growing more ticked off. I'd have to hunt quickly to fill my bag, because those girls would scoop up all the trash on this part of the beach, and I didn't want to have to hike too far from those hot dogs or Mrs. Thompson's whistle.

As their leader called them all into a circle to pass out gloves and order them to stay together, I stomped right through the middle of them, toward a plastic six-pack ring peeking out of the sand.

"Hey!" one girl said. "He's gettin' our litter!"

I pretended I hadn't heard her and stuffed it into my bag.

The leader laughed and said there was plenty of trash for everyone, and they all started grabbing any debris in view. "Ladies," she added, "remember to leave nature as you find it! We're here to collect *garbage*, not seaweed, sticks or shells."

"Even the broken ones?" another girl asked, staring at a handful of shell bits. "No snails or crabs can live in these. They aren't good for anything, so they're trash, right?"

I rolled my eyes as I walked between them. She saw me and frowned.

"No, Pearl—the broken ones are still *nature*. Let those be too, hon."

"Dumb girl," I said, and she bit her lip and looked like she might cry, which poked something inside of me and made me feel mean. She was just a little kid. But I passed her, snatched up a scrap of newspaper, and crammed it into my bag. I was a man on a mission.

An hour later, my bag was full and I'd walked farther than I'd meant to. I didn't see anyone from my pack. Maybe I had been too far away to hear the whistle. Maybe the hot dogs were gone. My stomach growled, angry at that thought, and I jogged back down the beach. That's when I noticed something in the water—*a tangle of trash?* No. It was dark hair. Small arms flailed from either side of it before the head and arms vanished below a wave. I slowed, staring, telling myself it was just some kid playing in the water instead of helping with the cleanup.

The hair and arms bobbed to the surface for a second or two and sank again. If there was a cry for help, it was too far out to be heard. No one seemed to be watching but me. Our beaches didn't have lifeguards, and no parent was nearby, eyes searching the surf. If you wanted your kid not to drown, you watched him. Anybody with sense knew that.

My heart sped when seconds passed and nothing came back up. I dropped the trash bag and ran to the edge of the water, scanning the surface. Nothing. *Nothing.* Had I just stood there watching somebody drown? Without thinking, I splashed out into the water in my uniform, shoes and all.

"Hey, kid!" I yelled, my gaze sliding over the water's choppy surface. Once I got chest deep, small rippling waves hit me in the face and kept me from seeing more than a couple of feet in front of me. I was such a *dumbass.* I hadn't shouted for a grown-up. I'd just rushed into the water by myself, like the stupid shit-for-brains my dad said I was.

Something bumped me, and I opened my mouth to scream, swallowing a mouthful of gulf water. Hands out to ward off whatever it was, I coughed and spit and saw a flash of blue and pink. *The drowning kid.* Grabbing instead of shoving, I pulled the limp body to my chest and backed up as fast as I could. A big wave knocked me down and both of us went under, but I held on and shoved my feet against the gulf floor until we surfaced. The face flopped toward me, eyes closed.

It was the girl I'd called dumb.

"No!" I coughed out, hooking my arms under her neck and

knees. I stumbled, yelling into her face. "Wake up! Wake up!" Dropping to my knees, I put her on the sand, but she didn't move. I didn't know what to do—people on TV breathed into people's mouths and pushed on their chests, but people on TV also did a lot of stuff that wasn't real like climbing up the sides of buildings or turning into vampires.

The girl's Scout leader appeared. "Pearl! Oh God!" Her hands shook as she pressed her fingers against the girl's neck. She laid her head on her chest, saying, "No pulse, no pulse, oh Jesus." She pinched the girl's nose shut and breathed into her mouth, but the girl's eyes didn't open.

I felt sunburn-hot, but I was shaking like I was sitting in a bucket of ice. People surrounded us, watching and mumbling, but I couldn't see or hear them clearly and I couldn't move. All I could see was the lady mashing on the girl's unmoving chest and breathing into her mouth. All I could hear was my own pulse, thumping like a drumbeat in my ears. I was alive and she was dead, and it was my fault for not yelling for an adult instead of walking into the water alone. And I'd made her cry an hour ago—her eyes dark, sad pools, like Mama's always looked after Daddy hurt her.

Then, like a fancy fountain, the girl coughed up water—*lots* of water. It gushed over her face as she jerked up, sucking in air, eyes flying open. She looked right at me, and not until I felt her hand tighten around mine did I know I'd been holding it.

The crowd around us cheered. I felt hands patting my shoulders and the back of my head as the lady started to cry, saying the girl's name over and over—*Pearl, Pearl, Pearl*—and thanking Jesus and God and finally, me. "You saved her life. Thank you. Thank you."

The past moments crashed around me like days instead of minutes. My eyes burned. My teeth rattled and my limbs quaked. I

18

clutched Pearl's hand, small and bronze in mine, and stared down at the dark hair tangled around her face, stuck to her cheek, and snagged around one of the Girl Scout pins on her chest—which rose and fell like it should. I gazed into dark eyes that were wide and *alive* and felt like I'd just learned something, but I didn't know what it was yet.

When the paramedics arrived, my den leader wrapped me in a beach towel and pulled me away, breaking my grip on Pearl's hand and hers on mine. "You done good, Boyce. You're a hero, you know that?"

There was a story in the paper and two pictures: one of my smiling pack leader pinning a shiny Honor Medal just above my left pocket, over my heart, and another of Pearl's mother, my parents, and Brent standing behind the two of us—both in our Scouting uniforms. The top of her head, a mess of dark curls pulled into a pink bow, didn't even reach my shoulder.

That was my one occasion of valor—more than some people can lay claim to, I guess. Too bad I was only seven. It's some kinda crap to peak before you hit puberty.

· · · · · · · · · ·

I don't always quit working at closing time. Most afternoons I'm wrapped up in the job and don't want to stop until I'm done, but sometimes there's just too much left to do whether I want to finish or not. I'd been considering hiring someone to help out, at least part-time.

I usually remember to throw the bolt and turn the Sorry, We're Closed sign on the front door at six o'clock even if I'm still working, but I was ass deep in the installation of a cylinder block when the hour turned. When the bell over the door clanked at half after, I swore under my breath and called, "I'm closed," glancing toward the doorway between the cramped front office and the garage.

Dad's old lawyer (and failed AA sponsor), Barney Amos, appeared there, his expression twisted into a permanent warped grimace from the accident that had mangled his face and left arm, almost gotten him disbarred, killed his six-year-old son, and made him quit drinking—one day too late. Austin Amos had started Cub Scouts with me. He'd have been twenty-two or so now.

"Hey there, Boyce," Mr. Amos said, one hand upturned like he was swearing to tell the truth, the whole truth, and nothing but.

"Hey, Mr. Amos." I wiped my hands on a rag and stood straight, rolling my shoulders and feeling the burn under my shoulder blades. "What can I do for ya?"

Barney Amos hadn't been to the shop in years, though I saw him around town often enough. Dad's attempt to quit drinking had consisted of two or three meetings followed by a binge that lasted the rest of his life. I knew where to place that blame, even if Mr. Amos tried to take a piece of it. It was all my dad's choice. Every bottle. Every swallow.

"Boyce, did your dad ever see another attorney? After he and I parted ways?"

I shrugged, shoulders objecting, feeling guilty for the appeal of the ice-cold beer waiting for me once I showered and met up with a couple of boys in town. Unlike my father, I would limit my intake. Unlike Mr. Amos, I wouldn't get behind a wheel until I'd sobered up.

"Not that I know of, but he wasn't exactly talkative about that sorta stuff." *Or anything else, except his opinion of what a fuckup I was.* "Why?"

Mr. Amos shifted position but remained in the doorway, his eyes falling to the floor, looking even more uncomfortable than his natural state. "Have you browsed through his papers? Thoroughly?"

When people answer a question with a question, it's never a good sign. "Legal papers, you mean? Not really. Why?" I asked again.

His crooked mouth turned up on one side in clear relief at my answer. "Ah, well then, I'd suggest you get to looking—the sooner the better. You're gonna need documentation to have his effects—the deed to the trailer, the garage, and the contents thereof—legally transferred to you. As well as the business itself."

I frowned. That made sense, but something about this needled, shoving his reasonable advice aside. "I'm his only remaining heir, so that's just formality, right?"

"Well sure, sure. But the law is kinda particular about following formalities in how property is bequeathed after someone passes."

"Okay. Well. What am I looking for in particular? A will, I guess?"

He nodded. "A will and any paperwork relating to the garage—business formation, tax forms, etcetera. Assuming it was still a sole proprietorship, you might have a few issues. Unless Bud incorporated formally in the past decade or so, then a new owner would have to reform it under his own name."

Incorporated formally? Yeah. That didn't sound like something Dad would have bothered doing. Since I'd turned eighteen, he'd paid me every week like I was an employee, tax forms and all—after he got a letter from the state or the IRS that put him in a three-day rage.

"And, uh, you might look for a divorce decree too? Maybe one from out of state?"

"Divorce decree... another formality?"

21

He nodded, eyes meandering over the lift, diagnostic equipment, and tools lining the walls. "As soon as you have everything, bring it by my office and we'll get everything filed. Pro bono, of course—the least I can do."

"Yessir." I might not hold him responsible for my dad's sobriety fail, but I also wasn't gonna piss on *free*. "I'll be by in a few days." There was something he wasn't saying, but I couldn't put my finger on it. I figured I'd find out soon enough.

Pearl

My phone trilled, the screen displaying a days-old shot of Mom at graduation. My heart stuttered before answering. She never called when she knew I was driving.

"Aren't you driving?" she asked as soon as I said hello. "I was going to leave you a voice mail. You shouldn't answer your phone if you're driving."

I sighed, relieved at her tone, which told me nothing was seriously wrong, and annoyed with her tone, which presumed that I was still six years old. "Mama, you can't call me when there's a ninety-nine percent chance I'm driving and then tell me I shouldn't answer when I'm driving."

"You could have let it go to voice mail."

"I hate voice mail. And you're apparently calling to tell me something that can't wait until I get home in"—I glanced at the clock—"a little over an hour? You raised me to fret first and ask questions later. Deal with it."

She huffed a resigned sigh into the receiver. "Fine. Your father forgot about an AMA event in Houston—*tonight*. And he's *speaking* at it." Dr. Thomas Frank, MD, FAANS, FACS, wasn't my real father. My biological father died before I was born, and Thomas married Mom when I was thirteen, adopting me soon after. I became Pearl Frank then, which sounded, as Melody Dover, my best friend from high school, would later say, like a total white-girl name—a thing Mama seemed all too happy about. I hadn't asked her opinion before requesting that *Pearl Torres Frank* be printed on my official diploma. I loved my stepfather, but I wanted a certified acknowledgment of my heritage—of where I originated and who I might have been.

I heard Thomas's good-natured mumble in the background, followed by Mama's sputter of incredulity. "Introductions require preparation too, Thomas! And no, you cannot just *wing it*. Madre de Dios!" Her accent was more pronounced when she got riled— something my stepfather enjoyed provoking just to hear it. Full-on Spanish, though? *Jackpot*.

"So you won't be home tonight," I interrupted, too relieved at the one-night respite from my impending confession to feel rotten over being relieved. "No problem. I've got my key. I'll see you both tomorrow."

· · · · · · · · · ·

I was stuck in the back doorway while Tux, meowing his displeasure at my parents' desertion, wound himself around my legs in a succession of figure eights. They'd only been gone a few hours, before which he was undoubtedly petted, cooed over, and fed a hand-chopped portion of fresh drum or whatever Thomas last caught when he took the boat out.

I patted Tux's tubby flank and pulled my overnight bag through the door. "You aren't fooling anybody with that *I'm wasting away* song of your people, cat. You're the most over-indulged feline on this whole island."

He was also the sweetest, which was why he was spoiled. He and Thomas had been living the ultimate bachelor life before Mama and I entered their lives seven years ago, but Tux had welcomed us as warmly as Thomas had—as though he'd just been waiting for some woman and her thirteen-year-old kid to move in and claim territory that had been his for years. He batted the zipper-pull on my bag while I called Melody, who'd just graduated from SMU and was home for two weeks before she moved back to Dallas to begin her new public relations job.

"Hey, girl!" she answered. "Home yet?"

"Just got in the door. My parents are out tonight. You busy?"

"Nope. Been home two days and I've had it up to *here* with Mom's bitching about the million and one things I'm doing wrong with my life—from my clothes to my career to how I'll never land a husband because I failed to find one in four years of college. It would serve her bony ass right if I just became a lesbian."

Right. Because women become lesbians all the time just to piss off their mothers.

"I don't think that's a feasible alternative for you, Mel."

"Yeah." She sighed. "I like men too much." Four years of college hadn't improved Melody's grasp of sarcasm. "Speaking of men—let's go out!"

She and her last boyfriend had broken up a month ago, and she knew the whole ugly story of Mitchell, but going out sounded more tiring than tempting. I'd hoped she'd catch me up on her personal life and local gossip like the adult women we were—while sharing a bottle of wine and lounging in yoga pants. I wanted to spend time with her before she left town though.

In high school, we were so night and day yet so connected that someone had dubbed us the yin-yang twins. That nickname likely resulted from our diverse outward appearances—even with her summer tan, she seemed paler and blonder next to my olive skin, dark hair and eyes. But to me, our bond, our yin-yang, was internal. We'd grown apart over the four separated years of college. I missed her.

"Melody, I'm not really in the mood to—"

"No worries—I'll drive!"

"*Mel.*"

"I'm jumping in the shower. Be there in an hour. Ha! I made a rhyme. See you around nine." *One, two*—"Hey, I did it again! TTFN!" She snorted and hung up before I could *Mel* her a second time.

I had to laugh. Nothing like a high school friend to drag you back to high school behavior. Melody, more popular, more outgoing, more everything—had always decided our social agenda, and I had always followed. We'd parted activities in one instance that surprised no one, however. While she tried out for the cheer squad junior year and was head cheerleader senior year, I joined study groups, volunteered at the marine-science center, and was our class valedictorian.

If nothing else, I could try my confession out on Melody before I handed it to Mama. Melody would be the one to understand my anxiety over disappointing my mother.

"Me-OW," Tux complained, purring like the brat he was.

To hush him up, I plopped a scoop of cold mac and cheese in his bowl—his favorite meal right after seafood. "You are so weird," I told him. "If you'll excuse me, I'm going to get ready for a night on the town. At least it's midweek. Hopefully the bars will be deserted."

chapter *Three*

BOYCE

Tourism had been the town's number one economic resource forever —even fishing came in second. But the flow of cash didn't stop the locals from bitching whenever hordes of out-of-towners showed up and invaded restaurants, crowded roads and the one grocery store, and jammed the beaches with sweaty bodies, Styrofoam coolers, and useless umbrellas that were demolished in the first stiff airstream off the gulf.

If you wanted to go out and avoid tourists this time of year— good luck with that. But your best shot was to hit a butt-ugly dive bar off the main strip. No bright tropical exterior, no palm-treed land-scaping, no view. The sort of place nonresidents would either over-look entirely or take one look at and think, *no way*. Like the Saloon.

After a basket of onion chips, a half-pound burger, and a couple of beers, I challenged Mateo Vega to darts on the pockmarked board hanging close enough to the door that there were stray dart tip holes *in* the door. As I lined up my throw, the door swung open and in walked Melody Dover, a girl I'd known since my hellish repeat of third grade, and Pearl Frank, who knew me better than anyone in this town. I hadn't seen either of them since they'd been home on winter break, more than four months ago.

"Oh, fabulous," Melody muttered, glancing at me before checking out the near-vacant room. "Remind me why we're *here*?"

The other two guys in my group—Randy Thompson and Vega's cousin, Bart—lounged at a table a few feet away, and a couple of old-timers sat side by side at the bar. There'd been a few other regulars in earlier, but they'd cleared out.

I ignored Melody—a skill I'd honed over the years until it was all reflex—but I couldn't ignore Pearl. She looked damned good, even in those sensible little clamdigger pants and flat shoes. Her hair was less wild than it used to be, but it still ran past her shoulders and down her back like a dark current. I tipped my chin as soon as her eyes met mine, and her answering smile was subdued but genuine.

She returned her attention to her friend, smile widening. "We want a quiet place to talk, Mel. This is perfect."

Melody, hot as ever and aware of it as ever, glanced at me over her shoulder. "That remains to be seen—all it takes is one loudmouth to ruin the peaceful ambiance."

"You should know, Dover." Sinking a dart just left of the bull's-eye, I refused to look at her.

She gasped but sounded more like a riled-up purebred than a grown woman. It took everything I had to hold back a laugh. Before she could spit out the smart-ass answer she no doubt had on the tip of her tongue, Pearl asked her a question and Melody turned to march toward a table along the back wall, yakking about some new job and forgetting to fire back at me.

Mateo's cousin Bart, who was nineteen going on idiot, leered across the rough plank floorboards, which were scattered with discarded peanut shells—the Saloon's idea of down-home decoration. "Thought you said there weren't no hot pieces of ass in this town,

Téo," he said, all but drooling at the sight of Melody's backside in shorts and heels.

That boy had no idea how close he'd come to a dart in the forehead. He could stare at Dover's legs all he wanted, but one word about Pearl and he'd have been sporting a skull ornament.

"Shut it, dickwad." Mateo swatted the back of his cousin's skull. "Those two are so far out of your league they might as well be on the moon."

Bart rubbed the back of his head, eyes following Pearl's best friend as she walked up to the bar. "Maybe. But it looks like they're slummin' it tonight, *primo*." He was up and swaggering her way before any of us knew it.

"This should be interesting," Randy said, settling back in his chair to watch. He crossed thin arms over his skeletal chest, chuckling, and I was glad to see him smile. He'd been released from prison a few months ago after serving time for running a meth lab in a trailer that blew to hell a few years back. He'd have been inside a lot longer if anyone had been there at the time. That or dead. He'd convinced the parole board he was determined to go straight, and so far, he was sticking to it. The same couldn't be said for his little brother, Rick.

"Oh *hell*." Mateo passed a hand over his face and turned away like he couldn't bear to watch. Two of his first three throws barely made the board at all.

"It's just Melody Dover, Vega—not the queen mother," Randy said. "Besides, your cousin could use a slapdown. Twenty bucks says he's about to get one." As we watched, Bart rested one elbow on the bar next to Melody, and she leaned away as he leaned closer.

I shook my head and threw another dart.

"Yeah. Except her father is my boss's boss's *boss*." Mateo was the assistant manager for one of the half dozen convenience stores in town, five of which were owned by the same company. Melody Dover's daddy was the divisional manager over half the state.

"Chill, man," I said. "Rover Dover's got nothing to report about you. God knows we can't do anything about the dumbasses we're related to." I pulled my darts from the board, thinking about my dad and my brother, and how different they'd been. Wondering where I fit between them.

"'Rover Dover,'" Mateo choked out under his breath. "I haven't heard that in years. Christ, Wynn, don't let her hear you say it. Between that and my ignoramus cousin, she'll have me fired in two shakes and then drag me through town from the bumper of that Infiniti her daddy just bought her."

Pearl

Of course I would run into Boyce Wynn on my first night home. Boyce Wynn—my guardian angel, the imaginary best friend of my childhood, my unprofessed adolescent crush, my dirty little secret. Or was that last one me?

Boyce saved my life when I was five.

It was my first beach cleanup day. I was an entry-level Girl Scout, determined to take home my troop's prize for the most bags of trash collected. Funny, I can't recall the reward I wanted so badly— one of those plush toys filled with plastic pellets. A dolphin? A whale? I don't remember. All I retained was my single-minded resolve to win whatever it was.

I'd defied stay-close orders and branched out a bit farther than allowed. Collecting trash along the water's edge, I spotted something that looked like litter but turned out to be a clump of floating sargassum—the seaweed scourge of the gulf. I'd followed it far enough out that my shorts were soaked to the waistband. So when a tiny jellyfish caught my eye, the first live one I'd ever seen, I didn't fret about getting my clothes wet. I wanted to see that translucent creature up close. It hardly looked real—gliding along the current as though it had been fashioned of fluid glass.

I hadn't sensed the slight drop-off coming until I took a step and plummeted, the water level abruptly reaching my shoulders. I didn't catch sight of the wave that knocked me off my feet immediately after that either, so I had no chance to draw a breath before being submerged, overturned, and disoriented. I knew how to swim, but this was no deep end of the pool where the water was motionless and I could see the blue-tiled bottom below and the clear sky overhead, just beyond the smooth, horizontal surface of the water. Here, murky water swirled in every direction. There was no up, no down, no air.

And then I glimpsed light. I propelled toward it, kicking and clawing, and burst out of the water. *Air.* I sucked in a breath before sinking again—nothing was underfoot. My brain knew I must have surfaced facing away from the beach because I hadn't seen it, but it seemed as if the beach had ceased to exist.

I kicked hard and surfaced again, both arms thrust high. Still no beach. I gulped a breath and got a bit of water too, and a reflexive cough exhaled the precious air as I sank. I swam up again, legs and arms tiring rapidly, knowing only that I needed to breathe—nothing else mattered. The jellyfish I'd pursued, or maybe it was another one altogether, appeared in front of my eyes like a dream, and then there were more of them. They puffed along all around me like miniature swimming umbrellas or beautiful, soundless ghosts.

My lungs demanded air but took in water. My vision darkened

and narrowed—the jellyfish swimming away, the sky fading.

My life didn't flash before my eyes—just one scene, one memory. In the kitchen of our tiny duplex, I inhaled the aroma of Mama's churros, fresh from the frying pan. She placed them, still warm, into a paper bag of sugar and cinnamon. It was my job to shake the bag and coat each one before placing them on a wire rack to cool, but I didn't want to wait. I broke one open as soon as it slid from the bag, the steam erupting and singeing my fingertips.

"Ow, ow, ow," I said, breaking off a piece and heedlessly scorching my tongue as well.

"You silly, impatient little thing!" Mama shook her head. "If you blister your tongue until everything tastes the same, what will you care if I feed you churros or meatloaf?"

I wrinkled my nose in disgust. Mama was a good cook, but as far as I was concerned, even she couldn't save meatloaf, which we ate at least once per week.

She looked at me then and yelled, "Wake up! Wake up!" But it wasn't her voice. The voice belonged to a boy—the big one who'd called me a dumb girl that morning. Mama always told me to ignore boys, especially the mean ones. They were *bad news*, she said. Besides, I didn't want to wake up. I'd show *him* that no boy would tell me what to do.

My chest felt like it was being crushed. Like someone heavy was sitting on me, pressing me flat as a waffle. Was that boy sitting on me? It hurt too much. I would have to wake up after all and push him off.

I sat up and my eyes opened and I threw up all over myself, but the puke was all water. I coughed and coughed, more water coming out. He was above me, looking down at me. His hair was cropped short, but so red in the sun it seemed to be on fire. His face wasn't mean. His eyes were full of tears, and I felt his hand, holding mine. I knew he was sorry, not bad news. I tried to tell him I forgave him, but I couldn't speak because my chest hurt and my throat was sore, so I squeezed his hand, and he held mine tighter. That's when I noticed there were people all around us, applauding and laughing.

I didn't think anything was funny, and neither did he. Miss Eilish, my Daisy leader, was crying, and she repeated my name about twenty times before thanking the boy and telling him he was a hero.

We got our pictures in the paper. I cut out the story and the photo with our names listed below—*Boyce Wynn and Pearl Torres*. It's still in the back of my first school yearbook, the newsprint yellowed, ink faded.

Afterward, I saw him sometimes at school, but I was two years behind him, so his classroom was in a different hallway and his class's lunch table was four tables away from mine. All his friends were other boys. They played basketball or football on the playground while I took my turn on the swings or played chase on the grass or hunted for frogs near the drainpipes after it had rained.

A year passed, and we didn't talk or say hello. I figured he'd forgotten who I was until the day one of his friends took the playground ball my friends and I were using to practice soccer.

"Give it back!" I yelled, my fists knotted at my sides.

"Us boys need this for kickball," the boy said, laughing. "Go play with dolls or something."

Boyce walked up. "Quit being a dick, Rick," he said, punching the ball from his friend's grip, bouncing it once on the packed ground before tossing it back to us.

"What'd you do that for, asstard?" his friend shot back, because boys liked to cuss out on the playground where the teachers couldn't hear. "They're just dumb girls."

Boyce looked right at me then. "No they're not." His mouth didn't smile, but his eyes did. He scanned the playground, zeroing in on a group of boys kicking a ball back and forth while heckling some girls sitting in the gravel beneath the monkey bars. "Let's go steal that ball from Clark Richards. Maybe he'll cry again."

"Yeah!" the other guys said, tearing off toward them.

"Thank you, Boyce," I said as he turned.

"You're welcome, Pearl," he answered softly, not looking back.

· · · · · · · · · ·

After shooting down Boyce's one-lining friend, Melody's mood improved. From her standpoint, even unwelcome attention had always been better than no attention. After explaining the responsibilities of a junior account executive at a public relations firm, she poked a lime slice into the neck of her Dos Equis bottle and shrugged. "So basically I'll be coordinating social media publicity for our housewares and pet-products clients."

Housewares and pet products? I couldn't think of anything that said *Melody* less.

"I won't just be posting stuff on Twitter or whatever. I'll be directing the production of market-savvy graphics that will be used for *all* the major social media channels."

For housewares and pet products. Her words sounded more like justification than new-career enthusiasm. Public relations was a long way from Melody's dream job when we were sixteen. She'd wanted to work in a museum or gallery, helping curate collections, discovering new talent, unearthing works of genius by historically overlooked artists.

"That's great, Mel. I'm sure they're thrilled to have you."

"Damn right they are." Her smile seemed counterfeit, and I wondered if that's how I'd have looked on my way to med school. "What about you? My best friend's going to be a doctor! Better you than me, girl. I am so relieved to be done with school. You'll have to come to Dallas some weekend, and we can go out for real." She glanced around the Saloon like it was a dump, and I realized she saw our entire hometown that way and had for a while.

I shifted and took a deep breath. "Yeah, about that. I decided I don't want to be a medical doctor after all."

Melody arched a brow. "But you got into Vanderbilt! And what else would you do?"

"You know I've always been interested in marine science…"

She stared. "Pearl—you can't be serious! You got into a top medical school. Do you know how many people are smart enough to even get into med school at all?"

About twenty thousand a year, I thought.

"And oh God. Your mama will shit a brick if you drop out."

"This is my life, Mel, not my mother's." We both knew what I wasn't saying. Aside from small, aimless rebellions, Melody followed the path her parents expected of her. Her previous relationship had ended when her boyfriend admitted that he had no plans to give her a ring after graduation, a discussion that had only occurred be-cause her mother began dropping wedding hints over winter break, like the next plot point on the map of her daughter's life—one she controlled.

Still, I wished I could take the words back. We'd been friends for a long time, and I had no room to judge. "I've already declined the acceptance. But hey, it's not dropping out if I never start, right?" I smiled, hoping for commiseration, at least, not disapproval. I antici-pated plenty of that from my parents.

"Oh. My. God. You're seriously going to stay *here* instead of going to medical school and getting the hell out of this craphole of a town? Have you freaking lost it?" She sat forward and seized my wrist. "Wait. Is this about Mitchell?"

"No. This decision has nothing to do with him." Not that he'd seen it that way—but I wasn't getting into that. "Melody, I'm not you." She jerked her hand away, inferring the thing I'd not meant. "I never wanted to move away," I clarified. "I've spent the past four years missing the open water like I'd misplaced a piece of myself. I don't want a big city life. I want a beach. I want the ocean. I want *this*. I've always loved it here."

She shook her head. "I don't get it."

"I know." I sighed, risking a glance across the bar where Boyce, done with his dart game, leaned back in his chair and laughed, engrossed in the animated conversation between Mateo and the guy who'd hit on Melody earlier.

Until he took a long pull from his bottle and shifted his attention to me down the length of it, like he'd been watching me all along, keeping me in his sights.

chapter *Four*

BOYCE

Living with my father had been a nightmare I woke to daily. That's why I never faulted my mother for getting the hell out when she had the chance. If there'd ever been a time he wasn't an abusive fuck, it was before I came along. When cussing and screaming and throwing things didn't make enough of an impact on her, he shoved and slapped and pulled hair. When he was stinking drunk, he landed punches.

Brent, nearly eight years older than me, started getting in the way of those punches when he was eleven or twelve. While I hid under my bed or in our closet—"Stay *here*," he'd order, as if I needed convincing—he would try to talk Dad out of whatever fit he'd worked himself into. He usually ended up with a few bruises for his trouble.

Days before my eighth birthday, I heard a car pull up out front after one of my parents' brawls. A minute later, the front door's rusted hinges whined, and then there was a man's voice, deep and unfamiliar. I scooted out from under the bed, thinking maybe the cops had come at last. Maybe they'd haul Dad off to jail and he'd have to stay there forever. I inched around the corner to watch. A stranger stood in the doorway, but he wasn't wearing a uniform. Dad was sprawled in his chair, passed out, a half-empty bottle on the floor, just below his fingertips.

Mom shot out of their room then, dragging a big black trash bag full of stuff. Her favorite purse—the one with fringe on the bottom and a peace sign of purple rhinestones glued to the front—was slung over her shoulder. I knew the red mark on her cheek would be dark by morning, and she'd tap makeup from a bottle and smooth it over and over until it looked like a harmless shadow.

The man took the trash bag from her hands.

"Mom," Brent said, his voice a harsh whisper, his hands balled at his sides. "Mom, take Boyce with you."

She glanced at the man in the doorway.

"Ain't takin' no kid," he said, turning his head and spitting a wad of chew into the yard.

She turned back to my brother. "Boyce has you," she said. "Y'all'll be fine. Your daddy only hates *me*." Her voice quaked as she stared across the room. "You know how to make him calm. I just get him more riled."

"Mom, please. He's just a little kid—"

The man hefted the bag and strode out the door. "Ruthanne," he said. A command.

Mom started after him before swinging back and lifting a hand to Brent's face. At fifteen, he was a head taller than her. "Y'all'll be fine, baby." Her voice was so low I could barely hear her. The rhinestones caught the beam of the floodlight outside and glinted like broken bits of purple glass. "Carl will probably change his mind, okay? Just give me some time to soften him up. I'll let you know where I am."

We never heard from her again.

• • • • • • • • •

Pearl's parents' house was on the bay side of town—a neighborhood of houses that looked more like a row of resorts than homes containing only one family apiece. There were docks out back of each one where yachts and fishing boats and Jet Skis were conveniently moored. The more monstrous ones with corner lots and backyards—like the Frank place—had swimming pools, each one just feet from the bay. There was an airstrip nearby too, for the rich fucks who wanted personal access to the ocean *and* the sky.

Until high school, though, Pearl and her mom lived in my part of town, just on the other side of the long block where all three schools huddled together—elementary, middle, and high school. Her mom worked for a doctor's office, scraping by like most working class folks did. I'd see them sometimes at the IGA, leafing through coupons in the cereal aisle while Brent just bought the cheap store brand, or on the public beach, splashing through the surf.

Once, Brent and I were fishing off the main pier when I caught sight of them. Ms. Torres was propped in a folding chair, reading, while her daughter constructed the world's most pitiful lump of a sand castle. A humid breeze carried the sound of their laughter when Pearl stood up and stomped it flat like she was Godzilla putting a butt-ugly building out of its misery. She collapsed on a beach towel covered in Disney princesses and spread her arms and legs like a starfish, and her mom handed her a wet wipe and a baggie of orange slices. Watching them made me ache with happiness and jealousy until I couldn't look anymore.

Brent had managed to convince Dad that we'd both been asleep when Mom left. That we had no idea how she'd run off or with whom. She hadn't left any clues for him to follow, either.

Thundering through the trailer, he'd trashed their room and anything of hers she'd left behind—as if that black bag hadn't been full of everything she cared about. As if she hadn't walked out on everything she didn't give two shits to take with her.

My first time through third grade began a couple of weeks after her escape. Needless to say, given that I had to repeat it the next year, that school year didn't go well. They say the brain can block painful memories, leaving gaps and voids in place of them, but it didn't work like that for me. I remembered everything.

My brother always tried to protect me, but I was a burden he never got clear of. I couldn't ever tell him I'd overheard that last brief, whispered conversation between him and our mom. His plea. Her lie. *I'll let you know where I am.*

I knew by his expression he didn't believe her.

But I had.

· · · · · · · · · ·

Everywhere there's a group of people, there's a pecking order, even in elementary school. Once you're promoted to fourth grade, you're no longer one of the little kids, and only the fifth graders can lord it over you then.

Unless forty of your classmates get promoted and you're the only dipshit left behind.

Like my brother, I'd always been big for my age. But being held back a year told the world I was dimwitted, too, so I stood out like a mutant idiot next to my new, younger classmates. I stooped low when we walked single file down the hallway to the lunchroom or the library. I folded my body like crumpled paper, hoping to be overlooked when we sat in a circle to read out loud—the most fucked-up thing any teacher ever invented. Invisibility was the superpower I wanted most, but I'd never been more visible.

Guys learn to talk shit to each other as soon as we can speak. It's what we do. Even with our friends—sometimes especially with our friends. But with friends, there are subjects that are off-limits. Like your mom running away from home with some random dude and leaving you behind like trash. Like your dad being thrown in jail overnight on the regular for being drunk and disorderly out in public. Like how dumb you must be to get held back in third grade.

Those are the subjects friends don't touch, but other guys pick up and throw like stones, because that stupid nursery rhyme—*words will never hurt me*—that's a goddamned lie. When it's bad and it's true, those words slip beneath your armor and slice deep. And if you fight back with the only weapon you've got—fists, in my case— you're the bad guy. Because their weapons were "just words."

I'd heard the word *alcoholic* before. My mom had said it to my dad plenty of times, when she wasn't calling him other things. Brent explained that *alcoholic* was a different way to say somebody was a drunk—a nicer way, because it made it sound like they were sick instead of making bad choices.

"Is Daddy sick or making bad choices?" I asked. When I was sick, I threw up and I had a fever. I stayed in bed and drank 7UP.

"Both, I reckon," Brent said. "But if you're sick and you never try to get better, at some point it just looks like bad choice after bad choice, and nobody cares if you're sick anymore."

The word I'd never heard was *whore*. I might not have known what it meant, but I knew it wasn't good because it was whispered and chuckled over and thrown like a spear when connected with *Boyce's mama*.

"What'd you say?" I asked the one who'd said the word. A guy from my new class. The grin disappeared from his mouth like it'd been wiped off. His eyes bugged and he swallowed hard but didn't answer.

"He said your mama's a whore." There were four of them, all smaller than me, standing stiff as statues with their hands balled into fists, looking ready to attack or run. It was like a pack of wolves thinking maybe they were gonna take down a grizzly.

"Shut up, Eddie!" the first guy said.

Eddie Standish stood farthest from me, so he was full of spit and gristle.

I grabbed the guy next to me by the shirtfront, swung him around, and used his body to tackle Standish. We went down in a heap, and the last thing I saw before the world went red was the fear on both their faces. I'd put that there. And I wasn't sorry.

I was also about to be expelled. *From elementary school.* Staring at the scraped-up fists on my lap as if they belonged to someone else, I'd been silent when Principal Jaynes asked, *What in heckfire were you thinking, young man?* I didn't mean to tell what they'd said about my mom, so I said nothing. I didn't want anyone to know. Two of the guys were still in the nurse's office, and two had talked to the principal before me. Now he was calling parents while I sat in the outer office, alone. Elbows on knees and head in my hands, I hid my face and imagined my dad showing up, his hands and clothes spotted with axle grease, his breath sour with whiskey and anger.

"I need to talk to Principal Jaynes." The voice was soft, but I knew who it was before looking.

Through my fingers, I watched the smiling lady on the other side of the counter and the small girl with her back to me. Her long, dark hair was somehow tamed into one fat braid that hung straight down her spine.

"He's a bit busy right now, Pearl. Can I help you with something, hon?"

Pearl placed her hands on the tall counter, which sat just under her chin. "I need to talk to him about the fight. About what those boys said. I was a witness."

My mouth went dry, my *NO* wedged in my throat.

The lady glanced over at me, then said, "Oh, well then…" She turned away and dialed the phone. Mr. Jaynes's deep, murmured voice drifted down the hall, answering the call. A minute later, Pearl was led into his office and the door closed behind her. When she came out, she flicked one glance at me as she passed. She was so tiny that we were almost eye-level with each other even though I was sitting down.

"You're better than them, Boyce Wynn," she whispered as she passed.

Pearl

Mama blinked at me as if she'd forgotten how to speak English. *Here we go*, I thought.

When she and Thomas had come home from Houston, I'd been out on the dock, staring across the shifting water at the closest sandbar across the channel and practicing my I'm-not-going-to-med-school speech. Not that those rehearsals curtailed the shock factor one bit, judging by her atypical muteness and the fact that her eyebrows had receded into the wisps of dark hair across her forehead.

When she found her voice, she said, "You've *canceled* your acceptance at Vanderbilt? As in—"

"As in I rejected the acceptance, yes."

Her mouth hung open for a moment before she clapped it shut, jaw locked. "What about Harvard? Michigan?"

It was my turn to hesitate, perplexed. I'd just told her I had made the decision not to pursue a degree in medicine, which wasn't specific to Vanderbilt or Harvard. In an effort to soften the blow, I'd added that I'd been accepted into the doctoral program in marine biology—which she was pretending she hadn't heard. "Um. I was waitlisted at Harvard, Mama, I told you. Michigan also. But—"

"Columbia?"

I shifted on the sofa. "I turned it down."

"Stanford?"

"Mitchell didn't get into Stanford, remember? I turned it down last fall in favor of Vanderbilt."

"Which you've just rejected."

I nodded, sighing. "Yes, but the rejection, the waitlists—none of this is relevant to what I'm trying to tell you. Becoming a medical doctor isn't what I want—"

"You are *not* throwing your future away, Pearl. I've worked too hard. *You've* worked too hard. You've never been afraid of any challenge—never in your life. Why now?"

She didn't know me as well as she thought, or perhaps she just selectively overlooked anything that made me seem less than the perfect daughter. I'd faced down fear plenty of times—though fear had nothing to do with this decision. If anything, I feared departing from the expected plan to do something that felt right but at the same time recklessly impulsive. I feared disappointing her—which I was clearly doing.

"Mama, my choice isn't about fear. This is about what I want to study, and how I want to live my life. This is about what's important to me—"

"No."

No? Oh boy. This was going even worse than I'd imagined. I stared at my lap, searching for the words to make her understand before this deteriorated into a total stalemate.

"Hello, Pearl—welcome home," Thomas said. He was halfway across the parlor by the time he noticed the tension permeating the room. His smile faded. "What's going on?"

"Your daughter doesn't want to go to medical school." Mama's voice was clipped. Plus she made it sound like I had no plan for my future at all.

"Oh?" Thomas appeared more intrigued than concerned.

"I've been accepted into the doctoral program in marine biology. Here."

Paused in the center of the room as though unsure whether he should stay or retreat, he glanced from my face to hers and back. "That's… interesting. What made you change your mind?"

"She is not changing her mind!" Mama interjected, as if nothing I'd said could breach her denial. "She's still on the waitlist at Harvard. She could hear from them any day."

"Mama, it doesn't matter—"

"What we've worked for all your life doesn't matter? What your father sacrificed his life for doesn't matter?"

I sucked in a breath, feeling the mention of my father like a blow to the chest. She'd told me their story—my story—once, in halting, hushed sentences, but she'd never cited his name as an inducement or reproach. Of course, she'd never felt the need. Until now.

"Essie…," Thomas began.

She said no more, her lips pressed into a taut line.

My parents—young, in love, and pregnant, had run to escape a

Mexican drug cartel defended by a gang he'd become involved with—leaving everything and everyone they'd ever known—to see me born in the US. To make a new life for the three of us. To give me opportunities they'd never had and a future safe from the violence under which they'd come of age. My father, not quite twenty, had fallen ill and died during the crossing in an overheated, airless truck; my teenaged mother had braved the loss of the boy she adored and separation from family and friends, and I'd been born on US soil—their first dream for me.

Mama cleaned motel rooms and houses while teaching herself to speak and write English flawlessly and attaining her citizenship. My earliest memories were not playdates or preschools, but libraries where helpful librarians kept me entertained with stacks of books and educational videos while my mother mastered computer skills. Her ambition paid off, and she eventually became the office manager of a busy pediatric practice. A few years later, she met Dr. Thomas Frank, whom she held at arm's length until she was sure he understood and accepted her priority: me.

My phone beeped a message notification—a welcome interruption, no matter who'd sent it. Glancing at the screen, I said, "I have laundry to do," as I bolted from the room and up the curving staircase.

Boyce:	Still hanging out with Dover, huh?
Me:	You know she hates when you call her that.
Boyce:	If you're trying to convince me to stop, that's one regretful line of reasoning right there. JS
Me:	As in I just gave you impetus to call her that more. *sigh*

Boyce: If impetus means ALL THE REASONS, then
          yes.

The first time I first heard Boyce call Melody *Dover* was a year
or so after his playground brawl with boys in his grade. I'd defended
him to Principal Jaynes after that fight. I'd never tattled on anyone
before, but no one else was on Boyce's side. I had to do it. Tall, with
a head of solid silver, square-shorn hair, an angled nose and sharp
jaw, our elementary principal made students cower without speaking
a word. My hands shook and my stomach threatened to heave as I
recounted the ugly things those boys said about his mother. I was
never sure if it was my testimony that helped him escape
punishment, but I liked to think I'd paid back a little of what I owed
him for saving my life.

Mama normally bought me one pair of new shoes at the
beginning of each school year and another in the spring. But in the
middle of third grade, my feet sprang forward two sizes after a
growth spurt that only included my feet, so we went to the Thrifty
Sense for something secondhand to tide me over. I went bananas for
a glittery pair of sneakers marked five dollars, and Mama consented
to buy them after asking multiple times, "Are you *sure* you'll want to
wear these every day until spring break?" I'd nodded and begged
until, sighing, she consented.

Melody Dover was a year ahead of me in school and one of the
rich girls, so I'd been completely off her radar. Until I showed up at
school in a pair of her castoffs.

"Look! That little turd is wearing my shoes!" she exclaimed to a
trio of friends during recess. "They still have the dumb pink
shoelaces I bought for them."

They all laughed or said, *Oh my God!* I kept walking toward the swing sets as if I hadn't heard them, but my vision swam and my face heated.

"Hey, you—those shoes were mine until I got *tired* of them and gave them away."

I stumbled, wishing I could melt and soak right into the ground.

"Bet you had to give them away because your big, fat, flappy feet outgrew them, Dover."

I recognized the voice addressing her, but I didn't turn around.

"Shut up, *Boyce*, you stupidhead. And don't call me by my last name! I'm not a boy!"

"Oooooh noooo, Dover called me a stupidhead." He laughed. "I think her bark is worse than her bite. Dover, Dover, *Rover* Dover— *woof.*"

His friends howled with laughter and started barking and repeating *Rover Dover* while Melody screeched for them to stop, and I kept walking away, no longer the object of her ridicule.

She had no memory of me or those shoes, evidenced by the first time we officially met—five years later, on our first day of tenth grade. I'd skipped ninth grade entirely, thanks to my stepfather's money, which paid for tests confirming my academic skill level. Though I was happy to be more intellectually challenged, advancing up meant the loss of my few friends. I barely recognized anyone in my first three classes, and no one seemed to recognize *me* in my new wardrobe of brand-name clothes. Depressed, I veered into the girls' restroom just before lunch, contemplating hiding in a stall for the rest of the hour.

Melody Dover was leaning over the chipped sink, staring into the mirror, sobbing and trying in vain to repair her dissolving mascara at the same time.

My first impulse was to turn around and leave before she saw me. She was spoiled and bitchy—something I'd experienced firsthand. "Um, are you okay?" I asked. I could have kicked myself. I shouldn't have cared if she was wretchedly miserable. She probably deserved it.

She turned, sniffling, the pale skin under her eyes smudged dark. "Everything sucks. *Everything*. My boyfriend is being a dick, my parents are assholes, and I just had a wicked fight with my best friend, who is being a total bitch!"

I stepped closer and handed her a clean paper towel, and she renewed her efforts to blot the mascara from under each eye. I'd never had a boyfriend. My mother and new stepfather indulged and supported me completely. I had friends, but no one I could claim as best who would also claim me. And I'd never fought with any of them.

Mascara blotted, Melody heaved a sigh and managed to look like a beautiful, sad girl. No red, running nose. No blotchy skin. No fair.

"Hey, those shoes are really adorable," she said, sniffling again. "Where'd you get them?"

For a moment, I thought she was alluding to those damned silver sneakers I'd dreaded lacing up day after day for two months, even though she'd never spoken another word to me. But her pale green eyes were wide and sincere. She had no recollection of what she'd done to me five years earlier, or my association with the nickname Boyce had invented that still made her livid.

"Barney's. In New York?" I answered.

Since I was only thirteen, Mama and Thomas had taken me along on their honeymoon. We'd stayed in a suite at the Plaza, where I had my own room and watched television all night in the king-sized bed in an attempt to obstruct all thoughts about what was going on in the adjacent bedroom. We'd spent our days shopping and visiting places like the Empire State Building and MoMA and Ground Zero. Evenings, we walked through Times Square and saw a Broadway show and ate at restaurants that made Mama nervous about silverware use and what she was wearing. Thomas had smirked in a charmingly smitten sort of way and told her she could eat her mushroom risotto with her soupspoon or her roasted duck breast with her dessert fork for all he cared.

"You went shopping in New York? Lucky!" Melody said. "Mama and I go shopping in Houston every spring break, but that's not *even* the same."

I shrugged, unsure what to say to a girl I'd wanted to punch in the nose for years, who was now regarding me with jealous admiration. We exited the bathroom together minutes later, and had been friends ever since.

Me:	Melody told me about your dad. I would say I'm sorry...
Boyce:	Yeah, don't waste your sympathy.
Boyce:	See you around while you're home?

I stared at his question, harmlessly asked—another behind it. Mama's words rose up: *You've never been afraid of any challenge—never in your life.* Untrue. So untrue.

I'd confided in one person when I received that acceptance e-mail over winter break. Not my boyfriend. Not Melody or my sorority sisters. Not my university peers—the ones applying for and in many cases not being accepted into leading graduate programs. Not my parents.

But I'd told Boyce without hesitation. I'd told him in the voice of someone who wasn't planning to follow that dream and disillusion everyone she knew in the process.

He'd taken one look at me and gotten straight to the heart of everything. "When are you going to stop being afraid to live your life, Pearl?"

No one ever asked me that. No one *knew* it. I was the valedictorian of our high school class. I'd gone away to college and worked my ass off, graduating with highest honors. I'd been accepted into more than one of the most prestigious medical schools in the country. I looked like I had life by the scruff of the neck, but that was an illusion. Because I was scared to death of who I really was and what I really wanted. And somehow he knew. He'd always known.

Me: Yes. I'll be here all summer.

chapter *Five*

BOYCE

I wasn't sure when Pearl would leave for medical school, or even where she'd decided to go, but she said she'd be around all summer. Which meant her boyfriend might come around again. He'd been here for a week last year, chatting up her parents and making douchebag cracks about the place we'd grown up. I'd only been around him twice, but it had taken a shit-ton of self-control to keep my fist from bashing all the jabs about our hometown right back into his mouth. He'd paraded his intelligence like it gave him the excuse to be a superior fuck to her too.

After he finally vamoosed, Pearl and I met up at our spot along the beach—an alcove cut into the dunes where one of the island's hotel monstrosities had built a private boardwalk to the public beach. Not many people came and went through the locked gate once it was dark, and the dunes—full of cactus and wild vegetation and the occasional snake—screened the beachside portion of the boardwalk from the lit patios and balconies of the hotel's occupants.

When I got there, she'd looked up from one of the wide, sandy steps and asked what I thought of him.

"He's a prick," I said, lowering myself next to her.

"Wow. Tell me what you *really* think."

I shrugged. "You asked, so I assumed you wanted the truth." She nodded, so I went one step further. "I don't like how he talks to you. I think he could hurt you, and it had better go no further than emotional damage or I'll have to end him."

She'd rocked back, head angling to the side like it did whenever she was trying to work out something complicated. Funny, considering I've always been anything but. *Boyce Wynn: what you see is what you get.*

"Jesus, Boyce. What did he say to make you think that?"

"It's not what he says so much as how he says it."

She frowned. My answer wasn't good enough for a girl who lived and breathed hard facts.

"Are you… jealous? I know Mitchell had access to opportunities you didn't have, and his family is supportive of his academic ambitions. But they aren't rich or anything."

She thought I was jealous of her boyfriend's awesome childhood or his fancy education? Fuck me. "Nothing to do with money or *opportunities* I wouldn't want even if they were offered. He's smart. I get it. And he makes damned sure everybody knows it."

I didn't know how to tell her that his bluster reminded me of my father, who'd terrorized everyone who could have cared about him because he'd known that he was a gutless coward, too scared to quit the bottle. His bullying hid his weakness. Her boyfriend was the opposite of my dad on the surface, but he was hiding something. Whatever it was, that motherfucker had concealed it well enough to fool her.

"So you don't like him because he's smart?"

Hell, she was clueless sometimes. "Yeah, that's it. Good thing Maxfield isn't a fucking brain, or I'd have had to hate his ass. Oh, wait."

She rolled her big brown eyes. "He's different."

If I hated people for being smart, I'd have been screwed day one. Pearl was the smartest person I'd ever known, and my best buddy from high school was right behind her—graduating from the same giant university, about to head north to some sort of bioengineering job in Ohio. "Yeah. Maxfield is different. He's not an asshole."

"Well, y'all have been friends forever—"

I laughed. "Not forever. We beat the shit out of each other in ninth grade." Right after the worst summer of my life, when we got the news that Brent had been killed in Iraq two months before he was eligible to get out. I'd expected to escape my father but instead found myself the sole target of his untempered rages. For some reason, Maxfield was the guy I took it all out on. Maybe because he was the only one brave (or idiotic) enough to call me on my shit.

I'd been on an unswerving path to become my father, and I hadn't even seen it.

"Melody told me about that fight, but I thought she was exaggerating."

"No exaggeration. I got this from it." I pointed to the small scar near my right eye and grinned. "No worries. He's got one too. We were opposite ends of a fuckup stick for a while there."

A smile touched her mouth and she shook her head, turning to stare out into the dark, arranging her thoughts before she spoke, as she always had. I stared at her, waiting for it. The moon was only a sliver over the water, softening the contours of her face, and starlight flickered in her eyes. The collapse and retreat of waves on the sand echoed the familiar soundtrack of our lives.

"I don't expect you to be friends with Mitchell," she said. "That would be awkward."

Yeah. That would be awkward. I'd wanted her for too many years. She was the bad habit I'd never broken, because I didn't fucking want to.

"I may be jealous, but jealousy isn't why I don't trust him," I said, and she turned her face to mine. I wanted to fall into the deep wells of her eyes. "I protect you, Pearl. It's just what I do."

· · · · · · · · · ·

Brent protected me until the day he left town. Our whole lives, he insisted that Dad was full of shit and I should pay no mind to his opinion of me or anything else. He blocked my punishments, deserved or undeserved—sometimes physically, but usually by negotiation. My brother was a born peacemaker, the kind of kid who'd stepped in to referee neighborhood disputes before fists could fly, which made his decision to join the Corps at eighteen all the more incredible to me. At ten, I thought all Marines were guys who liked to fight and shoot people.

He planned to serve four years, then go reserve and come get me. "If I believed they'd let me take you from him now, I would— but nobody lets little kids choose their guardians. And I'm barely an adult." He paced the airless room we shared at the ass-end of the trailer. He'd just graduated from high school and would leave for boot camp in California in August, when I began fifth grade. "When I get out, I'll be older. You'll be older—in high school. I'll get a decent job. We'll move to Corpus, and he'll never lay a hand on either of us again."

My brother was also a dreamer, but I figured that's how heroes were—it's how they changed the world—by dreaming how it should be, superimposed over how it was. I wanted to believe what he told me. I wanted to believe that when Brent came back Dad would be so glad to get rid of my sorry ass that he'd let me go.

Brent went to San Diego, and then Quantico, and a year later, after 9/11, to Afghanistan. After earning distinction for marksmanship in boot camp, he made lance corporal and then became a scout sniper. When I was fourteen, he was sent to Iraq. Dad hung a US flag in the window of the garage and accepted praise from everyone who stopped by to yack about how proud he must be to have a son serving our country—as if he'd had any fucking thing to do with it. As if he weren't the dead reverse of everything Brent stood for.

I hadn't been born with my brother's ability to defuse anger; I'd inherited my mother's knack for throwing fuel on it without even trying. It didn't matter what I did or didn't do, said or didn't say—I was the only one left to trigger his drunken rages. I was the motherfucking dipshit, the worthless dumbass, the pansy-assed son of a bitch, the useless shit-for-brains moron. I swallowed every word, except where Pearl was concerned. I'd done my one good deed when I saved her life, and I knew it.

When she came up to the middle school, she was still tiny and so quiet. She seemed more defenseless than ever. I didn't notice when she sat down at the end of the table Rick and I had commandeered for lunch the year before. The outcast table, we called it—but that didn't mean just any weirdo could plant his ass at it.

"Hey, dipshit—sixth graders don't sit with us," Rick said. He and I were dicked around enough by eighth grade jocks without welcoming guys who'd just be a magnet for more of their shit. I glanced up, expecting to see some skinny kid moving his ass along. But the person sliding her tray off the table was Pearl Torres.

"Shut the fuck up, Thompson," I said, looking into Pearl's dark eyes, which were almost obscured by glasses so large they hijacked her face. Her hair was wild—free of the braids or hair ties she'd always worn. "Stay," I told her. "It's okay."

She nodded and sat. Every day for two school years, she sat at the end of our table, shoulders hunched, hair partially obscuring her face, silently eating her lunch and reading a novel or doing homework. No one bothered her unless they wanted to pass through me. I didn't get in many fights in middle school. Brent had made me swear to stay out of trouble when he went to boot camp, and my dread of Dad getting called to the school went deep. But I was bigger than Rick's big brother, Randy, who was old enough to drive, so most kids just weren't that interested in pissing me off.

Pearl

"Evan arrived last night with his mannequin-to-be in tow."

I was almost reacquainted with the way Melody launched into impassioned conversations the second she slipped into my car, before she'd even fastened the seat belt or asked where we were going.

She yanked the door shut on my GTI, and I flinched at the force of the door slamming into the frame. "She's a Barb Dover replicant! All *Yes, honey* and *Whatever makes you happy, Evan*, like she has no damned opinions of her own and no intention of forming any."

Now probably wasn't the time to point out the hypocrisy in her judgment of her future sister-in-law.

"But hey—my parents are thrilled shitless. They'll finally have the daughter they always wanted. Evan even proposed with Grandma Bea's three-carat emerald."

I gasped. "What? But she bequeathed that ring to you in her will!" Melody's outspoken force-of-nature grandmother was the only member of her family who'd ever encouraged Mel to stand up for herself. She'd also suffered no qualms encouraging her favorite grandchild to rebel more often, claiming that her parents deserved it.

"Right. And what am I supposed to do? Sue my parents, my brother, and his Mom-clone to get it?" She choked up, and I didn't know what to say.

Mama and Barbara Dover had been in the same social circle since Mama married Thomas. Mama took pains not to gossip, but sometimes she'd come home from lunch or a Junior League meeting muttering in Spanish, and even if she spoke too quickly and softly for me to translate, I'd caught the word *Barb* on a few occasions.

"They know I can't do anything about it. This is how they punish me for breaking up with Matt instead of extracting a marriage proposal out of him." Her mother actually *expected* Mel to be engaged by twenty-two. Who *did* that?

"I thought Matt broke up with you?" *After your mother gave you a bridal magazine subscription for Christmas*, I didn't say.

She huffed a sigh. "No. He just didn't want to get married in the near future, or maybe ever, so I broke up with him. Mama had convinced me that if I did it right, he'd propose. But instead I spent two weeks with Ben & Jerry and Jose Cuervo, and nothing to show for it but an extra inch on my ass."

"So he didn't want to break up—he just didn't want to get married? Oh, Mel."

"Yeah, can we not discuss what a moron I am? I had a good relationship with a decent guy and I blew it. *Again*."

When we were in high school, Melody—and half the town along with her—caught her boyfriend cheating on her. Clark Richards and three of his varsity baseball *bros* had a visiting-college-girls orgy in a beach rental his father owned. One of the guys took video clips, which made the rounds of the student body like a lit fuse. It wasn't the first time Clark had cheated on her, but it was the only one caught on film, witnessed by just about *everyone*. I was never more proud of her than when she broke up with him.

She started going out with Boyce's best friend, Landon Maxfield, which I warned her against doing because I was afraid she was just going for a bad boy and she might get hurt again. But then she told me about their conversations. How he wanted to know her opinions and cared about her feelings. How he made her laugh. How his kisses did things to her that Clark's had never done.

Clark found out immediately, of course. No matter how sizable the population of this island becomes during tourist season, it remains a small town to those of us who live here, and nobody keeps anything private for long. He had batches of roses delivered to her house. He gave her a diamond-studded charm bracelet in a pink satin box, begging her to take him back and swearing to never screw around on her again. Her parents approved of him; his daddy was a big developer, even richer than they were. He was a year older, popular, and hot in a conventional, old money sort of way.

He was also a rat bastard cheater, but I couldn't convince her that even if *once a liar, always a liar* might not be a surefire judgment, it was a damned good presumption.

She didn't even tell Landon herself. In the west hallway the following day, her boyfriend informed him he'd been a rebound and nothing more. I didn't know Landon well then, but I knew he didn't deserve my best friend staring at the floor while her boyfriend told him he was trash.

Then Clark graduated and dumped Melody like their two-year relationship and all his promises meant nothing. I hadn't wanted to be right. I hadn't wanted proof that what goes around comes around.

"So, about you," she said as I pulled away from the curb. "You said you notified your mama that med school was a no-go, and you're still alive. So how'd *that* conversation go?"

"She's in full-blown denial. I'm pretty sure she's setting her sights on one of the waitlisted programs coming through. Like getting into Harvard or Michigan would make any kind of difference to me when I was sitting right there telling her what I want to be and what I don't."

She grunted a soft laugh and mimed blinders on either side of her face. "Mothers are good at ignoring what they don't wanna hear."

There was no reason to point out that blinders block peripheral vision, not the ability to hear. It came to the same conclusion either way. I'd described my vision of the life I wanted to live and who I wanted to be, and Mama wasn't having it.

I'd always thought my mother was superior to all other mothers because she'd sacrificed everything for me—the love of her life, her family and friends, the place she was born and raised. I assumed she'd forfeited these pieces of herself because she believed in me, because she meant to provide me with every chance to dream and reach and become. I assumed that what I dreamed and reached for and became would be my choice.

Until today, I hadn't understood that I was the one wearing blinders, and she was the one who'd put them there.

Boyce:	Meet up tonight?
Me:	Good timing. Dropping Melody off in a few minutes.
Boyce:	I'm all about timing, baby.
Me:	*insert eyeroll*
Boyce:	;)

chapter *Six*

BOYCE

Brent died when he drew enemy sniper fire. On purpose, according to the final report we got. To divert attention from half a dozen fellow Marines bent on storming a building where intelligence had pinpointed a nest of insurgents. A year later, he was posthumously awarded the Silver Star Medal for "conspicuous gallantry and intrepidity." The day he died, though, we knew nothing more than the fact he'd been killed.

It was June. Without a word, I walked past my father in his mute shock, through the open doorway. I got on my bike and pedaled to the Merry Mermaid, the tattoo parlor where Brent's girlfriend worked. Flying down the side of the road—past colorful stores and restaurants, imported palm trees, and out-of-towners laughing in rented golf carts that were street-legal in town—I was numb. The sky was cloudless, the sun straight overhead. The shadow my body cast was a shapeless, fluid blob, caught beneath the fat tires block after block. Without Brent, I was a formless, unconnected outline.

"I need to see Arianna," I said to Buddy, the guy who ran the place. My voice cracked on her name, like I was a squeaky preteen with a crush instead of a stand-in for the angel of death.

Buddy, silver-haired but lean and muscled, was the color of wet sand wherever he wasn't covered in ink. He pulled a pocket watch from the front pocket of his black Dickies, flicked it open and glanced at its face. "She's finishing up with a client—be done in five or ten." He squinted at me then, his forehead a canvas of baked-in creases. "You Brent's little brother?"

I nodded and tried to swallow, nearly choking on my own spit. I'd been to the shop a few times with Brent. Brent, who was dead. His last breath exhaled in a foreign country. His blood spilling out there. His heart stopping there. His eyes closing there for the last time. My fingertips went so cold I couldn't feel them. I could barely breathe. My eyes burned. I was like water trying to choose a suitable form—ice or vapor.

"You okay, son?" Buddy asked.

I shook my head, or thought I did. I wasn't sure. Maybe I didn't move at all.

Buddy's expression altered then, his pale eyes wide and piercing from the other side of the counter. He wasn't often startled, and his face wasn't familiar with the shape it took. "Brent okay?" he whispered, two words barely audible over the classic rock blaring from speakers set into the back corners near the ceiling. The vocals repeated the same line, louder and louder—*Do you wanna die? Do you wanna die?*—while the bass thrummed, keeping pace with the pulse in my ears.

Buddy turned as Arianna parted the threaded seashells strung on lines from the lowered ceiling, separating the front room from the corridor where the tattooists did their work. Unlike Buddy, her visible tattoos were confined to one arm, which looked like an incomplete puzzle. A blue-haired mermaid was pinned to the curve of her shoulder, sitting on top of an albatross I'd once made the mistake of calling a pelican. Brent had laughed until tears filled his eyes. A hodgepodge of patterns were scattered from her elbow to her wrist—outlines, empty of color. Unfinished.

Her tank and jeans concealed the tats on her abdomen, lower back, calf and hip—I only knew about that last one because Brent had slipped and told me and then made me swear never to say a word to her or anyone.

"She's the strongest woman I've ever known," he'd said then, a sort of awe to his voice. Staring up at our ceiling, he lay on his bed with an arm behind his head, across the thin stretch of dingy carpet from my bed.

"So you don't want her to get mad?" I'd asked, turning to watch him. It was the summer I turned eleven. The last summer we'd shared the cramped bedroom on the side of the trailer that leaned into the brick exterior of the garage—a setup that completely blocked two of the three windows. The lone working window was shoved all the way up, and a fan swung back and forth from a short dresser under it, pulling damp air from outside and blowing it around in a useless attempt to cool the room. We both stripped to our underwear and slept on top of our sheets every night. None of these efforts made much of an impact.

"No. Because I don't want to hurt her," he'd answered, and I wondered aloud why he would worry that someone he thought was strong could be hurt so easily. "She trusts me now. I swore I'd never hurt her, and I mean to keep that promise."

Four years later, he was dead, and I was the one who'd come to hurt her.

Whatever Buddy had seen in my face, Arianna saw it too. "No," she said. Her hands fisted at her sides like she could hold herself away from what I'd come to tell her.

Her client was some lady I didn't recognize—a tourist maybe, or someone from a nearby town who'd heard about her artistic skill. The smile slid from her mouth as she looked back and forth between Arianna and me.

"No," Arianna said again, a sob emerging with the word, sneaking out and grabbing at the thread uniting us—love for my brother—and jerking me awake when I wanted to be unconscious. The pain I hadn't really felt, blunted by shock until that moment, drilled through me like a lightning strike, fixing me to the ground before dividing me into a million scorched fragments. The tears didn't rise up. They gushed. My body didn't care if I was trying to be a man, trying to be tough and strong for my brother, for the girl he'd worshipped. A wail forced its way from my core and emerged, raw and ugly, from my throat. I went to my knees as Arianna rushed forward and sank to the floor with me.

"Are you sure? *Are they sure?* There's no hope? There's no—"

I shook my head, silencing her attempt to wake from this nightmare and make it untrue. "He's gone. He's gone."

Her slim arms surrounded me and her tears joined mine.

The day he turned eighteen, Brent had gone to the Merry Mermaid and requested the words *Semper Fi* be inked on his left delt, signaling his intention to join up as soon as he graduated high school. Arianna had done the tattoo, but it'd been far from love at first sight for them. Twenty-one and full of fire, she'd decided my brother was an idealistic goody-goody who was all talk and no action. "You'll probably just say *fuck it* by the time summer comes around, Boy Scout. You'll tell yourself there's no reason to go get yourself shot at. You'll head off to college next fall with all the other armchair crusaders."

He'd been goaded into angry silence at her presumptions, but that only lasted until he got home, at which point he was just plain angry and none too silent.

"Who does she think she is?" He tore his T-shirt over his head and tossed it on the floor, pacing. "Just 'cause she's all tatted and pierced and hot, she thinks she's so cool? Just 'cause she's older than me, she thinks she knows everything? She assumes she can size me up with one look? Judgmental *bitch*."

Brent rarely cursed, and I'd never seen him lose his temper over a girl. Which was why I was surprised when he went back a week later for another tattoo—and requested her.

When he got home that time, he was quiet. The bandage wrapped around his bicep, just under the scripted Marine Corps motto she'd put on his shoulder the previous week. When he un-wrapped it an hour later, I saw that she'd added the Marine emblem —a hostile-looking eagle sitting on a globe with an anchor through it.

"Thought you said she was a bitch?" The tattoo looked pretty cool, but still. I wouldn't let some obnoxious girl stick a needle in my arm. Not like I'd want a nice girl sticking a needle in my arm either. I shuddered just thinking about it.

"I was wrong," he said, examining her work in the bathroom mirror. "Be hesitant to judge people too fast, little brother. I know I've told you to trust your gut…" He caught my eyes in the mirror. "But sometimes what seems like a gut feeling is just pride pretending to be instinct."

• • • • • • • • • •

I was about to head out the door when I got another text from Pearl, asking if she should just come to the trailer. I stopped, glanced around. She hadn't come here while my father was alive. Not once in the fifteen years I'd known her. I wouldn't have let her if she'd wanted to—but she wasn't a stupid girl, and she'd never asked before.

The trailer was mine now, piece of shit that it was. I texted back: Sure, come on over. And then I tore around like a jackass, picking up trash and dishes and clothing and embarrassing junk mail I'd never given a first thought to, let alone a second. Minutes later, the front door rattled from her knock, and I was standing in the kitchen holding the cardboard box I'd just gotten from the crematory. Inside the box was a clear plastic bag holding Dad's remains, which looked like the gray stuff inside a vacuum cleaner. My father, reduced to a bag of dust. When I'd signed the paperwork, the crematory guy had figured out pretty quick that I wasn't interested in paying for some fancy decorative urn to house Dad's ashes. But what the hell was I supposed to do with this shit?

Pearl knocked again and I dropped the box on the table (*hello— dead guy on the kitchen table*), then picked it up and moved it to a chair. Maybe later I'd clear a space for it under the sink, next to the bug poison.

"Dumbass," I mumbled at myself. *Dammit*. That asshole was dead, and here I was still using his preferred nickname for me. Some parts of my life, I hadn't been sure he even knew my given name anymore.

"Boyce." Pearl smiled up at me when I opened the door. "It's a good thing your house is next to the garage, because it's too dark to read the house numbers, and they all sort of look the same."

I smirked. "C'mon now—the trailers in my neck of the woods may look the same, but they can be told apart by their distinctive landscaping designs. The Echols' place has that big cactus out front.

The Olneys have that dead tree with a couple dozen birdhouses hanging from the branches. And of course, the Thompson house has that pool and snack bar."

Stopping in the doorway, she glanced at my darkened neighborhood and then turned back, head angled and giving me a narrow-eyed look like I was pulling her leg and she knew it.

I took her arm and turned her, pointing. "See that discarded bathtub and commode next to their driveway? When we were kids, Mrs. Thompson filled the john with dirt and grew strawberries in it. Summers, we'd pull the garden hose over to that tub and fill it with water—it had a slow leak from a crack in the porcelain so we left the hose on a slow trickle—and we'd take turns swimmin'."

She laughed and so did I. A lot of my life had been crap. It would be easy to look back and only see the asstastic parts, but I couldn't look at Pearl's face or hear her husky little laugh and do that. I'd had a superhero for a brother. I'd had neighborhood friends, a beach in walking distance, a best friend I hadn't deserved but got anyway, and memories of this girl that I'd take to my grave. I'd survived my dad, and whether he meant to or not, he'd taught me a skill and left me with the ability to make a living from it. All in all, I was a lucky son of a bitch.

Pearl

The thought of Boyce and Rick "swimming" in that discarded bathtub—and eating strawberries out of a toilet!—should have been the saddest thing I'd ever heard, but I couldn't stop laughing and he didn't seem to mind. Unlike just about everyone else in my circle of friends, Boyce Wynn had no qualms about being blatantly inappropriate and ridiculing himself for it.

He shut the door behind me and walked into the trailer's kitchen, gesturing for me to follow. The refrigerator door rattled when he pulled it open. "Beer?" he asked, and I nodded, picturing him growing up here in this ramshackle trailer with his abusive father. What he must have endured. Popping the tops off two Shiner bottles, he said, "So, you're home for the summer. Boyfriend visiting this year?"

His expression was almost neutral, but I knew him too well, and he hadn't exactly curbed his opinion of Mitchell when I'd asked for it last summer. He also hadn't been far off base.

Boyce and I hadn't talked or texted during the four years I was away at school unless I was home for a weekend or during semester breaks. His actions—or lack of them, I suppose—had confused and hurt me at first, when I'd text him and get a word or two in response. Or nothing at all. I was lonely and homesick, and for some reason, he was home to me in a way that no one else was. Maybe because he'd remained here when Melody and most of my other friends dispersed to colleges all over the country.

We hadn't spoken since winter break, when I told him I'd been accepted into the doctoral program in marine biology. When he'd sized up my cowardice in one glance and guessed that I wasn't going to do it. When he'd said the thing about being afraid to live my life, delivered in the candid method I knew to expect from Boyce—no sugarcoating, no sidestepping politeness. I hadn't wanted that to be true, so hearing him say it kind of pissed me off.

Truth spoken out loud like that has a way of niggling at you from the inside, nudging your heart, tugging at your soul, lighting your mind with possibilities and sinking your gut with the risks behind them. Truth knows how to say *I dare you* and make you take notice, even if you'd rather disown it and remain insulated and safe.

That conversation had occurred before the ugly breakup with Mitchell.

"No. We, uh, broke up. A few months ago."

He blinked, still trying to pull his mask of indifference into place. Boyce was thoroughly capable of disconnecting emotionally. For years I'd watched him go cold with authority figures and peers and other girls, like he was insensitive to other people's rants or disappointments. No matter how scared or angry or dejected a normal person would have been, unless he was in the mood to punch somebody, he'd just shrug it off. I knew that ability must have been acquired in ways I probably wouldn't be able to handle the details of. He was never completely detached with me, though. Not when we were standing this close. He was a confusing mosaic of moods when it came to me, but never detached.

"Oh?" he said, his eyes glinting with something more than simple curiosity.

Sighing, I shrugged and took the beer. "Yeah. He wasn't too keen on my decision not to go to Vanderbilt with him."

The bottle in his hand paused halfway to his mouth. "You're going somewhere else, then?"

I nodded. "I'm going into the doctoral program here. The one I told you about before?"

"Marine biology, instead of med school."

Five months had passed since I'd told him that, but he'd remembered. Immediately. "Yeah."

"So you're staying here. Not just for the summer."

"The first two long semesters are on the main campus, and there will be some travel to different dive sites over the following few years to build my general knowledge base and then gradually work toward my dissertation focus. But the program is based here, so a year from now, I'll be here full time."

"Cool." He took a swallow and cleared his throat, staring at his haphazardly tied work boots. "That's really cool."

I stared at his hands—big, strong, dusted with light hairs, a few scars, and more recent scrapes likely due to his work. He'd grown out of fistfights. I had no idea where he stood on dating or relationships—whether there was a current girlfriend or a regular hookup or a series of them. He'd grown out of being talkative about that too. I wondered if he'd grown out of his desire for me. It had appeared when I'd given up on it and became a kind of game—he flirted and sweet-talked and stared, one brow cocked, shameless. I demurred, silently, as if both of us knew it would never happen, all the time wanting more. Ridiculously more.

By my second week of high school, I'd been absorbed into a new social circle—one I suspected had allowed me entrance based wholly on my new lifestyle and appearance. Not that I particularly cared. The worries about my few former friends—most of whom didn't even recognize me when we passed in the hall or when I sat down a row over in class—faded. I was no longer Pearl Torres, daughter of a Mexican immigrant single mother. I was Pearl Frank, stepdaughter of an established town surgeon. I didn't forget who I was, but it seemed like no one else—my mother included, sometimes—*remembered*.

From the opposite end of the hallway, I'd seen Landon first. He'd grown a bit taller and a bit more self-confident, no longer staring at the floor as he had in middle school. The boy next to him was taller and bigger, his short red hair contrasting sharply with Landon's dark in-need-of-a-haircut mane. Boyce looked like one of the seniors instead of a sophomore. Where Landon was quietly confident, Boyce was assertively so—his laugh deep and loud, his smile wide, his eyes, connecting with mine, sharp.

I was stunned by how quickly and surely he recognized me. We'd never had an actual conversation, had only spoken in passing, and not even that in over a year, since I was still in middle school. I'd seen him in town—at the grocery store, on the beach, driving past me and Mama in his loud black car. I knew he smoked. He had a tattoo on his arm (a Marine emblem—I googled it), which was illegal since he was still under eighteen (also googled).

Melody, staring down the hallway, said, "Ohh, there's Landon... And *ugh*, Boyce is with him. Great, he's looking right at me. Fuck."

She was wrong. Boyce was looking at *me*. As we drew closer, his gaze didn't waver. He said something to Landon, who glanced my way but whose eyes instantly shifted to Melody.

"Just *ignore* Boyce Wynn," she'd said as the four of us drew closer, the students around us just blurs of color. "He's a *dickhead*. I seriously can't stand him. God, I have no idea why Landon and he are tight now. They had a vicious fight last year—remind me to tell you about it later. Boyce jumped him in the hallway. He's also complete trash—his father is an alcoholic who runs a garage and they live in a *trailer*—total stereotype, right?"

Melody clearly didn't understand the term *stereotype*. Nor did she know a thing about Boyce Wynn.

As we reached them, her face morphed into a honeyed smile. "Hi, Landon."

"Hey, Melody," he said.

I waited for Boyce to inadvertently remind Melody of our humiliating elementary school connection, but he acted as though she didn't exist.

"Hey, Pearl," he said, staring at me like I was a double chocolate cupcake.

"Hi, Boyce." I felt the blush rise from my chest to my neck to my cheeks, and I turned my face away to conceal it. Nine years. Nine years, I'd waited for him to notice me that way, and now he had... when I was finally pretty.

chapter *Seven*

BOYCE

There was something about Pearl that had belonged to me since the moment I dragged her out of the ocean and onto the sand, but I hadn't understood the full scope of those feelings until I spotted her at the other end of the hallway at school—first day of September, tenth grade. My entire life flipped, narrowed, and focused when she came into view, and everyone else disappeared.

She was a mirage—all curvy little body and coils of dark hair pulled away from her face to uncover her big dark eyes and full lips. I'd been like one of those morons who couldn't see the value of a classic super car unless it'd been overhauled and restored. A true car buff knows the worth of a wreck sitting in a junkyard, rusting and waiting for its parts to be stripped. Pearl hadn't changed; I'd merely been blind and now I wasn't. Clothes, hairstyle, makeup—these were minor modifications, none of which would matter if she was lying under me in my bed.

A rush of heat and blood and want hardened my dick as though it meant to part the crowd between us and claim her right then and there. "Down, boy," I muttered.

"Huh?" Maxfield said, and I just shook my head, thankful for the mass of people and the strategically held notebook in my hands. He followed my gaze to Pearl and was immediately distracted by Rover Dover—thank God, because if he'd looked at Pearl that way, I probably would have shredded the fuck out of our friendship right there, without a second thought.

I'd been an idiot. A total fucking idiot.

· · · · · · · · · ·

She was staring at my hands—the one loosely gripping the neck of a Shiner bottle, the other hooked in the front pocket of the only jeans I owned that weren't marked with engine grease. Jesus, what I'd give to know what she was thinking. Was she lost in thought and staring aimlessly, or wondering if I remembered the feel of my palms and fingers skimming over her smooth, golden-brown skin?

My fingers curled against the denim near my groin, and her eyes skittered to the kitchen table, and then to the box in that damned chair—the label of which was clear as day: HUMAN REMAINS.

"Is that… your father?" she asked, pointing.

Goddamn. Even dead, he was fucking up my life.

I glanced over at the box as though I had to check to be sure what she was talking about. "Yep. I expected to get more satisfaction out of having him incinerated, even if that's what he wanted. I suspect he knew he would be a pain in my ass a little longer that way. If I'da buried him, it would be done and *done*. Instead, I've got to figure out what to do with a creepy-ass dad-in-the-box."

She choked a laugh, eyes dancing. "God, Boyce." For some reason, she'd always found me funny. In high school, I would catch her smirking at some idiotic remark I'd made, trying to hide it while her best friend bitched and fumed and called me all sorts of names as though I gave a fat crap. Both of their reactions just egged me on, of course.

"I keep thinking he's gonna pop up outta there like one of those damn windup clowns."

She shook her head, smiling. "Maybe you could scatter him from the pier?"

I frowned. "Not gonna happen. I told him I wouldn't be totin' his dusty ass to the water or performing some pointless farewell ceremony. He's gone, and I'm glad."

She angled her head, sobering. "I know you are, and I don't blame you one bit. But maybe dumping his ashes in the gulf would bring you some closure."

"Ain't no closure for me and him, Pearl."

"I understand," she said, and I hoped she didn't.

"Besides," I added, sliding back into the comfort of disrespectful humor, "I'm pretty sure he'd amount to pure-D marine pollution."

She chewed her lip. "What about our sandbar? We could dig a hole, dump him in, and put a big, flat rock on top of him."

Our sandbar. The one not quite the length of a football field from her backyard—if a football field was submerged under eight or nine feet of water. A couple of marshy, sea-grass-covered islands and a dozen or so sandbars—an extension of the nature preserve that ranged as wide as the town—stood between the wide-open bay and her neighborhood.

When I was in tenth grade, a guy offered to trade me a shitty aluminum boat with a sporadically working outboard motor after I found a working vintage Holley carburetor for his '69 Boss 429 at a scrapyard in Corpus. I took the deal because that ugly-ass boat could maneuver the pass from the backside of town around to the channel between that bunch of tidal marshlands and sandbars—across from which the Frank house occupied a corner lot on a dead-end street.

I don't know what I thought I was going to do from there—spy on her? Then I heard Dover talking her into having a party there the coming weekend when her parents would be out, and I knew trading a scavenged Mustang part for that leaky relic had been a stroke of luck. Or genius.

"I don't know, Mel... if anyone reports it—"

"As long as we don't invite too many people and don't build a big fire, no one will see. It'll be so cool. It's my birthday. C'mon, Pearl—pleeeeease? Clark can get his dad's boat that night and we'll ferry everyone there and back."

She blinked her lashes at Pearl like she always did at my best friend—who was a sucker for every damn cocktease move she made. If he'd just wanted a hookup, I wouldn't have cared—anything that screwed over Clark Richards was good, including his girlfriend getting some on the side from my boy. But he was all in, and she knew it. She twisted him into knots every time he saw her and then left him that way to bounce back to that rich asshole.

Pearl sighed and agreed to the party. The last thing Maxfield needed was to witness Dover and her dickhole boyfriend making out, so when he slid onto his stool at our lab table a couple of minutes later, I didn't tell him about it.

Come Friday night, I motored down the channel near Pearl's place, alone, beaching the boat as soon as I saw the glowing fire pit and heard the music. There were about a dozen of them—all rich kids, no townie losers—drinking and dancing around the low flames. I pulled the boat up behind a clump of marsh grass and watched, feeling like some kind of lurker sociopath. Pearl was dancing with a guy who couldn't keep his hands off her—a junior named Adam Yates. His parents were both dentists; when we were in second grade, they'd come to school to talk about teeth and pass out tooth-brushes and business cards.

My jaw steeled, but I had no rights where she was concerned. She wasn't mine. She'd never be mine. I wanted to leave, but for some reason I just sat right there like a masochistic jackass.

When the birthday girl passed out cold just before one a.m. from too many shots, Clark trundled her and several others into his boat, leaving behind the dick who'd been feeling Pearl up all night. Richards and Yates didn't bother to disguise the thumbs-up signal between them, but no one was sober enough to witness it but me. The rest of the partiers left with PK Miller when he said he had to make curfew with his dad's boat or his mom would chew his ass the rest of the weekend.

Pearl stumbled around, dousing the fire with sand and chucking cups and bottles into a trash bag, because *of course* she was prevent-ing fire and picking up trash, even hammered. Yates trailed along behind her, trying to take the bag or get her to stop. I was too far away to hear them. My fists tightened when he slid his arms around her and kissed her neck, but I did no more than stand up from the rock I'd been parked on for two hours because she seemed willing enough. Until he turned her around and did something she didn't like—too much tongue?—*goddammit*—and she gagged and shoved at his chest.

I abandoned my grass-hidden rock and ran. Before I reached her, he howled and went to the ground like a sack of hammers, and she yelped and staggered back.

When she saw me, she started and yelped. "Dammit, Boyce—you scared me to death! What are you—"

"Are you okay?" I demanded, grabbing her shoulders and turning her to me. I checked her face in the moonlight. Other than the fact that her eyes were so unnaturally wide that the white parts showed all the way around the brown and she was trembling, she looked all right.

She nodded, no idea how she'd scared the shit outta *me*. Yates hadn't moved a muscle, and her voice went soft. "Is he... is he breathing?"

I knelt, feeling for a pulse and refrained from saying *I hope not*, because then she'd probably insist that one of us do mouth-to-mouth, and neither fucking option for that was acceptable.

"His head hit my knee on the way down," she said.

Fingers at his throat (ignoring the urge to wrap my hands around it and squeeze), I found his pulse and struggled not to laugh. "I take it another part of him hit your knee just before that?" I stood. "He's fine, by the way. Or at least he's *breathing*."

She breathed a relieved sigh. "Boyce, why—and how—are you here?"

Confession is good for the soul, they say, but it's not so great for scoring points in a semi-stalking sort of situation. I couldn't stare into her eyes and lie, though.

"I heard y'all talking about the party in bio."

She frowned, more sober than I'd thought she was. "Then you must have heard it was a private party to celebrate Melody's birthday. You weren't invited."

Ouch.

She took two steps away from me before going straight back down in the sand on her ass, gasping and holding her knee. "Dang that hurts. Adam's head must be hard as a rock."

I knelt next to her, fingers inspecting her bare kneecap, all too aware of her soft skin and short shorts and how she smelled like a handful of flowers. "You've got a pretty good lump going here."

Her fingers slid between mine, testing the rapidly swelling spot. "Great. I should get some ice on it…" She frowned at Yates, who'd begun to snore, and then to the water's edge. "Clark just *left* me here? How the hell was I supposed to get home?"

"Surprise, Pearl, Richards is an asswipe. He took off with Dover and a few other people. Probably giving Yates time to make his move."

She glared—luckily at Yates. "*Make his move?*" Her gaze shifted back to me. "So how are you here?"

I shrugged. "I have a boat."

Studying the shoreline for the second time, she asked, "Is it an invisible boat?"

"Ha-ha." I pointed, chuckling. "It's down the beach a ways." I stood, swinging her up into my arms. "C'mon, bruiser, let's get you home."

Between the low drone of the bayside waves and the sensations crashing over me—her soft hair grazing my arm and my cheek, the feel of her body pressed against mine, the perfect weight of her—I almost didn't hear her question.

"Do you remember… when I died?"

I almost tripped on nothing. I crushed her tighter, unable to look at her. I could feel her eyes on me. "Yeah." The word escaped me, jagged, rough, and that day rushed back like a nightmare.

Her voice was low and full of wonder instead of the terror I'd experienced. "All I remember is jellyfish scattering and a flash of panic—just a few seconds, really. Then a sort of peaceful feeling, and the smell of Mama's churros, and darkness. Darkness, and then nothing."

I stopped by my boat but didn't put her down, staring into her face. Her dark eyes shimmered, reflecting the stars.

"And then there you were… staring down at me like you are now, but with the sun behind you instead of the moon," she whispered. "You had tears in your eyes. Why?"

Jesus fucking Christ, this girl. "I thought you were dead." My eyes burned, and I braced myself against the memory of the last time I'd held her like this—when she was heavy and lifeless, her head drooping over my arm.

"So did I. When I opened my eyes, I thought you were an angel —but those tears… And you were holding my hand."

I smirked. "Accusing me of being a player back in the day, Pearl?"

"I used to dream that you'd kissed me then, in front of all those people." Her gaze flicked to my mouth. "But you didn't."

Goddamn. I swallowed. "Well. I could kiss you now, to make up for missing my cue when I was seven."

Her lips twisted, just barely, and I waited for her to laugh, but she didn't. "Okay," she said, and everything inside me went still.

I lowered my mouth to hers, hovering a breath away. Our eyes locked and she didn't back down, didn't close her eyes like she was just yielding ground. She held my gaze like the lit end of a firecracker. I'd been kissing girls for years, had popped my cherry with an older townie girl on the beach the previous summer, right before I turned sixteen. But none of that prepared me for kissing Pearl. I was starting from scratch.

Pearl

When I mentioned the sandbar as a possible burial spot for his father's ashes, Boyce started to reply, hesitated, and then stared at his boots. I wasn't sure if I'd said something wrong or if he was remembering the same thing I was.

I was nearly twenty-one years old and a college graduate, but my mind could still summon every precious second of a kiss that had happened when I was fourteen. I couldn't decide if that was sweet or pathetic.

Adam Yates had been my first (unsolicited and revolting) kiss, not ten minutes prior. When he'd nuzzled the back of my neck, it was almost pleasant until he'd wrecked it with a slavering onslaught seconds later—all tongue and alcohol breath and drool. *Blech.*

I'd seen Boyce making out with girls on the beach or pushing them up against lockers to steal a kiss at school. Girls like Brittney Loper, who was dumb as a stick but stacked and sort of pretty. Hooking up whenever it suited her with whatever guy was interesting and interested, Brit was a carefree, perpetually cheerful pothead. Hating her felt mean-spirited, and honestly I wouldn't have cared what she did, except *Boyce.* Watching him with her made me spitting mad. And restless. And aroused. Which made me *more* furious.

I was appalled to realize that I was jealous. Not just of Brittney, but all of them. Boyce had been mine for years, or so my heart had—unbeknownst to me—decided, and now suddenly he was touching and kissing and who knows what with all those girls and I didn't want to see it or think about it *stop stop stop.*

I couldn't tell my best friend, who would think I'd lost my mind or needed to schedule an exorcism. I couldn't tell my mother, who still considered me her nerdy, quiet, undersized bookworm who hadn't hit puberty and who certainly hadn't dreamed and fantasized and hungered for Boyce Wynn's lips on hers.

So when I found myself in his arms that night, practically alone (passed-out Adam hardly counted) for the first time ever, when he said *I could kiss you now*, there was no way I was saying no. I wasn't capable.

He stared, eyes hard on mine, as if he'd misheard my whispered, "Okay." He pulled me tighter and leaned so close that we were exchanging breaths, but hesitated for a long, silent moment as if I might revoke my consent. I returned his stare, afraid he would say something funny or smartass or indifferent.

"Pearl," he said against my mouth. The subtle brush of his lips when he spoke my name spiked down my body and curled my bare toes and shot to my fingertips where they twisted into his T-shirt. "I'm gonna kiss you. Unless you tell me not to good and loud right now, I'm gonna kiss you, and I'm not gonna be sorry."

I didn't move a muscle, except for the tremors I was afraid he would feel. I couldn't distinguish that fear from desire, though perhaps those two emotions—where Boyce was concerned—had entwined until they were indistinguishable. His fingers grazed my shoulder, triggering a flood of goose bumps, and my thigh, triggering a flood of something altogether different. I mewled, a sound I had never made in my entire life, and he closed the microscopic gap between us firmly, his lips soft, warm, decisive. He claimed my mouth as if he was tasting me, coaxing me to taste him in return— *minty, spicy-sweet*—sucking my lower lip with a hungry growl, licking and teasing the upper, all slow, deep, unrelenting persuasion. He lifted me higher, closer, his tongue thrusting deeper, and my head swam.

And then I gave him mono. Or more accurately, Adam Yates gave *both* of us mono.

Me: Thank your stupid BF for me - Adam Yates
        gave me MONO.

Melody: That's what you have? SHIT. I got that in 7th grade. It totally sucked. ☹

Melody: Wait. You hooked up with Adam? I thought you kneed him in the balls and left him there?

Me: I DID. But not before he shoved his tongue down my throat.

Melody: What an assmunch.

Me: You think??

Melody: I said I was sorry! I didn't know Clark was going to do that!!! He's such a dumb boy.

Me: More like an aiding-and-abetting-an-attempted-rapist boy.

Melody: Adam wouldn't have gone that far!

Me: How do you KNOW?

Melody: You're right and I'm sorry and I told Clark if he ever did anything like that again I'd cut him off for a month.

Me: So can you bring me assignments in the classes we have together?

Melody: Sure. You're lucky on one thing, btw – we're dissecting a FROG tomorrow in bio. GROSS.

Me: What?!? *crying*

Melody: OMG. I know you want to be a doctor but I can't believe you WANT to cut open a disgusting dead reptile!

Me: Amphibian

Melody: Whatever!! I'm going to make Landon do ALL OF IT because Boyce is out sick too weirdly enough. Hey he didn't get mono from you did he?? Haha! JK!!!

While we were out sick, our best friends each lost their only remaining grandparent, and neither of us could attend the funerals. By the time we returned to school, there was a different vibe between the two of them. I liked Landon well enough, but Mel had a boyfriend, and though we had escalating evidence of Clark's douchebaggery, neither of us yet knew just how big of a tool he really was.

"Clark keeps asking me about Landon—like, suspiciously," Mel said. "As if I'd cheat on him! I'm not a cheater. If anyone should be mistrustful, it should be *me* after some of the rumors I've heard."

I'd heard them too—but Melody was the most beautiful girl in our school, they'd been together over a year, and gossip in a small town was often just chin-wagging jealousy.

"*You* believe me, right?"

"Of course," I said, meaning it. "Cheating in a town this size would make no sense. Everyone would know by yesterday."

What she was or wasn't doing with Landon didn't matter, though, because that was when Clark was filmed screwing the spring-breaking college girl. I arrived to find Melody ripping the teddy bear he'd given her into fluff-filled smithereens.

I picked up a severed arm. "Aww, poor Beauregard."

"Fuck Beauregard!" She snatched an empty box from the floor and began loading bear fragments into it. Next in—jewelry he'd given her, accumulated homecoming mums, dried flowers and printed photos, all torn into tiny pieces. "Let's go."

I drove to the public beach where she marched up to Clark, who had a girl on his lap. From the box I held, she showered him with armfuls of petals and photo bits and bear parts. She threw a bracelet at him and called him a cheating bastard.

Feet away, on the other side of the fire pit, Landon watched her, eyes blazing, tense and ready for Clark to do something stupid, and Boyce watched me, a lit cigarette in one hand and a koozied beer in the other. We hadn't spoken since that kiss, other than his usual juvenile quips during biology—the ones that drove Mel and Mr. Quinn insane and made Landon smirk and shake his head and had me biting the inside of my cheek to suppress my smile.

At first I'd been confused, then disappointed, and then angry. I'd worked my way to acceptance, like when I'd known I was drowning and there was nothing I could do. He'd merely gone back to being Boyce Wynn, who did what he wanted and who he wanted. And I'd gone back to being Pearl Frank—star student, social royalty, good girl.

But I couldn't forget that kiss. The fixed glint of his eyes across the fire said that neither could he.

chapter *Eight*

BOYCE

"The sandbar might work," I said, staring at my boots and still thinking about the feel of Pearl in my arms that first time—her sweet, sweet mouth and her unexpected surrender to being kissed. I wondered what she'd do if I pulled her into my arms like that now, standing in my kitchen. If I dared her to tell me no. Dared her to kiss me back.

She could have asked me to put my dad's ashes in a rocket launcher and light the fuse right then and I'd have done it. I cleared my throat and shifted, raising my eyes to hers. "Maybe back in a marshy part."

"Do you still have the boat?"

"Got a better one a few weeks ago—actual seats, no leaks in the hull." I smirked. "It's almost a damn yacht." Her stepfather owned a Cruiser 275—which had a sofa and a bed and a damned *bathroom* on board. But for guys like me, *ballin'* meant parking my ass on a padded chair for a day of fishing instead of a cold, hard metal bench.

"Mel's going back to Dallas Saturday morning. Can it wait until then?"

Her question was an ice bucket of fucked-up reality. What the hell made me think anything would change just because we were adults? I was still her dirty little secret. I downed the rest of my beer, shoved off from the kitchen counter, and tossed the bottle in the green bin by the back door. "Sure. Unless I just flush him before then."

Her laughter rang out, but the smile died off and her mouth fell open when she realized I might not be joking. "Boyce—you can't... do that? To your father?"

"You know as well as anyone what a sadistic motherfucker he was." *My mother, wherever she was, knew. Maxfield knew.*

I'd meant to unbalance her. I hadn't counted on this goddamned hunger for her approval. Her sympathy even. What the actual fuck.

She walked to me, eyes searching mine, forehead furrowed, and I couldn't move. Taking one of the fists at my side between her small hands, she said, "I know he made your life hell, Boyce, and it's going to take you a while to work through it. I'm sorry I judged you—I didn't mean to. You just shocked me a little, that's all."

My fist loosened between her palms. She saw right through me. She got me. It scared the hell out of me—how solidly she got me and how much I wanted her to, because that kind of need made me weak where she was concerned.

I nodded. "I wouldn't do it." *Lie.* If I hadn't been concerned about the substandard plumbing running to and from this tin can, I'd have already dumped him.

She quirked a brow, her lips pursed like she wanted to make some smartass comment.

"Okay, yeah I would," I admitted. "But he can wait till Saturday—he's not goin' anywhere. It'll give me time to compose a eulogy and get flowers."

"Right." She chuckled, sliding her hands away from mine. "So... this place is all yours now. And the garage?"

I nodded. She couldn't possibly be impressed with this shack masquerading as a home. "There's some red tape to process. Mr. Amos—Dad's old attorney—wanted me to look through his paperwork for a will, divorce papers, and anything to do with the business."

"Did your dad even make a will?"

I shrugged. "No idea. So far I haven't found anything but a bunch of useless crap. I took over running the garage almost two years ago—billing and accounts payable, dealing with the distributors, manufacturers we order from, that sorta thing, so that's already separated out, thank Christ."

"You've got your own business now, Boyce."

Maybe I should have been a little pissed that she looked surprised, but I wanted to beat my chest. *That's right—I run my own business. I am The Man.* In Pearl's defense, she wasn't the only one to be dumbfounded. I'd worked on my high school principal's SUV last week—not only fixed it quick, but fixed it cheap. When Ingram came in, she was gushing oil like a West Texas rig—left a line of it straight up the driveway and thought the whole engine was about to fall out. I told her that unless she'd been driving off-road or slamming over curbs like a bat outta hell, that scenario was improbable. I think she expected me to gouge her in revenge for what a bitch she'd been in high school, but I stopped giving a crap about her the day I took that diploma from her hand. A fifty-dollar part and one hour of labor and she was on her way.

"That's really cool." Pearl rinsed her bottle before dropping it into the bin. "Here I am, still playing the *what do I want to be when I grow up* game, and you've got it all figured out—a career, a place of your own. Independence."

"Jesus, Pearl—you're shittin' me, right? You could do anything.

Fixing cars is what I do—all I can do. And yeah, I'm lucky that it's also what I *want* to do. But you've got the world in front of you and the brains to do whatever you want. To make a difference in the world. Don't go acting like you should have it all figured out by now just because I narrowed down to the one and only thing I'm capable of doing without fucking it up."

She blinked at me. "You don't think I'm possibly screwing up, quitting med school?"

I grinned. "Lemme pass on a little Boyce Wynn wisdom. You can't quit if you don't start."

She laughed. "That's what I tried to convince Mel and Mama of. They weren't having it."

"Melody gave you crap? Your mama's one thing, but I thought Dover was your best friend."

If Maxfield had quit college one semester in, or moved home after graduation and said he wanted to work on his dad's boat instead of going after the work he'd trained to do, I wouldn't have given him any shit about it. Having each other's back is the foundation of any friendship. If your foundation is shit, your friendship is shit.

"Yeah, a bit. She was just alarmed, I think—afraid it was an impulsive decision. I never told her I was considering not going. In her mind—and everyone else's—me heading for med school and ultimately becoming a surgeon was never in question. It was just... presumed."

"You told me and not Dover?" *Interesting.*

"When I got accepted at the institute, yeah, you were the only one I told. Maybe because I knew you'd see right through me. You could see I wasn't going to follow through because I was a coward."

"Pearl—"

"It's okay. It was true. I *was* afraid of what people would think or say, afraid of disappointing Mama and Thomas and anyone who's ever had a hand in my education. I guess I still am. But it's my life. My choice."

"Damn right." I literally clamped my jaw shut to keep from asking her if *her choice* could include a night in my bed. One more night to try to cure this never-ending ache, though I knew—and I'd known for years—I'd never get over her.

As if I'd broadcast that thought into the room, she said, "I'll see you Saturday then?"

The words hung between us, thick and unsaid: *Dare you, Pearl.* "I close up at three on Saturday, but I'll have some end-of-week bookkeeping to do, and I'll need to clean up. Get Dad ready."

She rolled her eyes and laughed, and I pulled her into a hug for another round of self-torture.

Pearl

As I backed down the driveway, Boyce watched me from the top step of his trailer, both hands tucked into his front pockets. The tarnished porch lamp mounted next to the door left his face in shadow but shed a weak blue light over his shoulder, accentuating the shadowed lines of muscle along his arm—biceps brachii, brachialis, brachioradialis, triceps brachii, extensor carpi radialis and digitorum... I wanted to trace each one with my fingers, skimming the rock-hard curves and the valleys between them.

Back home less than two weeks and my long-concealed addiction had returned full throttle. I'd been so sure that college would abolish it—the two-hundred-mile separation, the thousands of guys on campus (there'd only been seventy-something boys in my entire high school), the parties and rushing and pledging, and last but not least the pressure that came with attending an academically distinguished university.

With my course load and sorority obligations, I hadn't had much time to date, so I'd only had two official relationships: freshman year, lasting a whopping six weeks, with a frat douche named Geoffrey who had no clue what the title of "boyfriend" actually entailed, and two years later, Mitchell. Between them there were a series of standard hookups and almost-but-not-quites, most of those encounters so clumsy and unsatisfying that they were happily forgotten.

In four years, nothing had erased or even dimmed my memories of Boyce. His kiss. His touch. The disorienting intensity of his gaze. I was a different person now, and so was he, but apparently those transformations didn't matter to this thing I felt. For my heart, he was a grounding wire, the needle of a compass, a gravitational pull.

For him, in high school, I'd been no more than a fixation, a conquest to be won. Before that, who knows? An obligation, perhaps—some odd sort of debt incurred the moment he'd saved my life. As I turned the corner at the end of his street, I glanced in the rearview mirror where he was still framed, half-eclipsed by the dark, a motionless silhouette.

My introverted psyche had always preferred to leave the acting out to others, so that on the surface I seemed to be the proverbial good girl. Focused and guarded. The soul of discretion and the mind of rationality, head to toe. But I had a secret center, and my flashes of rebellion were internal. My heart—carefully concealed and never worn on my sleeve or any other visible place—turned a blind eye and a deaf ear to reason. It *craved* what it wanted, and for years, it wanted one thing against all better judgment: Boyce Wynn.

The moment I resolved to give in to those inner desires took place in the middle of my high school graduation ceremony. Talk about never seeing something coming.

I sat next to Principal Ingram, waiting to deliver my inane valedictorian address to my forty-two classmates, their families and friends. Boyce sat in the audience, not-so-covertly texting or playing a game on his phone. Swinging my eyes away from him to avoid glaring while facing all those people, I spotted Mama, who was snapping dozens of photos of me, her lipstick-perfect smile wide beneath a black Nikon worthy of a professional photographer. I was graduating at the top of my class, with a full scholarship to the best university in the state, and her maternal pride was as insuppressible as it was embarrassing.

Thomas sat next to her wearing his crooked smile. He'd taken me aside that morning after Mama made me try on four different pairs of earrings, two necklaces (including her pearls, to which I put my foot down), and I don't even remember how many pairs of shoes (all-important, she explained, because they would be the only part of my ensemble showing beneath the royal-blue commencement gown).

"I know the spotlight is awkward for you, Pearl," he said. "But she's been waiting for this day all your life. You might as well grin and bear it."

Awkward was an understatement. I hated public speaking like nothing else. I would've faked a fever to get out of it, but my doctor-stepfather would have seen right through a feigned illness. I'd been screwed into near-perfect high school attendance; my only absences had been due to that bout of mono sophomore year.

I'd planned to resist looking at Boyce at all once I stood to give my speech, but that intention lasted about a minute. I wanted to know if he would watch me. Maybe because the things about me that everyone saw—my intellect, my potential—weren't what Boyce saw. Boyce saw *me*. He sensed my mushy center. He seemed to somehow know the body I was too self-conscious to show off, as if he could see right through my clothes. He stared at my lips like he wanted another taste of them. Like he might devour me, given the chance. Lord knows I didn't need to dwell on *that* while attempting to enunciate clearly for ten minutes straight.

On accident, I glanced Boyce's way to find his attention was pinned on me instead of his phone. My cheeks warmed and then my neck, as if caught beneath that spotlight Thomas had mentioned. I fought the temptation to fan my face with the index cards in my hand. My voice warbled, and I had to clear my throat. "Sorry," I murmured, soldiering on with the hollow *we will make the world a better place* section of my speech, cheerfully insisted upon by Ms. Ingram.

And then—Boyce winked at me. If I hadn't been marking my place with my finger, I'd have lost track of what I was saying completely. That wink shot straight through me, scrambling my insides and giving them all a solid yank. The hundred-degree stare that followed said he wasn't mocking me—he was sending me a signal. A dare, even. I shifted my gaze away from him, phony smile fixed in place while scanning the audience, unable to distinguish one face from another. Though it took monumental effort, I forced myself not to look at him again.

As I finished (*thank God thank God thank God*) and turned back to my chair, everyone cheered—more for the fact that the ceremony was nearly over than anything I'd said. But none of that touched me, because Boyce Wynn had, with a solitary wink, issued a dare. And I had resolved to take it.

chapter Nine

BOYCE

I'd returned to that sandbar a few times, alone—to the far side, less visible from the two-story houses lining the channel and man-made canals where Pearl lived. A few of our classmates had lived in her neighborhood. Jackholes like Eddie Standish, and decent guys like Joey Kinley, who hadn't thought he was the shit because his parents were loaded. My buddy Lucas Maxfield—he'd gone by Landon back then—had grown up in private schools, wearing name-brand threads. I reckoned he'd have been like Kinley.

In the middle of eighth grade, a few months before Brent died, Maxfield and his dad moved to town, bunking with his granddad just down the beach in a wooden-shack version of our trailer. They chartered fishing trips in the bay and the gulf, something it seemed like half the old guys in this town did—the half who hadn't retired here with piles of money. His dad still lived in that old house, running tours. He'd started bringing his truck in for service once I took over the garage.

After high school, Maxfield had gone off to college—same one as Pearl, though he said the student body there was bigger than our whole town and then some, so he didn't run into her often. She'd probably been smack-dab in the middle of coed social life—frat parties and the like (which I couldn't let my mind linger on)—while I was pretty sure he was the opposite. If I hadn't dragged him to parties on the beach for all of high school, he would've never gone. Both of them spent ninety-nine percent of their time not saying much, but Pearl could be surrounded by any level of crazy and just quietly observe like she was running an experiment. She had a watchful way about her. I sometimes imagined she studied me like that—as if I were an unidentified organism pressed between slides under her microscope.

Maxfield's silence wasn't like Pearl's. He had a simmering sort of hostility just under the surface, always ready to erupt. His silence was fucking scary. Which came in handy when we worked for Rick Thompson in high school—our *dumbshit era*, we called it later—collecting defaulted drug debts.

I'd only seen him lose his shit three times. I was on the other side of his fist the first time, when we were in ninth grade. He was smaller than me, but gave as good as he got, and we each wound up with a scar and a best friend. The second time was Clark Richards, who'd keyed *FREAK* into the side of his truck. (Idiot. You don't deface a man's truck and expect no retribution.) The last was Eddie Standish, supposedly for a two-hundred-dollar liability to Thompson for a bag of dank. In reality, Standish crossed one of Maxfield's moral lines while the three of us were having a little discussion over that debt, got his shit-talking mouth rearranged, and had to eat through a straw for a month.

I'd missed the fourth, final time—the one that got him hauled to jail. Some prick on the beach went after Thompson's little sister—who was still in middle school—and Maxfield stopped him cold.

Sitting in a cell scared him straight. He'd been different after—

got a job in town instead of working the boat with his dad or being Thompson's enforcer. Drove to Corpus for martial arts classes. Stopped skipping class and started studying—with Pearl in a few instances. Only the strength of our friendship and his general trustworthiness kept me from wanting to kick his ass over that. No more weed, no more fights. I didn't exactly follow his lead, but I graduated, which was something. After I helped him sell his truck so he could pay his first year's tuition, we rebuilt a shittily maintained Harley to take its place.

And then I watched him leave town, along with Pearl. Along with most everyone I knew, or cared to know. Two years later, Dad was diagnosed with liver disease, and I saw the first light at the end of the tunnel I'd been stuck in since Brent died. And then I looked around. If Wynn's Garage was going to be mine, it was going to stop looking like a damned dump. I started with a bottle of industrial-strength cleaning stuff—hosing down the counters, scouring years of grease and dirt away before moving to the plate glass window. I used half a bottle of glass cleaner and wad after wad of newspaper, scrubbing until the glass seemed to vanish.

As Dad's condition deteriorated, I gradually took over all the repair work, ordering parts and billing—keeping the books with the help of a new computer, accounting software I found online, and a few chats with Maxfield's dad, Ray. Over that last year, I ran everything and shuttled Dad back and forth to the clinic and the hospital besides.

Folks sometimes assumed, wrongly, that he and I might have mended some of our grievances in those last months, but the knowledge that they're dying doesn't transform everyone. Some people remain selfish bastards all the way to the ground. My father was one of those. Some people can't absolve what can't be reconciled. I was one of those.

I still met up with the boys: Randy Thompson (Rick's older brother, known as *Thompson Senior* when we were kids) and Mateo Vega, when he could spare a couple of hours away from his wife and screaming toddlers. Poor bastard knocked up his girlfriend—with *twins*—the summer after we graduated. Brittney and some of the other girls I cut my teeth on came around now and then, though they usually preferred to screw out-of-towners who'd give them an entertaining weekend and then get lost. Couldn't say I blamed them; I felt the same way. Occasionally one or another of them would start to hint about settling down, and that would be the end of that. There was only one woman alive who could settle me, and God knew hell would freeze over before that'd happen. My love life consisted of one-nighters and nostalgia fucks. No love, but it was fine.

Until Pearl said she was moving back home, and my heart woke up like I'd just set a live wire to it. I heard this saying once: *The heart wants what the heart wants*, and right off the bat I decided that even if that was true I'd never heard a more damned unhelpful bunch of bullfuckery. No explanation. No guidelines. No solution. Sayings were supposed to simplify shit, not complicate it.

The heart wants what the heart wants. Great. Now what?

Pearl

"This feels like the end of high school all over again," Mel said, glancing around her bedroom—now empty of her personality, so bare that it resembled a guest room. "Except I'm leaving for good this time." She deposited the last of a matched Louis Vuitton luggage set near the door and reached for me. "I'll miss you, you tiny little *chica*." She tucked her chin over my shoulder.

I returned her hug. "I'll miss you too. But you'll be back for holidays and Evan's wedding."

"Ugh, don't remind me. If you weren't here, I don't think I'd ever come back."

That wasn't true, I knew—when it came to defying her parents or exerting independence, Melody was all talk. The shiny blue Infiniti in the driveway was proof of that, as were the pics she'd shown me of her new apartment off Turtle Creek. Recent college grads couldn't afford a car or digs like that without help. In her case, help came with strings attached—such as not raising hell over her grandmother's ring going to Evan's fiancée.

"Then I guess it's a good thing I'm staying here," I said.

She pulled back, sighing. "For the record, I still think you're *crazy*. All those brains and you're going to use them studying sharks or seaweed or whatever? But you'll be the best at whatever you do. You always have been."

• • • • • • • • • •

Four years ago, Melody had thrown her arms up and said, "Let's make daiquiris!" as soon as my parents turned the corner at the end of the street on their way to their second honeymoon. They'd entrusted the house to their dependable, newly matriculated daughter for the coming week, because they couldn't imagine her doing anything remotely irresponsible—like invite a boy over in a harebrained plot to lose her virginity.

That thought made my insides coil tight as new springs. "It's not even one o'clock. Maybe we should pace ourselves?" I hadn't told Melody my plans for Boyce, and I wasn't going to. She might heartily endorse what I was about to do, but not who.

"Oh, fine." She pouted. "Let's go upstairs and decide what we're wearing to the beach party tonight then. I plan to be too hot and sexy for Landon to resist me."

"Mel…"

"I know, I know—don't say it. I'm not listening!" She'd botched her chance with him in tenth grade. I'd told her a hundred times that he was clearly the type to whom over is over, unlike Clark, who jerked her around until the day he loaded his Jeep and headed for Missouri State. We'd begun our senior year with her life in shambles because she was single, no take-backs, for the first time since ninth grade. Between bouts of fury, she moped. I wanted to shake her like a Magic 8 Ball that keeps giving the same undesirable answer.

"Also, your mama is on her way to *another continent*, Pearl. Live a little! Put on that hot pink bikini—the one we got at La Mode two months ago that I haven't seen on you even once? You can't arrive at college a virgin for chrissake. Wear that bikini tonight and you *won't*." She made virginity sound like a disorder.

My reason for holding back had nothing to do with morals or repression and everything to do with trust. While I understood virginity to have no real scientific significance, I was still intimidated by the notion of being that intimate with another human being. I'd spent my life in this small Gulf Coast town and knew everyone in my age range. Weekends and summers meant hanging out at the beach, sometimes tolerating a sloppy kiss from some alcohol-emboldened boy in the light of a bonfire. I'd had a few dates, some good, some not, and had survived a wave of gossip when Parker Guthrie told his friends I'd "given it up" in the backseat of his Bronco.

I hadn't bothered denying it because that would have required acknowledging the rumor, but my reaction wasn't good enough for

Mel, who started a rumor of her own concerning the size (miniscule) and shape (like a boomerang) of Parker's penis. He'd tried to prove otherwise with photographic evidence to the contrary, which got him suspended from school for a week and almost arrested. He'd been pretty much shunned the rest of high school.

At some point during the afternoon, Melody, visions of Landon in her head, came up with the idea of having a private pool party.

"There's no way Landon will come if Boyce doesn't," I said, hoping to deter her.

"You're right. Crap. I'll just have to convince both of them."

Later that night, we were on the beach with practically the entire senior class, and my brain was flooded with second thoughts. A party? In my parents' house, while they were out of town? Which would undoubtedly include sexual activity, alcohol consumption, and possibly drug use? I closed my eyes. Aside from being parentally and legally prohibited, it was just so *clichéd*.

Before I could back out, Melody began issuing verbal invitations. *Shit*. The party was happening. If I wanted something to happen with Boyce, it was now or never.

"There they are," Melody said, starting forward as my stomach lurched like the bottom had dropped out of it.

Boyce's eyes were already on me, ignoring Mel in her black bikini and sheer tank dress, glossy blond hair swept into a flawlessly mussed updo. Floral-patterned board shorts hung low on his hips, the dark orange and hot-pink blossoms the perfect adornment for a body that was nothing but hard and ripped and *male*. His pulled-low Astros cap shaded his face but couldn't hide the glint of his eyes. My hands fluttered down the center of my chest—ascertaining that I was still wearing the protective navy sundress—and I burned wherever my fingers touched, as if *he'd* touched me.

"Hey, Landon." Mel grazed Landon's arm with her manicured fingertips.

"Miss Dover." Landon clearly didn't give two flips. He looked more annoyed than tempted, but she wasn't ready to give up.

"We're throwing a spontaneous graduation party at Pearl's pool in half an hour. Her parents left for Italy right after graduation—so they won't be around. If y'all wanna come over, that'd be cool. PK and Joey are bringing vodka. Bring whatever you want."

Eyes on her, I still felt Boyce's gaze sliding over my skin again as certainly as I felt the warm breeze off the gulf. That wink during my commencement speech had replayed itself in my mind all day, driving me insane. I'd worn the fuchsia bikini under the sundress, at which point Mel had scowled and said I was almost-seventeen going on forty. Somehow, under Boyce's penetrating inspection, I felt naked anyway. I pretended to watch some semi-intoxicated boys screwing around near the bonfire.

"We've got a beach, in case you girls didn't notice," Landon said. "Bonfire lit, beer in hand. What would we want with a *pool*?"

I heard the trace of rancor in his voice and felt embarrassed for Mel, but he exchanged a brief glance with Boyce and then shrugged.

Boyce, ignoring Melody, addressed me as if he'd caught sight of my internal struggle and meant to challenge it head-on. "All right. We'll be over in a bit. Don't start the party without us."

They turned to go, and I released a cautious breath, nervous about my impetuous seduction plan, trying to approach it as logically as possible. I had no delusions about what a night with Boyce would mean to him. I just wanted what I wanted, before I went away to college to begin the eight years of intense coursework staring me in the face. Before Boyce fell in love or knocked up some girl and moved beyond my reach forever.

100

That thought made my chest tighten possessively, which felt an awful lot like panic.

There were at least two dozen people in the house by midnight. I'd locked the doors to my parents' bedroom and Thomas's study before anyone arrived and opened the french doors of the living area to the shale-paved patio. Dancing with my friends, I held a stereotypical red cup, still half-full. I took a sip from it and grimaced. Cheap beer didn't improve at room temperature.

Scanning the partiers for Boyce, I saw his friend Mateo smoking a bowl with Rick Thompson, whom I'd rather not have in my house. But there Rick sat, on my sofa, along with Brittney—still a stoner chick, still dumb as dirt. She laughed, uninhibited and openmouthed like a little kid. I tried not to glare at her. Brit had slept with Boyce multiple times over the previous three years, and she'd never been secretive about it. The only reason I didn't full-out despise her was the fact that she was mindlessly unaware how it hurt me to hear her spouting the torturous details in the hallways or the girls' restroom at school, in line at the coffee shop, on the beach...

Living in a small town could really suck.

Melody's eyes met mine from across the room. The party had been going for a couple of hours, but Boyce and Landon hadn't shown. When she'd invited them, they'd agreed to come right before walking off toward the beach road, where Boyce's black Trans Am was parked. If they were coming, they'd have appeared long ago.

chapter *Ten*

BOYCE

The numbers had been telling me for months that garage business had picked up, but I thought the difference was a passing irregularity. Folks catching up on overlooked maintenance work, not an actual increase. When I entered the initial end-of-month numbers last night though, there it was—six months straight of higher revenue. Several new local customers too—more likely to be repeats.

More *money* I could appreciate. More *work* was pushing me to the limit. Hiring help would make more sense than turning away business, so I made a note to contact my old auto-shop teacher to see about employing a kid to do simple but time-consuming shit, clean up, and schedule appointments. *Boyce Wynn: boss man.* Huh.

I didn't check the message alert on my phone until I took a five-minute break. After taking a leak and grabbing a Pepsi, I checked my notifications. The text I'd ignored, thinking it was likely Vega bitching about the Astros crapping out way early from any possible chance at the playoffs for another year, was from Pearl.

Pearl: Mel is on her way to Dallas. Is today still
           good for you?

Me:	Sorry. Busy as hell today and just got a break. Tonight works better. Want to get something to eat first?
Pearl:	Why don't I bring something over? Whataburger? ☺
Me:	You know I can't turn that shit down.
Pearl:	Avocado bacon? Vanilla shake, extra thick?
Me:	You trying to seduce me, Miss Frank?
Pearl:	You are perpetually sixteen. What time?
Me:	7 okay?
Pearl:	See you at 7. ☺

I'd known I was going out on a limb, suggesting that we go out somewhere together—in public. It would have been more of a shock if she'd said yes. That'd only happened once.

When Maxfield cracked a rib kicking Clark Richard's ass in high school, I'd followed her brand-spankin'-new Mini from school to her house in my '79 TA so she could pick up the stethoscope her stepfather kept in his dresser. Then she'd followed me to the Maxfield place to check him out. She'd been cranky that day, which hadn't been long after that kiss on the sandbar—a month or so, maybe.

The feel of her in my arms, the sound of her sigh and taste of her mouth when I took possession of it—she'd spun my head around that night. Three days later in bio, she'd barely looked at me, and I knew from the way Dover spoke to me that she hadn't told her. If a chick doesn't tell her best girlfriend something, it's either so unimportant that she forgot or something she's too ashamed to tell. Frankly, I didn't want to know which one of those I was.

I'd gone to that sandbar the next weekend, downed a six-pack of Budweiser, and seriously considered motoring over to Dr. Frank's floating dock, tying off my piece-of-shit boat to one of the cleats, and marching up to her door. In a rare burst of restraint, I'd settled for hoisting those cans one by one, toasting her in ways I thankfully can't remember the particulars of now, cussing and kicking sand like a moron.

More swearing followed when I booted a mostly-buried something hard enough to break my big toe. I landed on my ass, clutching my bare foot, furious that some inanimate object would dare to be in my way while I was throwing a tantrum like the oversize man-baby Dover had accused me of being after I'd burped the chorus to "Gold Digger" in class. My anger flagged when the full moon came out from behind a cloud, lighting the small, visible portion of my buried enemy.

With only hands for tools, it had taken me a while to dig up the entire shell, which was about the size of a football. Even half-trashed, I'd known better than to use a rock or stick and risk cracking it. I'd never seen a whelk anywhere near that big, and my first thought was how much Pearl would love it. Once I dug it loose, I swept off as much of the sand as I could, wrapped it in my T-shirt, and left it by her front door.

She'd brought it to bio to show Mr. Quinn, nestled in a towel-lined boot box like it was a puppy. The whole surface, every spiral indentation, had been cleaned and polished. Quinn had her walk it around the classroom so everyone could see it up close. "The light-ning whelk is our official state shell, ladies and gentlemen!" Quinn said, more excited than anyone else, as usual. But as Pearl circled the lab tables, even people who hated school and science in particular wanted to touch it. "Judging by its size, the previous inhabitant—a predatory marine gastropod, scientific name *busycon perversum*—was older than all of you."

When she sat down, our eyes connected across the scarred black tabletop while our lab partners examined the shell.

"That must've been one scary, big-ass snail," Dover said, and laughter broke our linked gaze.

I never did get that T-shirt back.

· · · · · · · · · ·

Pearl, standing in my doorway in shorts and a God-have-mercy pink tank top, holding a bag of burgers and two shakes, was an assault on my senses. I didn't know what to want first. My mouth watered and my stomach growled at the smell of those burgers, but when she stepped into the light my dick sensed that sweet little body feet away and said, *Fuck y'all, food can WAIT.*

"Thanks. I'm starving," I said, forcing those three words out like they were near impossible to form. Hoping she took my asshatted-ness for hunger—for *food*—I took the bag and turned toward the table to hide the way my jaw steeled, fighting to bring my body under control. That was the moment I realized I hadn't gotten laid in two weeks. No, more than two weeks—a month, maybe. I could have blamed the lack on being too busy or too tired to bother—God knows I was both—but what kind of loser is too busy to fuck? I'd go drown myself in the goddamned gulf first.

I hadn't even been attracted to anyone since I'd realized Pearl was coming home. That was the only explanation, whether I liked it or not. It didn't matter if I could probably go to bed right now and sleep ten hours straight. My body was more than willing to man up and perform like a superhero first—if I was fucking the girl who was currently pulling milkshakes out of a drink holder and setting them on the table right next to me.

My fingers itched to touch her. I'd barely stopped to eat all day and was starving, but her scent—oranges and flowers and a trace of saltiness, as if part of her belonged to the ocean she loved even though it had tried to kill her—was more potent than the smell of the food on the table. She peeked under both milkshake lids before leaning to place one at my spot. Leaning *over the damned table* to place it at my spot. My hands curled into fists, unable to look away from her perfect ass in those shorts and the sliver of warm bronze skin at her lower back when she stretched farther and her tank rose.

Hunger flared through me, a greedy flash fire of lust. I wanted to run my palms down her arms from her slim shoulders to her small hands, flattening them against the table in silent command. I would skim my hands beneath the front of that snug top, fill them with her soft tits. I would bury my face in the curve of her shoulder, inhaling her tangy sweetness. I would lap the tip of my tongue along the side of her neck, feel her pulse accelerate beneath her skin, suck her earlobe into my mouth and tug it with my teeth. When she leaned back against me, I would rush to untie, unbutton, unzip, tear open those little shorts and shove them down her legs, along with the lacy underwear my imagination conjured. Fingers sliding down her belly, I would slip one into her, adding another once she was soaking wet and her arms began to tremble. And then, fingering her with one hand while I unzipped my jeans and freed my ravenous cock with the other, I would whisper the words I've wanted to say to her for four years.

"Crap. They didn't give us any ketchup," she said, setting two huge burgers wrapped in greasy yellow paper at my spot and one at hers, flattening the bag and upending an extra-large box of fries onto it. "Do you have some?"

She turned, her head angling at whatever lunacy she saw on my face, and I struggled to understand the simple words she'd just spoken over the gradually fading vision in my head. Without replying, I twisted for the fridge, pulling it open and leaning into the cold. *Fuck.* I was acting like a grade-A jackhole, and I couldn't make it stop.

I just wanted her so bad. Still.

Pearl

The expression on Boyce's face before he turned to yank the refrigerator door open was furious—jaw rigid, eyes sharp as broken glass—and I had no idea why. He couldn't be angry that I'd brought him food? Maybe he'd reconsidered my idea for burying his dad's ashes on the sandbar. He'd claimed he couldn't have any closure, like it was an unattainable thing, but I'd hoped he was wrong. I'd hoped to help him find it.

Now I wasn't so sure he *could* find closure. Wasn't so sure I was the one to help him look.

I gripped the back of the chair, unable to shift my eyes from the broad, defined muscles of his shoulders and the vee of his back, flexing just outside the confines of his ribbed gray tank. His short hair was dark, damp. He must have showered right before I arrived.

"I figured you might be hungry, so I got you two burgers," I said.

He turned back to me after a strained, silent moment, a ketchup bottle in his hand. "You figured right." The anger—or what I'd thought was anger—was gone. In its place was raw hunger.

"Let's eat then." I took the bottle from his hand and smiled up at him.

He nodded once, more of a jerk of his head than a gesture of affirmation, and stepped around me to sit at the table. He worked hard six days a week, both manual labor and dealing with clients directly. I recalled how exhausted Mama used to be when she'd worked long hours at the pediatric office she managed. By the time she'd pick me up from afterschool care, she was often irritable from masking her annoyance all day. She'd tell me that working with the public was sometimes more taxing than the manual labor she'd done when she first arrived in the U.S.

"Sinks and floors and toilets don't snap at you for politely requesting a co-pay," she'd say, hands clenched on the steering wheel. "They don't insist on seeing a doctor immediately when they show up late, or let their children wipe their snotty noses on the chair cushions in the waiting room."

Boyce unwrapped a burger and took a huge bite, his eyes closing like it was the best thing he'd ever eaten. His shoulders lowered just a smidge. He inhaled a long, deep breath through his nose and let it out just as slowly.

"Good?" I asked unnecessarily.

Still chewing, he opened his eyes and nodded, releasing a sighed, "*Mmmm.*"

I compressed my lips to conceal my smug grin at having tamed the beast prowling inside him when I arrived. He smiled back, eyes crinkling at the corners, reading me like my analysis of him had been scrawled across my forehead. His insight was simultaneously comforting and unsettling. For most of my life, Boyce Wynn's smile had been three things to me: safety, warmth, and home, even as that same smile made my heart throb with longing for some shadowed, unreachable thing.

SWEET

· · · · · · · · · ·

Four years ago

"Just a *minute*," I mumbled from the top of the staircase—as if whoever was standing outside pressing the doorbell could hear me. I wasn't hungover, but I was groggy from lack of sleep. I'd lain awake half the night wondering why Boyce and Landon hadn't shown and wishing Mel and I had just stayed on the beach with them.

I veered around a girl snoring on the steps, recognizing Shania Fowler, who'd been on the dance squad with Mel and me. Arms folded beneath her face, she made falling asleep in the middle of someone's staircase look like a perfectly natural thing to do.

I heard the front door open just before Boyce Wynn's ticked-off voice echoed in the foyer. "What the fuck are you doing here?"

I hurried down the last few steps to see him leveling a homicidal glare at Rick Thompson, who—*the hell?*—had just answered my front door.

"Jesus, Wynn, come in or go the fuck away, but shut the damned door." Rick's hand shielded his eyes from the glare outside as he backed away from Boyce. "I'm not ready for daylight."

Boyce slammed the solid mahogany door shut, rattling framed prints hanging near the door. He noticed me over Rick's shoulder at the same time.

"Fuck!" Rick hissed, both hands cradling his skull. Someone on the parlor loveseat whimpered at the noise.

"What's he doing here?" Boyce asked me. Before I could answer, his gaze skipped over the passed-out girl on the stairs, the girl on the loveseat, and the guy wedged against the media center, drooling on the sofa cushion crammed beneath his head. There were probably people in various states of unconsciousness all over the house.

Arching a brow, I turned and walked back up the curved staircase, sidestepping Shania. I didn't look to see if he was following, but I knew he was.

I padded down the hall and into my room, kicking a romance novel under my bed as he appeared in the doorway. He filled the space—wide shoulders and broad chest, hands braced on the door-frame, elbows bent, biceps flexed against the sleeves of his close-fitting T-shirt.

My heart thrashed harder than the music had last night.

"Hi, Boyce." I stared into his dark eyes, unable to distinguish the green. From the opposite side of my room, they looked brown. Black, even. But I knew that up close, his eyes were the dark, multilayered green of a deep, thick forest.

"Hey, Pearl." He entered the room and slid his big hand over the antique glass doorknob. "Mind if I shut the door?" He watched me closely, his words deliberate.

"Lock it, too," I said, my voice warbling. I cleared my throat as the door clicked shut and he turned to pin me with those eyes.

He slid the lock into place.

Click.

Without moving nearer, he toed off his boots, which were always haphazardly laced at best. He pulled off his socks, one hand on the dresser.

"Why didn't you come?" I asked, and he paused, frowning in confusion. "Last night," I clarified.

His brow cleared. "Maxfield didn't want to mess with Dover last night."

"So… you went back to the beach?"

When he nodded, my imagination flooded with the probabilities that gesture implied. I wanted to scour those images from my mind. He wasn't going to come here to me after going there and—*stop*.

Chin lifted, eyes narrowed, I clenched my fists to keep from hurling things at him. "Did you find what you were looking for there?"

His shadowed smile made me angrier. Until he said, "Course not. I knew what I wanted and where it was. Last night was about bein' there for my boy. Right now is me bein' where I wanna be."

His gaze slid over me and I shivered. Lips pressed together, he started across the room, footfalls soundless, like a predator after small, easily spooked prey, but he slowed when I reached behind my neck to loosen the ties of my sundress. I pressed the bodice against my sternum, too chicken to let the dress drop to the floor, even with my fuchsia bikini underneath.

"Your shirt," I said, my voice raspy in the silent room. I'd meant to play music, light candles. But that was last night. Now my white linen drapes were pulled wide to reveal a blindingly blue June morning, all cloudless sky and gently rolling waves that shimmered as if millions of tiny mirrors floated faceup in the cerulean water.

Obediently, he reached behind his head and yanked his shirt off, tossing it onto the floor in his wake as he moved across the room, and my breath went shallow.

I'd seen Boyce Wynn shirtless hundreds of times. I'd watched him grow from a boy to a man. But filling my bedroom, a dangerous fantasy come to life, he was unknown—from the fully developed muscles other boys his age would willingly drug themselves with lethal steroids to get to the freckles darkening the smooth skin of his shoulders, trailing down his arms like smudges on a population map—densely inhabited deltoids moving to sparsely occupied forearms dusted with coppery hair.

Toe to toe, he stood a foot taller than me, one finger hooked in my loosened neckline. His lashes were dark except for the very ends, where they shone red in the daylight. "Let go," he said. His drawled command was soft, like a suggestion. "I wanna see you so bad."

I never imagined Boyce Wynn could speak so softly. I relaxed my grip on the dress, and it pooled at my feet.

His perusal of my bikini-clad body was slow and thorough. The tiny hairs all over my body rose, as if straining toward the touch he withheld. His eyes came back to mine and he arched a brow—dark, dark red, like his short hair. "Looks like I've got me some un-packaging to do." His voice had gone gruff.

I swayed at his words, assailed by too many sensations at once. His hands were at my waist, anchoring me, and my palms seared onto his chest. His skin was soft and hot. I inhaled the scent of him—subtle but spicy, piney, like the forest his eyes evoked. A boy who grew up on an island of sand and palms and scrubby dune vegetation shouldn't have a forest in his eyes.

His hands slid down over my hips and he pressed me close. Through his jeans, I felt the hard evidence of what he wanted pressed into my bare belly. *If it feels that big still covered up…* My breathing hitched at the thought.

One hand inched up my back and he untied the bottom string of my bikini top before sliding around front to stroke one breast, fingers teasing the nipple under the pink fabric. The mattress hit the back of my thighs as he pulled the upper string and the top came away. He stared while setting me on the edge of the bed, kneeling in front of me and pushing into the space between my legs. I watched, spellbound, as he lifted his chin and sucked a nipple right into his mouth, his hands beneath both breasts, cupping them as though weighing them.

My fingers forked through his hair. Soft and thick, it prickled against my palms. He stood then, lifting me, guiding my legs up and around his waist while his lips shifted to my neck, kissing and sucking gently. I grew dizzier with each lave of his warm tongue. One knee on the bed, he laid me back in the center and stood. I whimpered and he chuckled.

"I'm comin' back, sweetheart. No worries." He unbuttoned and unzipped his jeans. Shoved them down his thighs and off. "You first, or me?" he asked, hands at the strings of the board shorts he'd worn underneath the jeans. Through which a humongous erection was so, *so* visible.

"You," I whispered.

He untied the shorts, loosened them, and they dropped to the floor. And *oh*, I was right. Given the size of the rest of him, I shouldn't have been surprised. *How would that fit?* But his hands went to my hips, fingers hooking into the slivers of fabric on the sides of the pink bottoms, pulling them away, and there was no time to weigh the consequences of the disparity between us.

"You're a dream come true," he breathed, echoing my earlier thought about him, his fingertips stroking over my bare skin.

My eyes brimmed with tears at the wonder on his face—hadn't this boy seen a hundred naked girls by now? I was horrified he might notice, but he was riveted in his examination. His gaze followed that tantalizing, dragging caress, every inch of my skin flaring up in response. As pleasure engulfed me, the breath in my lungs caught and released, and I closed my eyes, fists white-knuckle tight on my bedding. My hips twisted and my shoulders rolled against the mattress. I couldn't lie still.

He moaned in response, his voice a growl of frustration. "My God, Pearl. You're going to kill me."

"How?" I asked, confused. If anyone would be rent in two at the end of this, it would be *me*. He moved between my legs and I stiffened, thinking, *Condom?*

He rose above me, turning my face with his fingertips. "You're too smart a girl to have unprotected sex—and I know that. I'll take care of you."

There were multiple promises in those words. I was naked on my bed with Boyce Wynn—but he was going slow and promising to be responsible and hadn't even kissed me yet. All my fantasies were being flipped on their heads.

"Kiss me?" I whispered.

He angled closer until his chest rested lightly on mine and then dragged himself higher, brushing my breasts with an incendiary friction that zipped straight to my core and forced a gasp from me. His mouth hovered inches over mine, his breaths deep while mine were shallow, erratic. I vaguely registered the feel of him as *other*— his body hard and heavy though he balanced his weight away from me.

Elbows on either side of my face, he stared into my eyes for a long moment before lowering his mouth to mine. Careful and measured, his kiss was everything I remembered. And then the first stroke of his tongue blazed through me, exploring the seam of my lips. I gasped again, drawing him in, my tongue swirling around his. Withdrawing, he teased my lips until they craved the spear of his tongue sliding between them.

I arched against him, wanting more, and he pushed back, his eager kisses plundering my willing mouth until I could scarcely breathe.

"God, Pearl," he panted, "you're gonna make me blow without being inside you—and that would be a goddamned shame."

"Night table drawer."

He didn't have to be told twice. He was back in less than a minute, sheathed and ready, kissing me until I sank my nails into his back, and then he positioned himself and drove into me.

I screamed. Tears streamed from the sides of my eyes and into my hair, but I bit my lip and tucked my head to his shoulder, mortified. I'd asked for this. Wanted it. I'd known it would hurt— Melody and I had discussed sex a million times—but *holy hell*. What she described as discomfort felt more like being stabbed with a flamethrower.

Boyce held himself utterly still. "*Shit*." He started to withdraw and I clutched his arms, nails digging into his biceps, because movement equaled a burn like a lit match. "Pearl…" His voice was pained. "Are you—?"

Crap. So much for a stealthy loss of my V-card. "I *was*," I mumbled, feeling every bit as dumb and inexperienced as I was.

"But— That assmunch you dated junior year—" He stopped, because I'd just proved *that* rumor untrue. "That sexy come-to-my-bedroom look— The striptease without so much as a kiss— You have *condoms* in your nightstand for fuck's sake! I thought— Jesus *Christ*. How was I supposed to know—" Again he began to withdraw and I cried out, equal parts pain and embarrassment. He froze. "What the *hell*, Pearl?"

How could I ever explain this? *Oh, you know, I've been in love with you since I was five and I wanted you to be my first. That's all.*

No, no, no.

The inferno below appeared to be subsiding, kind of. I took a deep breath and pulled my face from his shoulder, determined to be bold and fearless. The last thing this fiasco needed was for my declaration to be delivered in a squeak. "I'm going to college in three months. And I wanted this to be with you." Matter-of-fact. Logical. Very Pearl Frank. "Is that not okay?"

His freaked-out expression melted a bit, but his grimace lingered. "Why me?"

I licked my lips. "Because you want *me*. Not just *this*. Not just something to fill the time. You want *me*. You have for a while."

His brow relaxed and his mouth pulled up on one side. "I'm not exactly a subtle guy."

In spite of everything, I laughed. "No, you aren't." Swallowing lightly, I whispered, "I thought maybe you wouldn't have done it at all if you knew…"

Leaning to brush his lips against mine, his indignation melted away. "Hate to spoil your puzzling opinion of my principles, but you thought wrong. I wish you'd have told me. I could've made it so much better if I'd known." His warm breath fanned against my throat.

"So make it better now. It doesn't… doesn't really hurt at all anymore." A little white lie. Even if the pain had subsided, it was anything but pleasant. I was at a loss as to how the first man ever talked the first woman into trying this a second time. Then I looked into his dark eyes, which were crowded with an uncharacteristic mix of banked passion and self-reproach. *Ah, that's how.*

"I'm so sorry, Pearl."

"I'm not." The words tumbled out, startling him, but they were right. I wasn't sorry.

He lowered his mouth to mine again, kissing me softly, deeply, as he withdrew below. Before I could protest, he returned—more tenderly than before. His biceps trembled beneath my hands, and I knew he was using every ounce of control to keep from hurting me.

I trailed my fingertips over his solid shoulders and down his back as he pressed deeper still, his kisses drugging me. The discomfort began to melt away, to be replaced with a fierce, building ache. Progressing slowly to longer, deeper strokes, he countered those movements with his mouth rather than mirroring them—his tongue driving deepest when he pulled back, teasing the surface of my lips when he thrust inside.

"Boyce?" I breathed, beginning to move along with him, though the motion was foreign and some small part of me felt ridiculous. I wasn't sure if I was doing it right.

He slowed and I arched against him, wanting the opposite of slow.

"Ah, dammit." He closed his eyes. "You. Feel. So. Fucking. *Good.*" His eyes flashed open and he steeled his jaw, filling me completely and going stock-still, watching me.

My breaths came so raggedly that they'd turned into inarticulate whimpers, and I knew the orgasms I gave myself weren't going to compare to this. Nothing in my experience assured me of this—but I knew it was true. I writhed under him, *so close*, wanting him to *move*. "Don't stop. Please don't stop."

"No intention of that," he murmured, pressing his forehead to my shoulder and pulling out, slamming back into me a second later. "Jesus Christ, girl. *Goddamn.*" He raised his head and swirled his tongue over the margin of my ear and I moaned, teetering on the verge and terrified to let go. "*Fuck* me, Pearl," he said. "I've got you. *Fuck. Me.*"

Everything under my skin from my jaw to my toes clenched tight at once—muscles and veins and nerves and blood—and then released, pulsing, gushing like a dam breaking open, and I cried out for the second time, but for the most opposite reason possible.

That time he did too.

chapter *Eleven*

BOYCE

I pulled my bellyaching TA onto the road, the loaded boat trailer filling the rearview mirror. Using a classic sports car to tow a fishing boat—even a small one—wasn't ideal, and I tapped the steering wheel in unspoken apology. The municipal harbor was only a quarter mile or so through town, and lately I hadn't gotten much chance to take her out on the water anyhow, but the recent increase in business meant that renting a slip at the marina might be less of a fantasy than it was a few months ago.

"I guess I've never been in your car before," Pearl said, clicking the seat belt over her lap. Her gaze roamed over the dash, the floorboards, and my hand on the knobbed gearshift between us. "It's really... clean. Your place too. Very tidy."

I chuckled. In terms of everyday living, we knew so little about each other. She wasn't familiar with all my habits and quirks any more than I was familiar with hers. "Expected me to be a slob, huh? Surprised?"

She chewed the edge of her lip, trying to hide the familiar cheeky twist of her mouth. "A little."

I'd run around picking up before she showed up, but it could have been worse. *Was* worse; she hadn't seen Dad's room. If not for Mr. Amos having me search his shit for legal paperwork, his decades' worth of hoarded crap would have been at the curb a week ago. "How do you know I didn't just clean up before you came over?"

"Why would you?"

"To impress you, of course." I flashed a wink at her. "Did it work?"

"It's just me, Boyce." She dropped her gaze and smoothed her hand along her thigh. "You don't have to do anything to impress me."

My fingers tightened on the gearshift. "Because you already think I'm awesome, or because you never will?"

Her eyes flashed back to mine, startled. "You saved my life." Her voice was soft but steady. She returned her gaze to her lap and then forward, and the setting sun made her dark eyes glow. "I've been impressed with you since I was five years old."

I glanced at her profile and then stared out the windshield—as if I couldn't drive this road blindfolded. I wrestled to swallow the lump that rose in my throat, ashamed of the way I hankered after those words. The way I needed them and hadn't even known it until she'd said them.

When we got to the marina, she jumped out and helped remove the tie-downs and push the boat into the water, and I tried to return to the easy teasing she was used to. "At home with launching a boat, Pearl?"

She climbed into the boat, turned it on and reversed it off the trailer.

"Lord, girl—do you fish too? I might have to fall in love with you." Well, *hell*—where the fuck had that come from? I should just bite my damned tongue off.

She hitched the boat to the dock cleat before she looked at me. "Be careful how you throw that proposition around, Boyce Wynn. A girl might take you seriously."

I parked the car and trailer in the near-empty lot, grabbed the dad-in-a-box and cooler from the trunk, and jogged back over to the boat, waiting for her response to cut off my air, to give rise to the Mayday warnings my head sounded whenever I felt cornered or suffocated or obliged. But there were no orders to retreat, and the only distress signal in my head told me to make that girl fall so hard for me that she'd never wanna get back up.

When I hopped aboard, she was sitting in the passenger seat of my Gambler, texting. I didn't ask who and she didn't volunteer it. When she looked up, tucking the phone into the front pocket of her shorts, she stared and I threw her a questioning look.

"Your hair, with the sun behind it like that," she said. "It looks like it's on fire. Like those medieval paintings of saints and angels, with the rings of light around their heads?"

Damn if I wasn't on fire right now, conjuring up the last time we were on that sandbar. The first time I claimed those plump lips. "I'm neither of those things, Pearl."

"So you say."

"So everybody says."

She crossed her arms. "Well, everybody is wrong."

I couldn't help laughing at that. Angels and saints don't fantasize about doing a girl like Pearl over a kitchen table, or most of the other ways I'd imagined taking her. "There's my stubborn girl— so dead set on being right. So which am I? Angel or saint?"

She blinked and blushed dark pink, rising like dawn from chest to throat to cheeks. I wasn't sure I'd *ever* seen Pearl blush. I hadn't even said anything that suggestive in view of the teasing, flirting nonsense she'd tolerated for years.

"I suppose you'd be my guardian angel, wouldn't you?"

Her answer slammed into me. I hadn't expected her to choose either.

Once we picked a spot to beach the boat, she grabbed the cooler while I pulled the box and a small shovel from the hatch. I went back for the blanket and stack of firewood I'd stored there last night. The sun was almost gone—just a sliver of it loitering on the horizon like it meant to cause trouble, lighting the sky a violent red-orange. It lit the very edges of Pearl's dark hair as well—bits torn free of her ponytail during the trip over. On her, it was less halo and more like she'd dipped the ends of her hair in red dye.

We both stared at the box. I'd never known a moment of softness from my father. He hadn't earned the right to my grief, not even a slice of what I'd felt when I lost Brent. Why, then, did the knowledge that he was right there, in that box, dead but not buried, make something in my chest ache like it might crack?

"Boyce." Pearl's voice was soft. Her touch was soft as she pressed the shovel into my hand. "Let's choose a spot and get this over with. And then we'll make a fire and have a beer. C'mon." She picked up the box and waited until I stamped toward the marsh grass and started digging.

· · · · · · · · · ·

"You sure that wasn't illegal?" I asked, tossing the last log on the fire.

"Maybe. Probably we should've procured some sort of permit. Good thing my silence can be bought with a couple bottles of Shiner and a perfectly dug fire pit, huh?" She grinned and I laughed, which felt really good.

June wasn't a month that required a fire for warmth—not by a long shot. The heat of the day and the never-ending humidity felt like sitting under a lukewarm wet towel, even if the south wind off the gulf was cool. But Pearl had always liked campfires on the beach. Sometimes, back in high school, I'd catch her staring into the flames like she'd been hypnotized. So I used the shovel to dig a pit, and now we were parked on a blanket between the open cooler and the blaze.

She lay back and looked straight up. "God, I've missed this sky, all crammed full of stars. I could be here all night, tracing constellations." Stretching a finger to connect the pinpricked dots overhead, she said, "There's Ursa Minor—the Little Dipper."

I had a splintered memory of my mom, holding me on her lap, using my finger to outline skeleton patterns in the sky—Ursa Major and the sea serpent and Leo, my birth constellation.

"Most stars fade out in big cities because of light pollution—all the headlights and streetlights and landscaping lights. So much artificial prettiness at the expense of real beauty," she said. "Nothing makes me feel how small and insignificant I am, how fleeting life is, like the sky and the ocean. And here they are, in one place."

"You want to feel insignificant?"

"I want to feel what's *true*. And the truth is our lives are short and so often they seem to mean nothing. Even lives that seem important, like scientists who discover cures to horrible diseases or humanitarians... If we step back and view human beings—all of us—as part of the history of the universe, do we matter?" She paused, sighing. "Do you think when we're dead, we're dead, or that we become something else? It seems so pointless otherwise."

Leaning back on my hands, I stared into the dark where the

water lapped at the sand. "What does?"

"Life."

I pushed my alarm aside. Pearl wasn't suicidal, just muddled over weightier matters than most people contemplated or worried on, because they couldn't really be solved. That, I got. It was the place we'd always met. "Those are some big questions. Pretty sure lots smarter people than me have argued over those things for a long damned time." I smiled down at her. "No one seems to have reached an agreement, near as I can tell."

"Yeah, I know." She turned on her side to face me, folding her arm under her head. "But what do *you* think?"

I chuckled and glanced at the empty bottle just behind her on the sand. She was a little two-beer lightweight who got all metaphysically curious when loaded instead of drunk-dialing an ex like everyone else. No surprise there. "What difference does it make what I think? My opinion doesn't matter in anyone's grand scheme of things."

"It matters to me," she said, dark eyes probing mine as if I had the answer to her philosophical uncertainties and she meant to dig it loose.

I pondered her question, unsure it had an answer and even less sure I was capable of finding it. "Okay. Well. I think life is like a test on a subject we came in not knowing much about. We do the best we can, and we find out after it's over how we did. Or maybe we don't ever find out. But when you say my opinion matters, doesn't that eliminate the option of life being pointless?"

"My life, because your opinion matters to me, or your life, because yours is the opinion that matters?"

"Both." I paused and she waited for me to gather my thoughts. "What if all humanity is like a mechanical creature—made up of millions of parts, all working together, but sometimes not? Parts break or wear out or malfunction and have to be replaced by other, newer parts. And that keeps the whole thing going indefinitely, as long as new parts exist to replace the old ones."

She flopped onto her back and sighed. "But we're still just interchangeable parts then. We'll eventually wear out and get replaced and not matter."

I grinned and shook my head. "You're making a sorry case for *pointless* with that pity party. None of us live forever—we all learn that early on. But maybe you're one of the important parts. Maybe my dad served his purpose when he fathered me, and I served my purpose when I pulled you out of that ocean you keep wanting to dive back into."

She was quiet for a heartbeat before turning her head to look at me. "That's not true, Boyce."

When she didn't say anything more, I lit a cigarette and dug my toes into the sand at the edge of the blanket. The breeze pulled the smoke out over the water where it dissipated into the darkness.

"You're trying to figure out where you fit," I said. "That's one of the cool things about you. The fact that you care about things like what kind of difference you can make and how to make it. That's why I can't believe people like you, people like Brent, would be born into the world for no reason."

"I didn't—I didn't mean he—"

"I know you didn't. Maybe I can't be impartial where you and Brent are concerned. I've always been a self-centered son of a bitch, y'know. Everything eventually comes back to how it affects *me*." I took a drag and smiled down at her. "Looks like that includes your existence, sweetheart."

Pearl

When Thomas brought that enormous lightning whelk shell in with the morning paper, I knew Boyce had left it for me. I hadn't seen him or heard him leave it, and I wasn't psychic. I just recognized his shirt—a green baseball tee with dark green three-quarter sleeves. He'd filled it out better than any boy on the actual baseball team would have, and the green in his eyes, usually indistinct from across the lab table, glowed when he wore it.

I had no idea what it meant that he left that shell on my front porch. At fourteen, the motives of sixteen-year-old boys baffled me in general, but Boyce—kissing me cross-eyed one night and acting like it hadn't happened a few days later—left me bewildered.

Crusted with barnacles and marsh weeds, packed full of sand, the shell would have been an odd gift for anyone but me. I loved it, apart from Boyce and his intentions. But I loved it all the more because he gave it to me. I spent the day digging the sand out of the deep aperture and scrubbing the outer whorls and crevices with an old toothbrush. Once it was clean, I polished it with mineral oil and set it on my desk.

"I wonder who put that shell on our front porch and why?" Mama asked at dinner.

I shrugged and stared at my plate.

I didn't find out why he left that shell at my doorstep until over two years later—the first and only time Boyce was ever in my bedroom, the day after we graduated.

The fact that I was lying on top of my comforter buck naked—next to an equally naked Boyce Wynn—seeped into my consciousness slowly. Though I'd thought long and hard about who (Boyce) and how (protected) I'd lose my virginity, I couldn't say I'd seriously contemplated the where or when. In my fantasies, the set-ting was always somewhat ambiguous but always dark. Because of course it would happen somewhere private, romantic, and dark. Not *at ten a.m. on my own bed with at least a dozen people in the house.*

After discarding the condom, he collapsed next to me. I stared at the embossed patterns on my ceiling as the sounds of our breathing slowed simultaneously and our shared muteness became a whole different sort of loud. My bikini and sundress were on the floor, on the opposite side of the bed. On the opposite side of the boy lying next to me. The bedding was in disarray beneath us, but not enough to dive underneath without making an awkward spectacle of myself.

I suppressed a panicked giggle. I was lying on my bed with a boy in the bright light of day, *naked as a jaybird.* I'd rocketed past both *awkward* and *spectacle* a ways back.

That was when he rose up on one elbow and pointed at my desk. "Still got that whelk, huh?"

Pretty much the last subject I expected to discuss at this juncture was the shell that had been sitting on my desk for two years.

"Um. Yeah." I wondered if I could grab the edge of the comforter and roll myself into it without looking like a lunatic. Or a burrito.

"I knew it was meant to be yours the minute I found it. So whatever happened to my T-shirt?"

I blinked as his eyes flicked to mine, and then, as if he'd just remembered the fact that *I was completely naked*, his gaze moseyed—a Boyce Wynn pastime if ever there was one—over every exposed peak and valley to my toes and back.

"Do you want it back?"

"What?" His eyes returned to mine finally, but his stare was incisive, his pupils dilated, dark.

"Your T-shirt?"

He grinned, his warm palm splaying across my stomach. "Screw the T-shirt. All I want right now is round two—if you're game."

Desire surged over me in a landslide as his hand slid higher, thumb stroking the underside of one breast. From the feel of things against my hip, *he* was definitely *game*.

He was kissing me before I finished nodding yes.

· · · · · · · · · ·

Sleep was impossible in that bed, four years older but not much wiser when it came to Boyce. It was midnight before I got home from our trip to the sandbar. I'd watched him dig that hole and stare into it for several minutes before emptying the contents of the bag and refilling the remaining cavity with soil and sand. Not a word was spoken. Even so, Bud Wynn had been laid to rest in a manner he didn't deserve—with more respect than he'd ever shown his youngest son.

Melody had texted me earlier, letting me know she'd arrived safely in Dallas and asking what I was doing without her. *Not much*, I'd responded, revealing nothing about what I was doing or with whom. Boyce and I had never made our relationship—whatever it was—public. We'd both taken pains to do the opposite in fact. I'd persuaded myself for years that it wouldn't be understood by anyone who knew us, but now I questioned why I cared if anyone understood. The secrecy wasn't all me, though. Boyce hadn't ever broadcast it either, or even told his best friend. Lucas had given us puzzled looks the few times we ran into each other that summer between high school and college. He wouldn't have watched the two of us like we were an unsolvable equation if he'd known.

Melody: I still can't believe you want to stay there,
         GF. That place is VOID of anything or
         anyone worth doing! Dallas is sooooo much
         better. Promise you'll come visit!!

Boyce had returned from parking the car then, dropping his dad-in-a-box into the bow hatch and steering the boat down the canal, toward the bay.

Me: Sure. Maybe this fall. ☺

Slipping my phone into my pocket, I'd glanced up and forgot what I'd been about to say. The sun had begun its descent on the horizon, and at that exact moment it framed Boyce just as as it had that day on the beach when I'd woken up from drowning to his face hovering above me and his hand grasping mine. Art History, freshman year, I'd memorized various terms for the light surrounding him that day—*halo*, *nimbus*, *glory*—used to depict saints and angels.

Boyce had laughed and urged me to tell him which of those he was, as if daring me to liken him to either. He'd stared at my lips, and they'd prickled as I recalled, like a film on fast-forward, every blessed moment of their possession by his mouth.

Saint, he most definitely was not.

Twelve

BOYCE

Ruben Silva was the only teacher I respected in high school—as much for his awe-inspiring size as his mechanical know-how. I'd given him some hell, but he'd known the best way to deal with me was to threaten to kick me out of his shop or call my dad. I'm sure he never thought I'd end up running my father's garage alone, but neither had I. If not for how much I craved the purr and smell of a revving motor and the feel of grease on my hands, my old man would have lost me to dealing weed to tourists long ago. I'd come close enough as it was.

I figured Silva might know a kid who'd jump at the chance to be paid to change oil and spark plugs, plus get an occasional hand in a more complex engine repair. It was worth shutting down a little early to go chat with him after he finished his first week of teaching driver's ed. We met in his shop where two kids leaned under a hood while he directed whatever they were working on.

"Summer class, Mr. S?" I asked, crossing the concrete floor, offering my hand.

He was still the biggest man in town and had been since he was seventeen—the high school's only wrestler to ever win state. Rumor had it he'd turned down an offer to go pro to care for his terminally ill mother and stayed after she passed to finish raising his little sister, who went on to college and then law school.

"Well I'll be—if it ain't Boyce Wynn." We shook, his mitt still engulfing mine, though not as noticeably as it had when I was his student. "Making me proud, son."

I swallowed and nodded, grateful when he turned toward the students.

"No formal class. Just a few students who were more automotively curious than the rest. We meet in the afternoons, work on their cars or donated vehicles—repair work, restorations. Gives 'em something to do besides bein' thugs all summer." The would-be thugs eyed us over their shoulders. One wore safety goggles. The other was holding a wrench. "*Adams*," Silva barked. "*Goggles*. God dammit, these kids. One of 'em'll put an eye out and who'll get blamed? *Me*."

I chuckled, having heard this exact same tirade a hundred times years ago, directed at me more often than not.

He waved a hand at the Adams kid. "Come meet Mr. Wynn." It threw me for a loop, hearing *Mr. Wynn* from Silva—*about me*. To me, he said, "This is the one we talked about. Ignores orders half the time but a natural under the hood—like you. Has some potential beneath that know-it-all façade."

"Ain't no façade, Mr. Silva." The kid smirked, chin lifted. "I know a *lot*." This was Silva's recommendation for my first employee? A smartass who sounded about twelve and looked like a scrawny twig in those coveralls?

And then the kid sat down in the wheelchair I hadn't noticed and wheeled quickly around a stack of tires and a toolbox, heading our way. My misgiving morphed into disbelief.

"Boyce, this little twerp is Samantha Adams. Samantha, Mr.

Wynn."

A *girl.* In a *wheelchair.*

Her brass-blond hair was chopped short and stuck out in every direction, and her eyes were gray as an angry fog rolling into the gulf. "It's *Sam.* Jesus, Mr. Silva." She scowled at her teacher and shook my hand like she meant to crush my fingers.

She yelped when I squeezed back.

"Sam."

Withdrawing her hand and flexing her fingers, she sized me up. "So how much is the pay and what hours do you expect me to work?"

Goddamn. Who the hell was interviewing who?

"Minimum wage, and we can talk hours if I decide to hire you."

"If? So what do you have a problem with—my chair or my gender or my sexual orientation?"

Jesus Christ, I was ready to throat-punch Silva. I had a sneaking suspicion he was about to pay me back and then some for every smartass retort I ever made or rule I ever disregarded in his class. "Better flick those chips off your shoulder," I said. "I don't give a rat's ass about the first two, and I don't want to know details of the third."

Her eyes narrowed. "Meaning you have a problem with it?"

"Meaning the only sex life I have any interest in is my own, which—let's just throw this out there right now so we're clear—is none of your damned business. I may be swamped and need help, but not at the expense of pissing off my customers. If you want the job, convince me you won't be a bitch or a whiny brat and tell me what you can do for *me.* I run a garage, not a nursery."

She blinked, silent, which I assumed wasn't usual for her, and my phone buzzed.

Pearl:	Hey. I know you're probably busy tonight but I have a problem and I don't know who else to talk to.
Me:	Never too busy for you. Just tell me where.
Pearl:	Your place? When can I come?
Me:	You tell me, I'll be there.
Pearl:	Now?
Me:	Come on then, girl. See you in a few.

I glanced down at Sam, who was chewing her lip. "I have to get," I told her. "Think about the job and come by Monday if you want it. We'll do a one-week trial."

She frowned up at me. "One week? Isn't trial employment usually like a month or ninety days?"

"It's however long I say it is. Take it or leave it." I turned to Silva and stretched my hand out over Samantha Adams's head. "Thanks. I think."

The bastard had the nerve to laugh.

Pearl

The "highway"—two lanes, one in either direction, with stoplights—was clogged with summer vacationers. Even so, it only took ten minutes to get to Boyce's place. He was sitting on the top step of his trailer, smoking, one booted foot resting a couple of steps down on the cracked concrete and the other crossed beneath it. The dark plaid shirt—sleeves rolled up, unsnapped with a navy tee underneath—looked good on him. I tried to remember the last time he hadn't looked good to me and couldn't.

The doors to the garage's two bays were both shut, though it wasn't yet six. I parked in the driveway and got out.

"Close early today?" I walked the worn dirt path from the garage drive to the trailer's front door. I couldn't see his eyes; his sunglasses were too dark.

"Yep. Had an errand to run up at the high school." His forearm flexed under the light brush of copper hair as he turned to stub out the cigarette in a makeshift ashtray—a ceramic pot three-quarters full of sand.

"Really? Doing what?" I ripped my gaze from his arm when he turned back.

"Hiring one of Silva's students to help me out in the garage, hopefully." Grimacing, he reached to scratch the back of his neck. "I don't know though. Might be more trouble than it's worth."

"I think it's a great idea."

As I reached him, he shrugged and stood. "We'll see, I guess. You said you had a problem? Come on in and let's solve it."

If only it were that simple. I'd never thought of myself as helpless, but Boyce was running a business and his *life*, and I had no job, no money of my own.

I followed him into the trailer, which seemed darker in broad daylight than it had when I'd come over the other night. We both removed our sunglasses.

As if reading my mind, he said, "Sorry it's so dark in here— trailers aren't exactly famous for great lighting design. Your eyes will adjust in a minute, but I can switch on the lamps if you want. I could walk around in here blindfolded, so I don't really think about it."

"It's fine. I didn't prepare a graphic presentation or anything. I just need to talk this out. You sure you don't mind?"

"'Course not. You can always come to me—you know that." He sat on one end of the sofa and I took the other. "So what's up?"

We leaned into our respective corners, facing each other.

"I just finished my first week of class. It's an adjustment from work I did for my BS, and even more so from what I ever imagined doing as a postgrad, but I love it. My two classes are small—just a handful of people. I already know everyone. We took a boat out and gathered samples to help one of the professors run lab tests, and it was nothing like being an undergrad at a huge school where you have little to no autonomy. He was like, 'Go do this,' with almost no direction, which was like being a peer instead of, you know, a minion. A *low-ranking* peer, but a peer."

He smiled. "Sounds great. And I'm not hearing the problem."

Closing my eyes, I sucked in a deep breath. "The problem is I got accepted to Michigan. Med school."

"I don't understand. Thought you said you weren't going."

"I applied to several schools, and I was actually accepted to the majority of them. When Mitchell and I chose Vanderbilt, I turned the other acceptances down. But I was waitlisted at two—Harvard and Michigan."

"At the risk of showing my hick side, what does that mean, exactly—being waitlisted?"

"It means you met the qualifications, but other candidates met them better, so they got the offers to attend. Waitlisted applicants are put in a queue. You only get an actual acceptance if enough of the candidates ahead of you decide to go elsewhere and you're high enough on the list. I got an acceptance letter today—which Mama opened before I got home."

"Ah. So she's all fired up about you changing your mind."

I chuckled joylessly. "*Fired up* is a good way to term it. I want to do exactly what I'm doing, but she's made it really clear that she and Thomas don't support that decision, which could mean I'm on my own financially. I know this will sound incredibly naïve and immature to you—but I've never had to take care of myself in that way. I grew up understanding that there were things I couldn't have because Mama couldn't afford them. I never asked for anything I perceived as unreasonable, but I was still a kid. I wasn't always sure. After they got married, money was no longer an impediment. What I got or didn't get was based on factors like safety or whether it would distract me from my studies. Things that had little or nothing to do with the expense. As a result, I'm… I'm *spoiled*."

Sitting forward, he leaned his forearms on his thighs and his eyes promised the frankness I both wanted and dreaded. Boyce never lied to me. That was why I often sought him out when others might have made more sense on the surface—because he told me, bluntly, the truth as he saw it.

"I grew up shifting for myself instead of being looked after," he said. "It was do or die and I chose *do*. But I think there's a difference between spoiled and privileged. Your best friend thinks she has a right to anything she wants without earning it. That's spoiled. Privileged is what anyone with sense would want for their kid. Your needs were seen to. Most of your wants too, maybe. But that's nothing to feel guilty over. And it doesn't mean your parents get to decide your life for you."

I'd never thought of it that way. Privileged was something I became when Mama and Thomas married, though compared to the hand Boyce was dealt, I'd been privileged my whole life. Since he used her for an example though, I felt the need to defend Melody. "Mel's parents have always dangled material things in front of her to manipulate her, you know. She earns what they give her by relinquishing any claim to make her own choices."

The answering set of his jaw told me he would always fight granting Melody any sort of concession for her overindulged behavior. I couldn't blame him. She'd been unkind to his best friend in high school. He didn't know her like I'd come to know her, or the lengths to which her entire family went to control her.

"Hmm," he said. "Maybe the difference is your mama didn't have to manipulate you because up till now, you and she wanted the same thing where your future was concerned."

He was right. I couldn't remember a point where I hadn't regarded the world from an analytical perspective. All my mother had to do was support those innate desires—no tactical guidance required. This was my first deviation from The Plan for Pearl's Future.

"Oh God." I put my face in my hands in full, miserable comprehension that this was it—or not. This would be my sticking point or the point where I ceded control over my future. It was my choice.

BOYCE

"Plans tonight?" I asked her at the door, ready to text Thompson and cancel for tonight without blinking an eye.

She glanced up, the little crease between her brows signaling her concern over what I'd said or the decision she had to make. Me and my stupid fucking mouth. She wanted me to give her the straight-up truth, but that didn't mean I had to be a dick.

"A group of us are going out," she said. "It's the first official weekend here for the incoming class. Those of us who chose summer start, at least. I'm the only townie, so I'm supposed to know where to go. I'm also the only one who did premed as an undergrad, so I have to prove I don't have a stick up my butt... although I'm pretty sure they all assumed I didn't make the med-school cut."

"You set 'em straight on that?"

"No." She shrugged, pushing her sunglasses on and digging keys from her bag. "I guess I'm kind of afraid they'd all think I'm as irrational as everyone else does."

"Not everyone," I said, coaxing a crooked little smile from her.

She squeezed my forearm—one second, maybe two—but my skin burned where her fingers skimmed. "Not everyone. Thanks for that."

I watched her drive away for the second time in a week, waiting until she turned the corner before I turned to go inside.

Randy Thompson and I headed to Avery's every Friday after work for chicken-fried steak the size of a platter, buttery potatoes, and iced tea. The ritual had started in high school with Maxfield, Vega, and Thompson's younger brother Rick. Randy had been a senior when the rest of us started high school. He'd been dealing then, mostly weed. He hadn't gotten into the harder shit until later. Since coming home from Jester, Randy had been living with his parents in the home he grew up in, across the street. He worked at his mom's shop now, which sold island-themed décor, T-shirts, and jewelry Randy made.

"That Pearl's car over at your place earlier?" he asked, swiping a forkful of steak through a pool of potatoes and gravy.

"Yep."

"She graduated with Maxfield last month, right?"

I nodded, chewing. I'd meant to go to the ceremony, but between Dad's final trip to the hospital, the increase in business, and the eight-hour round trip, I hadn't been able to get away.

"Cool. And Maxfield's heading to Ohio?" Thompson was no idiot. I didn't discuss Pearl with anyone, and he was no exception. "He coming home first?"

"Not sure he considers this place home. But yeah—he'll be here in a couple weeks."

"Cool," he repeated.

Our waitress, Honey, arrived with the pitcher and topped off our glasses with fresh-brewed tea so dark I grabbed two extra packets of sugar.

"You boys staying outta trouble?" she asked. Thompson stared at his plate. A childhood friend of his mom, Honey was probably more familiar with the details of his time in Jester than the rest of our small town.

"Yes, ma'am, we are." I winked, grinning. "Unless you're offering to lead me astray. Don't tease me now."

She swatted my shoulder. "You stop that flirtin' or one of these days I might take you up on it just to watch you run outta here like your pants are on fire."

"Oh, they're on fi—"

"Hush!" She laughed, shaking her head before moving to the next table.

We ate in silence for a few minutes, and my thoughts wandered to Pearl for the millionth time since she'd come home. I'd never imagined her moving back here to live. She'd be gone for a few months come fall, but after four years of her absence, a few months was nothing. Unless she returned with another boyfriend. Someone from her program, maybe. I'd watch her grow older, settle down, have children. I'd know those children existed because I'd saved her life, and that fact should make me proud, but it made me want to throw the table across the room.

I set my fork down before I bent it.

"I'm never going to live it down," Thompson mumbled.

His assertion felt like something I'd think about Pearl, and I had to shift gears. "Honey didn't mean—"

"I know," he said. "It's not what she said so much as…" He sighed. "It feels like there's some implication under every word anyone says. Some reference to the fact that I'm a fuckup. I'm always expecting it, whether it's actually coming at me or not."

"I learned a while back not to let other people define me," I said. *Except Pearl.*

"Easier said than done when your permanent record includes a set of convictions and prison time."

I took another bite, considering. It was true that he'd dug a big hole for himself and then nearly buried himself alive, metaphorically speaking. Digging back out would be a bitch, and there were some options—some possible futures—he'd thrown away forever in the process. That sucked. "What's that saying? Nothing worth having is easy?"

Like Pearl. Had there ever been a possible future with her—one I'd never believed in?

Thompson sighed. "Sometimes, though, I just want it to be easy." His prison release came with mandatory AA meetings twice a week, monthly appointments with his parole officer in Corpus, and a year's worth of random drug testing. If he failed at even one of those things, he'd go back in and nobody would give a goddamn except his mom. And me.

"You can do it, man. You *are* doing it."

"Thanks, Wynn." He glanced at me and back at his plate. "For what it's worth, that girl should wake up and see what she's missing before it's too late."

I didn't reply. If I'd had a lick of sense four years ago, I wouldn't have wrecked even the snowball's chance in hell I might've had with her. I'd never been able to forget the look on her face the first time I saw her—*after*. It was officially summer, and it felt like half the state was partying on the beach. I'd been a bit wasted that night, so my reaction had lagged. The sight of her on the other side of the fire was a violent jolt—every fantasy I'd ever ached for personified. It had only been ten hours or so since I'd left her bed, but I wanted her more than I ever had.

Her eyes went wide and her mouth formed an *O* made silent by the distance between us, and I had the fucking idiocy to be confused when she stepped back and out of the campfire's light. By the time I figured out why, she was gone.

I'd pushed the girl off my lap, staggered to my feet and walked straight—or straight as I could manage—to where she'd been, but she had dissolved into the dark and the summer swarm of people as if I'd imagined her there. I tried to convince myself that she'd been a hallucination, that her crushed expression was a nightmare I could still prevent, but I knew better.

She didn't answer my dumbass texts the next two days (*What's up?*), and when we finally ran into each other at the gas pump, her eyes slid away from mine as we small-talked. I hadn't gone to my knees and apologized. I hadn't told her she was all I wanted and always had been. I convinced myself that I could weasel out of it without that sort of humiliation.

A week later, I heard she'd gone off to some university in Georgia for a premed program for high school graduates instead of working at the marine-science center all summer like she'd planned. She was gone for six weeks, and when she came back, we'd backed up to the day before I spent three hours in her bed, foolishly thinking I was making her mine.

Pearl

Dinner conversation focused on research projects, the cheapest bars, the awful reality that the nearest Starbucks was almost an hour away, and affordable student housing that would have cost thousands per month on the open market for the beachfront view alone, even with ancient appliances and doors warped by decades of humidity.

As usual for me, I'd been quiet during class so far, only contributing when I was one hundred percent certain of what I was stating. My colleagues could tell I wasn't going to be a burden, but they had no idea of my passion. I knew most of them assumed I'd scrambled for a biology-related graduate studies field when med school shut its door in my face. Maybe they even thought what Mitchell had—that I'd only chosen what was close and safe.

But I didn't want to be safe. I wanted to do research that would make a difference, targeting oil corporations and lobbies and politicians and any other entity that threatened the fragile balance of the estuaries connected to the gulf and the life teeming beneath the surface. At times I felt every bit as miniscule and marginalized as those individual organisms. But I had to try, whether I was ultimately listened to or ignored.

Over blackberry cobbler and caramel-drenched flan, the conversation turned to land-derived nitrogen pollution and my mind wandered. Odd, because I was interested in the topic. More odd, considering what pushed that subject matter to the side and hijacked my thoughts—Boyce Wynn's hard, freckle-dotted forearm and the electric current that shot through my fingertips when I'd touched it.

I had an obsession with male forearms that could be traced back to the middle school lunchroom where I shared a table with Boyce every day. I was far too timid to ogle flirtatiously, but furtive staring from behind my goggle-sized glasses and unruly preteen hair was simple, especially when I brought a novel from the library. I was mesmerized by the visible copper hair and the sharp line of muscle linking elbow to wrist—the breadth of which called for big-faced watches and leather bands and led to strong hands.

Hands. Those hands assumed a different meaning after—*ugh.* I was an adult woman, and it had been *one time*. I hid my face with my coffee cup, making a drawn-out pretense of careful sipping while trying to breathe, trying to forget Boyce's big hands on my hips, stroking, kneading, lifting…

"Pearl?" Shanice's voice broke through my reverie.

"What? Sorry?"

Chase restated something about mollusks and the effects of large-scale sea grass destruction. Suitable adult, doctoral-student conversation. *Right.*

． ． ． ． ． ． ． ． ． ．

I got all the way to Sunday before Mama brought up Michigan again. Thomas was on the patio grilling while she assembled a salad and I sat at the kitchen table outlining notes from journal articles about chemical dispersants used to clean up oil spills and the effects they had on fragile ecosystems.

"When are you going to respond to Michigan? What is the deadline?" she said, chopping the heads off radishes that were the color of Mel's favorite lip gloss. "You don't want to miss it." She kept her eyes on the knife slicing through the knobby veggies one after the other, her tone merely inquisitive, as though we weren't having a struggle of epic proportions beneath the surface.

"Mama… I'm not going to Michigan. I'm sitting here studying for a marine biology course I'm enrolled in *right now*. I know you're disappointed, but I've made my decision. Please let it go."

The knife stilled and her eyes flashed up. "You cannot be serious, Pearl!" She shut her eyes and mumbled something too soft to hear, likely a prayer for patience in Spanish, and then, "I should have never allowed you to omit ninth grade. That counselor at your school—he said you were *advanced* and you needed to be challenged

143

by more difficult classes. And what has it led to? You are a college graduate at only twenty. Too young to make this sort of decision for yourself—to throw away your future because of a breakup—"

"That is *not* what this is about—"

"We understand not wanting to go to the same school *that boy* will be attending, but to throw away the opportunity—"

"Mama, are you even listening to—"

"You cannot live here and do this."

We stared across the space between us as her edict rang in my ears, the knife no longer thumping rhythmically against the cutting board. My mouth fell open, words crowding through my head but failing to organize themselves into anything coherent.

She found her voice first. "I have never put my foot down with you before, but I am doing it. This is too important." Nothing in her expression suggested that she was bluffing or promised a retraction, but that was typical for Mama. Just not where it applied to *me*.

I remembered Boyce's theory that my mother and I had simply never disagreed about the direction of my future… until now. "So if I decline my acceptance to Michigan and stay here—*in a doctoral program*—I can't live at home?" My voice emerged stronger than I'd assumed it would.

"Yes," she said.

I nodded, closing my notebook and textbook. My hands were shaking. "Okay."

As I reached the base of the stairs, she called, "Supper will be half an hour!"

When I got to my room, I tried to text Boyce, but the autocorrect made nonsense of my attempts and I gave up and pushed Talk instead. I shut the bedroom door as he answered.

"Hey, what's up?"

"You were right—she's expecting me to cave. She says I'm not old enough to know my own mind. That I can't live here if I decline my acceptance. I don't know what to do—student housing is full and it's *June*. Even the crappiest rooms for rent in town are either booked or cost a fortune—not that it matters because *I don't have a job*. What am I going to do? Housing is full for fall too, but I thought I could get an apartment for the nine months there and— God, I'm so clueless! I just *assumed* they'd pay the rent—" I choked on the last word. I'd never once in my life fought with my mother. I'd been so self-righteous about the difference between my relationship with her and Mel's with her mother, when all the time it was no different.

"Pearl? Did you hear me?"

I took a trembling breath, hating my panic. Hating my powerlessness. She couldn't force me to go to medical school, but how would I pursue what I wanted to do? I had options. I had to have options. I just had to figure out what the hell they *were*.

"I'm sorry. I didn't... I didn't hear. I'm just trying to think." I closed my eyes and swallowed. *Think. Think.*

"It's not much, but I have a spare bedroom," he said. "You know you're welcome to it."

chapter *Fourteen*

BOYCE

I had just asked Pearl to move in with me. I had just asked Pearl Frank to move into my two-bedroom, one-bathroom, piece-of-crap tin can of a trailer that *butts up against a garage*. And damn if the bedroom I offered her wasn't still chock-full of thirty years' worth of squirreled-away *junk*, for fuck's sake.

I'd spent the afternoon at Mateo and Yvette's place watching the Astros pull out a win over Chicago and being used as a climbing wall by Alonso and Arturo. As I handed off a twelve-pack to their mama at the door, they'd run up and attached themselves to my legs, one wearing the Astros second baseman jersey I gave him on their birthday last month and the other in full Batman gear, cape and all. To be honest, I've never been sure which was which. They've always looked like miniature replicas of their daddy and each other.

Now, still holding my phone, I came around the corner to find all four Vegas staring at me from the table where we'd just sat down to Sunday supper. "What?"

"Mama says no phone calls at the table," miniature José Altuve said. "It's *rude*."

"There's still food on your plate," pint-sized Batman added.

"Hush, y'all two. Rules for daddies and little boys don't apply to guests." Yvette blinked innocently. "So... who was that?"

I pulled my keys from my pocket. "Um, I gotta go."

She turned wide eyes at her husband, who was chewing.

"What?" he asked her.

"Boyce never gets up from food. Certainly not *my* food."

She had a point. This was a first.

"I'll explain later," I said, thinking *or not* and turning toward the door. "Uh—thanks for supper, Yvette."

Poor Vega would be subjected to the third degree before I got my TA backed into the street. Too bad he didn't actually know anything.

. . . .

From her minute-long silence on the phone, I'd guessed Pearl was as bowled over by my proposition as I was having said it. But she needed somewhere to live for the summer; I had an extra room. I'd have offered the same thing to Maxfield or Thompson or Vega... who were all *guys*. Though it had been known to happen, I'd never even wanted girls to stay over after sex. I'd always reckoned that was because I lived with my dad, but he'd been in and out of the hospital for months and I'd had the trailer to myself most nights. He'd been dead for four weeks. Neither made a lick of difference. I was flat-out opposed to hookups getting cozy in my place.

Yet the notion of Pearl *living there* hadn't bothered me enough to keep it from coming out of my mouth. I hadn't even hesitated before offering it. If anything, I was ready to talk her into the idea. Sort of like signing up for voluntary *torture*.

I left the keys hanging in the lock when I got home and walked straight to the closed-off master bedroom. After wasting two evenings and half a weekend searching for the documents Mr. Amos had asked me to find, I'd rid the room of cans and bottles, bagged up an ass-ton of odds and ends and pointless documents, and pulled the door shut on the rest. The old man had amassed piles of statements, bills, and junk mail mixed with mildewing stacks of *Field & Stream*, *Car and Driver*, and the *Hustler* mags I'd stolen and stuck beneath my mattress until I discovered the Internet and real girls. His closet and dresser were crammed full of clothes that should all be trashed. Ditto the bedding. *Shit*—and the soiled mattress. No fucking way I was allowing Pearl Frank to lie down on that.

Pissed at myself for putting off this chore, I wished I could set fire to the whole room like I had that damned recliner. But that chair had been worthless, and this room meant freedom to Pearl. I pulled the keys from the door, grabbed a box of heavy-duty trash bags from the garage, and started separating useful from useless.

Four hours later and an ass-ton of black bags stacked at the end of the driveway—where they'd sit until garbage pickup Tuesday—I heard back from Pearl. We'd agreed that she should have dinner with her parents and hope her mom did an about-face, but where parents were concerned, I never held my breath.

Pearl: No change. Thomas seems opposed to her
        ultimatum, but he won't contradict it.
        Boyce - that car doesn't belong to me.
        Neither does my phone. I've never felt so
        stupid and naïve.

Me: You didn't see this coming. Stop blaming
        yourself. Do they know you're leaving? Will
        they take your car away?

Pearl:	I'll tell them tomorrow. I've packed my clothes and plan to ask them to leave my phone on long enough for me to get my own, but if I'm determined to be self-sufficient, I can't justify taking the car. I can walk the few blocks to class from your place, and I'll have to find a job nearby. Guess I'll be doing lots of walking.
Me:	We'll work something out.
Pearl:	Are you sure about this? I'll pay you rent once I have a paycheck.
Me:	The hell you will. Like I told you earlier, I would do this for Maxfield or any of my close friends. It's less than three months and you're a tiny thing. You won't bother me none.

With those lying words, I pictured her shampoo and bodywash and razor in my shower, bras and panties hanging over the rod, her in a towel, blow-drying that mass of dark hair in my bathroom... *Goddammit.* She would bother the hell out of me. Just not how she was thinking.

Pearl:	Okay. I'll come over after class tomorrow. What time do you finish up? I'll need a ride back to your place after I leave my car at home. At *their* place, I mean.
Pearl:	I didn't think I'd graduate college and be immediately homeless, haha. ☹
Me:	You're not homeless. Just a little transient. ☺
Pearl:	I don't know how to thank you.

149

Me:	No need. Just take it and go do your thing.
Pearl:	See you tomorrow. Goodnight.
Me:	Yep. Nite.

I texted Thompson about using his truck to haul the disgusting mattress to the dump tomorrow and he responded: NP I'll git er done without asking why. Shouldn't take more than a week to get a new one in there. In the meantime, Pearl would sleep in my bed, and I'd lie wide-awake on the sofa, struggling not to visualize her sweet little body curled up in my sheets, her soft mouth falling open with an eager sigh when I stroked a hand over her hip to pull her closer, her sleepy eyes blinking slowly as I woke her to a need that I would fill.

I was fucked. I was so, so fucked.

· · · · · · · · · ·

I was up until two a.m. cleaning the bathroom after battling that goddamned mattress out the front door in the middle of the night. My neighbor, Mrs. Echols, eighty if she was a day, flipped on the floodlight at the corner of her place—blinding me momentarily—and glared out her bedroom window, clutching her robe to her chin. I propped the mattress against the side of the trailer and saluted, and she snatched the curtain closed.

After a quick shower, I fell into bed and slept like the dead until the alarm went off at six. Not the best day to face on four hours of sleep, because I'd forgotten all about my surly probationary employee until she wheeled into the bay where I was testing fluid levels as part of a tune-up. Her father walked up behind her, sizing me up with all the friendliness of a rabid dog. *Jesus Christ.*

Despite the fact that I felt like I was hungover and wished they'd just turn around and leave, I wiped my hand on a rag and stuck it out. "Mr. Adams? Boyce Wynn."

He shook as firmly as his kid had last week. "Philip Adams. I understand you've offered Samantha a job."

"*Dad*," she growled and he grimaced.

"Sam, I mean."

I nodded toward the scowling kid in the chair. "We've agreed on a one-week trial to see how we get on before I extend an actual job offer."

"And she'll be paid for the trial week?"

"*Dad*."

I ignored her and nodded once. "Of course."

He pursed his lips, looking around the shop as if inspecting it for safety hazards—which he probably was. "She's brought her lunch. When should I be back to pick her up?"

"*Oh my God, Dad.* I said I'd *call you*."

Philip Adams had to be the most even-tempered guy in town. His daughter wasn't going to find that kind of patience here. I'd park her at the end of the drive in two shakes and call him myself if she mouthed off to me like that.

"Two or so should be fine today, if that's convenient." That was when Pearl's class ended, though at the moment I doubted Sam and I would make it to two.

"I'll be back at two, Sam." He patted her rigid shoulder and glanced around once more. "Unless you need me sooner."

She sighed like she was barely surviving the embarrassment he was causing her, and he nodded once and walked back to his truck, probably used to her shit because he had to be.

When he was gone, I said, "Hope you don't mean to treat my customers to a helping of that attitude or this job'll be over right quick."

Her short, spiky hair looked lethal, but it underscored how small her head was and made her almost appear vulnerable. "What attitude?" *Until she opened her mouth.*

"Really?"

She stared at the hands fisted in her lap for a long moment. "He doesn't want me working. He doesn't think I'm capable of doing anything on my own. Like *at all*."

"So he's protective."

"*Over*protective, you mean."

"There're worse things." When her lips parted—no doubt to argue the point, I held up a hand, thinking about Pearl. "But it's good to learn to do for yourself. Otherwise they'll keep doing for you. And you don't seem to want that."

"I don't."

"Good."

She glanced around the shop, her silence dialing her back to vulnerable. "So I'm here," she said. "What do you have for me to do? I've been working on cars since I was ten. I'm real good at diagnostics and replacing fuel lines and—"

"Keep your shorts on. If you're lucky, I might let you help replace a battery by the end of the week. For now, I need the tools along the back wall organized."

She gasped as if I'd insulted her ancestry. "Seriously?"

I cocked an eyebrow at her and said nothing, and after a minute or two she harrumphed like she was a Mrs. Echols clone and wheeled to the back wall. Good freaking Christ. Between waiting for Samantha Adams to vamoose and waiting for Pearl to show, six hours felt like a hundred.

Pearl

Boyce's place was so close to campus that it took me less than three minutes to get there. If I hadn't gotten stuck behind a golf cart, the trip would have been even quicker.

I parked at the curb but remained in the car. A pickup truck sat in the driveway of the garage, where a man lifted a girl into the passenger side. As he went to buckle her in, she swiped the seat belt from his hands and fastened it herself, then leaned out to pull the door shut. He shook his head, folded a wheelchair into the truck bed and strapped it down. Boyce exited the right-side bay wearing the same resigned expression Thomas got when Tux tore through the house like a dust devil for no conceivable reason, knocking things askew as he went. Thinking about my stepfather and cat made my chest ache right down the center.

One eye squeezed shut against the afternoon glare, Boyce lifted his hand in farewell to the people in the truck as he scanned the street and then spotted my car. His mouth, halfway to a smile from the squint, lifted into his familiar grin as he sauntered toward me. "Right on time," he drawled as I opened the door and popped the trunk.

"I'm nothing if not prompt. That's one of my distinguishing characteristics." I slung my backpack over my shoulder and we lifted three suitcases from the trunk.

He grabbed the two largest and led the way to the trailer I would call home for the next ten weeks. "I hadn't noticed that one."

I faked a gasp. "Really? I'm appalled at your inattention, Boyce Wynn! I'm known everywhere for my punctuality."

He turned at the bottom step, his eyes sweeping over me, and I shivered despite a heat index that topped a hundred. "Guess I've always been distracted by your more... visible features."

Oh *God*. I had no chance of remaining sane for seventy days if he was going to toy with me like that the whole time. Nothing turned me on like his flirtatious banter, no matter how preposterous it got, even if I knew full well he'd never restricted it to just me. I pinned my lips together and stared down at my pink Sperrys—which probably made me look like a prude who was disconcerted by a little flirting. I had to let him think it. If he knew how the sound of his voice made my mouth water and those teasing remarks melted my insides, I'd be in so much trouble.

I raised my eyes to his when he said, "Hey." He stood just inside the open doorway, watching me closely. His grin was gone and his tone was cautious, as if he thought I might turn and run back to my car. "I've been handing you those harebrained lines forever just to provoke that little smirk of yours, but I'm just playing. You have nothing to fret over with me. I hope you know that."

I nodded, unintentionally giving him the smirk he'd summoned, and walked up the steps and through the door.

He led the way across the living room, past a small bathroom that emitted the aroma of at least a gallon's worth of bleach, and into a stark bedroom containing an old dresser and a bed frame.

"Had to ditch the mattress," he said, turning to me. "Got a new one ordered this morning. It'll be here in a week."

I swallowed. "Okay." Of all the possible scenarios I'd imagined for this summer, living in a trailer with Boyce Wynn hadn't been one of them. A trailer that at the moment contained one bed. "I guess I'll just sleep—"

"In my bed."

My hand, gesturing toward the living room, froze midair. I've heard people say *My heart stopped*—which of course isn't possible unless you've just *died*—but I now understood where the perception might originate. "Uh."

"I'll take the sofa," he said.

Embarrassment washed over me. He wasn't propositioning me. He was being courteous. I lowered my hand, half-convinced I'd fallen into an alternate universe where my mother kicked me out of the house and Boyce Wynn was *proper*. "You don't have to do that."

He arched a brow, his eyes glowing with mischief. "You want me to sleep with you?"

Or not.

"I... I meant I'll take the sofa."

He shook his head once. "That wouldn't be very gentlemanly of me, Pearl."

"I'm moving into your home and not even able to pay you rent. Or repay you for buying a mattress. Also I'm shorter than you, so I'll fit better. On the sofa, I mean. And it's only for a week. I'm not forcing you out of your own bed—"

"All right, all right." He held up a hand. "But if you get uncomfortable, or lonely..." He winked. "My offer stands."

With that proposition, the world righted itself.

· · · · · · · · · ·

The cowardly side of me wished Mama would be out when I got home. I could leave a note and my car keys on the kitchen counter, park my car in its garage spot, and climb into Boyce's car, avoiding the confrontation altogether.

But it was Monday afternoon—she'd be home planning the week's meals and supervising the weekly housekeeping service, and Thomas would be at the surgery center seeing new and prospective patients. If I'd wanted to avoid them both, I'd have waited until

Friday, when she did volunteer work and he took the boat out all day. And I couldn't leave without a face-to-face explanation, as much as I dreaded it.

I'd focused on how she would respond to my failure to fall in line with her stipulations for continuing to receive their financial support. I hadn't given much thought to what her reaction might be to where and to whom I was turning—to Boyce. She had no more idea of our relationship than anyone else did. But seeing his Trans Am in the driveway—watching me leave with him after I let her know I couldn't yield to her ultimatum? It wasn't hard to imagine exactly what she would think.

Freshman year of college, she'd been none too thrilled when I told her I needed an appointment to get birth control. Thomas talked her off the ledge by pointing out the maturity and responsibility it had taken to make that request. Even so, when Mitchell visited last summer, she'd put him in a guest bedroom downstairs, though we'd been exclusive since the beginning of junior year. Mama and I didn't really discuss sex. I knew she'd rather I wasn't sexually active, though I think she was glad I was sensible about it. She'd known me all my life, though—what else would I be?

I knew where her need to disregard that I had a sex life originated—my unplanned existence. She'd never once made me feel unwanted, but I knew the story and connected the dots. If it weren't for me, she and my father would have had time to plan a safer passage from Mexico. He might have lived.

I pulled into the wide driveway at the edge of the cul-de-sac, and Boyce pulled in behind me. "I don't think this will take long," I said, walking up to his open window.

"I'll come in with you."

"It's better if I go in alone. I want her to concentrate on what I'm saying, not who's with me. If you come in…" I shook my head. "I just need her to know it's *my* decision."

His jaw tensed. "Okay. But if you need me, call or text or yell and I'm there."

I nodded. "I'll be fine." My stomach lurched when I glanced toward the house. "If you're one of those guys who freaks out around tears, though, you might wanna get prepared. I hate disappointing people I love. I might cry." My eyes filled just verbalizing the possibility, and he looked like I'd just told him he might need a big injection in a highly unpleasant location.

As I turned, he caught my wrist. "Pearl—I can't imagine anyone ever being disappointed in you."

When I walked into the kitchen, Mama had finished putting away the fresh food and was organizing pantry items and fussing at Tux, who issued piteous meows while circling her ankles, begging for a snack. I picked up an empty grocery bag and folded it, gathering my courage.

"Did you process the withdrawal?" she asked when she saw me.

"I'm not withdrawing, Mama. I'm not going to Michigan." She froze and I pressed on. "I understand your requirements for living here, and I just… can't. I'm sorry to disappoint you and Thomas, but this is my life. I have to do what's right for *me*. So I'm moving in with a friend for the rest of the summer—Boyce Wynn? He has an extra room and he's close to campus."

I hadn't ever known my mother to be speechless. Without waiting for her to emerge from her stupor, I left my house and car keys and my credit card on the counter next to a package of brown rice and a small bag of cat treats. I hugged her stiff shoulders and walked back outside as quickly as I could manage while blinded by tears. Boyce didn't say a word when I curled into the seat, sobbing, but he reached over and took my hand as we pulled onto the road.

chapter *Fifteen*

BOYCE

Damn. I'd only seen Pearl cry once—right after I took her virginity like some ignorant assclown who didn't know jackshit about how to make sex satisfying for a girl. I was mad at her for not telling me—until she said she'd thought maybe I wouldn't have gone through with it if I'd known. She couldn't have been more off target with *that* assumption. I'd all but wanted to plant a flag that said *FIRST* on one side and *MINE* on the other.

I was a goddamn idiot at eighteen.

"You gonna be okay?" I asked her once we were back home. "I was planning go out to the garage and get some work done. I've got a brake job to finish up and a transmission that's— Well, I reckon you don't need the particulars…"

"I'm okay." The words scratched their way out of her throat.

I pulled the extra key off my carabiner and let her into the trailer before putting it into her hand, but didn't follow. Two hours later, I scrubbed the grease off my hands and arms and went inside, unsure of my strategy if she was still crying. The only weepy girls I was familiar with were depressed drunks, which I took pains to avoid.

Pearl was sitting at the kitchen table, which looked like a

backpack full of textbooks had exploded on top of it. No tears, thank Christ. Her legs folded up in the chair, she was tapping away at a small laptop. Her hair, wound and piled on top of her head in a knot, was too stubborn to be contained. Long, wavy chunks of it fell down her back and over her ears. I knew how soft and thick it would feel between my fingertips.

"Hey," she said, twisting in her seat when I shut the door. Aw, *hell.* She was wearing glasses. I hadn't seen her in glasses since she was thirteen, but these weren't the chunky, thick-lensed sort she had back then. "I saw some cold cuts in the fridge. I thought we could make sandwiches for dinner…" She tipped her head to the side and blinked as I fought to focus on what she was saying once I'd realized she was talking. "Unless you've already got plans. I'm sorry, I didn't even think—"

"No," I blurted, cutting her off. "No plans. Except you. Tonight." *Fuck.* What was wrong with my brain? She was just so damned cute. White shorts and black tank, barefoot, thin blue-framed glasses outlining her dark eyes, hair pinned up but trying its best to escape—and *holy shit* I wanted to take it down. She was wide-eyed and watching me like I'd lost my ever-lovin' mind.

"Sandwiches. Good." I pointed across the living room. "Gotta shower."

I turned, stalked straight into the bathroom, and shut the door. Hands gripping the edge of the sink, I stared into the mirror and took a breath. Ten weeks and she'd be back in Austin. She'd come to me because she had no one else to turn to. I wasn't gonna try to turn that into something it wasn't. We were friends. Like Maxfield and me.

I laughed and turned on the water. Yeah, no. Not at all like Maxfield.

Those glasses though. *Fuck me.*

I took a hot shower and rubbed one out to take the edge off. If I'd been imagining some other girl on her knees, water plastering her hair to her back and streaming over her face and tits while her small hands grabbed my thighs and her mouth worked me over, it might have succeeded. Instead, I turned off the water, and the itch to walk out there butt-naked, pick her up, and take her straight to my bed was even worse.

"*Goddammit.* How is that even possible? *Hell.*" I held the towel over my face, mumbling to myself like I was fucking mental.

I dried off and realized I'd come straight into the bathroom with no clean clothes. Even with the south door to the garage open all day, it was June—hot and sticky all day long. No way I was putting that sweaty shit I'd been wearing pre-shower back on, and this towel was just big enough to cover my ass and my nuts. Barely.

I swiped the dirty clothes off the floor and opened the door, steam billowing out behind me like smoke rolling from the doorway of any bar in town on a Friday night. That was the answer, right there. I needed to go out and do a little flirting, a little drinking—go out and get my ass *laid*.

Halfway across the living room, I looked up to see Pearl standing by the table, holding two plates piled with ham sandwiches. She'd cleared a place where I'd sat the only other time we'd eaten together, and the spot next to it. My stomach roared in appreciation, and I focused on that gnawing hunger instead of the one prowling around a bit lower.

"I'll be right out," I said, glancing at her face as I passed and realizing that she wasn't looking at mine. She was staring at my usually covered-up parts. *Hell, yes, baby—look your fill.* Every muscle in my body flexed instinctively, each one challenging the rest for her attention.

The plates clattered to the table and she tore her eyes away from my bare torso. "Uh, okay. Sure. I'll just be… here." She cleared her throat, hands fluttering to pick up the few potato chips that had bounced off the plates when they'd come in for that rough landing. I didn't get much time to gloat, because *damn* if she didn't lean across the table to slide one of those plates to my spot, and *damn* if I didn't apparently have a new favorite fantasy that wasn't so different from the original.

Except this time she was wearing those glasses.

I slammed my bedroom door way too hard, stomped to my dresser, and ripped the drawer halfway out. Tossing clothes onto the bed, I set myself to breathing just like I did when I weight-trained to failure to surpass a lifting rut: Focused. On. The. Goal.

What the fuck is the goal?

I thought about her flustered face of five minutes ago. Pearl wasn't an innocent little high school girl anymore. She was a woman, and women had needs. I'd filled a sizeable amount of those sorts of needs since I was fourteen. Truth be told, I probably hadn't filled any but my own for the first few years, but I sure as hell knew how to fill them now.

I'd met her ex. No way that dickweed satisfied her regularly, if ever, but she'd spent four years in college after I'd obliged her with eliminating her virginity. My teeth clenched at the mental image of her with the sorts of college guys who came here during spring break and over summer vacation. Ninety-five percent of them were varying degrees of pretty-faced, muscled, rich, arrogant fuckers, and that was being generous. There were some, like Maxfield, who were honest about what they wanted—going after girls who wanted the same. As much as I hated the thought, I hoped she'd found a few guys like that instead of one after the other who'd be all smooth-talking and attentive just long enough to get into her cute little shorts.

Not helping.

If I didn't have to stick my face in the freezer multiple times a day for the next ten weeks, it would be a damned miracle.

Pearl

When Boyce exited the bathroom and sauntered through the living room and past the kitchen, I stood there staring like I'd never seen a guy in a towel. A towel that could win a prize for being the smallest bath towel ever made.

The question I'd been about to ask—something about whether he preferred mayonnaise or mustard or what he wanted to drink—melted into a mushy puddle at the bottom of my brain. My last comprehensible thought was, *Holy mother of God.* Eyes on the floor and unaware of my ogling, he rubbed his short hair dry with a hand towel. Every rock-solid muscle of his right arm, shoulder, and pec expanded and contracted with the effort, forming shifting arcs and sharp lines that rearranged the landscape under those familiar freckles and the droplets he'd not yet toweled away.

An Internet search for *unfair* could include a GIF of him in that moment and a link to a biological explanation of the riot that occurred inside my body and the mental chaos it triggered. I couldn't speak or move or form a single judicious plan to make it stop. As he drew closer, my traitorous mind projected a full-fledged fantasy behind my eyes.

Without pausing or stopping or asking permission, he would turn and walk straight to where I stood gaping and take the plates from my hands. "We'll eat *this* later," he'd say, placing the food on the table. Sweeping me into his arms, he would walk to his room and drop me on his bed, where my clothes would obligingly slide away with a few strategic pulls of his fingers. He would yank the damp towel from his hips in one movement and thrust into me in the next, his mouth seizing mine in a searing kiss—lips enveloping, tongue plunging inside, stroking deep and hard—

"I'll be right out," he said, snapping me from the spell I'd fallen under. I dropped the plates to the tabletop, scattering chips everywhere like a total goofball. Gathering them, I refused to meet his eyes, certain he would see every pathetic craving I'd nurtured since I was too young to know what those cravings meant.

Minutes later, he emerged from his bedroom clothed in shorts and a white T-shirt, and I crunched one chip after another and pretended to read.

Slathering a layer of mayo on his sandwich, he said, "Thanks for making supper," his voice uncharacteristically soft. The gentle pitch poured over me, warm and hypnotic.

I forced my lips into a relaxed smile and risked a quick glance up. "Thanks for providing the ingredients." Hoping he couldn't read my mind, which was threatening to resume my erotic fantasy *in slow motion*, I stared back at the page and highlighted a random line, unsure what it even said.

"Yep," he said, carrying his plate to the living room and turning the television on, volume low.

Eventually, the words on the page in front of me organized themselves back into intelligible details and data charts, and my rational thought processes returned.

"Sure you won't take the bed?" Boyce said, breaking my concentration. The television was off and a glance out the window showed it had grown full dark. My laptop time read 10:21 p.m. "I feel like an asshole handing you sheets for the sofa."

My neck popped as I stretched for the first time in two hours. I took the sheets from him and stood. "I would feel like an asshole bumping the person who's sharing his home with me out of his own bed. I'll be fine."

He stared down at me. "You sure you're fine?" he said, and I knew he wasn't talking about the sofa.

I nodded, my throat too full for words to escape. I'd stopped checking my phone an hour ago. This was real. I was on my own. When I'd first left home for college, it had taken some adjustment being away from Mama, away from my home, Mel, high school classes, everything and everyone familiar—including Boyce Wynn. Unlike my dorm suitemates, I'd gone home for the weekend three times before Thanksgiving break. My classmates seemed so much older and more experienced, so ready to be all grown-up. I just wanted to go home. My third trip home, I'd laid my head in Mama's lap and told her I didn't want to go back. I knew what she'd say and knew she'd be right, even if I didn't want to hear it.

"You don't mean that, *mija*," she'd said, stroking my hair off my face. "You're a little younger than everyone else. That's all it is. I'm here whenever you need me, but you don't want to miss this opportunity. Take that brain of yours and go do what you're meant to do."

She was right that time, and by second semester, I'd acclimated.

This time she was wrong.

• • • • • • • • • •

Sleeping on that lumpy sofa was one step above sleeping on the floor, and my discomfort was exacerbated by nightly dreams about my roommate. I prayed to God I didn't talk in my sleep.

I fell into Boyce's daily routine, not having much choice since my location on the sofa put me smack in the middle of it. He woke early every day and went out the door in shorts and sneakers. I'd feigned sleep as he crossed the dark living room, but quick window checks the past two days told me he was going into the garage. An hour later, he'd come inside to shower, change into jeans and steel-toed boots, make coffee, and wolf down a breakfast that would have hit my maximum daily calories in one go.

I joined him at the table this morning after pouring a cup of coffee into one of a dozen mugs imprinted with fishing wisdom. This one read "A bad day FISHIN' is better'n a good day WORKIN'!"

Still groggy, I nibbled a piece of toast. "Do you work for an hour and then eat breakfast?"

"Not working. Lifting. Got a bench, barbell, a few plates, and some dumbbells out there. It's the best time to work it in. Too tired by the end of the day." He shoveled another bite of eggs and sausage into his mouth and flipped through a stack of paperwork. His hair was still damp.

"Hmm," I said, staring into my coffee as if my imagination hadn't just lit up like the bioluminescent phytoplankton that sometimes invaded the gulf during fall and winter nights.

I started guiltily when someone knocked on the front door.

Boyce frowned, backing his chair away from the table. It wasn't even eight a.m. "You expecting anybody?"

I shook my head, and he stalked to the door and jerked it open, blocking the doorway. His shoulders lowered and he exchanged a subdued sentence or two with the person on the other side. He nodded and shut the door partway before crossing back to me.

Mama, I thought.

"It's Dr. Frank," he said. "If you don't want to talk to him—"

"No. I'll talk to him." I braced myself before going to the door, but seeing the concerned face of the only father I'd ever known splintered my resolve. "Hi, Thomas." I swallowed and blinked at the burn in my eyes.

He opened his arms and I stepped into him. "You okay, little girl?"

I huffed a tearful laugh. *Little girl*. "Yeah."

After a moment, he patted my shoulder and we separated. "Listen, I know your mama put her foot down. But I bought you that car, and I have a foot too." He gestured toward the drive, where my little red GTI sat. I almost ran outside to hug it.

If this was their idea of manipulation, it was downright cruel. After three days without it, I missed my car. Having transportation would make my life a hundred times easier, but that didn't mean I was caving. "I'm not changing my mind. I've made my decision."

"I see that, honey, and I'm not asking you to." He scratched his chin, clear blue eyes inspecting me closely. "But can I at least ask how much this decision has to do with that boy?" He nodded toward the interior of the trailer. "Or the other one?"

They'd known nothing of my relationship with Boyce, and what they knew of my ex was that our parting was unpleasant but I'd gotten over it quickly. "Nothing. My breakup with Mitchell wouldn't scare me away from something I wanted to do, and Boyce has only ever encouraged me to do what I want to do."

"I see. And your decision reflects a desire to be a marine biologist, not just a desire to *not* study medicine? Because there are other alternatives—"

"It's what I want to do, Thomas. And medicine isn't. I'm sorry."

"You don't have to apologize to me." He chuckled. "I'm not that easily insulted."

"Mama's still angry though." I wanted him to contradict me but knew he wouldn't.

"She can be a bit... obstinate." He arched a brow that said she and I were two peas in a pod. "But it'll work out." He took my hand and pressed my key ring into it. I couldn't help noticing that my house key was on it as well. "I've got a few postsurgical appointments this morning. If I could hitch a ride to my office, I'd appreciate it."

Throwing my arms around his neck, I whispered, "Thank you. Let me get dressed—I'll be out in ten minutes."

When I got outside, he and Boyce were standing at the mouth of the garage, hands in pockets, talking. Looking my way, Boyce angled his head in a single nod and disappeared inside the garage.

As I pulled into the street, Thomas said, "I take it you and Boyce Wynn are... *closer* than your mother and I knew?"

I nodded, my face warming at the type of connection I was allowing him to imagine between us, but I wasn't in the mood to make excuses about where I was sleeping. Or not sleeping.

chapter *Sixteen*

BOYCE

"Dude, your girlfriend is *hot*."

That wasn't something I'd ever expected to hear from a female employee—if I'd ever contemplated the idea of a female employee. If I *had* contemplated it, let's just say she wouldn't have been anything like the girl watching my roommate of seventy-two hours climb the steps to the front door.

Pearl had pulled up five minutes ago and parked her little import on the gravel drive next to my TA. She'd grabbed her backpack from the backseat and waved a hand as she crossed the yard, glancing back at Sam before turning toward the trailer. We hadn't discussed my employee, and this was the first day she'd arrived home before Sam's dad arrived to pick her up.

"She's not my girlfriend."

"What're ya—*blind*?"

"I was."

I said no more, hoping Sam would return to tightening lug nuts with that torque wrench. We'd wasted five minutes bickering about why she couldn't use the pneumatic wrench to do it. (*Because you need to learn how to tighten them using exact measurements first—*

by hand, I'd said. *But the pneumatic is faster*, she'd whined.) I finally stopped arguing with her and just stared until she started applying some elbow grease.

"Well, that's cryptic," she said, arching one blond brow.

"My roommate is not up for discussion. Neither—as I've already made plain—is my sex life."

"Or lack thereof."

"Shut it." *Man.* Silva must be laughing his ass off over pawning this kid off on me. "Tell me what you do if the threads are oiled instead of dry."

She rolled her eyes so hard her head followed the movement. "Reduce the torque."

"Good, genius. By how much?"

"Um, fifty percent."

I laughed and she scowled. "Not unless you want this guy to lose his wheels heading down the highway and come back to cuss you straight into the gulf, if he comes back at all."

"Hey, y'all need something to drink?"

Sam and I both turned toward Pearl's voice. She was holding two cans of Pepsi.

"Thanks!" Sam said, smiling. *The hell?* With that blond hair poking in every direction, her face looked like a happy cartoon sun. I hadn't known she could *be* happy. "I'm Sam, by the way." Or *friendly.*

Pearl handed each of us a can and smiled back at Sam. "I'm Pearl. So Sam—you're Wynn's new employee?"

"*Provisional* employee," I said, popping the top. "She's got one more day to prove herself. I'm still on the fence."

Sam's eyebrows shot toward each other like magnets and her mouth tightened into a knot. If she'd had laser vision, I'd have been sliced up one side and down the other. Leaning halfway out of her chair, she plunked the can on the concrete and put all her effort behind that torque wrench, fighting to keep from smarting off to me in front of Pearl.

Pearl caught my eye with a tiny *shame on you* shake of her head and that damned smirk I'd do almost anything to set off.

I tipped the can back with a quick wink, taking a long swallow to hide my grin from Sam.

· · · · · · · · · ·

In clearing out Dad's room, I'd discovered things I'd forgotten he had and things I'd been unaware he had. Time-pressed to empty the room, I'd tossed anything worthy of keeping into a box I put aside for later inspection. Between Pearl moving in and Sam showing up, I'd forgotten about the box and my appointment with Mr. Amos until it popped up on my phone's reminders.

I separated tax forms and any documents that looked business-related from birth certificates and photos I'd known nothing about—two or three of my mother and a few dozen of Brent and me, but none past the age we were when Mom left. I unearthed the flat box containing Brent's Silver Star Medal. Inside, along with the Medal, were his dog tags and a laminated photo. I slipped the chain over my head and dropped the tags into my shirt.

The photo was a selfie of Brent and Arianna on the beach. Behind them, the sun was coming up over the water. It was scratched up like it had been in a wallet, taken out often. He'd probably had this photo with him—either on him when he died or with his effects. It had been eight years, which some days felt like a century and some days like yesterday. I flipped it over.

Arianna had written: *Your home is right here next to me ~ A.*

In my mind, my big brother had always been older and stronger than me, but he'd been my age when he died—twenty-two—and now I was weeks from turning the age he'd never be. The only decent parts of me were there because of him. Tears that hadn't come when Dad died came all too easily for the brother who'd been more of a father to me than my old man had ever been. But when Brent was a boy, getting called words a kid shouldn't even hear, taking punches from a full-grown man to protect our mother, to protect *me*, who'd stepped in to be a father for him?

· · · · · · · · · ·

Mr. Amos's office was the front room of his wood-frame house off Palm Drive, where he lived alone. I parked in the driveway, next to a well-used boat sitting on a trailer, ready to be hooked to the white Silverado backed up to it. A couple of palm trees and a massive oleander shrub shaded the porch swing to the left of the doorway. The only way I knew I was at the right place was the wooden sign hanging beside the front door that said *Barney Amos, Attorney at Law*.

I handed over the box full of possibly significant papers and checked out his office walls and shelves while he examined them. In addition to his law school diploma (Loyola—I'd heard of that one), there was a pic of him with fishing buddies, one with the mayor, one of his daughter on her wedding day, and one of Austin—a smidge older than Mateo's boys—holding a bass as tall as he was. In Cub Scouts, we'd called him Bug on account of his eyes.

I'd forgotten Bug had a sister and couldn't remember her name, but she looked a lot like him—same thin nose and big eyes. She'd been a few years ahead of us in school and moved away with her mom after the accident. Despite a DUI conviction, Mr. Amos—so wasted he hadn't known what had happened until the next day—hadn't been held responsible for the wreck. A drag-racing kid had run a red light and T-boned the passenger side of his car, flipping it three times, killing Austin instantly and permanently injuring Mr. Amos in ways both obvious and not.

During one of his few AA sponsor visits with Dad, I'd heard him say, "If I'd been sober, maybe I would've heard him coming and hit the brakes. Maybe I wouldn't have been in that intersection. Maybe Austin would be alive."

Dad didn't give a shit, I guess. Wasn't moved the way I was, thinking about Bug, who would never turn seven. Frozen at the age he died—just like Brent.

"No new will or divorce papers, Boyce?"

"No sir, none that I could find. What happens if there's no will? And maybe he just didn't keep the divorce papers? I can imagine him lighting them on fire well enough."

"Yes, yes—that's true, but it's a little more complicated than that. Have a seat, son."

I sat and watched his face—the right side of it, anyway. The left side, in its permanent droop, gave no clue to whatever it was that made him stick a finger behind the collar of his shirt and give it a yank like his tie was on too tight even though he wasn't wearing one.

He took a deep breath through his nose and folded his hands. "Bud had a will, Boyce. It was made before your mama quit town. I have a copy of it here." He placed a palm on a paper-clipped set of documents.

Seeing as how I'd been searching that damned trailer high and low for a will, it seemed odd that he had it. I waited for him to explain, because I couldn't for the life of me figure out what the hell was going on.

"It names your mama as the primary beneficiary. I drew it up myself—after insisting that he and Ruthanne each needed a simple will because they had minor children. My intention was to protect you and Brent." He took another slow breath, lips pinched. "I was hoping you'd find a new will, revoking any previously made. But more importantly, I was hoping you'd find divorce papers."

"I don't understand," I said, but that was a lie. I got the gist of what he was saying. I just couldn't wrap my head around what, exactly, it meant. Because there was no goddamned way it meant what it sounded like.

"I've sent to Austin and the surrounding states for a divorce decree, but nothing's come up yet. In the absence of a divorce decree, which would invalidate any wills made prior to it—"

"Are you seriously about to tell me that even though she left us—left *him*—fifteen years ago, she's going to get the trailer and the stuff in it?"

I hadn't thought the man could look more pained than he normally looked, but I was wrong.

"Assuming she's alive and was still married to your father upon his death, your mother is entitled to everything that belonged to Bud. If there hadn't been a will, she'd still inherit all their community property, because she is—as far as I can find—his legal spouse."

I sensed there was more and what it was before he said it.

He swallowed and unloaded the worst of it. "If he never incorporated Wynn's Garage—I've spent the past two weeks searching but can't find any evidence that he did so—then the garage was a sole proprietorship, indistinguishable from the individual upon his death. Making it part of his estate."

Holy fucking shit, this was not going down. "So I own *nothing*? I've worked for my dad since I was thirteen years old—unpaid for the first several years, not that it stopped him from having me do every oil change and tire rotation that came in. I took responsibility for everything when he got sick. I've done *everything* for the past year—"

"I understand, Boyce, and this is as inequitable a thing as I've ever—"

I stood. "I have to go."

He nodded. "I'll have to institute a search for her. If she's worked or applied for credit, an apartment, a loan of any kind—it won't take more than a week to find her." He grappled with his collar again. "One last thing. I made a will for her as well—a duplicate of your dad's with him named as her beneficiary—which made her my client. I will not represent her against you, but I can't represent you either. It would constitute a conflict of interest in the eyes of the court."

"Well, fuck," I said, in one of the many understatements of my life.

Pearl

Saturday afternoon, I was studying when a knock rattled the front door. Besides Mama and Thomas, only Melody knew where I was living. As I expected, she'd gone utterly silent when I called and told her, like that dead calm right before the worst part of a squall hits. "Mel?" I said, and she sputtered to life, firing interrogations without waiting for answers and citing all the reasons she was certain I'd gone off the deep end.

Mel was in Dallas though, so whoever it was had probably come for Boyce, who'd taken a box of documents to the attorney who was helping him sort his dad's affairs.

I'd spent the morning in a futile job search, the details of which wouldn't quit replaying in my head. Most places had already hired for the summer, and I had no job history or employable skills to entice the few that had an opening. Dressed like it was rush week instead of a Saturday in the most laid-back town on the coast, I'd filled out applications and smiled until my face ached. Everyone had the same questions: Have you worked retail? Waited tables? Run a register? Worked with the public in any way, shape, or form?

No, no, no, and no.

When the knock sounded again, I tiptoed to the door. There was no peephole, so I lifted a mini-blind slat. *Brittney Loper*. She turned my direction and I dropped the slat.

"Boyce, I saw you. Open up, dammit."

I was so not in the mood for Brittney Loper.

Granted, I was never in the mood for Brittney Loper.

"Boyce, *c'mon*! I need you."

Oh *God*. Hoping she didn't mean what I feared she meant, I turned the bolt and pulled the door open to cutoffs, boots, and a tank sporting the name of one of the touristy bars on the main drag. Her chest could still influence gravity. I wanted her to look worse for wear, but she didn't. Blinking thick lashes and tilting her head full of dirty-blond hair like an adorable puppy, she checked the metal numbers tacked into trailer's siding and then the existence of the garage next door.

Why hadn't it occurred to me that his life included *this*. Boyce was a man. Men had needs. Needs that would be filled by women who looked like Brittney, if they looked like Boyce.

Her gaze swung back to me. "Pearl Frank? Right?"

"That's me," I gritted out. "Boyce isn't here, Brittney. He'll be back in an hour or two."

"Whoa. I didn't know you and Boyce—" She snorted a giggle. "*Ah*, this explains a whole helluva lot! But I thought you were away at college or something?"

"I graduated." *What* explained a lot of *what*?

"Cool. And you decided to move back here... for Boyce? That's kinda—"

"No, that's not—"

"—sweet."

"—why." *Sweet?* Was she high? Knowing Brit, that was entirely possible. "I just needed somewhere to stay, and Boyce has a spare room since..."

"Since his worthless turdass of a father kicked it, *finally*. That guy was barely a step above my old man."

A step *above*?

"So when will Boyce be back? An hour, you said? Because my piece of shit truck is shaking like a tweaker between hits." She pointed a thumb over her shoulder at the beat-up pickup in Wynn's driveway. "I dunno what I did to it, but it's pissed. I gotta have that thing to get back and forth to work or I'm screwed."

Even Brittney Loper was employable.

That's uncalled for, my conscience tut-tutted. "I have the opposite problem. Working car, no job." Small talk? *Shut up, Pearl.*

"But your mama is married to Dr. Frank. Don't they, y'know, give you money?"

My face warmed.

Before I could answer, she added, "If you and Boyce ain't getting busy then why are you living here instead of there? I haven't been to the Frank place since we graduated, of course—what was that, four years ago? But shit, girl, they'd have to pry my ass outta there with a crowbar if I was you." A crease popped up on her forehead. "Unless Dr. Frank—"

"God. No—*no*. He's great. I just had a little disagreement with them about what I'm doing next. They expected me to go to medical school and I... don't want to." Why was I telling *her* this?

"You know you're an adult, right?" she said slowly, as if I were dense. "You went to college even! Not married, no kids... You don't have a kid, right?"

"Uh, no."

"Free as a bird. And look at you—you're a cute little thing. If you wanted Boyce, you could land him. Honestly, if you'd been a bitch in high school like your best friend was—no offense—I wouldn't point this out, but I mean *be real*. Plenty of the dipshits we went to school with are still living with their mamas, but Boyce has his own place and his own business. Sure, he was a fuckup in high school—weren't we all—well, not you—me and Boyce and Rick, *etcetera*. But Boyce turned out pretty decent I'd say, and Lord-have-mercy hot to boot."

I snapped my mouth closed once I realized it was ajar. "I thought you and he... uh..."

She laughed, displaying a mouth full of white teeth. I meanly concentrated on her small overbite. "Well, yeah, but it's never been anything serious between us. *You*, though. You've got the goods. He'd be an idiot not to go for it. Just make him work for it. Boyce doesn't set store by anything that comes too easy, if you get my drift."

• • • • • • • • •

Boyce was silent when he returned, dropping the box in his room, checking the fridge and shutting it without removing anything. Unless he'd eaten while he was out, he'd missed lunch.

"How'd your meeting go?"

He shook his head but didn't reply, staring out the window into a backyard that had been allowed to go wild.

"That bad?"

"I'll figure it out." His eyes shifted to mine and away. Just as I meant to press him to let me listen or help, he said, "I missed my workout this morning. I'm gonna go do that."

He left his room five minutes later and headed straight outside wearing unlaced sneakers, mesh shorts, *no shirt*, and dog tags I'd never seen him wear. My body threatened mutiny at my self-imposed celibacy while sharing quarters with *that*. As soon as the door shut behind him, I went to stand six inches from the AC unit in the window, which couldn't blow cold enough to cool my feverish skin. I'd handled Boyce Wynn in bits and pieces all my life, but living with him was testing every bit of willpower I had.

My body didn't get it. I couldn't deny that I wanted him on a purely physical level, but if I gave in to that, my heart would wake up and want more. I couldn't play that game with Boyce. He would break me.

Even if I'd experienced brief moments of wishing I could be more than a friend he found attractive, I had never let myself imagine him falling in love with me. Exception: those few hours between our only time together and seeing him on the beach with a girl on his lap—a *temp fuck*—that's what he and his friends called the tourists' daughters they hooked up with.

Playing house had put relationship mirages in my head where none existed before. Or maybe I'd just been able to repress them before now. Damn Brittney Loper and her cruel promptings to *land* the boy I'd loved all my life.

Nine weeks, two days.

"I forgot to tell you—Brittney Loper came by for you," I said when Boyce came inside.

He paused before pulling the fridge door wide and staring inside. "What did she want?" The waistband of his shorts was damp with perspiration.

"She said her truck was shaking."

He grabbed a bottle of premade iced tea and a small tub of grilled chicken and turned around, his lips quirked. "That can't be abnormal for her." His shorts hung lower than they had an hour ago—showing off the sweat-sheened ladder of muscle notching his abdomen and sculpted chest.

"*Boyce*."

"What?" He chuckled, spearing slices of chicken with a fork and wolfing them down.

"Double standard much?" I snapped, pointlessly angry.

"All right—down, ethics police—I'm just playing. God knows my TA's been known to *shake* now and again."

I wanted to punch him, but he probably wouldn't even feel it. He looked like a bodybuilder, skin oiled to highlight the hard-won cuts and rock-solid curves.

"She say when she's coming back?"

I stared down at my book. "She said she'd come back tomorrow. She's at work now."

"Tomorrow's Sunday—that's my only day off."

"I guess she believes she has a… special influence with you."

He grunted. "The fuck she does. No one has influence over my Sundays." When he finished off the chicken, he tipped the iced tea back and drank all of it without stopping.

Efforts to keep my eyes glued to the open book in front of me were a giant fail. I watched him through my hair, ready to feign total concentration on the text I was supposedly reading at the least indication that he was about to notice me *staring like a creeper*.

"I'm gonna grab a shower and go out. I'll probably stop and check Brit's truck." He turned to look at me and my eyes dropped to the textbook. "Wanna go with, get a beer?"

"No thanks. I've got to get through this chapter." *Bullshit.* I was more than caught up. There was just no way I was going to go watch him flirt with Brittney or the vacationers who'd begun to show up en masse in the past two weeks. *And when he brings someone home— which could happen tonight?* my practical side asked. I was of a mind to tie and gag my practical side. "I have to apply for more jobs tomorrow too."

"No luck this morning?"

"Zero. But I'll find something," I said, professing more confidence than I had. "I just have to keep looking."

Seventeen

BOYCE

Brittney plopped a shot of Cuervo down on the bar in front of me. "Where's Pearl?"

I asked if she wanted to come along. She said no—as usual. "We're roommates, Brit, not married."

"You wish."

"What?"

"Oh, c'mon, like you haven't thought about it. Or at least one part of it." She grinned. "And y'all would make some cute babies."

My mouth dropped open like I was bent on catching flies, and an image flashed through my mind like a video clip: *I opened a door and a kid ran up and attached itself to my leg—a kid that looked like Pearl the day I met her*. I closed my eyes briefly to clear it, but that image stuck like it'd been welded to my brain. "The hell? Why would you think a guy my age would be thinking about shit like that?"

She snorted. "If a girl like Pearl Frank doesn't make you think of putting a ring on it, you're a bigger idiot than I thought. Best fish or cut bait, Boyce Wynn, before that girl gets a better offer."

I scowled, no retort coming to mind—a damned unprecedented

state of affairs for me.

"I'm just sayin'! No need for a hissy fit."

My teeth gritted. "*Subject change*. When's the last time you've had your tires rotated?"

She arched a brow.

"You said your truck was shaking? Having the tires rotated and balanced would be the easiest, cheapest fix if that's the problem. Unless you've had it done lately." I sipped the tequila, back on solid ground.

"Well, hmm. I got new tires for graduation."

I put the shot glass down. "As in four *years* ago?"

"Boyce, tires ain't in my wheelhouse. I know beer and liquor. I know how to make my grandma's pecan pie from scratch and biscuits and gravy that'd make you cry they're so good. I know good boys and bad boys and how to turn the former into the latter. I do not know *tires*."

I held up a hand. "Bring it by tomorrow, late morning—but text me first. Thompson and me are going fishing early."

"Rick?"

"Naw—Randy. I haven't seen Rick for a while. Last I heard from Randy, Rick was living somewhere outside Houston."

Her mouth tightened. "Me neither. Not that either of them were geniuses, but I'da never thought Randy would turn out the levelheaded one of them two. He was one crazy motherfucker, and now he's selling T-shirts and making jewelry."

A guy two stools down was trying to get her attention by waving and clearing his throat.

"Well. Enough reminiscing—I got drunks to serve."

"Hey!" the guy said.

"Keep your shorts on, sweetie—I'm coming." She slapped the

bar. "See you tomorrow, Boyce. Oh—Jesus, I almost forgot! My great-great-aunt—the one who runs the inn? Her front-desk girl is preggers, and she's just been put on bed rest. She needs somebody smart who presents well, won't steal shit, and can work weekends. I figured Pearl fit that, so I called Aunt Minnie and she was all over it. Tell her to stop by tomorrow if she's interested."

. . . .

By the time I returned home, it was raining. The trailer windows were dark, so I toed my boots off on the stoop and went inside in wet socks. Pearl was asleep on the sofa, sheet pushed to her waist, wearing one of her old dance troupe T-shirts. I couldn't resist the urge to wander closer and stare at her for one short minute. Curled on her side, knees tucked high and hands folded below her chin, she sighed in her sleep. Her hair was loose and wild, covering the white pillowcase.

Goddamn Brittney and her talk of rings and babies when just trying to get this girl to be seen in public with me was as good as repeatedly bashing my head against the wall. When I could lose everything I'd built in the two shakes it would take Barney Amos to find the mother who left me with a man who talked with his fists.

. . . .

When I woke, I assumed it was because of the crack of thunder that shook the trailer, and I turned onto my side, prepared to sink back into sleep and hoping this shit let up before five a.m. Otherwise, my fishing plans were screwed.

The flash of lightning seconds later lit my room through the open blinds of the single window. One second, maybe two—just long enough for me to catch sight of the figure in the doorway.

"Pearl?" I leaned up on an elbow.

"Is it always this loud during storms? Or should we be concerned?" Her voice was reed-thin.

Dr. Frank's place was a stone fortress compared to this tin box that was designed to be pulled off its foundation, loaded onto a set of wheels, and moved on a whim. Besides that, the Frank place was on the bay side of the island. They didn't get the brunt of storms rolling in from the gulf like my neighborhood did.

"It's always this loud. Nothing to be worried about." Just as I said that, thunder from that last strike roared and the vibrations shook the floor. Pearl jumped visibly, and I bit the inside of my cheek to keep from laughing. "C'mere." I scooted into the center of the bed and held the sheet up.

She hesitated, wheels grinding away in that brain of hers. I couldn't accuse her of overthinking. I wanted her, and I could tell she wanted me from the looks she'd been trying to mask over the past week. I was all but daring her to cross that line and let me give us both what we wanted. I wouldn't make the first move, though, even if she joined me. The power of whether we just fell asleep or whether I kept her wide-awake for the next hour or three was in her hands.

I wouldn't make the first move, but I'd damn sure make the second.

Lightning lit the room again—several seconds of it—multiple strikes. The next crash of thunder would rattle the walls for half a minute straight. She paused for all of about one second before crossing the room and sliding under the sheet, but she hugged the edge of the mattress with her back to me, no part of her body touching mine. She curled up like she had been on the sofa, waiting for that first loud, angry clap and the echoing bellow just behind it.

I dropped the sheet over her just as the boom came like a rifle shot, transforming into a wind-powered rumble that rocked the trailer and everything in it. By the time the last of it faded, her back was pressed against my chest, her hips tucked against my abdomen. My arm lay across her rib cage, but my hand rested against the mattress in front of her. I made no move to reposition closer or farther away. A few more similar strikes ensured she didn't leave, though none were as bad as the two or three that had sent her scurrying to my door.

Just as I was sure we would drift off to sleep, she shifted onto her back and turned her face toward mine. I hardened instantly but didn't move as we stared at each other. The hums and aftershocks of wind and rain went on outside—more lightning, more thunder—but it was moving on up the coast and none of it seemed to trouble her now.

She made another quarter-turn, facing me full on, and I swear I'd never held myself so still. Finger on the trigger, I waited, motionless, for her clear signal.

Her fingertips stretched up and curved against my cheek. *Not yet.*

Her warm lips touched the edge of my jaw with a barely there kiss. *Close.*

The pad of her foot skimmed along my shin, bare toes trailing down, and she angled herself alongside me tip to toe, cradling my rigid, hungry dick against her belly like a welcome home. *Almost.*

My hand drifted to her back, my fingers charting a careful path through her T-shirt as I drew her in tight, palm sliding down her spine, pressing her flush against my chest, dipping into the bow of her lower back as she released a quiet moan. When my hand slid to cup her hip, I said, "You ready?" and she nodded.

Now.

Pearl

His mouth covered mine, his tongue spearing home as he turned me onto my back—nothing gentle, nothing measured—just raw possession and claim staked. I hadn't wanted time to think anymore, and he didn't give it to me.

Clutching his bare shoulders and the arms that surrounded me like indestructible bands, I gave myself over to every trembling response he lured from the buried recesses of my heart. As the storm ebbed outside and sporadic volleys of lightning shone through the window and flickered across the room, he peeled away my clothes and kissed me until I was gasping into his mouth and surging against his hand.

I whimpered as he held his body inches away, hovering over me, so close that I could feel the heat radiating from his skin. With a muffled chuckle, he kissed and teased his way over my breasts and ribs and belly, his lips and tongue stroking unerringly. His hair was soft against my palms as he drifted lower, and I writhed and arched, craving his touch, the feel of his body against mine.

His hands connected with my thighs, and I wailed like I'd waited for days as he dipped his head and slicked his tongue over me before plunging it inside. Arching like a bow and fisting the tangled sheets beneath me like I was clinging to the surface of the earth, I panted a garbled expletive and almost cried. There was no way I could hold still, no subtle response possible.

"Mmm," he hummed, and I came undone.

He slid up my sweat-slicked body and into me, reclaiming my mouth in the same instant. I convulsed around him, my brain screaming about protection to no avail, drowned out in waves of bliss as he cradled my head in one hand, turning my face for a deep, slow kiss as he rocked into me and came, his mouth breaking from mine to utter my name and, "*Godfuckingdammit*."

Foreheads pressed together as if fused, we panted. I closed my eyes, panicked that everything I'd ever felt for him would spill out.

When he withdrew and dropped to my side, he rolled onto his back and dragged me close in one movement. His chest still rose and fell, and I watched my hand ride up and down, curled over his heart. I slanted one leg over his and he tightened his hold, but neither of us spoke. Heart rates decelerating, limbs relaxed and languid, our echoed breathing patterns returned to normal, and the comprehension of what had just occurred presented itself.

I took stock. I'd come to his door like a panicked child, afraid of the sort of thunderstorm I'd never enjoyed but had survived dozens of. He'd invited me into his bed with no seductive propositions or wisecracks. I'd turned to face him. I'd run my fingers over the soft scruff at his jawline and then kissed him there. He'd been hard against my stomach. *You ready?* he'd said, and I'd nodded.

I tried to be sorry and couldn't. What a lie that would be, and I wouldn't tell it. Not to myself. It wasn't just as good as I remembered. It was—impossibly—so much better.

Finally I mumbled something about the bathroom and slipped out of his arms. The night table drawer was ajar, and a condom wrapper was on top, empty. I hadn't noticed him reach for it, but I hadn't noticed much of anything past what he was doing to me. I plucked my T-shirt off the floor and pulled it on as I padded from his bedroom, through the kitchen, and past the living room with my disheveled sheets on the sofa as I'd left them.

I washed up in the dark by the light of the lone porthole window over the shower, unable to look myself in the eye just yet. What now? Back to the sofa? I had no idea of the time, but there'd been no hint of dawn through the windows as I passed them. The rain was still falling, quietly tapping against the roof and windowpanes, but the lightning strikes had abated and the menacing winds had calmed like exhausted toddlers after a tantrum.

Boyce was just outside the bathroom when I opened the door. He caught my hand as I passed and pulled me close, tipping my face up and kissing me tenderly, slowly—nothing like our turbulent coming together moments ago. By the time he released me, I was light-headed. I turned and walked to the sofa, sitting and then curling under the sheet, my mind more muddled than ever. What did it mean? Anything? What had I done?

Minutes later, he exited the bathroom, walked directly to the sofa and scooped me up, sheet and all.

"We're not done yet," he said, and my heart launched into a staccato beat as he carried me back to his bed.

This time everything was slow motion. He drew me astride his body, his hands enveloping my face carefully before sliding into my hair and pulling me down for long, deep kisses. Once he was sure of me, his fingers wandered down my arms and back, caressing over my shoulders, along the center of my back to finally duck beneath my shirt and set fire to my skin. His kisses gentle but insistent, he gripped my hips and pressed me against the hard length between my legs.

This time I was aware when he reached into the drawer. Aware when he tore open the wrapper behind my back and tugged me up on my knees while he rolled it on before pressing me back down, hands at my hips, impaling me, filling me. His face disappeared beneath my shirt as I came down and he rocked up. I felt but couldn't see him tug a nipple into his mouth, swirling his tongue round and round the tip until I moaned, then sucking so forcefully it was almost painful before alternating to the other, his hand moving to cover the first sensitive, wet nub, pressing his palm to my breast like a blessing.

This time when I began to come, he flipped me onto my back and pressed deep, one hand between us, thumb and forefinger stroking lightly—once, twice, three times—until I bucked and screamed with the unbearable pleasure, cresting and shuddering until I thought it would never end. Before the tremors subsided, he withdrew and surged home, setting me off once more when he came, my name in his mouth before he kissed me like it was the last time.

· · · · · · · · · ·

I woke with a start and sat up, heart hammering. Full daylight streamed through the window across the room as if the thunderstorm had been a hallucination. *I'm late.*

No—it was Sunday. I heaved a relieved sigh and then listened for Boyce's presence outside the bedroom, but every sound I detected originated outside—the squawk of seagulls scavenging a few blocks from the beach, the hum of a car passing on the street, the low horn of a tanker or cruise ship out in the gulf. I was alone.

I pulled the sheet back, revealing my bare legs below the worn T-shirt twisted around my torso. Scooting to the edge of the bed, I realized I was a bit sore. It had been five months since I'd broken up with Mitchell. Returning to my comfort zone after the breakup, I'd thrown my full concentration into academics and earned a 4.0 in my final, most challenging semester. I'd had little to no social life outside the Chi-O house. Attending compulsory spring events with guys who were friends, I declined any actual dates and sidestepped hookups, preferring the use of my hand and my imagination as a sexual partner. No misunderstandings, no complications.

Little wonder I'd responded so forcefully to Boyce's skillful attention last night. *Oh my stars*. I'd never, ever nearly cried during sex… except for the first time—also with Boyce—but that was due to pain, not ecstasy. I'd always thought *It hurts so good* was a silly expression, a fictional ideal.

Wrong.

My shorts were folded on the night table, next to a note scribbled on the back of a list of auto parts.

> *Gone fishin' (always wanted to write that to somebody). Back around 11. Brit is bringing her truck by late morning but she's supposed to text me first so she shouldn't bother you. BTW - she says her aunt needs a front desk person at the inn on Cotter. She told her about you. Sounded like you could show up and it's yours, if you're interested.*
> *B.*

Boyce had left me a note to tell me where he was and when he'd be back… but Brittney Loper was bringing her truck by, despite her supposed lack of influence over his Sundays. I fought back the surge of jealousy that made my eyes burn. Boyce wasn't mine. We'd slept together last night, but that didn't mean he belonged to me.

Brit had been friendly yesterday and had possibly arranged for me to land a job at an inn. After my initial job-search failure, I wasn't willing to look that gift horse in the mouth.

I grabbed my shorts and the note and went to shower. When I got out there were two messages and a pic on my phone—from Mitchell. I tapped Edit and my thumb hovered over Delete, but I couldn't do it. My curiosity got the best of me. I wanted to know what the hell he had to say.

> Mitchell: I got an apartment in the Hillsboro West End area. It's biking distance from campus on nice days. I think you'd like it. The pic is the view from the patio.
>
> Mitchell: Anyway. I wanted to apologize one more time. I know you deleted my messages after we broke up instead of reading or listening to them, and I don't blame you. I was such a jerk. I guess I'm just hoping you read this. I'm so sorry, Pearl.

"*Be* sorry, asshole," I muttered. So much had happened in the past five months. So much had happened in the past *twelve hours*. Mitchell didn't deserve to know any of it. He didn't deserve an *I forgive you…* even though I'd reneged on all our plans and didn't tell him until I had to.

I didn't regret my decision, but if I'd just told him about it earlier, I could have avoided these pangs of conscience. I closed the message without answering or deleting it, unsure which to do. No rush, either way. Besides, I had a job to land.

Brittney Loper's words reverberated in my head and I wondered what had made her think them. *If you wanted Boyce, you could land him.* I didn't want him to just want me in his bed. To manipulate him into promises or arrangements because of that want. I wanted him to love me like I loved him. I wanted to be his only. But no one had ever been Boyce Wynn's only, and I wasn't foolish enough to view that as some sort of challenge. He wanted me sexually, yes. But interpreting desire as proof of love produced a counterfeit result, born of immeasurable evidence and hidden formulation and a vague hypothesis with no falsifiable alternative.

He was a magnet and I was a magnetized entity. One week was all it took to submit to the magnetic field that trailer had become, and there were nine weeks to go. The only question was whether his undivided attraction would last the whole nine weeks—whether my heart would be shattered before the time was up or I would shoulder the pretense of being the one who left, my dignity intact, outwardly.

I had what in science is known as a hindsight bias. When it was over I would say I had known all along how it would end, because I'd been here before. It could be argued that I would influence the result—that my wrecked heart would be a self-fulfilling prophecy—but I couldn't see how that mattered one way or the other. And that's when I knew how far gone I was.

chapter Eighteen

BOYCE

Sunday afternoon I'd sent Brit packing with balanced tires and orders to get a new set as soon as she could afford them when Pearl texted me. She not only got the job, they wanted her to start right away. Aunt Minnie—who was about a hundred—had taken a spill over Katy Perry, the inn's reception dog, and fractured her femur one week before her knocked-up front-desk girl got put on bed rest.

If I were Pearl, I'd have thought long and hard about the bad luck making the rounds there before signing on, but she'd always been a logical sort of girl. Luck one way or the other wouldn't faze her because she'd never believed in it.

She came home around ten thirty, tiptoeing through the trailer for no good reason because I was wide-awake, staring at the ceiling and praying for a gully washer despite the fact that there was a two percent chance of rain and not a cloud in the goddamned sky. She fell asleep on the sofa while I tossed and turned and cursed the fact that my pillow still smelled like her.

Sam showed up Monday morning, full of beans because she'd survived her trial period and was now a bona fide employee. We were working on a routine brake job under the lift I'd set low so she could see and reach everything. I pulled my weight bench over so I didn't have to squat. I'd never worked on an underbody while seated, but it was damned sight more uncomfortable than I'd have thought.

"You were in the Marines?" she asked, all offhand like she thought I'd start spilling war stories if she was sneaky enough. Since I'd rolled the sleeves of my T-shirt to my shoulders, she had stolen several veiled peeks at my tat, not near as wily as she thought she was.

"No. My brother was." I didn't elaborate and didn't intend to.

She was quiet for a minute, taking in that word—*was*. When I spoke of Brent to someone unfamiliar with his story, which was rare because I didn't speak of him at all if I could help it, a strained moment always passed during which I hoped they'd heard everything that word implied. People could express sympathies all day long and I would nod and accept them, but I didn't want to discuss the loss of him.

"My mama was too."

I glanced at her downturned face and wondered if Silva had known this. *Of course he had*, that sly bastard.

"I got the tattoo on the third anniversary of 9/11, three months after he was killed in action," I said. "He had the same one."

"Did you mean to join up too?"

"No. Brent—" *Damn* if his name spoken aloud didn't still lance through me. "Brent was the Marine. I was always the grease monkey."

She smiled faintly. "That's what my dad calls me. His grease monkey."

"You're a monkey all right. A damned ornery monkey." I was sure she'd have some comeback at the ready—likely one that proved my point—and we'd leave the grim discussion of dead brothers and mothers behind.

"Dad says he'd rather I be cranky all the time than pretend to be happy when I'm not."

Not exactly the retort I'd expected. I handed her a wrench and pointed to the bolt she needed to tighten.

As she turned it, she said, "My mama got out when she got pregnant with me. Dad's never told me if she meant to stay out or go back. I think she meant to go back. But then, you know, *me*. With all *this*." She pounded a fist on the arm of the wheelchair and stared at her lap. "She killed herself when I was three. I don't remember her. But in every picture we have of her, she's *smiling*."

I didn't know how the hell to respond to that, so I didn't. I was at a loss for what Silva was thinking, sending this kid to me. I couldn't fix her. All I could do was give her a job, though working had been a savior of sorts to me once I allowed it to be.

"Congrats, monkey—you just replaced brake pads all by yourself."

She rolled her eyes. "It's not like I've never done it before."

"Ever gotten paid to do it?" I shot back.

She blinked and her mouth quirked a little on one side.

"Don't waste time being smug. Get to work on the next one."

• • • • • • • • •

The mattress delivery was scheduled for Wednesday, so I slapped a coat of paint on the walls of Pearl's bedroom Tuesday evening while she was at work. That room hadn't been painted since *ever*. When she came home, I heard her rummaging for something to eat in the kitchen, washing up in the bathroom, and finally opening the creaky door to that bedroom across the trailer. I'd left a window up for ventilation, but the searing fumes had snuck under the door anyhow.

"You painted the bedroom?" she asked the next morning when I came in from lifting. She hadn't yet moved from her spot on the sofa. She usually got up about the time I grabbed a final cup of coffee before heading out to the garage. In her little sleep-rumpled T-shirt and shorts—with nothing, I knew now, underneath—she'd stand there folding the sheets and stacking them on the end of the sofa while I fought the urge to cross the room, pull her to my lap and kiss her until she begged me to lay her down.

I stopped halfway to the bathroom, fists clenched tight. "Reckon it needed it." I'd driven my muscles to fatigue not ten minutes ago, and it had done nothing to stem the want of her. "The mattress should be delivered later today. I forgot to buy sheets, but I have an extra set you can use."

Just when I was calling myself ten kinds of dumbass for setting her up with a bedroom when I wanted her back in *my* bed, she said, "Thank you, Boyce."

"Yep."

I was a patient man. I'd survived being beat and cussed and outlived the asshole who did his damnedest to make every day of my life a living hell. I'd withstood being branded a troublemaker when all I wanted was to be invisible. I'd done what I had to do and refused to sweat the nuts and bolts or suffer remorse over what couldn't be changed. My life was simple. I fished a little and drank a little. I worked hard and I fucked hard. I'd outgrown fighting, but if the situation called for it, I could put a boot in someone's ass they'd never forget.

I was a man who'd loved this girl from the moment she'd come back to life and saw no one but me. Now she was closer than she'd ever been, right when I was on the verge of losing everything I'd spent years building and becoming. It was the cruelest switch life had ever thrown at me.

. . . .

Just after the delivery truck showed up, I got a call from Barney Amos, who didn't beat around the bush this time. "Boyce, I traced your mama to Amarillo, where she's been living for the past twelve years. I got ahold of her an hour ago. She asserts that she and your dad never divorced. Will or no will, disputing her claim wouldn't be something I'd advise, though you're welcome to seek other legal counsel." He sighed heavily. "You'd best start setting up a plan B."

I pointed the delivery guys to the bedroom and waited until they carried the mattress set inside and out of earshot. "Did she already know about Dad? And Brent?"

"She knew about your brother's passing, but not Bud."

I walked out onto the stoop, lit a cigarette, and took a long drag. The sky was too bright and blue for my world to crash and burn today. "Did she ask about me?"

"I told her what a fine young man you've become. That you'd been running Wynn's ever since your dad got sick." He hadn't answered the question—not directly, at any rate.

"When'll she be here?"

"I'm not sure what her circumstances are, and it's near seven hundred miles there to here. At the soonest, it'll be a couple days. More'n likely three or four."

My life was set to blow to hell in somewhere between forty-eight and ninety-six hours. I could almost hear the *tick tick tick* counting down. This whole shitty scenario hadn't been real before. Now it was.

SWEET

By the time I lost Brent, I hadn't expected to ever see her again. I hadn't presumed her dead. I'd just presumed her gone, as if she'd vanished into thin air the night she left. I'd spent a year or two pining for her to come back, crying myself to sleep face-first in my pillow so Brent wouldn't hear. When he left for boot camp, I couldn't handle the double loss. To survive his absence, I let her go.

Then Brent died, and I knew neither of them was ever coming back. No one came back. Not for me.

Pearl was off tonight, so we'd planned to fry up the drum I'd caught Sunday along with a bagful of fresh okra Sam brought me from her dad's garden yesterday. Sam wasn't fond of okra, so she was happy to get rid of it and Pearl was happy to take it. I was less sure. It was free *okra*, not free beer.

"I straight-up dropped a hundred-dollar beaker in the lab today," Pearl said, plopping a pat of butter and a pinch of salt into the rice. "I was so mortified—I must've turned ten shades of red. Everybody froze, including me, until Dr. Kent said, 'Well it ain't gonna sweep itself up. Broom's in the *broom* closet.'"

I chuckled at her vocal imitation. "He sounds like a good ol' boy."

"Yeah, but he's such an actual genius I think regular people exasperate the hell out of him. He's usually cantankerous. I thought for sure he'd make some sort of example out of me for being clumsy with the lab equipment. I'd have deserved it."

I watched her soak okra slices in buttermilk and coat them with cornmeal and spice. I'd grown adept at cooking fish a hundred ways, but vegetables were always raw or microwaved. I had no patience with anything that required a recipe. She'd made fresh iced tea too, in a pitcher I didn't know I had.

"Maybe he thinks you're hot," I said, turning the fish in the frying pan.

Her laughter tumbled out like a song I wanted to replay over and over. "Boyce, jeez! He's old enough to be my grandpa." Her dark eyes glinted as she slid the okra into the pan alongside the fish.

"Baby, if he ain't dead yet, you're hot enough to wake him right up." I winked, nudging her from prim and proper to hot and bothered. She wouldn't look at me, and her cheeks shaded pink. When she added salt and butter to the rice like that task demanded her full concentration, I didn't have the heart to tell her she'd just done that two minutes ago. I'd always loved getting her flustered and unbalanced with a bit of flirting and then catching her and setting her upright before she knew what was what.

That thought brought to mind the thing that would unbalance her in a way I didn't want. Once we sat down to eat, I said, "I need to tell you something."

"Okay." She waited, wide-eyed. I wasn't sure what she thought I was about to tell her, but whatever it was, she was off the mark.

"My mother is coming back to town in the next few days. Seems she and my dad never got divorced. They did make wills—leaving everything to each other. But that doesn't matter as much as the fact that he died still married to her."

Her lips fell apart. "So she'll get everything. Including the *garage*?"

I nodded, unsurprised that she'd caught on faster than I had.

"That rotten *bastard*. How dare he have you running his damned business and taking care of his sorry ass and never tell you this?"

Pearl rarely cussed. She had to get pretty pissed to let loose like that. I bit back a grin at how cute she was when she was spitting mad.

"After the first year or so he never brought her up, drunk or sober." I shrugged. "I'd always assumed they'd divorced somewhere along the way. I assumed I was his sole heir. Mr. Amos says I could fight it, but this is a community property state and they were still legally married. I'd lose. And I need my savings to do whatever the hell I'm doing next."

She laid her hand on mine, and I knew right then there was nothing I wouldn't do to make her mine, short of dragging her down with me.

"What *will* you do next?"

"No idea," I said, which wasn't the whole truth. I had one short-term plan—a proposition I intended to make. I wouldn't share it with her, though. If she knew the details, she'd never let me go through with it.

Pearl

I'd never wanted to give somebody a piece of my mind like I wanted to give it to Bud Wynn in that moment. Too bad he was dead. All I could do was hope hell was real and he was in it.

My sorority's social director, Jen, had been pre-law, and her parents were both attorneys. She'd explained the basics of trust funds and inheritance transfers and prenups to any of us who weren't familiar with the legal pitfalls of saying *I do* and later saying *I sure as hell don't*. I'd assumed that if Mitchell and I got married, we'd be doing so as doctors—equals. If it didn't work out we'd arrange a reasonable, equitable split.

I'd never considered what happened in a situation like this— where a divorce should have happened but hadn't. Boyce's mother had run from an abusive husband, leaving her share of marital property behind. I couldn't justly fault her for wanting her share—I just hated what she might take from Boyce. He wouldn't know what she intended until she showed up, but I'd learned two things from Jen's warnings and a bit of Internet research: she was probably entitled to everything, and when it came to money and inheritance, people lost their damned minds.

"You have a personal account in your name, right? Separate from the business and your dad's accounts?"

He nodded, staring at his plate. "There's not a whole lot in it. I've been channeling most of the garage income back into the business, replacing crap diagnostic equipment, buying new tools. I got advice from Maxfield's dad when I first took over, and he told me to keep the business money completely separate and pay myself a salary. I wish I'd given myself a fucking raise a year ago." He chuckled. "But thank Christ I listened to him or I'd have lumped it all together like a dumbass."

"Boyce, there's no way you could have seen this coming," I said—his words to me when Mama had told me I couldn't live at home and pursue the life I wanted. Little did I know I'd be echoing them back to him about his own mother. I took a bite of rice and nearly spit it right back out. "Aauugh! How much salt did I put in this?"

He laughed and arched a brow. "You were a tad distracted."

Lord, was I ever. I downed half my iced tea in an attempt to dilute the salt and battled the urge to fan myself like a swooning twit. "Maybe you shouldn't distract me while I'm cooking."

He leapt from playful to predatory in two seconds flat. "But I like distracting you."

His mouth curved into the lazy half smirk I knew so well, and his gaze dropped to my lips. When I licked them (combination nervous habit and enough salt on that rice to choke a horse), our eyes connected. There was nothing guarded in the deep green of his.

It was official: when it came to Boyce Wynn, I was the quintessential swooning twit.

· · · · · · · · · ·

The inn was over a century old but had been reincarnated multiple times. In one form or another, it had survived a fire, a tidal wave, and a lengthy economic downturn. My semi-official title was Front Desk Person, but that hardly covered the responsibilities of the position. By my third shift, I'd unclogged the ice machine with a screwdriver and a couple of swift kicks, placated a returning guest when another guest refused to vacate the room they'd reserved, and set mousetraps in a storage closet after a guest freaked out that the scratching noises she heard in her room overnight were evidence of a haunting—part of the inn's folklore.

Minnie assured her that the inn's resident spirit meant no harm. "Alyce was a former tenant who'd lived a happy life here and didn't want to leave. She had a touch of the OCD—not diagnosed back in those days, y'know. She's been known to sweep the floors at night. Maybe that's what you heard?"

"It did sound like sweeping!" The woman agreed while I fought to maintain a straight face and worried whether my boss actually believed what she was saying.

When the door shut behind the guest, Minnie reached beneath the counter and pulled out a box of mousetraps and a jar of peanut butter. "Ghosts they'll stay for, rodents they won't."

The room (and storage closet next to it) was upstairs, and Minnie was under strict orders not to climb the creaky staircase with her cast and cane. "Don't let it snap on your finger," she said. "It'll take your nail clean off."

I was less worried about trap springs and more worried about squeezing into a narrow closet with a territorial horde of mice.

In my last hour of the night, I'd been summoned three times to a room shared by three college boys—first to deliver fresh towels, then extra pillows, and then to change a lightbulb in the ceiling—which I accomplished standing on a chair while they stood around watching. Their last call was an invitation to join them in some whiskey-shot pregaming before they went out. I declined.

As I locked up the office and drove home, I thought about Boyce's mother. Specifically, where would she stay when she arrived? I'd spent one night in the new bed, but I could be back on the sofa in a day or two. Or sleeping in my car.

BOYCE

I had a picture in my mind of my mother's face, but it was fifteen years old now and had been stored there by a kid. The night she left, she was in her early thirties—skin unlined, hair a darker copper than mine and taller than me, though not by much. Next to my father, she'd been pretty and small and fragile.

I knew Brent had taken his disappointment in her to his grave, though he hadn't been given to resentment toward anyone but our father. He'd never said a bad word about her to me, but I would never forget the look on his face the night she left. Once she was gone, it was clear as day he hadn't hoped or planned for her to return. That faith had been mine. He'd known better.

The woman standing on the top step when I opened the door Sunday evening was a faded version of my memory. Her hair was carrot-red with an inch of dark and gray roots, her face lined from years of smoking and sun and God only knew what else. Only her hazel eyes were untouched by the years.

"Boyce—my God, you're bigger than your daddy was," she said. "Bigger than Brent too."

Brent, standing in this very doorway, begging you to take me with you. "He was fifteen the last time you saw him," I said. "I'll be twenty-three—"

"Next month. I know."

I inclined my head once, at a loss for what was supposed to happen next.

"Can I come in?" she asked.

I stood back and she walked into her former home, glancing one way and then the other. "It looks just the same," she said, as though she'd expected Dad might've redecorated in her absence. The only modifications he'd made were installing the flat-screen and replacing a lamp that broke years ago when he punched me and I landed against the table it sat on.

Trailing her fingers over the sofa, she stared at the square of less-soiled carpet where Dad's chair had been before I lit it on fire in the yard. Mrs. Echols, watching from her corner window, had called the volunteer fire department on my mini-inferno, but by the time the first truck pulled up that chair was a smoldering bunch of coils and charred wood. I hosed it down with the extinguisher I kept on hand in the garage and the first responder called off the emergency, noticeably disappointed.

I followed her into the kitchen, where Pearl's laptop, notebook, and a couple of textbooks covered half the tabletop. She pointed to one. "*Dynamics of Marine Ecosystems*? Are you—"

"That's my roommate's stuff."

Her mouth tightened, lips a flattened line. Her eyes shifted toward me and away, and she cleared her throat. "I hadn't really meant to do this right off, but I'll be needing my bedroom, of course. Since it's my house now."

From the constricted feel of my jaw, I knew my face mirrored hers. "Well. That didn't take long."

She flinched. "I don't intend to kick you out, Boyce—this place is yours too. I just didn't think you might've rented a room out to some stranger so quickly."

She didn't understand that *she* was the stranger. How could she not see it?

I stole a glance at the clock on the microwave and shot Mateo a text to tell him I wouldn't be over for supper. In three hours Pearl would be home from work, and I wanted this settled before then. "Let's get this over with," I said, reaching into the fridge to grab a beer. When I gestured to her, she nodded and I grabbed another one. "I know what you're entitled to legally, but I've built a life here without being aware you were going to come back and take it from me."

She lowered her bottle. "I told you I don't mean to take anything—"

"Then why are you here? If that's the truth, leave."

We stared across the table until her eyes shifted away and she said, "I left here with a trash bag full of *nothing*. While he built that business, I lived in this trailer day in and day out, cleaning his clothes and cooking his meals and raising his babies and abiding his slaps and punches when everything I did wasn't good enough. It was *hell*."

I counted to three in my head, fist clenched so tight around the bottle in my hand I was surprised it hadn't cracked. "I'm well aware of what it was. You left me and Brent here in it."

Her eyes welled. "What else was I supposed to do? I had no education, no job, no money of my own—"

"Brent would've helped you."

She dashed a tear away. "He couldn't do anything to help me—he was just a boy."

"Yeah. He was. But he stepped up and became both parents to

me that night, just like you knew he would."

"Whatever you think of me now, I tried. For years, I tried. I earned my due, putting up with that man for sixteen years—"

"Brent put up with his shit for longer. So did I. My brother's due—*your son's due*—was a hole in the ground after years of looking after a child he got saddled with raising while he was raising *himself*."

She burst into tears and ran for the bathroom, and my head fell into my hands. I felt like an asshole. An asshole who'd kept that shit bottled up far too long. I'd never looked at my home or Wynn's Garage as compensation for two-plus decades of taking shit from my father. Neither would have ever measured up. I saw these things as part of the life I'd built for myself. And now she was taking that, whether she admitted it or not.

Five minutes later, she returned to the kitchen. "As I said, *you* are welcome to stay." She was holding some kind of hair apparatus that belonged to Pearl. It had been in the bathroom. "But your *roommate*"—she air-quoted—"has to go. Are you even charging her rent money?"

I learned a long time ago that feeling powerless made for rash decisions. The only way to reduce the risk of doing something asinine in such a situation was to take your power back before that moment when you reacted without weighing up your choices. Instead of answering her, I asked, "Am I expected to keep running the garage I thought was mine?"

Her chin jerked up at the change of subject. "Your father should have told you we were still married. That wasn't my fault."

I ran a hand over my jaw like I was mulling things over. "Maybe you're right. But my ignorance is about to be your problem, because unless you know how to pull a transmission or change a spark plug, that garage's income comes to a halt tomorrow, seeing as this is not only a community property state but an at-will employment state." *Thank you, Mr. Amos, for passing on that info.* "And I'm about five seconds from *I quit.*"

It took her a moment to absorb what I'd just said. She exhaled heavily, her chin falling a notch. "What do you want?"

• • • • • • • • • •

Me:	She's here. She wants her room back, so I moved your stuff to my room and I'm taking the sofa. I'm sorry. I feel like shit about this.
Pearl:	DON'T feel bad on my account. I'll sleep on the sofa. I got used to it. I'll be fine. Are you okay?? How is it? It must be weird.
Me:	Weird, yeah. I don't know her. She looks familiar but she left before I turned 8 for fuck's sake. Brent was only 15. He was the age I am now when he died.
Pearl:	Oh Boyce. ☹
Me:	I told her you were my roommate and she's fine with it. Also you're sleeping in my bed and I'm taking the sofa. PERIOD.
Pearl:	Okay.
Me:	Okay then.

• • • • • • • • • •

I hadn't seen Maxfield since spring break, when he came home with a girlfriend for the first time. I gave him shit about settling down to one girl, but he was so seriously fucking happy it made me realize just how *unhappy* he'd been before her. I'd hardly ever seen the dude smile in all the years I'd known him. From the beginning, I'd figured him as one of those unstable emo types. His mood was either grim and quiet or violent and homicidal—nothing in between.

We had never spoken about what had fucked him up so bad, but he'd come here in middle school carrying some heavy shit. I'd made it worse for a while, but I liked to think I'd atoned for the dick I'd been at first—in my own way, of course. Not like I gave him candy and flowers.

He'd introduced me to his girl, Jacqueline, as his best friend from high school.

"Ah, so *you're* the one responsible for all those tattoos and this?" she'd asked, reaching up to tap a finger on the ring through his lip. That thing still made me shudder to look at it. I'd had to leave the room when he got it done because once Arianna pulled out that wicked curved needle, I knew I was either going to pass out or puke.

"Yeah, that'd all be my fault. Sorry." I'd only suggested the tattoos on his wrists. The rest of that shit was all him, but I wasn't gonna rat him out.

Then she threw her arms around me and said, "Thank you," while he stood there with a smartass grin on his face.

I had no fucking idea what to make of any of it, so I hugged her back until he said, "All right, that's enough appreciation," and pulled her back to his side. I laughed because I'd never seen him get territorial over anything but that old truck of his. It was about damned time he got to feeling that way over a girl who felt the same way about him.

Even to Maxfield, I'd never confided anything about what was between Pearl and me, but he had come close to guessing when I asked him about her last fall. They went to the same college, and I hadn't seen or heard from her since I'd told her I thought her boyfriend was a prick. I'd always told her the truth when she asked for it, but that didn't mean I wanted to hurt her or push her away.

When Maxfield asked about our relationship, saying, "One of these days, you're gonna have to tell me," I'd changed the subject.

Now they'd both graduated and he was home for a spell, visiting his dad before heading to Ohio to work. *Ohio.* Right there was proof of why five-year plans are bullshit. If anyone had told me five years ago that Maxfield would move to Ohio and Pearl would move back home, I'd have said they were high.

We met at the Saloon. "Shit, man—no facial ornaments and I can see your ears," I said. "Have I ever seen your damned ears? I'm not sure. You look almost respectable."

"Says the guy who owns his own business." He knew better than to express sympathy for my *loss.* He'd known my dad better than any of my friends except the Thompson kids, who'd lived across the street and got eyefuls of his drunk-ass shit on a regular basis.

"Yeah—about that…" I slammed my first shot.

He sat forward, frowning. "What's up?"

"A buncha shit, so let me get it all out first." When he nodded I said, "First, my parents weren't divorced. Long story short—I own nothing. The trailer, the money and the garage—all hers."

"*Shit,*" he said.

"Second, Pearl moved in with me." His eyes popped wide and I could see the questions forming, but I held up a hand and he shifted in his seat, silent. "She decided not to go to med school. She's staying here to study marine biology instead, and her mom was none too happy."

"Jesus—they kicked her *out?*"

I nodded. "More or less."

"So you gave her a place to live."

"Everything was fine until my mom came back to town last week and moved into the trailer. Now I'm sleeping on the fucking sofa, Pearl and me are sharing my closet, and all three of us are sharing one bathroom and one thousand square feet of space."

"What the *hell*, Wynn? You've been working there since I've known you and running the whole place for what, two years? All that time under the justified belief that you'd inherit it… and now you're working for your *mom*?"

"Yes and no. I assumed the garage would be mine, and I was dead fucking wrong. It is what it is, and I can't change it. That said, I don't intend to stick around long-term to get dicked over by another parent. But Pearl needs a place to live, here, until mid-August. She has to spend the first two semesters in Austin, so she's working at the inn to save for a deposit and rent on a nine-month lease there."

"*That* I think I can help with. Hang on." Maxfield pulled his phone out of his pocket and dialed. "Hey, Cindy … Yeah, everything's great. Listen—a friend of mine from high school—my class valedictorian? She's starting the graduate program in marine biology here, and they spend the first year on the main campus *there*. She needs somewhere safe and cheap to live. Do you think—"

He broke off and I held my breath.

"Yes. Exactly." He nodded to me, one thumb up. "Great. Let me know and I'll have her call you. Her name's Pearl Frank … Thanks, Cindy. Bye." He hung up and grinned. "She's checking with Charles, but that's a formality. I lived in the apartment over their garage for four years—just vacated it two days ago. It's quiet, private, cheap, and close to campus. She'll love it."

"Goddamn, Maxfield. I don't know what to say."

"Pearl was my friend too—I wouldn't have made it through high school without her help. So… how about you tell me what's *really* going on? I know she was a challenge for you in high school—the one girl you wanted who wouldn't give you the time of day—"

"That's not exactly true."

He lifted a brow.

So I spilled it. Not all of it, because some things are meant to be private. But I told him about the day I saved her life and how she saved mine by being the one perfect thing in my nearly twenty-three years, and I admitted that she'd ruined me for any other woman the summer before she left for college.

"Wynn—she's *living with you*. Have you told her how you feel? What you want?"

Not unless taking her to my bed counts. "I've got nothing to offer her. Not now."

He sat back and rolled the bottle back and forth in his hands, stabbing me with the icy look that'd scared people shitless in high school. Came in handy when the two of us were collecting overdue weed payments for Rick Thompson. I was grateful on more than one occasion that I'd made a friend of him because he'd had a side of crazy even I wouldn't go to. People saw my wrath coming if I was gunning for 'em. Maxfield's just fucking exploded out of nowhere.

"Whatever happened to *I'm Boyce Fucking Wynn*?" he asked. "That guy wouldn't let anything get between him and something he wanted this bad."

I barked a laugh. Ah, damn. *Boyce Fucking Wynn.* My high school motto. "I'm not that idiot anymore, man."

Glancing around the overcrowded bar, he bit the spot where that lip ring used to be. I'd learned it to be his one tell—fucking with that thing with his teeth or tongue or a finger. I waited for whatever blunt truth he was about to shell out, set to be kicked in the gut by it, considering his hesitation to spit it out.

"Here's what I'm hearing. Ownership of that garage made you feel worthy of her. For the first time, maybe." He signaled Brit's coworker for another round as my heart pounded slow and hard. He leaned up, eyes locked on mine. "I worship the ground Jacqueline walks on, and I'm not ashamed to say it. I love her, man. If that's how you feel, all I can say is don't give up. Don't fucking give up."

Pearl

Boyce's kitchen wasn't as welcoming since it had become Ruthanne Wynn's kitchen. It felt off-limits to me unless he was there too. She didn't say anything to that effect, but the hostile weight of her silence when we were alone in that small space said it all.

At first I attempted to study in Boyce's bedroom, but the lighting wasn't ideal. Two of the windows were inches from the brick wall of the garage, and the third was shaded by a crepe myrtle that hadn't been pruned in years. He and his brother had grown up on an island just as I had, but no one would have ever have known that from their dimly lit, barely ventilated bedroom.

I began studying on campus after morning classes and lab research—either in the library or the glassed group-study area between the offices, labs and classrooms. On Tuesdays and Thursdays, when I had evening shifts at the inn, I didn't bother to come home between school and work. Days I wasn't scheduled to work at all, I came home after six when Boyce closed down the garage for the day.

Though Ruthanne and I didn't have conversations—our exchanges were limited to the barest need for words—I got the feeling she thought I was working some angle to take what was hers and encouraging her son in that direction. Admittedly, if I could have conceived a strategy for him to regain what he'd worked so hard to build, I'd have suggested it to him. My motives would have surpassed her comprehension, though, as they had nothing to do with taking from her and everything to do with giving back to him. I'd always believed mothers sacrificed for their children to keep them safe and happy. Ruthanne's mothering heart—if it beat in her chest at all—seemed to lack that impulse.

Those musings yielded anguished thoughts about Mama and how much our falling out hurt. My birthday was coming up—a day she'd always, always made a fuss over. I couldn't think about her without my eyes stinging. She'd built a nice life for herself, yes, but only after she ascertained I would benefit as well. If Thomas hadn't been prepared to love me too, she'd have kicked that door shut with no hesitation. I decided it was time I extended an olive branch. I wouldn't alter my academic course. That was set. But I could open the door for her pride to forgive me for it someday.

Ruthanne's sidelong looks extended to any time Boyce and I were together, especially when we came in from our new nightly routine—sitting out on the step where we talked about our days while he smoked and I sipped iced tea. I didn't ask why he'd stopped going to bed before I got home, assuming it had to do with her tendency to watch television until almost midnight from the sofa he slept on.

"I feel bad that you can't go to bed at your usual time," I told him one night, stirring the granules of sugar in the bottom of my glass. I also missed watching him pad across the living room in the early dark, sweaty and pumped after a workout and heading for the shower. In the bedroom, I slept until my phone alarm told me to get up. By then he was at work in the garage. "If you'd take the bed, you wouldn't have to rearrange your schedule. I go to sleep later than you anyway. I can bed down on the sofa after she goes to her room."

He took a long drag and flicked the ash from the end of the cigarette before answering. "I offered you a room when I asked you to move in, not a sofa." There was clearly no arguing with him on this point.

"You're more obstinate than you used to be, Boyce Wynn." *But just as protective.*

"Yep."

Several minutes of quiet followed. We waved to Randy when he pulled into his driveway across the street and watched June bugs hurtling and wheeling drunkenly, attracted to the porch light. Staring up at the sky, I felt as unmoored as the stars appeared to be, though internal nuclear explosions and gravity bound them. I wondered how Boyce figured into the way I'd always felt rooted to this place. Whether he was my internal combustion or my gravity. Or both.

Through the closed door behind us, the murmur of the television snapped off.

"She always gives us the weirdest look when we come in from sitting out here or when we're making dinner," I said. "Why do you think that is?"

He turned and stubbed the cigarette out. "I reckon she made assumptions about you and me that aren't panning out."

Oh. *Oh.* "Having to do with you sleeping on the sofa? As opposed to, uh, with me."

He nodded. "That and the fact that you're in graduate school and working to support yourself. You're young and hot, but you aren't using your looks to bait your hook, lure in some guy who'd take care of you. Pretty sure she thought you'd take off when I no longer owned the garage."

I sighed. "So she thinks I'm using you." Which spoke volumes to the worth she placed on her son for everything he'd become, apart from and so much more than what he did or didn't own.

"I don't give a shit what she thinks. You shouldn't either." He turned to take my chin between his fingers and tilted my face up. "You hear?"

"Yes," whispered from my lips.

His touch—so unbearably soft—muted everything but the *thump thump* of my heartbeat. He examined my mouth from inches away, his fingers slipping down my throat, taking the measure of my pulse, his eyes dark, masked by the shadows from the dying day. I swallowed and his grip widened and caressed the margins of my neck, delicate as a warm breeze on damp skin. Goose bumps skittered down my arms and my mouth burned to be kissed.

He pressed his lips to my forehead and said, "Good night, Pearl," before he rose and disappeared inside.

Mama drilled two things into my head growing up. The first was a goal: that I be able to provide for myself *well*. The second was an assertion that being alone was better than being with the wrong person. We'd been far from wealthy, but we were comfortable. Thomas—clearly the *right* person for her—worked hard to get her to admit it. Even when she capitulated, they argued about the size of that rock he slid onto her hand. She worried that everyone in town would think she was a gold digger. He said everyone in town would think he was a cradle robber, so they were even.

She'd taught me two things by example: to crave independence —which had sort of backfired on her when I refused to go to med school—and to fiercely, unapologetically shield and protect any child I might have. But none of that left me with any inkling of what to do when the person I wanted most to defend, to *save*, was a grown man.

chapter

Twenty

BOYCE

Before my mother turned up, Sam had grown used to daily chitchats with Pearl when she came home from class. After dumping her backpack inside, she'd come out to the garage with cold Pepsis and let Sam show off whatever she was working on that day. I tried to put a stop to it once, pretty damn sure Pearl was as uninterested as a non-mechanic could be in the dirty details of a head-gasket repair, but she told me to hush and let Sam finish.

That night during supper, I'd told Pearl there was no need for her to suffer through one-sided conversations about transmissions and oil pumps just to keep from hurting Sam's feelings. The kid loved cars more than anyone I've ever known aside from myself, but she was bright enough to comprehend that most of the time even people who brought their cars in just wanted us to do the work—they didn't want to hear a speech about it.

"There's actually a connection between describing something to someone and learning it at a deeper level yourself," she said. "When I was a sophomore, I tutored a couple of my Chi-O sisters who were struggling with first-year biology. Pretty simple stuff. But breaking those basic concepts down and explaining them actually helped *me* in my more advanced courses."

She'd tutored Maxfield through practically every class at the end of junior year when he'd been half a fuckup from failing out. "So you're letting Sam bore the crap out of you to help her."

"It's ten or fifteen minutes." She smiled. "Very little can bore the crap out of me in fifteen minutes. Besides, I remember you and Lucas discussing cars and car parts in high school, so animated and engaged that anyone watching y'all would've thought you were talking about boobs."

"Oh, we discussed those plenty often too."

She rolled her eyes. "I'm sure."

Sam had formed something between a little-sister thing and a crush on my roommate, so she noticed when Pearl stopped coming home after class. "Where's Pearl?" she asked after several no-Pearl days, all *no big deal* except for the way her voice rose like a cracked bell, not quite in tune.

"She's avoiding my mother."

Leaning into the engine next to me, Sam pulled up so fast she almost fell over. "Why?" she said, grabbing hold of the front end briefly to right herself, ignoring the way I lunged for her arm. She never asked for help. If she needed something, she demanded it. *I can't reach. Lower the lift.* After she was in the truck and screwing with the radio last week, her dad told me she'd been born with a spinal disorder, adding that she'd been scrapping her way toward self-reliance since birth. Big surprise. *Not.*

"What'd your mom say to her? Did you let your mom kick her out?" she asked, her fist balled like she was prepared to sock me if I'd had anything to do with Pearl's disappearance. "I thought this was your place. Did *you* kick her out?"

"Settle down. *Jesus.* Nobody kicked anybody out. It's...

complicated."

She frowned at the worn-out hose in her hand, halfway detached and briefly forgotten. "I'm pretty smart, y'know. I can follow complicated."

I sighed. "Fine. But you can't talk to Pearl about it. At all. Understand?"

She felt for her chair's handles and lowered herself into it. "Why not?"

I stared at her.

"Okay, *okay*," she huffed. "I never see her now anyway."

I finished detaching the coolant hose while I spoke. "My dad died in May. He and my mom—who took off when I was seven—never divorced, which was news to me. So everything is hers—including the garage. She thought I was just going to run the place for her until she sells it or whatever she plans to do with it. Fuck that—but I promised Pearl a place to live until mid-August, so I worked a deal with my mom. I'll stay and keep running the garage until Pearl moves back to Austin. Then I'm gone."

"She's moving away? And… you're leaving town?"

"I can't stay and watch my mother pull to pieces everything I've built. I have to get the hell out of here, at least for a while."

"So I won't have a job anymore either, come fall." Her crushed tone was hell.

I nodded. "Sorry about that, Sam."

She stared into her lap. "Sorry about your dad."

"You don't need to be sorry about him. He was nothing like your dad. He was just something I survived."

She scratched her thigh with a grease-lined fingernail, thinking. "What do you think will happen to Wynn's Garage? Obviously your mom isn't gonna run it. She never even comes out here."

"Don't know. Don't care." I wished like hell that was true.

"This *sucks*," she said.

She had no idea. I had less than six weeks left with Pearl.

Pearl

A few months ago, I read an article that linked anxiety to inattention to accident-proneness. *Fascinating*, I mused, and didn't think about it again—until now.

During lab this morning, I dumped a petri dish full of phytoplankton and the water in which they were swimming on my shirt. Thankful no one noticed, I refilled the dish and conducted the series of measurements as expected, but this was three for three. First the beaker. Then last week I'd tripped over a taped-down cord in the lab and sloshed scalding hot coffee over my hand, which *might* have gone unnoticed had I not spit out a Boyce Wynn-worthy string of curses right after. ("*Nice*," one of the visiting undergrads said, sending me a flirtatious grin, because being chatted up is what a girl wants *when her hand is on fire*.)

I might have been inured to the sulfurous odor emanating from my shirt, but I knew Minnie wouldn't welcome me smelling like a science experiment during my four-hour shift at the inn, and the liquid had left a conspicuous blotch of discoloration as well, so I went home after class to change, cussing my recent spate of careless-ness while acknowledging the thrill that zipped through me at the excuse to see Boyce during the day. I missed my weekday chats with Sam too.

Since Ruthanne kept her hail-battered Ford coupe parked on the gravel next to Boyce's car, I'd begun parking my GTI on the street on the opposite side of the trailer. Inside, she sat on the sofa, alternating her attention between her phone and daytime television. We ignored each other, per usual. I dumped my backpack on the kitchen table and grabbed two Pepsis from the fridge.

Neither Boyce nor Sam had seen me arrive when I wasn't expected home, nor did they see me back away from the mouth of the garage, processing the conversation I'd overheard.

I put the sodas back into the fridge as my thoughts spun, stretching and twisting like they'd been threaded through a taffy machine. Boyce had no hopes or remaining aspirations concerning the garage or his relationship with his mother. He had continued working for her for one reason: the promise he'd made to me.

All I could do to help him was free him to *leave*.

Shouldering my backpack, I left the trailer, snuck to my car and drove to Thomas's office as if on autopilot. Once inside I recalled that Tuesday afternoons were reserved for surgery consults and emergency postsurgical checkups. There were five people in his small waiting room—the equivalent of rush hour. I nearly burst into tears.

His nurse, Talisha, opened the door to call a patient back, glancing up from the chart in her hand to spot me standing like a lost puppy in the middle of the room. "Well hello, Pearl! What are you—" She halted mid-sentence and reached to take my arm. "Come on back, honey. Mr. Gardner, you just head on down to room three. We'll be right with you."

One minute later, I'd been escorted into Thomas's inner office, handed a cup of water, and left to sit on the sofa he used for an occasional afternoon nap. An ornate clock sat atop the doorstop edition of *Gray's Anatomy* in his bookcase and ticked the seconds away—ninety or so of them by the time he slipped through the door and shut it behind him.

"What's happened?" he demanded, walking to sit beside me. He took my hand and focused his clear blue gaze on me.

"I need to know if there's a chance… that I could move home." My lip wobbled and I swallowed, bracing myself. "Without quitting my program—"

"Good God almighty, *yes*! Your mother has been beside herself. She can't sleep, barely eats, cries constantly—I've never seen her like this. *Please* come home. I've tried to talk her into calling you, but she's convinced that she estranged herself from you with that unreasonable med-school stipulation. I didn't think we were going to survive your birthday tomorrow."

I began to sob and leaned onto his white-coated shoulder, relieved at every word he'd said but miserable at the reality of leaving Boyce—our nightly talks, his appreciation of my sorry attempts at preparing dishes my mother could make a million times better, the coffee he programmed to start ten minutes before he knew I got up, every kiss we'd shared and all we never would.

"Pearl, tell me what's happened." Thomas's jaw was rock hard, his hands bracing my shoulders so he could see my face. Anger brewed in the gaze he leveled on me, and his grasp tightened. "Did you and Boyce Wynn have a falling out, or is it something worse?"

"No—it's…" I took a deep breath. "Fifteen years ago, his mother left his abusive father, and Boyce and his brother—and now she's back. She's taken the bedroom Boyce promised me. I'm sleeping in Boyce's bed and he's sleeping on the sofa. We're all sharing one bathroom—"

"Say no more, honey." He slid his arms around my shoulders. "Trust me—just come on home. Everything will be fine."

• • • • • • • • • •

Thomas had his office manager reschedule later appointments, and I waited in his office until he saw patients who'd already arrived. Following him home after a month's absence, I turned my stereo low and reviewed possible scenarios despite his reassurances that Mama would welcome me home. I'd imagined letting her know I was doing fine and taking care of myself—easing her worries while discouraging further disputes or ultimatums. I hadn't anticipated coming to her with an entreaty to move home.

I chewed my lip as we entered my neighborhood and fought tears when we turned into the cul-de-sac. I parked in the driveway, not my spot in the three-car garage, but Thomas beamed, waiting by the back door. I was less sure of what awaited me, which must have shown on my face.

He hugged an arm around my shoulders when I reached him. Opening the door, he called, "Essie! I've brought you something. Come and see."

We walked through the mudroom and into the kitchen as Mama appeared in the opposite doorway, far less put together than usual, and pulled to a halt.

"Pearl?" she said, as if I might not be real. Her eyes filled with tears. "Pearl?" she repeated, coming across the kitchen, arms spreading. "Oh my God. Oh my God."

I went into her arms, relieved. "Mama. I've missed you so much."

"*Mija*, you're here? You've come home?" At my nod, she began sobbing. "*Perdóname, por favor!* I'm so sorry, *mija.*" We cried into each other's necks, and she held on to me like she'd never let go.

"*Me-OW*!" Tux bellowed, trotting as quickly as his stubby legs would carry him to twirl his whip of a tail around my legs and fuss at me for my absence, the same way he had every time I'd come home during semester breaks.

"Tux is right," Thomas said. "This reunion calls for steak on the grill." He gathered us both in his embrace and squeezed. "Come on, Tux. I think Mama might allow you a few table scraps tonight. Better take advantage, little man."

"Merrrow," he agreed.

"I have work tonight," I said, sniffling. "At six."

We all shifted just far enough apart to view each other's faces. The creases between their brows matched, and they blinked as if I'd spoken gibberish.

Thomas recovered first. "Where do you work?"

"At the inn."

"Can you stay until your shift begins?" he asked.

"Yes."

"How about a chat on the patio and three iced coffees? You girls go on outside, I'll be right out." He looked at Mama then, and something passed between them. "It's time to tell her, Esmeralda."

Her eyes refilled with tears and she nodded as an ice-cold trickle of trepidation tore down my spine.

Twenty-one

BOYCE

During our nightly meeting on the top step, there was something different about Pearl. She was quieter—no gossip about her shift at the inn. My stories about Sam's red-faced reactions to the things customers sometimes left out in the open when they brought their cars in—polka-dotted panties in a backseat, a sealed box marked *fecal matter* resting on a dash ("There's poop in that box! *Poop!*" Sam said), a strip of condoms curled in a cup holder like a roll of stamps—all produced the ghost of a smile instead of laughter. She leaned her head on my arm and I fell silent, smoking and leaving her to her thoughts.

Once my mother had closed herself into her room, Pearl and I went inside and took turns in the bathroom. I was bedded down on the sofa, lights out, when she came out wearing a thin-strapped blue tank and shorts. I nearly bit my lip in half to keep from moaning my appreciation of it, of her, *of her in it*. "Good night, Pearl," I said, doing fuck-all to conceal the lust in my tone, but *damn*. Instead of answering, she walked toward me, silent. The light from the bedroom behind her glowed dimly, outlining the curves of her body as she walked up to me and held out her hand. I sat up, taking it, and she tugged softly.

No idiot, I allowed myself to be led to my bedroom. She closed the door behind me and switched off the light. The window was open wide, the fan oscillating in front of it like it meant to lift itself right off the dresser, but the night air remained sticky and hot. The only AC units were in the kitchen and the bedroom my mother occupied across the trailer. We were going to be sweat-covered in two minutes flat, but I didn't give a single goddamn if she didn't.

"You want me to lay you down, sweetheart?" I asked, pulling her close, hands sliding to cup her ass as she nodded. "Done." I leaned down to kiss her full mouth, my dick springing to attention in my boxers, fully prepared to give her whatever she wanted, however she wanted it.

She opened that warm, pretty mouth wide and pressed her pliant body into mine, arms looping around my neck, fingers raking across my scalp and forking through my hair. I groaned right into her and she sucked my tongue hungrily, swallowing the garbled sounds that said my body meant to *own* hers. My dick surged jealously and I fought like hell to banish the vivid fantasy of her mouth taking me deep because I wouldn't last five seconds if I let those images run loose in my head. And then she dropped to her knees.

"Holy *shit*," I ground out as she pulled my boxers down my thighs, and then not one coherent word left my mouth.

I paid no heed to the urge to guide her because she didn't need any goddamn directions. My fingers sank into the silky, dark waves of her hair and I just held on, watching as the sway of her head followed the warm stroke of her tongue and the constriction of her throat. Three seconds from exploding, I tugged at a handful of her hair, almost relenting when she shook her head no. "*Next time*," I panted, half-sure I would drown her with the force of my release because my body wasn't used to the amount of self-denial I'd been requiring of it lately.

The suctioned pop as her lips left that swollen, greedy head was my breaking point. I fell to my knees and turned her onto her hands and knees, yanking her shorts over her hips and pulling her bare backside into the saddle of my lap while choking out, "Okay?"

"*Yes*," she groaned and I plunged deep, one hand braced on the floor, my opposite arm locked around her middle, palm pressed to her belly and fingers slanting low to stroke her as we shuddered into waves of climax from that solitary thrust.

Nuzzling her hair aside, I kissed the back of her neck, tongue lapping down the soft arc of her salty skin, and she trembled and convulsed again with a soft moan. I hummed my approval, placing soft, sucking kisses across the beautiful jut of her shoulder blade and still shaking from the intensity of my release—I'd never experienced anything like it. I'd never come that close to losing control.

Oh. *Shit*. No condom. No condom. *Fuck*. My grip around her slackened, but I didn't release her because her arms were quivering visibly. I was still supporting most of her weight.

"Oh…," she said, angling away from my lap and tucking her chin to glance at me over her shoulder. "We forgot—"

"I've never had sex without a condom, and I've never had any, um… infection issues."

She slipped her shorts back up and I did the same, processing the fact that in a decade of sex with too many girls and women to recall, this was the first time I'd outright fucking *forgotten* to grab a rubber first.

"I… I had my yearly check after… I'm clean, too. But…" But *pregnancy*, she didn't say aloud.

I heard it anyway.

228

My dumbass brain went straight for a vision of Pearl pregnant with my child, and God help me, I wanted it. Wanted it so bad I had a hankering to pick her up, carry her the ten steps across the room to my bed and fuck her again to double my chances. What in hell was wrong with me?

"I'm sorry, Pearl—I was so—" *Distracted by lust. Out of my mind. Crazy for you.* My head thumped back against the door. I was so fucked.

"I was too." She turned and sat on the floor in front of me, her eyes heavy-lidded, watching me, probing desolate corners of my heart that never saw the light of day. I dipped my head to kiss her sweet lips, dumbstruck—always dumbstruck by her, top to bottom and back again. We sank toward each other, kissing until we were both breathless. "I'm tired." She sighed, eyes blinking open. "Will you lie down with me? We need to talk."

We got up and moved to the bed, stripped the covers back, and lay down facing each other.

"I went to see my mother this afternoon, before work. She's retracted all her med-school demands." She laid her palm over mine, and I closed my fingers over the back of her hand, but I could barely feel her touch because I knew what she was about to say. "I want to thank you for giving me a place to live and the ability to stand on my own—or as close to it as I've ever come. I'm keeping my job. No more allowance or credit card, though they offered the return of both. But I'm going to move home. Especially with your mother here—it's the right thing for both of us."

Every cell in my body argued that letting her leave was the farthest thing from right—for *me*. But this decision wasn't about me. It never had been. "When?"

"Tomorrow."

I reached to trace the soft skin at her hairline. "Your birthday," I said, sliding a strand of hair behind her ear and following the curve behind her earlobe. I settled my hand on her neck, fingers massaging the back of it, palm absorbing her fluttering pulse.

"Yes." Her voice shook and her dark eyes each reflected the square of moonlit window. A tear streamed from the corner of her eye into her hair. "I'll miss living with you, Boyce."

My name in her mouth just then pierced right through me. Thompson once told me that he'd gotten stabbed by a guy in prison. "You'd reckon it'd be a sharp pain," he'd said. "But it's not. It's like getting punched really fucking hard. So hard that it bruises down deep inside. At first your innards are all surprised—like *How did something hit me there?* I didn't even know I'd been shanked till I saw that dickhole standing there all crazypants, holding a fucking shiv *with my blood on it*. Creepiest damned thing ever happened to me—looking at him and thinking, *That motherfucker just killed me.*"

Thompson was lucky—the homemade blade missed everything vital. He recovered.

The knowledge that Pearl was moving out—that I'd pulled her so close just to lose her forever—was a deep punch to the gut. A punch that in reality was a stab wound I might never recover from.

"Jesus, Pearl," I whispered, more worship than curse.

When I angled above her, she drew me down for a long, deep kiss, her body growing restless as my hand slid from her neck to her chest, palming those perfect tits and tugging her nipples gently through the barely there tank I'd not had time to remove the first time. "Won't be needing this tonight," I said, lifting it over her head and tossing it to the floor. "These neither." I drew the shorts down silky-smooth legs that would shortly be spread wide and then locked around me.

I paused to stare at the tempting little road to hell lying there in my bed for the two beats it took to ditch my own shorts and no longer. If loving her was gonna be the death of me, I saw no reason to dawdle.

Pearl

When I woke this morning, everything was the same—at first. I leaned to turn off my phone alarm, bleary-eyed. The bedroom door was shut and I was alone. I was also butt-naked.

As I pulled on the tank and shorts I'd worn for about ten minutes before Boyce stripped them off, the night came flooding back, not that it had far to go since it hadn't ended until early morning. A shiver went through me at the thought, and my body temperature must have spiked several degrees because holy cow, that room was suddenly an oven.

I padded into the kitchen and poured a mug of coffee, then went back to Boyce's bedroom and dragged my suitcases from the back of his closet. As I packed up everything I'd brought with me weeks ago, I replayed yesterday afternoon's conversation with Mama in my head. I'd been too shocked to be angry at her confession, though I worried that bottled-up emotion could rise up and slap me silly any minute. She'd kept so much from me—evidence of how childlike I had still been in her eyes, college degree and all.

I'd perched on the edge of one of the chairs facing the water, anticipating a critical diagnosis and trusting it would be something highly treatable, caught early. Not fatal. *Please God, not fatal.* Her expression terrified me—eyes like dinner plates, chin quivering, hands knotted in her lap like they'd been superglued to each other.

"What did he mean by *time to tell her*?" I prompted. "Tell me what, Mama?"

She swallowed, flinching when Thomas pushed the sliding glass door aside to join us. I waited, tensely silent, as he handed glasses to each of us and took a seat next to her, across from me.

"Your father," she began and then stopped, swallowing again. Thomas placed a hand over hers and she took a shaky breath. "The story I've led you to believe about your father is not... wholly true."

I was so relieved that no one was *dying* that it took me a moment to absorb what she'd said. "What do you mean, not *wholly* true?"

"It is true that we grew up together. That we fell in love. That he was intelligent and had dreams of becoming a doctor. It is untrue that he died trying to escape Mexico."

"How... how did he die?"

"He was executed by the drug cartel—"

I gasped.

"—which he belonged to."

My mouth fell open, but I could only shake my head and think *What?*

"We were sixteen and seventeen when he was recruited. Boys of poor families follow the temptation of money all too easily, and we were from very poor families. The money, the power, the violence— they changed the boy I loved into someone I no longer recognized. But that transformation took place gradually. It took me too long to see it, and once I did, I thought I could change him back." Her voice hitched. "The first time he hit me, I blamed myself."

"*Mama.*" My eyes welled with tears.

"He appeared sickened at the mark of his hand on my face. He cried like a child and begged my forgiveness. I pled with him to leave the cartel. He swore that if he remained just a little longer, we would have enough money that he could go to university to follow his dream. I argued that the deeper he got, the more impossible leaving would be. But he was a charming, persuasive boy, and I loved him.

"The next time he hit me, I fell against a large urn and it toppled over onto my hand. My face scraped against a broken fragment." She touched the scar at her temple. She'd cited a childhood accident for that mark and the little finger on her right hand that didn't bend. Her aunt had set the broken bone with a stick, she'd said, shaking her head as if the whole incident was sad but funny.

Hot tears tracked down my face. This story didn't fit the woman I knew.

"The last time, he brought me home unconscious and told *mi abuela* I had fainted and hit my head. I woke and said nothing to contradict him. I pretended I couldn't remember his fist flying at my face. When he left, I collapsed at her feet in tears because I knew... I knew I was pregnant with you, and I thought there was no way out.

"'Have you told him about the baby?' *Abuelita* asked, and I shook my head. 'Then you will never tell him. You will go to the United States and make a new life for yourself and your child. You will be safe, because you will never return.'

"She took me to the room she shared with *mi tía* and knelt by the bed. She pulled out a box covered in dust, filled with old papers. One was my birth certificate. My parents died, as I told you, in a car crash. But before that, they'd crossed the border into Texas with my brother Jasiel, found work, and had me."

"Which made you a US citizen," I whispered.

"Yes. They made a home near Brownsville. My mother worked in a hotel kitchen. Jasiel began school. But the construction site where my father worked was reported for hiring *illegals*. He was deported, and Jasiel. They thought that because of my citizenship, my mother would be allowed to stay, but the *anchor baby* exemption was a myth. Immigration officials deported her as well, and she would not leave me behind. They died only months later—I can't remember them."

"And my uncle?" *A man I hadn't known existed until two minutes ago.*

Her red eyes refilled, tears spilling down her cheeks. She held tight to Thomas's hand. "I haven't seen my brother or any of my family since the night I left Matamoros. Jasiel took me to the US Consulate with my birth certificate and Mexican identification and every peso *Abuelita* had scrimped and saved for years. I had just turned eighteen. I was granted a passport and allowed to enter the US two weeks later. Alone."

• • • • • • • • • •

Avoiding a glance into the garage for fear my anguish was too visible, I stowed two suitcases in my car and went back to get the third and my backpack. Inside, I stood staring at the bed I'd only shared with Boyce twice, overwhelmed with the eerie sensation of overlooking something vital.

I didn't want to leave him, that much was plain as day—but I recognized my selfish pining for what it was. I would not remain here and let his mother use him. *If you love something, set it free.* The rest of that insufferable adage didn't even matter, because there was no *if*. The only way to free him from her coercion was to walk out his door and release him from the promise he'd made to me.

I took a deep breath, determined to paste a smile on my face and walk to the garage. Say good-bye. Assure him that we were good.

Pretend that I hadn't just stood in the center of his bedroom ripped open, heart bleeding out on the floor, aching for him worse than I ever had before. I'd known, in part, what I was wading into and how much it would eventually hurt, but I wouldn't make it undone now if I had the power to unravel time.

I turned and there he stood, hands planted on either side of the doorframe as though he'd hold me prisoner in that room if he could. *Ah, damn.* My heart was still capable of wishful thinking, poor ignorant thing.

"Were you gonna say good-bye?" he asked.

"Of course." I tried to smile, but all I managed to do was bare my teeth and raise my top lip. *I must look nutty as a fruitcake*, I thought, lowering my chin so he wouldn't see through my charade and ordering myself to get a damned grip. "I was just about to come out to the garage. You didn't have to come in."

"I did, actually—I have something for you. Today's your birthday, after all." He reached into the closet—top shelf—and pulled down a plain cardboard box, a foot square, flaps folded shut instead of taped. "I can't wrap anything worth a shit, so I didn't try. Figured you wouldn't mind."

I smiled up at him, taking it. "I don't. Wrapping paper is overrated and environmentally unsound."

He inclined his head toward the box. "Wait until tonight to open it?" His gaze dropped to the floor, thick lashes falling against his cheeks. "After whatever you've got planned to celebrate your bein' twenty-one, I mean."

The boy who'd seen the inside of Ms. Ingram's office more times than any single person I knew in high school—usually for cutting up or smarting off in class—was *shy* when it came to gift-giving? I wondered if he'd ever given anyone a gift, and how long it had been since he'd received one. My heart ached, because I knew the answer to that without asking.

"I'm having dinner with Mom and Thomas tonight, but I'm going out with classmates Friday to celebrate—La Playa and then some barhopping. Would you… want to come?"

His eyes lifted to mine and he was quiet for a long time. I realized he might have Friday-night plans. Plans he wouldn't want to confide and I damn sure wouldn't want to hear.

"I could do that, if you're sure you want me along," he finally said. "I usually meet up with Thompson Friday night for supper, but I think he can survive without me."

Senseless relief filled me—it was only a matter of time until our lives went in opposite directions, after all—but today, I'd take it. "I'm sure. If you're sure Randy won't mind."

One corner of his mouth lifted in a half smile brimming with secrets. "He won't mind."

I hefted the box that held my birthday gift. It wasn't heavy. "Can I shake it?"

"Maybe a little. Just don't drop it."

As clumsy as I'd been lately, I decided shaking was right out. "What if—oh, never mind." I waved a hand.

"What if what, Pearl?"

"What if you call me tonight when you go outside for your evening smoke? And I'll open it while we're on the phone."

He smiled. "Deal." He took the box and set it atop my suitcase and slid my backpack from my shoulder to the floor. "One more thing before you go." His voice rumbled softly like the idling hum of a powerful engine.

His cool hands framed my face, and I inhaled the citrusy smell of the oil-removing soap he kept by the aluminum sink in the garage.

His eyes crept over my features one by one like he might never see them again. When he reached my lips, his hands slid into my hair, cradling my head. As he bent to kiss me, I rose on my toes to meet him. Tears streamed from the corners of my eyes, and I knew he felt them connecting with his palms, baptizing his miraculous hands and giving me away.

Brow creased in confusion, he touched his thumbs to the tears. "What's this then?"

"When will you leave town?"

His frown deepened and I realized my mistake.

"Why do you think I'm leaving?"

Me and my careless mouth. "I... I just assumed," I stammered, knowing my eyes were telling him what a liar I was.

"Ah, dammit Pearl." He sighed, mouth tight. "Did Sam tell you?"

I shook my head. "I overheard you telling her what you were doing for me. I'd meant to call Mama this week to let her know I missed her. What you told Sam just gave me incentive to do it. We needed this break because it's past time she began regarding me as an adult, but we also needed the reconciliation." *And I needed to know the truth about my father.*

An hour later, sitting in class, I realized that he'd deflected my question about when he planned to leave town. I had no business wanting him to stay when I would be gone before the end of August. I'd asked to move home to liberate him to go find his future. My longing to be part of that future didn't figure in.

· · · · · · · · · ·

Four messages were on my phone when I checked it after class.

Mama: Happy birthday, Mija. We'll see you
          tonight?

Melody: Hey chica – FINALLY 21!!! WOOHOO!! Sorry
          I'm not there. ☹ Scratch that. Sorry you
          aren't HERE. When you come to Dallas this
          fall we will party our butts off. K??? Miss you!

Lucas: You're welcome – it's a great apartment.
          Heads-up, the Hellers' daughter Carlie may
          elect herself your new best friend, and a
          bossy orange cat may show up at the door.
          Francis considers the apartment his and I
          didn't disabuse him of that notion. Carlie
          takes care of him and will keep that up if
          you don't want to. Jacqueline and I plan to
          fly down for Thanksgiving. Dad's meeting us
          there. If you'll be in town, J wants to meet
          you.

Mitchell: Happy birthday, Pearl. Thinking about you a
          lot lately. Hope you're doing well. I miss you
          and wish we could at least be friends.

I told Mama I'd be home after lab. I sent Mel a winking
emoticon and *Miss you too!* I thanked Lucas for the tips on Carlie
and Francis, assured him that I would welcome a friend and a guard
cat, and told him I'd love to meet Jacqueline. My first, second and
third instinct was to ignore Mitchell, but he wasn't getting the
message. By the time I was unpacking in my old room, folding
clothes into the dresser and stacking textbooks on the desk, that text

was like a burr under my saddle.

I set the lightning whelk shell he'd tried to destroy on my desk, finger tracing the whorls, and then I picked up my phone.

Me: I'm fine, and I wish you all the best, but we can't be friends, Mitchell. We're done. Please don't text me again.

I deleted the conversation, deleted his contact information, and blocked his number just as Boyce's familiar smirk showed up on my screen and the ringtone he'd never know I'd set for him years ago played softly.

"Hello there, Mr. Wynn."

chapter

Twenty-two

BOYCE

She sounded happy. *Good*. I wanted to be the one who triggered it, but I'd rather her be happy the rest of her life without me than be the thing that made her sad. The tears she'd shed after I kissed her this morning had hung over my day like a storm brewing out over the water but never making landfall. I couldn't for the life of me think what I might've done to hurt her, but I had no damned clue why she'd been crying.

"Hey, Miss Frank. How was the birthday?"

"It was good. I heard back from Lucas—I texted him last night to thank him for arranging the apartment. He said he and Jacqueline are coming down for Thanksgiving and meeting his dad at the Hellers'. Are they related or something?"

"I think his dad went to college with them. Maxfield's known them his whole life." I blew a stream of smoke away from the phone, as if she were sitting next to me instead of in her bedroom two miles and two thousand reasons away from me.

"The first thing I thought when I read it was that I can't stay there for Thanksgiving, because I won't see you unless I come home. And then I realized I don't even know where you'll be in

November."

"Maybe I'll come see you there. I've been tied to the garage for years. Now I'm not." I wondered what in hell made me say that. I kept meaning to let her go, but I kept holding on.

"I would like that." She went silent for a moment. "How does that feel, to be free of it?"

Like I had a sense of purpose and a place in the world and it evaporated. Like I got cut loose on the ocean in a rowboat. "I don't know yet," I said, both fact and fib.

"I'm going to open my box now. Okay?"

"I feel like a dick making a big deal about it. It's just… something I thought you'd like. I dunno. Hope it's not too lame."

Through the phone, I heard the scrape as she pulled flaps of cardboard apart and the crumple of the old newspapers as she peeled them aside.

"Oh, Boyce," she said.

Relief washed over me, and I pulled in a drawn-out dose of nicotine to prolong the high. "It's not as big as the last one, but the day you moved in with me I noticed the spire was cracked on that shell. Been hunting for a new one ever since. I found one that was perfect but still inhabited. I knew how you'd feel about me evicting his ass, so I put him back in the water." Her soft laugh confirmed I'd nailed that decision. "I almost gave up and bought one on eBay, but that would be like cheating. Anyhow, I found that one last week and Thompson polished it up at his mom's shop. Glad you like it."

"I love it. I'll always love the first one you gave me too, cracked or not." She paused. "Mitchell broke it on purpose, you know."

"He *what*?" I should have kicked that douchebag's ass when I had the chance.

"During the last argument we had—the night we broke up. He

was pissed when I told him I wasn't going to Vanderbilt. He walked to my bookcase, grabbed the most important thing on it, and smashed it against the wall. That was the final straw for me."

"I knew that guy was an asshole. What business of his was it if you decided not to go to med school?" *That shell was the most important thing on her bookcase?*

"We were going to go together, get an apartment, blah blah, and I changed my mind at the last minute. I kinda didn't tell him for a month or so either."

I laughed, imagining that little prick throwing a tantrum, but I sobered up at the next thought. "Did he ever hurt you?" She was quiet a beat too long. "Pearl, goddammit—"

"Once—which he swore was an accident and I—*ugh*. I was stupid—"

"The fuck you were. You've never been stupid a day in your life. Trusting and sweet and too goddamned forgiving, maybe." *Well, there you go. Damnation.*

"Don't think I'm a *dumb girl* anymore, huh?"

I scrubbed a hand over my face and hung my head. "Jesus Christ I was a dick of a kid. I'd kinda hoped you'd long forgot that."

"You made up for it." I heard the soft smile in her voice and took another deep drag to keep from telling her all the ways she could demand I make up for it and keep making up for it as long as she wanted.

"About Friday. Why don't I pick you up and be your designated driver so you can go wild and celebrate your fill? I'll get you back home safe." *Fuck if I wouldn't rather get you back to my bed safe.*

"Okay."

• • • • • • • • •

Thompson and I shuffled our Friday night supper to Thursday. "Maybe we can stop somewhere after, get in a game of pool?" I asked.

"Let's not go nuts, man. We're responsible adults now," he said, chuckling and sifting through the envelopes and flyers in his hand.

"Hey there, Boyce," his mom called, walking down to the mailbox at the end of their drive where we stood talking.

Thompson handed her the mail. "Goin' to supper with Wynn tonight instead of tomorrow night, Mom. That okay?"

"Sure, hon," she said, squeezing his arm. "Maybe your dad and I will go out too, and I'll save that fried chicken for tomorrow."

He slid an arm around her and kissed the top of her head. "See, Wynn. This is why I'll never marry, right here. Because I was both lucky and unlucky enough to have the perfect woman for a mom."

She shook her head and patted his chest, her lips fighting a smile. "Crazy boy of mine." Towering a foot over her, Thompson was a skinny twenty-six-year-old ex-addict, ex-con who lived at home and worked for her, but you could hear in her voice that he was still the little boy she'd taught to tie his shoes. "I've hardly seen Ruthanne, Boyce. Y'all are sharing the place now that your daddy's gone, I see." The twist of her mouth said everything she thought about my father, and probably a bit about my mother as well. "How's that going?"

"S'all right." *Not.* At least our schedules were off enough that we barely crossed paths. She hadn't even noticed yet that Pearl moved out yesterday. "I'm probably going to be leaving town soon... I haven't rightly decided where to yet."

"So Randy said." She looked up into my eyes.

I hadn't remarked the years on her until that moment. Her sons' shenanigans had taken their toll, but she'd never lost the faith and optimism I remembered from my childhood, and the increased smile lines just served to make her look kinder.

"You'll do well in whatever you decide, Boyce. I see your brother in you." Seeming to know she'd just knocked the breath out of me, she patted my arm and turned back to her son. "See you later then, Randy. Y'all boys have a good night. You both deserve some fun."

. . . .

"So Pearl moved out and *now* you're taking her on a date?" Thompson chalked his cue and sank two balls.

I watched him line up his next shot and threw back half a Shiner. "Not exactly. Her group is taking her barhopping to celebrate her turning twenty-one. I'm just… tagging along. As her designated driver."

"Hell, man—twenty-one? Thought Pearl was in your and Rick's year? She's barely older'n Amber—and Amber's still got two or three years left at A&M." His little sister was the only Thompson kid to go to college. He sank one of my stripes and cussed.

"Pearl moved up a year." I lined up my shot and sank one ball in the far corner.

"And the folks you're tagging along with—they're all grad students? Scientists? Fuck, Wynn. That setup would intimidate the shit outta me, and I've been to *prison*."

He'd nailed it. Not much unsettled me, but being the soon-to-be-jobless mechanic among a bunch of *academics*—got that word from Pearl—*was* fucking intimidating. But she'd never asked me to go out with her—in public—before. *Hell* if I was saying no.

"Brit swears there's wedding bells in your future."

Scratch. "Dammit, Thompson." I glared, and he chuckled. *Christ.* Why couldn't Brit limit spouting her damned ridiculous speculations to me? "Since when have you and Brit been getting cozy?" I asked, which shut him up right quick. They'd had a falling out when she'd defected to his little brother in high school. Brit went where the weed was back then. Meth wasn't her poison, and she wanted nothing to do with it, which meant she'd stopped wanting anything to do with Randy.

"She's stopped by the shop a time or two since I got out." He replaced the cue ball and sank his last two solids and then the eight ball. "Nice to know how I can finally beat you at pool, man. Mention the word *wedding* and you go down like I jerked a knot in your tail."

I grabbed the triangle to rack the balls. That word didn't rattle me as it related to Pearl, except in the utter impossibility that I would ever be good enough to make her mine.

Pearl

"Most people are *away at college* when they turn twenty-one, Mama. I'm a college graduate."

She wrung her hands. "I understand that, *mija*. I'm only worried about your safety. You're telling me you're going to go out and drink excessively, on purpose… it's just not like you."

I sighed. Getting wasted on a regular basis wasn't something I'd ever done—that much was true—but I hadn't abstained altogether. Even if alcohol hadn't played a prominent part in my college experience, I'd done my share of partying and suffered the crappy hangovers to prove it. Not that I was going to confess that.

"Boyce will take care of me." I raised my left hand and placed the other atop the *Better Homes & Gardens* on the coffee table. "No alcohol poisoning. No driving drunk."

Her jaw locked.

"What?"

"What about *him*? What good does it do for you not to drive drunk if *he* may do it?"

Jeez. "He won't. This was his idea, Mama—he promised to be my designated driver for the night, and there's no one I trust more."

"I see." She arched a brow, looking at me, but then she blinked, lips parted, dark eyes locked on my face. "What's happened between you and that boy in the past few weeks, Pearl?"

I was tired of denying his importance to me. There was no reason to hide it, not anymore. Not after living with him half the summer. Not when he was leaving, maybe forever. "It hasn't been just the past few weeks, Mama. Boyce and I have been close friends for a very long time." Close friends who'd shared moments in his bed that made my toes curl in my boots just thinking about them. "I trust him completely. You can trust him. I'll probably be hammered when I get home, but I'll get home." *Safe and sound*, he'd said.

"He seems like a decent young man," Thomas said. "Been running that garage alone, hasn't he, since his father died?"

"He's been running it alone since his father got sick a few years ago. He was half-running it when we were in high school."

"So Wynn's belongs to him now?" he asked. Thomas drove Mama's Mercedes and his Nissan pickup to the dealership in Corpus when they needed maintenance. He'd never used a mechanic on the island.

"No. His parents never divorced, and there was a will leaving everything to his mother. The garage, the trailer, *everything* belongs to her now. She abandoned Boyce and his brother—who died in Iraq right before Boyce started high school—to fend for themselves with an abusive, alcoholic father. I don't blame her for running from him—Boyce doesn't blame her—but he was *seven*! How could she *leave* him there?"

Mama said nothing, but her lips pressed so tight they'd lost color and her hands were tight fists. She'd left her home and everything she'd known to protect herself and *me* before I was even born. I'd watched her refuse everything Thomas offered until he extended his proposal to adopting me, until he swore to love and care for me as if I'd been his natural-born child.

Thomas frowned. "I remember when his brother died. Brent Wynn. True hometown hero—decorated for bravery postmortem, I think. I had no idea about their father. Will Boyce remain at Wynn's working for his mama, then?"

I shook my head. "We think she just wants whatever cash she can get for it now. He built that place up to what it is now, thinking it would be his. He's proud and strong, and he's survived things I can't even let myself think about. Now he's losing the one thing that mattered to him—that garage. He'll probably find a job as a mechanic, but not here. He can't stay and watch her dismantle everything he's done."

I pulled at a loose thread on my skirt to hide the desolation I felt at the thought of his departure. Once he put down roots elsewhere, a rift would begin to form between us. It was inevitable. There would be nothing for him here anymore.

• • • • • • • • • •

La Playa was always packed wall-to-wall, but on Fridays it was overrun. There were usually as many people waiting for a table as there were people eating, but the owner was one of Boyce's numerous satisfied customers. We'd been seated at a pieced-together table for ten in less than twenty minutes.

I had introduced Boyce as my best friend. "He's generously volunteered to be my DD for the night and get me home safe, so none of y'all are stuck with that job," I added. Everyone chuckled and a few people said *Thanks, man.* "First round of margaritas are on me! And your iced tea too, Mr. Wynn," I said, nudging his solid arm with my shoulder.

As soon as the drinks, baskets of chips, and bowls of salsa arrived, someone posed the inescapable question: "So Boyce, what do you do?" Kyle wasn't a total jackhole, but he could be an intellectual elitist. He was still learning not to make discriminatory remarks about *the locals* around me.

"I'm a mechanic," Boyce answered. His right hand lay fisted on his thigh. Otherwise, he looked wholly unruffled.

"Ah," Kyle said, flicking a glance my way. "Cool." His tone didn't imply *cool* so much as a sense of superiority. Boyce didn't give two figs about that and never had.

"Where do you work?" Shanice asked, blinking big dark eyes at him while curling a springy coil of hair around her finger, a thing I'd assumed studious doctoral students were incapable of doing. *Wrong.* "I'm sure my hand-me-down Pontiac will need some work over the next few years. I'd love to know someone who could keep it running."

"Yeah, me too!" Milla said, her blue eyes skipping over Boyce's torso and arms.

His dark green T-shirt was just snug enough to show off the muscularity of his broad chest and defined arms. I prayed the low growl in my throat would remain there, unheard. There was no good reason for me to be territorial. *Oh, yeah?* my brain snarled, flashing images of Boyce hovering over me in the darkness, that chest and those arms bare under my appreciative hands. *Dammit.*

Gustavo slid an arm over the back of Milla's chair with a perturbed scowl. They'd been an item for about two weeks, and the rest of us had wagers going on how *that* would end. Prediction: *messy.*

Battling the desire to stake a claim on the beautiful man next to me in all manner of unacceptable ways, I sympathized with Gustavo. I had nothing against Shanice or Milla... but I wanted to knock their brilliant heads together at the moment.

"I'm at Wynn's Garage," Boyce answered.

"But your surname is Wynn—correct?" Kaameh asked. "You are the owner, then?"

I rarely saw Kaameh because she was working on her dissertation. She was also the research assistant for Dr. Kent—the professor whose grant-funded research focused on oil spills and their effects on the biodiverse marine habitats of the Gulf Coast. I hoped to take her place when I returned from Austin.

Boyce's jaw twitched, but he produced a thin smile. "Actually, my mother is the owner."

Her eyebrows arched high and she returned the smile. "Your mother is a mechanic too?"

He shifted in his seat, and I wished my colleagues would stop giving him the third degree. "No. My father died recently and ownership passed to her. I do all the repairs and run the day-to-day operations."

"Oh—I'm so sorry for your loss. Please excuse my prying. Your mother is fortunate to have a responsible son looking after her business."

He nodded but said nothing.

"So you've known Pearl her whole life?" Mahlik asked him from my opposite side.

Boyce gave me a lazy smile. "Close to."

"Yo, man—has she *always* been clumsy?" he asked. Everyone laughed and I hid my face in my hands—knocking over my half-full margarita in the process.

"Pearl, clumsy?" Boyce chuckled, quickly mopping up the spill with his napkin before it left the tabletop and dribbled all over my lap. "Naw, man. Not at all."

· · · · · · · · · ·

I felt the bed beneath my back, but the room was spinning around it. Boyce removed my boots and sat next to me in the dark, brushing the hair from my face. "Stay," I whined, reaching for him, clenching and unclenching my hands like a toddler begging to be held. "I'm not sleepy."

He chuckled softly. "Pretty sure you're gonna be asleep any second, sweetheart. You're pretty well hammered."

"You calling me a cheap drunk, Boyce Wynn?"

"No ma'am. I'd never call you a cheap anything."

I puckered my lips and tried to look sexy, and he bit down on his lower lip, which he did when he wanted to laugh and was trying not to. I loved that full lower lip and wanted to lick it.

"That's nice," I said. "You're nice. No, better than nice. You're *sweet*."

By the moonlight streaming through my big, open window, I could make out the shape of his generous mouth—the white of his teeth and slight upturn of his lips. The chuckle he'd tried to stifle escaped. "Sweet? Me? Now I *know* you're trashed." He leaned over me, hands on either side of my shoulders, imprisoning me between them.

"No, no, no, you are! You are. You're so, *so* sweet. That's why I love you."

• • • • • • • • • •

My head throbbed like a rowdy neighbor resided on the opposite side of my headboard, bass thumping through the wall. Unlikely, as the room next door was an unused guest room. That pulsing beat was all internal. *Ugh.*

I was grateful someone had pulled the drapes closed because my retinas couldn't tolerate the bright light of a summer day just yet. They would burst into flames. Turning toward the wall, I eased onto my side in slow motion, but half of me was slower to follow—limbs rubbery and brain loose inside my skull, sloshing side-to-side before settling into the new position.

I remembered now. *Boyce* had shut the drapes before he left. He'd taken care of me as promised—drove me home. Carried me upstairs. Put me to bed. He was so, so sweet.

My aching eyes flew open. Oh no. *Oh no.* Breathing slowly, I shut my eyes and concentrated hard enough to hurt, fighting to remember.

That's why I love you.

Twenty-three

BOYCE

Earlier in the week, I'd changed Wynn's hours of operation on the door and the website. No more official Saturday hours, though there I was at nine a.m. the very next Saturday, replacing an engine. One of my regular customers had assumed his compact sedan could make it through some water on a low road that turned out to be two or three feet deeper than he'd assumed.

When he had it towed into the shop on Tuesday, I put it up on the lift so Sam could get a look at the damage a little bit of water could do when it got sucked through the air intake.

"Whoa," she said. "That dumbass is screwed." Sam had no patience for stupid, not that I could blame her.

I hated making those types of calls, but I'd learned it was best to spit out the facts and let people deal with them how they would. "Well, Bobby, you've hydrolocked your engine."

"Is that bad?" he asked.

"Um, yeah. Pretty bad." I told him I'd hold off doing anything until he authorized it, because it was going to cost a couple grand. Poor guy was nearly in tears when he called back to tell me to do it. He'd probably swerve around two-inch-deep puddles for the rest of his life.

Diagnosis required concentration. Doing the work, not so much. My mind was free to chew on everything that happened last night—and there was plenty to ponder.

Pearl had answered the door wearing a mouthwateringly short denim skirt and boots. A little white top that sorta twisted around her a couple of times and tied in the back just about finished me off. I caught sight of that bow at the small of her back when she turned to call good-bye to her mom, and all night, every time my hand grazed it, it was all I could do to beat back the image of giving it a tug and unwrapping her like a sugary, melt-in-your-mouth piece of candy.

Her friends ranged from tolerable to pretty cool. Over dinner they did a little scientist shoptalk that I couldn't follow, but after a few drinks they slipped into stories about lab mishaps, research trips, and gossip. We hit several bars within a three-block radius. The second was a karaoke place I generally avoided at all costs because I didn't sing and had no desire to listen to other poor fuckers who couldn't but thought they could. It wasn't my circus though, so I just smiled and said, "Yes ma'am." By that point they all treated me like I was one of them, except one dickhead who wanted Pearl though she seemed oblivious to it. *Kyle* tested the limits of my patience all night long.

When he grabbed her hand and hauled her onstage to sing a duet, the only thing keeping me from busting his jaw wide open was the fact that I was *the best friend* and I'd promised to look after her, not beat the shit outta her friends. But then he couldn't sing for shit and she sang her parts—a tad slurred—directly to me instead of to him like most people did during duets. The desire to wipe the floorboards with him eased off, and my eyes never left her face as she serenaded me with words I wanted her to mean.

Her older colleague, Kaameh, looked back and forth between us, but I held my straight face and pretended not to notice her studying my reaction. Near unbearable when I wanted to stalk up to that stage, pick Pearl up, take her straight through the back door, and press her up against the wall outside. I wanted to untie and unravel the folds of that white shirt until I freed her from it, push that little skirt just high enough to get my hands underneath, and tell her to wrap her shapely legs around me, boots and all. I wanted to kiss her until she couldn't think. Until I couldn't think. Which wouldn't take more than two seconds of her pretty little mouth under mine.

By the third bar, Pearl was drunker than I'd ever seen her. I shouldn't have liked that, but damn, I did. She giggled and leaned against me and said, "Hiiiiii, Boyce."

She pulled me out on the floor to dance, something I wasn't fond of doing until right then, with her. Under the light of a disco ball, we two-stepped to Lonestar and slow-danced to Green River Ordinance, and she twirled around me to some damned boy band I was happy not to know the name of while I made sure she stayed upright.

At the end of the night when I drove her home, she curled in the passenger seat with a silly smile on her face and fell asleep. I carried her to the front door and her stepdad let me in, chuckled at the pint-sized snores coming from her, and led the way to her bedroom. I didn't let on that I knew and remembered exactly where her bedroom was.

"I take it she had a good time tonight," he said.

"She sure did. She may regret it in the morning, but she enjoyed it fully."

She came to when I laid her on the bed. I took her boots off and set them out of the way and moved the wastebasket closer. I wanted to help her out of that shirt and skirt—neither of which would be comfortable to sleep in—but I reckoned that was inadvisable under the circumstances of parents hovering just down the hall, waiting for me to leave.

Then she told me I was sweet, which was a cockeyed, harebrained, undeniably drunk thing to say. "That's why I love you," she added before nodding off, and everything tangled and froze—the heart in my chest, the breath in my lungs, the thoughts in my head.

I stumbled into the hallway and down the staircase like I was the one who'd downed margaritas and shooters like they were going out of style.

Before I reached the front door, Dr. Frank came out of the kitchen and pressed a bottle of water into my hand. "Thought you could use some rehydration for the road. Listen, I know it's late, but if you've got a minute, I had a question or two about the garage."

Still dazed, I mumbled, "Um, sure," and followed him into the kitchen. We passed the table and sat at the granite bar on a couple of barstools like we were just two guys shooting the shit instead of me and Pearl's stepfather at near three o'clock in the morning. I twisted the cap off the bottle of water and swallowed half of it.

That's why I love you.

Dr. Frank knit his hands together on the bar, pointing his index fingers toward me as he spoke. "Pearl says your mama's taken ownership of the garage and intends to sell it off. That accurate?"

I nodded once, knocked catawampus by Pearl's drunken confession. Would she mean it sober? "Yes, sir. She's just waiting for the official transfer to go through."

"Have you—or has she—had a business valuation done on the garage? To know its worth as a going concern versus auctioned liquidation of the property, tools, and equipment?"

Auctioned liquidation. That jerked me right back to earth. I had no damned intention of hanging around to witness that and didn't particularly want to discuss the likelihood. "I handed the spreadsheets over to Mr. Amos, her attorney, but I have a decent idea of it since I've been doing the accounting for a couple of years now."

He rubbed his chin and then said, "The probability that your mama will find a taker for that place without you at the helm is low. She's more likely to break everything up and unload it piecemeal, I'd guess."

Meaning *liquidation*. Yeah. Got it. "I reckon so," I said. I liked the man well enough based on how Pearl felt about him, but there was only so much of this rubbing-salt-in-the-wound shit I could take.

"So she might be interested in selling the whole thing, lock, stock, and barrel, to a singular entity." He laid this statement down like he was placing a hand of cards faceup on a table and watched as the purpose of his questions hit me.

"To *you*?"

"Possibly. I'm always on the lookout for investments, especially here on the island, particularly small, locally owned businesses. It's good for my personal property value and my practice that this place maintains its laidback, small-town image. That said, you, as the current key employee, would have to be part of the deal—that'd be an associated agreement. If you're not game, I'm not game."

"Are you… suggesting that you'd buy Wynn's and I'd work for you?"

"I'm planting the idea in your head. We probably don't have a whole lotta time, but we've got a few days. Mull it over. If you are interested, I'll get my CPA in touch with your mama's attorney and get a look at those numbers. There's due diligence that'd have to happen before any deal, you understand, handshake or paper."

I drove home in a stupor, as unprepared for the next shock of the night as I was for the first two.

• • • • • • • • • •

I'd just fallen asleep when I heard a pissed-off voice—a *male* voice—that sounded as if it came from inside the trailer. As I grabbed the wooden bat from under the bed and threw my bedroom door open, I heard my mother's equally worked-up voice and the sound of a slap.

Without a second thought, I ran across the space between the bedrooms and busted through her locked door. A man I'd never seen had her by the shoulders. "Hands off!" I roared, bat up, and he released her and sprang back with his palms in the air like I was a one-man SWAT team.

"What the fuck, Ruthanne?" he yelled, eyes wide. "What the *fuck*?"

The lights were all on in Mom's room, which made her handprint on his face real visible.

"Who the fuck are you?" I spat, keeping the bat up and over my shoulder, ready to knock a home run with his head if he came at me. I outweighed the guy by at least seventy pounds. Unless he was armed and fast, I'd kick his ass to hell and back before he could count to ten.

"I done told you I live with my son," Mom said, chest rising and falling. She jerked the housecoat she wore most of the day, every day, around herself and tied the belt.

"You made it sound like he was a kid." He pointed at me. "That ain't no kid!"

"No shit," she said, a hand braced on her hip. "Better not lay another finger on me."

Keeping an eye on me, he raked a hand through thinning, greasy hair. I figured him to be younger than her by a decade or so, but that didn't make him a prize. He had the same weedy look Thompson had when he was sent to Jester—scrawny and lean, no muscle tone. "Why is he here, Ruthanne?" he whined. "Thought you said this place belonged to you."

"He runs the garage, Riley."

"So? You're gonna sell it all off anyway. He's gotta go." He glared in my direction and I glared back.

Her eyes flicked to me. "Me and him have a deal. He gives me the cash that garage earns every week, and I let his little *spic* girlfriend live here for another month."

I clenched the bat in my hand, teeth grinding, and fought to breathe normally when my mind and body were begging me to swing that bat in every direction, consequences be damned. "Pearl is gone," I gritted out. *Thank God, thank fucking God.* "And I can be gone tomorrow. Hell, I can be gone in ten minutes. In which case you're responsible for the cars I haven't finished fixing, settling the end-of-month debts, balancing the books, and figuring out what the *fuck* everything is worth, because I'm nothing but a fucking *employee* with *no fucking liability* for *any of it*."

"Shit," Riley muttered, lowering his hands but leaving them where I could see them. I didn't lower the bat. "When do we get the fuckin' money, Ruthanne?"

"As soon as I sell this dump, that's when—just like I told you." She spread her hands. "You shoulda kept your damn job and stayed in Amarillo—"

"I don't need you tellin' me what to do, woman!" He jabbed a finger at her and started toward her but halted when I stepped forward too, bat at the ready to knock him into next week. Wide-eyed, he twitched and pointed that finger at me. "*Goddammit*, junior, you best step off."

Christ on a fucking cracker, my mother had picked another winner.

I arched a brow. "Or else what? I'm the one holdin' the bat, asshole."

I *did not* need this shit. Nothing was stopping me from backing across this trailer, throwing everything I owned in my TA and leaving town in a cloud of dust. There was something to be said for a future wiped blank and laid bare, unhooked from the past. But what if I didn't want to be unhooked from my past? If I took off, the opportunity Dr. Frank had dangled in front of me would dissolve, and I would never know if Pearl meant those words she'd said.

"I'm going back to bed. I have work tomorrow—starting in about five hours. So if y'all are planning on killing each other, shut the *fuck* up about it."

I had Bobby's waterlogged engine pulled by noon. I hadn't heard from Pearl, but I was pretty sure she'd spent most of the day cussing the existence of alcohol. She'd probably never remember what she'd said to me, but I would never forget it.

Pearl

Brain still sloshing inside my head and stomach heaving with any sudden movement, I lay in bed until noon, calculating my chances that Boyce would interpret my drunken admission as inebriated hogwash. And whether I wanted him to.

After wrestling out of my outfit—not quite as cute smelling like stale cigarettes, beer, and sweat—I pulled on a big T-shirt, brushed my teeth to offset the I-just-licked-a-carpet taste in my mouth, and wound my riotous hair into a knot before descending the staircase one slow step at a time, gripping the handrail until my feet touched the cool marble of the ground floor. Mama had left me a note next to a basket of still-warm blueberry muffins—she and Thomas had gone into Corpus for lunch and errands.

Tux purred, winding around my legs until I gave him a fat blueberry, which he ate. Mama always said he was so pampered he'd be toast in the wild. I wasn't so sure, because that cat would eat anything. On the other hand, macaroni and cheese didn't grow on low-hanging trees.

Picking at my muffin and waiting for coffee to brew, I scrolled through my colleagues' Instagram posts from last night. Boyce was in several and Lord almighty, he looked good. I'd always thought he was hot, but lately my eyes loved everything about him—every single thing—as if I no longer saw him through the same lens.

Kaameh had posted a pic of us dancing: Boyce laughing down at me—one hand at my waist, fingers grazing the tie that kept my shirt wrapped tight, and me on my toes—smiling up at him, hair falling in waves down my back.

At one point last night, he'd leaned in close and asked, "So what happens if I pull this little string in back and spin you around?"

High on the delicious punch of his hot breath in my ear and the scrape of stubble grazing my cheek, I bit my lip to stifle an impending giggle. I was under the influence of both alcohol and Boyce Wynn—a dangerous combination. "You'll find out what I'm *not* wearing under this shirt."

His eyes burned like green fire, and I knew if we'd been alone I would've been spinning like a whirligig. "Mmm-hmm," he said.

I stared at that picture, and a snapped undercurrent zinged

straight to my core as if he were standing in my kitchen, his hands on me, urging me to come undone under the influence of his firm touch.

Me:	Thank you for taking care of me last night. I'm alive. Mostly.
Boyce:	You're welcome. Feeling the effects today are ya?
Me:	GAH. My brain hasn't stopped sobbing and asking if we're gonna die. So glad I asked for today off work. I'd have been facedown on the keyboard all day. I rang in 21 good and hard.
Me:	Well that came out wrong. :-/
Boyce:	I'm biting back so many witty comments right now out of pity for your incapacity to retaliate...
Me:	Gee, thanks.
Boyce:	Any regrets?
Me:	No. No regrets.
Boyce:	Good.

No regrets.

Not a lie, applied to last night. Not the whole truth, applied to the length and breadth of the relationship Boyce and I shared. Harriet Beecher Stowe wrote, *The bitterest tears shed over graves are for words left unsaid and deeds left undone.* That night on the beach years ago—when I caught sight of that girl sprawled on Boyce's lap—all I felt was quick, hard betrayal. And on the heels of that blow, I just felt stupid. I had never questioned whether I should have stood my ground. Whether I should have demanded to be more to him than just another hookup. Whether I *was* more.

Pearl Torres Frank always did the smart thing, and accepting the way things were instead of railing against that all-too-predictable conclusion and exposing my naïve heart for what it was seemed the smart thing. But leaving those words unsaid—*I wanted to be your only*—was also the cowardly thing. My one moment of regret in my twenty-one years.

Twenty-four

BOYCE

For the first time in a long time, I was trying to sort out a concern I couldn't discuss with Pearl. After Sunday supper at Mateo and Yvette's place, Yvette locked herself in their bathroom to take a bubble bath and read a book with a near-naked dude on the cover whose ripped chest and abs said, *I got all this by spending most of my time at the gym. I don't actually have time to run a billion-dollar corporation or screw anyone for longer than maybe fifteen minutes.*

I'd noticed Pearl shoving that exact same book under her stack of sheets at the end of the sofa before the night of the storm.

"Your woman reads this stuff?" I asked, picking it up off the counter.

Yvette snatched it out of my hand and rolled her eyes. "Later, loser," she said, and her sons fell all over each other giggling.

"Trust me, dude. Her reading that stuff is *all good for me*," Vega said.

"Hmm," I said, filing that away for later.

Vega and I kicked back on his porch with a six-pack of Coors and a pack of Camels while the boys played on the two-story fort we'd built in their backyard last summer, and I told him the details of

Thomas Frank's proposition.

"I've never heard anything bad about the guy," he said. "But that garage should have been *yours*, Wynn. You'd be going from being *the boss* to being an employee."

I took a drag, watching the boys take turns going headfirst down the slide. "Can't do shit about that, man. Yeah, it sucks, but Amos says she'd have gotten half of everything fifteen years ago in a divorce—court-ordered—and maybe he'd have had to sell the garage back then to give it to her. I dunno, man. What's done is done. I just don't want to cut off my nose to spite my face, you know?"

"I hear ya." He paused to take a sip and holler at Arturo for throwing rocks over the back fence into the neighbor's yard. "What about the trailer—would you have to like...*rent* it?"

"Good point. No idea."

One of the boys tore by us, the other one right behind him with a Super Soaker the size of my arm. "Oh *shit*," Vega said about one second before his kid turned and sprayed him smack in the face, knocking the can right out of his hand. He jumped up, grabbed the hose and turned it on, then ran after the two of them, who shrieked like they were being chased by that dude from *Saw*.

Watching them, I remembered when we'd found out Yvette was knocked up. They'd been arguing over the fact that his chief activities after graduation were playing drums in a band that had little ambition and less talent, smoking weed, and playing *Gears of War* while stoned. Then one day she'd announced she was pregnant, breaking up with him, and moving to San Antonio to live with her older sister because her parents were super religious and freaking out and she couldn't deal. We sat staring up at her from his parents' sofa, mouths ajar and controllers forgotten in our hands.

"They're making me tell you, so consider yourself told," she'd said, hands fisted at her hips. "But you're a child, and a child can't raise a child. I'm done, Mateo." Her voice shook. "I'm just done." She walked out the door crying. He mobilized two minutes later and ran out the door after her—they'd lived two houses down from each other all their lives.

He quit the band and got a job the next weekend—manned up like no one I knew had ever done. When they found out she was having twins, I asked him why he hadn't taken that free pass. He said, "Those babies and fatherhood scared the fuck out of me, but I kept thinking how scared she probably was too because she's *in it*, you know? And I just want to be in it with her."

I asked myself now if anything could happen with Pearl that would scare me—waiting another fifteen years, or her name with *doctor* in front of it and *PhD* after it, or a baby, or promising to love and cherish her, or her needing me for *any damned thing ever*.

Nothing. *Nothing* scared me like the thought of losing her. Which just meant I had to do everything in my power to see that didn't happen.

Pearl

I'd barely sat down in class Monday before Shanice, Milla, and Chase clustered around me.

"So. *Boyce*," Shanice said.

I'd always sucked at concealing my emotions when confronted with something I hadn't sorted out, and where Boyce was concerned I was disastrously unsorted. I felt the longing scuttle across my face before I could quash it. Accustomed to seeing him daily, I had been back home a week and had only seen him once—which had taken place in the company of eight colleagues... three of whom were scrutinizing my raised eyebrows (I lowered them), my fidgeting hands (I shoved them under the table), and my shrill, innocent-but-not-really voice (I vowed to remain silent after squeaking, "What about him?").

They exchanged the shrewd glances. "Told you," Chase said. If I remembered correctly, he'd picked up a guy at the karaoke bar who followed us to the next place. So had Shanice. My colleagues were making the most of pursuing graduate degrees in a place lots of people came for vacation. "She's *definitely* into him. You said his name and I swear her pupils dilated."

Pupils! *Dammit.* I pressed my lips together and hastily jerked my game face into position. "He'll be leaving town soon."

"But he said he runs that garage for his mom," Shanice said. "I wasn't kidding about my POS Pontiac. That thing is *not* happy about the humidity here. It's been sputtering every time I start it. Besides, *you're* here, and he didn't look like he wanted to go anywhere."

"His mother is going to sell the garage. And he's... going to leave." As the words fell from my mouth, they became real. They tugged until they pulled that pretense of *I'm fine and unscathed and it's no big deal* right off. I couldn't break my fall, and for the first time, I didn't want to.

"That sucks," Chase said. "He looked *really* into you."

"Are you going to be okay?" Milla asked, a tiny crease between her brows.

"I don't know," I said.

No, I thought. *No, I'm not.*

Twenty-five

BOYCE

On Wednesday, Sam told me she needed to leave early for an appointment with her therapist, which she swore up and down was a complete waste of time and energy. "Dad won't even fucking listen to what I want," she said, crossing her arms and scowling like Vega's boys did when they were confronted with something green on their plates.

"Get any good drugs outta the deal, at least?"

More sheltered than her rough-and-tumble attitude implied, she went slack-jawed, eyes bulging. When I laughed at the utter disbelief on her face, her expression sank right back into its routine glower. "I only take drugs when I *need* them," she said, hints dropping from that statement like shrapnel shells.

I'd looked up spina bifida on the Internet—she'd told Pearl her diagnosis during one of their *Here's how I change a spark plug* interactions. I was more impressed with Sam's tenacity in the face of that shit than I would ever let on, mostly because she'd probably hurl one of my own tools at my head and say she didn't need *any damn pity*.

"Do *you* do drugs?" she snapped.

I lifted the battery she'd just detached out of the hatchback. "I did when I was your age." I decided against telling her I wasn't just *doing* them at her age, or that I smoked the occasional joint *now*.

"So you think I'm a pussy because I think drugs are medication and not for recreational dumbassery?"

Whoa, Nellie. "Nope." I lifted a shoulder, unpacking the new battery. "I was a dumbass at sixteen. I laughed because you sorta look like an anime hamster when you're shocked. Also, full props for *recreational dumbassery*."

She smirked, so I guess the anime hamster analogy was acceptable. *Christ.*

I set the new battery in place. "You've got a few minutes before your dad gets here. Hook 'er up."

After Mr. Adams picked Sam up, I turned the Closed sign, locked up, and went inside to shower, ignoring Mom and *Riley*— who had decided he didn't have to abide by my *no smoking inside* rule since I didn't "own the place." Saying horseshit like that amused the fuck out of him, so I'd quit speaking or listening to him altogether. For five days running they'd rolled outta the bed I'd bought for Pearl around noon, stumbled out of the room I'd painted for Pearl, and parked their asses on the sofa watching daytime television, drinking my beer, and picking redneck fights with each other.

I hadn't seen her since Friday night—or Saturday morning. We'd texted a few times and talked a couple. She had let me know earlier in the week that everything was cool regarding our no-condom fuckup.

"Oh good. *Phew*," I said. What I was thinking: *Damn*, which I sure as shit kept to my fool self because she would *not* have shared that reaction.

I knew she was confused when I begged off seeing her, but I blamed Riley's appearance and the need to get a few things at the shop settled. Both were true—no way I was allowing her to cross paths with that jackass, and I had some serious shit to nail down before I saw her again.

"You won't leave without seeing me, right?" she'd asked last night.

"No way."

I heard her answering sigh and almost caved. I wanted to talk to her about her stepfather's offer, but I couldn't. I wasn't going to tell her until I had something to fucking *say*. Until I'd removed the obstacle that stood between us. Until then, I was spinning my wheels, scrambling for enough solid ground to pull myself out, and I'd be damned before I'd drag her into the mud with me.

"Where're you going?" Mom asked as I crossed the living room. "Ain't the garage still open?"

"Not today."

She said something else I ignored, then came to the door and hollered at me as I fired up the TA and cranked the stereo like I didn't see or hear her. She hadn't been around for my teenage years. I reckoned she had it coming to her.

· · · · · · · · · ·

Dr. Frank closed his office door behind him and reached to shake my hand. "Boyce, good to see you. Have some questions for me, or have you reached a decision?" He sat behind the desk, and I took one of the chairs facing him. The positions were familiar enough that all sorts of smartass comments were pouring into my head. But this wasn't school and I wasn't in hot water. I was a businessman speaking to a potential investor.

I sat straight as a rod, pressing a fist to my thigh to pin down my leg, which wanted to judder a mile a minute. "You've made me a real fair offer, Dr. Frank, and I've got no reason to turn it down. But—and I'm sure I'm going about this all wrong—I have a proposition of my own."

He nodded and sat forward. "All right."

"I started working for my father ten years ago. He was an asshole, pardon my language, but he knew cars and he passed that know-how down to me. If I told you I'd thought that garage would be mine since then, that would be a lie. Truth is, I didn't have any kinda goals or plans when I was a kid. I just... did what was easiest."

What was easiest was surviving the loss of Mom and Brent and ducking my dad's fist, but by seventeen I could've shaped up. I could've followed Maxfield's lead and got the hell out. I chose not to, because staying required nothing. It was so fucking easy.

I'd dug my own hole, and it was time to dig myself out.

"A couple years ago, my dad was diagnosed with liver disease. He never quit drinking, so he was ineligible for a transplant. He was going to die fast and ugly and we both knew it. Once I knew—or *thought* I knew—Wynn's was going to be mine, everything shifted in my head. How I saw the place, the customers, my work, my connection to this town—everything changed. So the thing is—I know I can do the work. I can run the place for someone else." I swallowed. "But what I want is to own it."

"Oh?" His brows rose and he steepled his hands on his desk. Dr. Frank seemed like a good-humored, plainspoken sorta guy. He'd gotten his MD from Baylor in 1986—diploma on the wall behind him—which meant he and my dad had been of an age. But whereas my dad had been a hard-living son of a bitch who believed a man taking care of himself was for pussies, Thomas Frank had a George Clooney thing going on. I could see how his sexploits got to be part of local folklore before I was even born.

And then he met Pearl's mom.

"There are two paths to owning Wynn's: purchasing it—cash on the barrel—or financing it," he said. "I assume you don't have the funds on hand to buy your mama out." I shook my head, as he knew I would. "So that leaves financing a business loan. How might you feel making payments on something you thought was yours?"

"Well, I reckon that'd depend on the terms of the loan." Thank Christ I'd looked this shit up last night.

He smiled. "My initial assumption was that your mama would sell Wynn's to me at a fair price and I would pay you to run it. If you were to take on a loan for that property, you'd have to make that payment every month, as well as support the business and yourself. That's a lot to ask of a young man with marketable skills who could command a steady salary and undertake no risk instead."

Working for him was the easier path, and it should have been tempting, but it wasn't. "I'm probably shooting myself in the foot to say this to the guy offering me a job, but I'm not sure I'd bring the same amount of dedication to something that isn't *mine*."

He eyed me more closely. "All right. Just a moment." He pulled up some software on his computer and entered numbers and turned the monitor toward me. "My CPA sent over property and business valuations yesterday—both asset-based and income-to-value. Here's the possible range of the loan payment amount—high to low—depending on what she'll sell it for, at a typical rate of interest."

I braced myself for something between barely doable and hopeless.

"That's—less than a grand per month? For—uh, principal *and* interest? That's all? I could do either of those."

He nodded. "You'd have to pay taxes and insurance separately, but I'm sure you have a good idea what those will be since you've already been keeping up with them. I'm glad the upper limit looks doable, but why don't we see how close we can get her to the lesser amount?"

"Are you… are you saying you would be willing to loan me the money?"

"Confession—I looked into your credit history as well."

"Ain't much there," I said. "No car loans or rent paid. One credit card I don't much use."

"What I see is that you live within your means when a lot of people your age don't. You took responsibility for a business and built it up instead of squeezing what you could get out of it or abandoning it. I'd be proud to invest in you, Mr. Wynn."

My throat squeezed tight. I couldn't swallow, and I sure couldn't trust my damned self to answer. I nodded and stuck out my hand and we shook.

Pearl

By the time I was at work Thursday night, I couldn't take it anymore. Almost a week had passed since I'd seen Boyce. He'd told me not to come over, and I knew he had his hands full running Wynn's, watching over Sam, and dealing with his mother and her boyfriend. But my heart only knew I missed him.

I had my excuse when I remembered that his birthday was six days away—exactly two weeks after mine—or exactly one year and fifty weeks before mine. He'd flunked third grade and I'd skipped ninth, throwing us into the same forty-three person graduating class in high school.

Some people might have called that destiny, but I wasn't one of them. I'd never believed in the illogical concept of fate—owing an A on an exam to a lucky hat or attributing a touchdown to a preordained miracle. Fortunate outcomes were the result of hard work or happy accidents. There was no correlation between wearing a hat and earning an A. It was coincidence.

Like Boyce spotting me in the water seconds before I would have drowned. Or the two of us ending up in the same biology class in tenth grade because Mel and I made the dance squad and we had to switch out of last-period biology and into Boyce and Landon's section. In life, bad things happen, good things happen, and we do what we can to encourage one and prevent the other. Boyce was one of the good things in my life. One of the best things. I wanted to be one of his best things, even if someday all I'd be was a memory.

I decided to give Boyce a birthday gift that would make amends for those he'd never gotten. Something he'd have loved as a boy but would still love as a man. It didn't take much deliberation to know what that thing was. A lifelong supporter of Houston's exasperatingly subpar baseball team, he'd once told me that he'd never actually been to a major league game.

I pulled up the Astros' schedule on the inn's antiquated computer.

Me:	Someone has a birthday coming up... but I have a little problem with your gift.
Boyce:	Oh?
Me:	It would intrude on one of your Sundays.
Boyce:	But my birthday is on Wednesday...

Me: Yes, but your *gift* isn't on Wednesday.

Boyce: Okay...???

Me: You said no one has influence over your Sundays.

Boyce: That has nothing to do with you.

Me: You sure?

Boyce: Yep. Positive. So what is this gift??

Me: I'll tell you more on your birthday. If you're still here and want to see me?

Boyce: Let's get something straight that I should have already said. I'm not leaving. I'm busy as hell right now and I know you are too with classes and the inn, but I'm here. I don't want you coming over because of my mom's shit-for-brains BF hanging around. That's the ONLY reason.

Me: I miss you. ☹

Boyce: Same. Yes I want to see you Wednesday. That's all I want for my birthday. Let me take you out.

Me: You taking me out wouldn't be much of a birthday – besides, I asked you. I'll pay.

Boyce: Like hell you will. I'll pick you up at 7.

Me: Stubborn man.

Boyce: Yep. ;)

• • • • • • • • • •

The frosted cupcake the waitress set in front of Boyce was almost the size of a salad plate and boasted one lit candle standing in the center, weeping wax from top to base.

"You gonna sing 'Happy Birthday' to me all sexy like you sang that Lady Antebellum song?" He leaned over the candle from across the table, one brow cocked, mouth drawn up on one side. Lord have mercy, he was mischief incarnate.

"I think you endured enough of my singing on *my* birthday-celebration night." I crossed and uncrossed my legs under the table, half-embarrassed, half-itching to blow that candle out and climb into his lap. Or run down to the rapidly darkening beach and hurl myself in the water because it was suddenly beyond warm in the burger joint we'd chosen.

"Naw, baby—you can carry a tune."

The way I'd sung that song that night—right *to* him, hips swaying and lips puckered—oh. My. God. No wonder everyone at school thought we were hooking up. "Psssh! If by *carry* you mean *mangle ruthlessly*."

He laughed, that tiny flame from the candle dancing in his green eyes. "Sounded just perfect to me."

"Then you are clearly tone-deaf, thank God. Now blow that candle out and make your wish."

"Yes, ma'am," he drawled, extinguishing the flame in one short burst. Another naughty smile pulled at the corners of his mouth. "Am I gonna get my wish?"

He was in a wicked mood, and God help me, I loved everything about it. I leaned an elbow on the table, my chin cupped in my hand, and batted my lashes twice. "I suppose that depends on your wish."

The waitress arrived with the check and Boyce shoved three twenties in her hands without looking at it. "Keep the change," he said, grabbing my hand and stalking to the door.

"Boyce—our bill was only like thirty-four dollars—"

"Worth it," he said, not slowing. He shoved the door open and pulled me into the twilight-purple evening. The temperature had cooled from roasting to sweltering with the sun's departure.

I stumbled over a rock in the gravel-strewn parking lot—flip-flops and I had a shaky relationship lately—and Boyce immediately turned and swung me into his arms. I slid my arms around his neck and stared up at his taut profile. "Are you mad? Did I say someth—"

"Not mad. Not mad *at all*." He stared down at me, turning to thread through the haphazardly parked cars without slowing. "I have to kiss you. I have to touch you in very publicly inappropriate ways. *Right now*." He leaned closer as I went molten from the center out, breath quickening, every individual part of my body pulsing fiercely all at once. "I wanna fuck you, sweetheart," he murmured, setting me down against the passenger door of his TA and absorbing my shocked gasp with his mouth, his hands cupping my face as he kissed me. When his lips released mine, we panted, eyes locked, inches apart. "I'm afraid none of that made sitting in the Lodge in full view of a few dozen people a good idea."

I shook my head. "N-no. Staying would have been… inadvisable."

He chuckled, opening the car door and kissing me again. "Get in. No seat belt."

I nodded and obeyed as he circled to his side, glancing around the lot. No one was near us, but the lot was far from deserted. The dusking sky caused streetlights to pop on, but they cast a feeble amount of illumination. *Oh my God, was I considering DOING IT in his CAR?* That was disturbing and uncharacteristic and illegal and—and—*so hot*.

His door slammed shut and he lowered the windows partway. He shoved his seat back as far as it would go and reached for me, pulling me astride his lap. He kissed me, hands pushing under the back of my shirt and unhooking my bra. Lifting the hem just above my breast, he nudged one loose cup aside and took the nipple deep in his warm mouth, sucking and humming.

My head fell back and all I could hear was my own low moan and the pounding acceleration of my heartbeat. I pressed against his erection instinctively, squeezing my thighs on his hips and grinding against him, and he gripped me closer. His hand on the bare skin of my back was so hot he could have left a rosy handprint between my shoulder blades.

Releasing my nipple, he filled one hand with my breast and pulled my mouth back to his with the other. Our kisses were hungry and the humidity-heightened temperature in the confined space spiked. His lips moved down my throat and he murmured softly, "*Goddamn*, beautiful girl. Can I make you come for me like this?" Placing soft, sucking kisses at the base of my throat, he moved his hips, thrusting upward as though he were already inside me.

Damn. These. Shorts!

I gasped, clutching my thighs tighter. "I… I can't…"

"Spread too wide without me inside you?"

I nodded, biting my lip.

"Turn," he said, lifting and rotating me to sit on his lap facing out. In the last row of the lot, the TA faced nothing but a rickety fence, tall weeds poking through the warped, splintered slats.

I laid my head back against his shoulder—missing his mouth on my throat, my lips, my breast—and I wanted to wail, *How is this better?* Then he unbuttoned and unzipped my shorts and thrust his hand right down the front of them.

"Ah, that's it," he murmured. "Right. *There*. One? Or two?"

I writhed and groaned, shutting my eyes to our surroundings and yielding control to his intoxicating words and searching fingers.

He chuckled. "Two it is."

"Oh... *God*." I panted.

He licked and kissed my neck at the pulse point just under my ear, his left hand cupping my right breast, pinching the nipple gently as if linking an erogenous connect-the-dots triangle.

"That's my girl." The vibrations of his voice rumbled through me, a grounding bass to the orchestral maneuvers of his hands and mouth. His thumb circled and pressed as his fingers thrust deep, curving and caressing. "I wanna watch you come, baby. That's all I've dreamed about since the last time I was inside you—kissing you again, touching this sweet little body again, all warm and tight and wanting me to lay you down and fuck you deep and hard."

I jolted and came apart, clapping one hand over my mouth to keep the people in the restaurant across the lot from hearing me.

Twenty-six

BOYCE

One hand covering her mouth and the other gripping my forearm like locking pliers, she was a mind-blowing sight. I shocked the hell out of her, but she loved it because she trusted me, and every time I touched her I felt that surrender. This girl was all brainy respectability on the surface and blazing-hot daredevil underneath. I knew this. I'd known it for a long time. I was just too fucking stupid to comprehend what it meant—that she needed a man like me.

I couldn't get enough of her, and I knew deep in my gut that I never would. I wanted to take her home and love her all night long, but I had to get my mother and her ignorant dickhole of a boyfriend out of my goddamned trailer first.

I heard voices nearby—a group of folks who'd just finished supper, lazily weaving through the lot toward their car. I zipped and buttoned Pearl's shorts, pulled her shirt into place, and turned her on my lap like we were just sitting there kissing. A little naughty, but nothing like what we'd been up to two minutes ago. She was still trembling from that release, her head on my shoulder, her curvy little ass pressed against the raring-to-go length of my dick—*sorry, buddy, not tonight*—and her feet in the passenger seat, toenails painted blue as the deepest part of the gulf.

When the approaching voices broke through her awareness, she stiffened, glancing over her shoulder out the open window.

I tightened my arms around her and kissed her forehead. "No worries. We're just two people sitting in a car having a *right friendly* conversation. They won't pay us any mind."

She relaxed, laughing softly, and tucked her head beneath my chin as if she was listening for my heartbeat, which was likely going lickety-split under her ear. "So about *your* gift…"

"Mmm-hmm?"

"I'll need you Saturday morning through Sunday afternoon." She paused.

"All right." *What in hell?*

"Okay. Good." Her fingers tickled back and forth over the forearm she'd just been hanging on to for dear life not five minutes prior, as if she was gentling me. As if any moment I might rear back and tell her no. "I'll pick you up around eleven. Dress like you are now, and pack a change of clothes for Sunday plus whatever you'd bring for an overnight trip. You don't need to do anything else."

I wasn't exactly experienced in overnight trips. Accidental overnights in somebody's bed—yeah. Those involved condoms, re-wearing whatever I'd shucked off around two a.m., and hoping the girl had mouthwash in her medicine cabinet or at least gum in her purse. If I was planning on an overnight with Pearl, I'd bring clean clothes, a toothbrush, and condoms. Damn straight, condoms. *Please God tell me I'm gonna need condoms.*

"Where are we going?" I'd never been so curious in my life— and that was saying a lot, because I was born curious.

She leaned her head back on my arm, black eyes gleaming in the darkness and lips curved into a playful grin. "That's a *surprise*,

Boyce Wynn." A welcome gust of wind off the gulf blew through the car, lifting one long curl across her face. It stuck on her lower lip and she reached to pull it away, and I was knocked sideways by how much I loved her. She must have seen the realization cross my face, because her hand slowed. Her smile faded. "What?"

I smoothed one finger between her brows. "I have a surprise of my own is all. I'll tell you this weekend."

"No fair."

I kissed her with every possessive, *damn the torpedoes* desire surging through me, my tongue sweeping through her mouth and caressing her shy little tongue, encouraging it to come out and play. When it darted out to tease my upper lip, I drew the tip into my mouth and gave it a soft, leisurely suck before allowing it to retreat back into her mouth. When I pulled back, she blinked up at me, winded and dazed.

"I never swore to play fair, sweetheart," I murmured.

• • • • • • • • • •

Dr. Frank called me Friday to tell me that he, his accountant, Barney Amos, and my mother had met and reached an agreement for a cash purchase of the property and everything on it. "We'll meet Monday afternoon to sign the papers and hand her a cashier's check. She's agreed that she and *Riley* will vacate the premises as soon as they have the check in hand." What he thought of Mom's boyfriend was plain, just in the way he spit that douchenozzle's name. Like it left a rotten taste in his mouth.

I knew the feeling. "I'd feel better if she was getting the money without him, but I guess that's her business."

"It is. I agree that he's a piece of work, but it's her decision what she puts up with—unless you've seen his ill-treatment turn physical."

Riley must've felt small, sitting there with a doctor, a lawyer, and an accountant—like he was the butt end of that joke. All it lacked was a bar and a punch line. When men like him felt small, they got meaner. He'd probably been all spit and swagger in front of them—lording over her.

"If I'd seen any evidence of that, he wouldn't have been at that meeting because he'd be in the hospital. If he smacks her around, they've both hidden it damn well from me."

"Damn shame when a woman puts up with that kind of treatment. I've seen it time and again in my line of work, but I'll never understand it." He heaved a sigh, switching gears. "So. Are you sure about purchasing Wynn's? I'm prepared to have you work for me instead, if you've had second thoughts about taking on that loan. Now's the time to speak up."

"No, sir. Truth is, I think abiding this hardship to get that garage has been a good thing, in a way. Instead of feeling that the place was dumped on me like a ton of bricks, I not only chose this, I'm gonna earn it. Thank you for offering me the ability to do that. I want Wynn's to be mine. I'm sure."

"All right then. Give me a couple weeks or so to get everything filed and clear, and we'll proceed with your loan from there."

• • • • • • • • • •

I'd insisted that Pearl text me when she left her house so I could walk directly out the door without her coming up to knock. Half an hour ago—when I started packing—I'd realized I had no luggage. In the back of my closet, behind the box of photos I'd gleaned from Dad's room, I unearthed my high school backpack. Luckily, I'd barely used it in high school, so it wasn't in the nasty shape it should have been. I was a grown man—going on an overnight trip who knows where—*stuffing my shit in a backpack.* Jesus.

I hitched it over my shoulder and said, "Back tomorrow," to Mom and Riley, who were sitting on the sofa, smoking. It wasn't yet noon, so they weren't roused enough to respond before I jerked the door shut behind me.

Pearl pulled up and popped the trunk on her little car. I tossed my backpack next to her leather duffle, which had some kind of initialed design all over it and probably cost more than a new set of tires.

"Have I ever driven you anywhere?" she asked when I folded myself into the passenger seat and slid it back so my knees weren't under my chin. She was a sight with her hair pulled into a ponytail, big dark sunglasses, and a little sundress showing off her smooth bronze legs and shoulders.

I slid my aviators on. "Nope."

"Well, settle in. We've got a three-and-a-half-hour drive—*after* we get off the ferry, which currently has a forty-five-minute line, according to the website."

Three point five hours… "Houston?"

She sighed. "Wow—yes. Bonus points for speed. I knew you'd figure it out once I got on 59, but sheesh. We aren't even to the first stoplight."

"Bonus points, eh? What exactly do these points go toward?" I asked. "I might want to rack up a few more before we reach our destination."

Sitting ramrod straight, her full pink lips pursed tight, she slid me a sidelong look over the top of her sunglasses and then scrutinized the road ahead like we were battling rush hour traffic.

"Maybe you won't need any points tonight."

Whatever smartass retort I might have prepared went up in flames.

It'd been years since I'd gone farther out of town than Corpus. The long stretches of highway with nothing for miles in every direction but grass and crops and cows felt cosmic—as if there was nothing beyond any of it but more of the same, forever. And then we'd go through a town so small that if you blinked you'd miss it, or I'd spy a big decrepit barn set back from the road—roof half caved in, paint peeling—and I'd think, *Somebody used to keep livestock in there and now they're all gone. Did they move? Die? Did they live a good life, out here in the middle of bumfuck nowhere?*

We stopped for gas and barbeque in Wharton.

"Still not going to tell me what we're doing in Houston?"

She took a huge bite of her turkey sandwich, a bit of barbeque sauce running down the side of her hand. "Uhn-uhnn." She licked the sauce off her hand—her pink tongue darting out to catch it before it got far—and I contemplated my potato salad like I was trying to figure out the recipe. God*damn*.

I took a bite of my sandwich. Took a sip of iced tea. "There's a game at Minute Maid Park tonight." I grinned. "Pirates are in town for a four-game series."

She scowled. "Dammit, Boyce!"

I lowered my sandwich. "Are you serious? We're going to a *baseball game*?" I couldn't stop my voice's inflection from climbing sky-high right at the end.

Her scowl melted and her words went soft. "Yeah. That was the surprise."

I shook my head. "What's that thing Mrs. Thompson used to say when one of her kids startled her, bringing unauthorized critters in the house... *Well butter my butt and call me a biscuit!*"

Pearl chuckled. "I didn't think actual people said that."

"Oh hell yeah—when Randy dragged a baby possum into the kitchen one time, she blurted it right out. That thing liked to gave her a coronary on the spot."

"Oh... my... *God*." She laughed until she snorted.

"I'm serious! I'm *surprised*—so bonus points for that. Not that you'll need 'em." I winked. "I aim to show you my sincere appreciation any damn way you want it."

She swallowed. "Just to remind you..." She leaned closer so the couple at the next table wouldn't hear. "It's broad daylight outside, and the parking lot is *really really small*."

"Guess you'll have to wait, then."

"Guess you will, too," she said, all wide-eyed innocence, sucking down the last of her iced tea through a straw I was suddenly *very* jealous of.

Pearl

Boyce was like a kid at Christmas—though as soon as I had that thought I couldn't bear to think what his Christmases must have been like.

When I pulled up to the valet at the Magnolia, he mumbled, "Holy shit," before he got out. I handed the valet the keys and Boyce grabbed the bags from the trunk. "S'ok, I got 'em," he told the impeccably uniformed porter who attempted to carry them to the front desk. He stood silently as I checked us in and didn't speak another word until I opened the door to the room. "Holy. Shit," he repeated, making no move to enter.

I walked in, heading for the window, and he followed. "Thomas and Mama always stay at the Magnolia whenever they're in Houston. I'm using their points for the room. This building is almost a hundred years old, and Minute Maid Park is"—I opened the drapes wide— "right there."

He came to stand next to me and we stared at the park.

"They let you do that? Use their points to stay with *me* this weekend?" He was still holding both bags, as if he might bolt right back out of the room with them.

I took them from him and set them aside. "They didn't want me staying at some seedy motel in the middle of Houston." I took his hands and leaned to put my chin on his chest. He stared down at me. "So… have you noticed the bed?" I asked. "The one right there behind me?"

His gaze flicked over my shoulder to look at it. "It's big."

I bit my lip at that straightforward observation and the way his eyes darted around the plush room. I wondered if he'd ever slept in a king-sized bed. Or seen one. He reminded me of Mama in New York on my parents' honeymoon—a bit overawed.

Distraction—that's what he needed. "We've got an hour until dinner reservations at an awesome steakhouse between here and the ballpark. Just don't wrinkle me."

His arms slid around my waist, dragging my hands behind my back, and that dark red brow angled up. "How do you propose I keep from doing that? Especially when I aim to toss you right in the middle of that bed in a couple seconds to build your appetite for round two later tonight."

I turned to hide my smug smile and pulled my heavy ponytail aside, and he slid the zipper down my back at an agonizingly slow pace. "I did say we only had an hour, right?"

He sped it to the bottom and spun me around to pull the dress down my arms. "I aim to please, ma'am."

"I believe you." I leaned up to kiss his scruffy chin. "So do I."

· · · · · · · · · ·

Over dinner, Boyce told me what Thomas was doing for him. I was so stunned and grateful and *happy* I started crying.

The waiter hovered politely out of earshot and Boyce leaned closer. "Why are you crying?"

"I just... You were going to leave town, and now you're not, and... I don't know. Because I'm happy?"

He shook his head. "So because you're happy, you're crying?"

I laughed once and patted my napkin under both eyes. "Yeah."

"Women do understand why men get confused over these kinda responses, right?"

"Of course not," I said. "We give you all the clues. You just have to read them."

He angled a brow. "That right there is a trap."

· · · · · · · · · ·

When I came out of the bathroom, Boyce had switched off all the lights but one. He sat in the middle of the bed in boxers and a gray tee, watching me cross the room. "Thank you for tonight," he said. "Nobody's ever done something like this for me."

I shook my humidity-defeated hair loose from the elastic and slid the band onto my wrist. Boyce's green eyes flared. I might lament my hair's irrepressible nature, but he liked it. He liked the glasses I was wearing too. Liked removing them, as if they were one more item of my clothing he was confiscating. I pulled at a coil of hair and twisted it around my finger, and his mouth tightened.

"I'm glad you had fun," I said. "Sorry they lost, though. At least it was just one point."

When he smirked, the action always came from his left side. Left eye crinkled at the corner. Left corner of his mouth angled like it was pointing at something. One barely-there dimple in his left cheek. He ducked his chin, staring, and my whole body strained forward, needing his touch.

"A one-run loss is aggravating, but they lose a *lot*. Us diehards are conditioned to it. Watching that game live and in person—being there with all the other fans—it was fucking awesome. I don't even care who won."

"Is that true?"

"Okay, not the last part. A win would have been nice. Shocking and miraculous, but nice. Everything else is true, though." He angled his head as I put both palms on the bed and then a knee. "Is that... my shirt?"

I crawled onto the bed, wearing the green-sleeved baseball tee he'd used to wrap that lightning whelk shell in years ago. It hung to mid-thigh and the sleeves—three-quarter length on him—were almost at my wrists unless I rolled them up. "Maaaaybe."

He reached for me and I took his hand.

"I have something I want to discuss," I said. "It's about..." *The night after.* My heart balked and the words jammed in my throat. It had been four years. Maybe I didn't want to talk about it.

"About...?" he prompted, pulling me to sit on my knees, facing him.

"That night, on the beach—"

"Stop." He brushed the ridge of my knuckles with one finger, traced zigzags up each digit to the short, unpolished nail and back. "I know what you think you saw that night. No. What you *saw*." He tucked a bent finger beneath my chin to coax my gaze up to his and held it there with the urgency in his eyes. "Sweetheart, there was no one but you that day. That night. That summer. And every single day since then.

"Nothing had happened with that girl and nothing would have. Nothing *did*, even when you ran off. I was high—we were all high— but I'd been waiting for you, hoping you'd show. I couldn't see anyone else. I wanted to call, tell you how I couldn't stop thinking about you. But I was following the stupidest advice guys have ever passed around—*don't call too soon. Don't look too eager.*

"I thought a little weed would take the edge off. When I saw the look on your face—" His jaw tightened and his hand curled around my chin. "You didn't see me come after you, did you?"

I shook my head, forgiveness filling me up, ready to overflow and saturate us both.

"I don't know how long I looked for you that night. There were so many people, and I was so ignorantly fucking *stoned*." He ran a hand over his face and sighed. "And then it took a few days before I wised up and thought *fuck the guy rules*—because they could never apply to who you were for me. But by then you'd left town for that internship. When you came back, it was like that morning had never happened. I convinced myself that I wasn't good enough for you and never would be."

My eyes filled. "Boyce—"

"I hurt you that night, and I'm sorry. I can't promise you I'll never be an idiot because I'll probably be one before the end of this conversation, but goddammit, I swear I'll never hurt you like that again."

He stroked a thumb over my lips and leaned to kiss me. I opened to him, my last fear dispelled.

"I talked to Maxfield about you when he was here last month." He slid my glasses off and put them on the nightstand.

"You did?"

"I did. He told me if I love you not to fucking give up."

Oh. "Do you?" I whispered.

"Love you? Oh hell yeah. When I pulled you out of that ocean, you woke up and stared up at me like I was worth something. I fell for you right then and there. You're the only woman I've ever loved, Pearl. It's you for me or no one."

"But I'm leaving in three weeks. I'll be gone for nine months."

He skimmed his warm hands up my forearms, pushing the sleeves to my elbows. "It's a four-hour drive, baby, not the moon. I'll go there. You'll come here. And I'll wait. Nine months is nothing when I plan to hold on to you for the rest of my life."

Twenty-seven

BOYCE

Thanks to our predinner warm-up on that goddamned amazing bed, I figured round two could be unhurried. I wanted to mosey over every soft curve. I wanted to savor the taste of her because Christ, every square inch of her tasted so good. I would lay her down and plunder that sweet, willing mouth until she said my name like a prayer.

"C'mere, you little thief." I pulled her onto my lap. Her naked backside slid onto my bare thigh and answered my question about what was under that seven-years-missing shirt of mine. "I'm done talking." I leaned to outline the curve of her ear with my tongue. "Except for a little dirty play-by-play detailing all the ways I intend to fuck you, that is," I whispered, and her mouth fell open on a soft moan.

"Wait," she breathed. "I have one more thing to say."

I was gut-kicked when I leaned back and saw tears in her eyes, and I held myself stock-still. If I could have stopped breathing, I would have.

She took a deep breath. "I love you too."

I processed her tears in relation to those words—words I'd been waiting two weeks to hear her say sober. "So this is one of those *happy* crying things, right?"

She choked a laugh. "Yes."

The relief broke over me and I grinned. "See? *Learning*."

"Is that a Wynn-win?" she asked.

She giggled when I arched a brow. I'd all but forgotten the dumbass self-pun I'd invented in high school. "You did *not* just say that. First, though, this stolen shirt you're wearing. This was my favorite shirt, you know. *For shame*, young lady. I should turn you over my knee."

Her eyes widened. I wasn't sure which I'd done more—shocked her or turned her on. Hopefully a bit of both.

"As I recall, Boyce Wynn, you *gave* this shirt to me."

I looked her over—lying back in my arms, her head braced against my bicep. *Smirking.*

"I reckon I did leave it on your front porch." I chewed my lip as if I was considering her line of reasoning. "And it does look better on you than it ever did on me, though I looked pretty damned hot in it, judging by the looks you'd sneak at me from across the lab table."

I reached to sketch a finger down the side of her face, skirting under her jaw and down her throat. I traced the line of her collarbone to her arm and down to the ring finger on her left hand. *Forever* stretched out in front of us in a way it never had. My desire for her, my need of her, had rocketed right past this moment and into the distance as far as I could see.

I'd seen Arianna fall apart and shut down when we lost Brent, and it took her a while to come back from that dark place. She'd thrown herself into her work, and a few years ago, Buddy, nearing seventy, transitioned ownership of the tattoo parlor to her. She seemed content with her life, though she did tell me once, "I'm probably never going to be a mommy, so I'm counting on you to give me a niece or nephew to spoil someday." I didn't even know how the fuck to respond to that sentence. When my brother died, she was only twenty-five, but she had never let anyone else in, and I guess I could understand why.

As much of a nightmare as Dover's high school shit had been, Maxfield had gotten over her bitch ass by the time he left for college. But for three years running, he didn't say much about anyone when he came home. I'd known he had friends there, but he was a natural loner. I figured that damned cat might be as close as anyone would ever get until Jacqueline—the girl who made him smile like a dog with a T-bone at just the thought of her.

Mateo and Yvette Vega were the real deal—high school lovers made good. They'd been together since a game of spin-the-bottle paired them up in fourth grade. I was close enough to the action to know how close they came to losing it though. Vega had swaggered since he could walk, but he was one loyal son of a bitch. If he'd fucked up with Yvette, he'd have never forgiven himself.

Along her collarbone, Arianna had two thinly scripted tattoos. On her right: *Life is fragile*. On her left: *Love is risk*. I knew both of these things to be true, but the thought of losing the girl in my arms through my own idiocy outweighed every threat of how life could take her or how she might leave me.

"Hey," she said, her hand rubbing slow circles over my heart. "Where'd you go?"

Her hair was a wild waterfall, tumbling over my arm to pool on the white comforter. She'd given in to the muggy coastal heat and, I suspected, the way I wound those silky coils around my fingers anytime I got the chance. Her eyes gleamed, fastened on mine, dark as night. I stared, and she stared back, her small hand still massaging my stinging heart, like she was bringing me to life. Maybe she was.

"Nowhere, sweetheart." I inched the shirt's hem up and let the fabric catch a taut nipple. "I'm right here." I made slow loops around that stiff little bud with a fingertip. "I think I could be persuaded to pardon the loss of my shirt on one condition."

"Wh-what's that?" She panted.

I laid her flat and kissed her, wrists caught above her head and that shirt of mine bunched up and out of the way. As I took one rosy nipple in my mouth and inched my hand south at leisurely pace, she began murmuring soft, tempting pleas. I kissed down the center of her chest and dipped my tongue into the tiny hollow of her navel on my way down, parting her thighs and kneeling between them. Her breath quickened when I drifted lower to kiss her stomach. "Now where were we...?"

"Your c-condition?"

I shucked my T-shirt and shorts, ripped the condom package open and rolled it on, slowing at the raw fascination in her eyes as she watched me. "Spoke too soon," I mumbled. I lay over her, kissing her. "No conditions."

Her hands skimmed over my hipbones, fingers digging into the flexing muscles, thumbs caressing the sensitive spots she'd located on either side of my happy trail that I hadn't known existed until she found them.

"I want you," she whispered between kisses.

"Take what you want from me then. It's been yours all along."

She took me at my word, sliding her hands to my hips and pulling me in, hard. When I rocked into her, I was convinced we could've powered the whole city of Houston on the surge we generated.

• • • • • • • • • •

Monday afternoon, Mom and Riley came home from the title company and packed their shit into the bed of his truck. They hadn't brought much. They'd sold her coupe to a wholesale dealer for a few hundred bucks because they'd just received a cashier's check for six figures. Thinking themselves loaded, they were headed back to Amarillo to show off.

Odds they'd blow through that money inside a year? Pretty damned high.

Riley leaned on the truck, smoking, while Mom came to talk to me in the garage. Sam had gone for the day before they'd returned, so it was just the two of us.

"You're welcome to stay, Mom. He's not," I said, qualifying the statement, "but you are." I forced myself to uncross my arms and hook my thumbs in my jean pockets. My offer was genuine, and I didn't want my aversion to her taste in men to make it look insincere.

"I appreciate that, Boyce. But a woman needs a man in this world—or at least I do. It's too bad you had to meet Riley under these circumstances. I think y'all woulda got along otherwise. He can be nice. He's just a little overly distrustful and protective is all."

Uh-huh. I didn't reply. Absolutely nothing would ever make me like that arrogant, snake-in-the-grass fucker. If he was protective of anything, it was first and foremost his own welfare.

"It's real lucky I got a buyer who's interested in the garage, you know," she said then. "So you can keep your job." *As if she'd hunted down an investor herself, making sure he'd look after* my *interests.* Somewhere in her head, she maybe even believed her own bullshit.

I had no mind to divulge anything about the secondary purchase that would occur in two or three weeks. Dr. Frank's offer to me was literally none of her business.

Riley had apparently finished his smoke, because he honked the truck horn. "C'mon, Ruthanne!" he hollered out the window. "We're burnin' daylight."

She reached to hug me and it was just plain weird. Like hugging a stranger, but sadder. I reckoned I should tell her I loved her, but it wouldn't come and I couldn't say those words where they weren't meant. I wasn't sure what I felt about her one way or the other.

"Have a safe trip home—or wherever."

"We thought we'd run up to Eagle's Pass for a few days before we head north."

I frowned. "The casino?"

"Don't look like that—Jesus H. Christ, you're as judgmental as your brother was. Riley likes to do a little gambling now and then. So what? We deserve some fun."

Because of how hard you both work? I bit back.

She reached up to lay her hand on my face. "Take care now. I'll let you know where we land—maybe you can come visit."

"Okay, Mom," I said. I studied her face, tried to commit it to memory, but five minutes after she left all I could remember was how she looked when I was a kid—laughing, screaming, cowering from my father's hand. Promising my fifteen-year-old brother she'd let him know where she was, right before she walked out the door.

I wouldn't be holding my breath for that call. Not this time.

Pearl

I'd always scheduled social engagements around academics. While high school friends thought this indicated a harebrained dedication to my education, in college my peculiar lifestyle choice was less peculiar. Most of my friends were either equally studious or they comprehended the reason I was when the term ended and I'd netted another 4.0 semester.

Mel's questions: "What about *parties*? College is all about parties."

That was one of the things I'd loved about being in a sorority—whole semesters of events were planned in advance. I set calendar reminders for all scheduled events, along with course project due dates and exams. If something spontaneous came up and I could fit it in, great. If it would interfere, I begged off. No one cared.

"But what about *boys*?"

Please. There's never in the history of boys been a shortage of the ones willing to hook up at the drop of a *What's up?* text.

"Okay, but what about actual relationships?"

I'd never craved the company of any of my boyfriends when they weren't around—not Mitchell or Geoffrey or the two or three who didn't last long enough to become official. I wasn't impatient for the next text, wasn't anticipating the next touch. I didn't get why anyone felt like that, ever. From the outside, that kind of attachment resembled obsession. Like an unhealthy fixation. Like *Get some therapy, ASAP*.

Now here I was, utterly infatuated—with a guy I'd known practically *all my life*. I wanted to spend every waking minute with him. When I wasn't with him, I contemplated the next time I would be. I *daydreamed* about him. I had never daydreamed about anyone. *In. My. Life.* I told myself that this preoccupation was all due to the novelty of it. That it would wear off eventually, and I would be able to get through a few hours in a row without thinking about him.

And then I wondered if I wanted that to happen.

I'd worked an evening shift for six of the twelve days Boyce and I had been official. Our first two evenings out consisted of dinner or driving into Corpus to see a movie, after which I would go home so I could study. I knew he wanted to make a good impression on Mama and Thomas—not asking me back to his place to spend the night, *or at all*. But when he brought me home, he'd lean back on his Trans Am, slide his arms around me, haul me onto my toes and kiss me good-night until I wanted to shove him into his own backseat in my parents' driveway.

And then came last Friday. Six days since our weekend in Houston. I couldn't take it anymore. When I got in his car, I said, "I was thinking burgers and beer tonight."

He nodded, pulling onto the road. "Sounds good. Got a place in mind?"

I fussed with the seat belt and dug around in my bag, striving to sound offhand. "Maybe Whataburger… and beer out of your fridge?" I felt his eyes on me but pretended I didn't for fear of blurting out something far too candid. Something like *Forget the food—drive straight to your place and take me to bed.*

His hand tightened on the wheel as if he could read the subtext under those words. "All right."

When we got back to his place, he switched on the lamp in the living room, dropping his keys and sunglasses on the end table while I went to the kitchen, flipped the switch on the dinette's light, and pulled plates from the cabinet. Boyce took ketchup and beer from the fridge and reached around me to set the bottles on the table, silent. Inches separated us. I felt the heat of him behind me like a furnace and I shivered, wanting to turn into his arms but frozen with confusion over his six days of gallant behavior.

I didn't want gallant from Boyce. I wanted his rough, commanding hands on me. I wanted the boy who couldn't pass me in our high school hallway without leering. Who'd noticed any sliver of visible skin that was usually hidden. Who'd loved making me bite the inside of my cheek to keep from laughing at his outrageous, uncouth outbursts while teachers fumed and well-mannered classmates rolled their eyes.

When his big hands gently grasped my shoulders, my breath hitched.

"Pearl?" His warm breath fanned over my ear. His thumbs hooked under the straps of my tank and caressed a lazy line, back and forth.

A powerful tremor shot through me and he stepped closer, his hands sliding down my arms to press my hands to the table. His body bracketed mine, his boots on either side of my canvas flats, his long legs and arms holding me in place against the table.

Enveloped by him, I slanted my head back onto his chest and closed my eyes, willing him to continue. His hands left mine and stole beneath my top—warm palms on cool skin. They slid up over my rib cage and my lace-covered breasts. Inhaling slowly, the tip of his nose following the line of my pulse, he kissed his way to the base of my throat. He hummed one sound on exhale, low and deep, lips progressing back the way they came, hands tightening on my breasts.

"Perfect," he murmured, taking my earlobe between his lips and sucking, his tongue stroking.

I was grateful my hands were braced on the table because my knees buckled.

His hands fell to my waist and unfastened my shorts. In two seconds, his fingers slid into me. "God*damn*. So *wet*." His words were hoarse, bringing me to the brink.

I pressed my bottom against his hard, denim-swathed length in combination of mute plea and invitation—I wanted him inside me. *Just like this, right now.*

He pushed my shorts and underwear lower bit by bit, squeezing and worshipping the flesh I'd never celebrated as I did in that moment. "So fucking beautiful. I want to take my time loving you, but—"

My shorts fell to my ankles, panties trailing after, tickling my calves.

"*Jesus*, Pearl."

I almost cheered when I heard his zipper lower, felt his skin against my hip.

And then, "Shit—I have to get—"

"I renewed my prescription," I said. "You can—you don't have to—" *Gah. Why was it so awkward to just say, "I'm on birth control! Carry on!"*

But I'd forgotten—this was Boyce. He didn't need a roadmap.

He raised me to my toes, pressed my elbows to the table with one arm angled across my chest to keep me just above the flat surface, and guided himself into me. His growl of satisfaction, the way he held me and filled me and the fact that he was leaning me *over a kitchen table* all joined forces to pitch me over the edge. I was convulsing around him by the second thrust.

"That's my girl," he rasped, following me.

After that moment, we were like a couple of unsupervised sixteen-year-olds who had just discovered sex. We rushed through dates to give ourselves more time at his place after. No surface was off-limits, no position too contorted to try, even if we ended up laughing like idiots and abandoned two or three attempts as failed experiments, happily finishing in more familiar positions.

Last night, we hadn't actually made it into the trailer first. We pulled onto the gravel driveway and were kissing before our seat belts were off.

SWEET

Boyce's eyes burned when I slid onto the center console and then backward into the back seat. He crawled over after me and with some maneuvering we ended with me astride his lap, my flouncy skirt barely covering my thighs, shirt unbuttoned, front-closure bra open, his hands beneath the skirt, opening his fly and guiding my hips, his mouth alternately kissing and sucking until I came so hard my toes numbed.

As he caught his breath, head resting back against the seat top, he chuckled. "What in the world made you do that? And for the record that is *not* a complaint."

I cuddled against his chest. "I've never done it in a car before," I admitted.

He tipped my face up, caressing my cheek. "Well, sweetheart, you just earned the award for best backseat fuck I've ever had." He kissed me. "I can't clearly remember having done it before, in fact."

"Good," I said, my tone prim, as if I'd harrumphed the word.

He laughed and I scowled.

"Let's go inside and I'll make up for being a tactless jackass. I'm making you dessert tonight." He fastened my bra, buttoned my shirt, mostly, and stuffed my underwear into his front pocket. "I bought ice cream. And chocolate syrup. And whipped cream. And cherries. Wait till you see what I got planned for those cherries."

I blinked, my brain filling in the blanks.

He grinned, fingers stroking up and down my thighs on either side of his. "Um-hmm—that's right. When I said I'm making you dessert? I meant I'm making you *into* dessert. And I'm going to enjoy devouring every fucking delicious bit of you."

I got home late and studied into the wee hours of the night, not caring one whit that I was missing sleep for every extra minute I spent with him. Retraining myself to concentrate in class was difficult but doable. Wiping the smile off my face when I thought about him was impossible. In days, I would be moving away for nine months. I had time enough then to learn to endure long weeks without him.

• • • • • • • • • •

Thursday afternoon the doorbell rang. I was expecting a box of textbooks I'd ordered for fall, and our mail carrier always came in the afternoon, so I didn't check before opening the door—an action I instantly regretted.

"Mitchell? What are you doing here?"

"I texted you and you didn't answer. I called you and didn't get your voice mail. Which means you blocked me. You *blocked me*."

I'd seen Mitchell angry, but there was more to this than anger. His eyes were bloodshot, and bulging like overinflated balloons. He filled the doorway, hands braced on the frame.

Mitchell was usually put-together—laundry-pressed shirts, hair styled. But his blue button-down had a visible stain on the pocket and was beyond rumpled—so creased it looked as if he'd slept in it. His hair was lank, hanging over his forehead.

He should have been immersed in medical school coursework and studying and team-building—not driving fifteen hours, one way, to confront an ex-girlfriend who'd broken up with him seven months ago. There was no reason—*no reason*—for him to be *here*. A spear of dread cut through me, and despite the heat, I battled the urge to wrap my arms around my chest. I tried not to cower visibly.

"I wasn't trying to hurt you." I swallowed and took a deep breath, striving for calm. "I asked you not to contact me again. If you'd complied with that request, you wouldn't have known you were blocked."

"What if I needed you? What if I had an emergency and I needed you?"

I shook my head. "You don't *need* me," I said, attempting to soothe his agitation. "You have your family. You have friends—"

"I don't have *anything* thanks to you."

"What—what does that even mean? We *broke up.* I said I wished you well and I meant that, but I don't owe you my time, I don't owe you my emotional support, and I *don't* owe you any further explanations." Annoyance doused my desire to pacify his baseless fury. "It's *over*. Please leave."

I moved to shut the door and he blocked it with a shoulder and shoved it open. It bounced into the wall from the impact, and I flinched and stepped back. Tux shot up the staircase behind me and I found myself wishing he knew how to dial 911. No one else was home.

I backed across the foyer, judging my options. I had three. My first instinct was to try to get around him, make it out the wide-open front door and scream for neighbors instead of retreating deeper into the house, but I'd have to practically go *through* him. He wasn't as big as Boyce, but he was a man. *Nope.*

I could run through the kitchen and mudroom and into the garage, but I'd have to hit the button to raise the garage door. Mitchell was a runner. If he was right behind me—and he would be—he could easily reverse the door and I'd be trapped.

Option three: get to the keypad in the kitchen and press the panic button, which would call the security company.

Without another thought, I took off for the kitchen. I swatted a barstool over and heard him trip over it, cursing, as I jammed the panic button. He caught up and grabbed at my arm when the phone rang seconds later—probably the security company calling to ask the nature of the emergency or the code in case someone had pushed the button accidentally.

I only managed to knock the handset off its base before Mitchell threw both arms around me, imprisoning my arms at my sides. The phone skittered across the counter, still ringing. If no one answered, they were supposed to send the sheriff, the volunteer fire department, and probably an ambulance. I stomped Mitchell's instep, and he grunted and loosened his grip enough for me to elbow him in the gut. I lunged out of his grasp, turning to run for the front door.

That was when we heard the rack of a shotgun and Mama's voice at the door to the mudroom. "Get back, *pendejo*." She leveled the barrel directly at his chest.

I reversed course and ran to stand behind her. Mitchell glared, hands half-mast, but didn't move.

I was eight or nine when Mama bought the Remington 870. We were making dinner one night when we heard a knock at the front door. She looked out the window, didn't recognize the guy selling candy door-to-door, and called, "No thank you." Furious that she wouldn't open the door, he banged his fist against it for five minutes, shouting racial slurs. We'd both started at the slightest noise for weeks after, and I'd taken to sleeping in her bed, too scared to be in my room alone.

So she did something she'd sworn to never do—she bought a gun and we both took lessons. It hadn't been used for anything but target practice since.

"Get out of my house," Mama said, nothing in her voice negating her willingness to unload a round of buckshot in his direction.

Mitchell's face held a tempest, barely contained. He backed out of the kitchen, but he sneered his last words as though my mother wasn't shepherding him out the door with the barrel of a shotgun aimed at his chest. "I thought you gave up Vanderbilt and *threw me away* because you wanted to do marine biology. Not because you wanted to fuck that trailer trash."

A siren sounded in the distance as he bolted out the door. We heard his car squealing out of the cul-de-sac as Mama locked the front door and I ran to the window. He was gone. *It's a good thing I wasn't holding that shotgun,* I thought. *I'd have shot him.*

BOYCE

When I collected overdue weed payments for Rick Thompson in high school, I got downright gifted at judging who was going to be a problem and who would cave after one look at my size or Maxfield's merciless expression. When Pearl's ex showed up at the garage, I didn't waste time deliberating over likely whys and wherefores. Mitchell Upstone was going to be a problem. That was plain.

Sam and I were in the middle of her first supervised solo engine replacement—something she'd been looking forward to all summer. I prayed to God she didn't set off on a rant at the sudden change in plans.

"Samantha, there's really nothing more for you to do today. Call your daddy and go on home. I'll see you tomorrow."

"What?" she said, her bristly blond head whipping up, a squall brewing in her gray eyes. She must've learned to read me in the past few weeks, though, because she tugged her phone from the pocket of her overalls and dialed, sneaking a surly glimpse at our unwelcome visitor.

When Sam's dad pulled up, Upstone quit pretending to examine my tools and read my certificates and gave me his full attention. The look he gave me was cold-blooded—no expression to speak of. No scowl, no narrowing of his eyes. His eyes looked dead, matter-of-fact, and that was a cause for concern, because his true interest didn't lie with me and we both knew it.

I waved a hand to Mr. Adams and Sam as they drove away. Wiping engine grease from my fingers, I got straight to the point, my tone all false calm. "We got business, motherfucker?"

He angled his head. "You remember who I am?"

"Yeah, I remember who you are. You're Pearl's *ex*. So I'm wondering what the fuck you're doing here." *Here in our town and here at my place of business.*

"I came to see Pearl, of course. I hadn't realized until I got here that I've been an idiot, not realizing you and Pearl were fucking around all this time. I get it now. I get it, and I'm here to… *encourage* you to cease and desist."

I'd advanced one step of the fifteen feet or so between us before he reached into the back of his waistband and whipped out a pistol he'd hidden under his slept-in shirt. He held it low, but it was aimed at my chest, and he'd removed the safety and cocked it without looking at it, which meant he knew what he was doing. *Fuck.*

"What's the weapon for, Upstone?" My hands balled into fists at my sides.

He flinched at my use of his name. "It's just here to inspire you to listen instead of react in what I imagine is your customary Neanderthal manner. I'd like us to have a chat about Pearl. What is and isn't acceptable going forward."

I hated her name in his mouth. "And you've run this by her?"

He chuckled, and I wanted to bash his face in. "She's mulling it over at the moment."

Everything stilled. "So you've seen her today."

"Saw her today, saw her leaving here last night… After the two of you *fucked* each other for two hours in that shitty trailer you call home—I assume. Highly unlikely you were having a philosophical discussion."

I calculated the last time I'd heard from her—a couple of hours ago when she was leaving class. She was due at work in three hours.

"Where is she now?"

His slow smile made the monster inside me bend the bars on the cage I'd put him in. "Oh, I imagine she's still at home."

"You need to understand something, Upstone. You hurt Pearl, I'll kill you."

He chuckled as if I was too simple to understand what was going down. "I love her. I wouldn't hurt her. Oh—did she tell you otherwise?" He laughed again. "She likes to be the center of attention, that girl."

Right.

A car drove by, and his stance faltered slightly. "Let's go inside the trailer, Wynn. You can give me a *tour* of your extensive property."

"Let's not. Whatever we have to discuss, we can discuss here." I'd never wanted to wipe a grin off anyone's face so badly.

"Oh, I don't think so. Inside, now, or I'll have to revert to my secondary plan, and I'd really rather not do that. And in case you're wondering? I'm an excellent shot."

"Planning on shooting me, then?"

His jaw flexed. He was getting more riled with me by the second. "The firearm is just here to level the playing field between us—self-defense, you understand. That said, only a pussy-assed moron carries a gun he has no intention of firing to a conversation with a belligerent redneck." He gestured toward the trailer with the barrel. "But let's talk. Maybe we can reach an agreement that will work for all of us."

That lying sack of shit didn't intend to reach anything but my elimination, but there'd be no happily ever after with Pearl if he was wanted for *murder*. As batshit as he was, he knew that much. She was in danger of this sociopath's delusions, and I was the only thing standing between the two of them.

I walked to the trailer and he followed a few feet behind. Even so, I could feel the barrel of that gun like it was jammed right into the middle of my back.

Pearl

Sheriff Walker wasn't all that impressed with the fact that my ex had shown up and shouldered his way into the house, tried to keep me from calling 911, and had to be persuaded to leave at gunpoint. He was equally unimpressed that we hadn't gotten a license plate number or the make and model of his car. Mama saw a blue sedan in the driveway when she pulled in, so I knew he wasn't driving the white Corolla he'd had while we were undergrads.

Walker heaved an overworked, underpaid sigh. "Look. These sorta squabbles happen all the time with young folks—boys with too much testosterone and pretty girls who like to be the focus of a little drama—until it gets out of hand."

I clenched my fists in my lap. "We broke up months ago, and I *do not welcome drama*."

He raised his unkempt brows and quirked his mouth knowingly as if to say, *Sure you don't—and yet here we are.*

"*Idiota*," Mama mumbled, her posture mirroring mine.

My phone alert sounded—a text from Sam. I typed in my lock code three times before I got it right; my fingers felt like prosthetics.

> Sam: Some weird guy showed up at Wynn's and Boyce made me leave early. He called me Samantha and he never calls me that. They didn't seem friendly and I didn't recognize the guy. He looked like he needed a shower BAD. I couldn't get a pic of him without being really obvious. I took this pic of his car and plates though.

My hands shook. "I have the car and plates. It's from Tennessee—maybe a rental. He's at my boyfriend's business."

Sheriff Walker rolled his eyes. "All right then, lemme have it." He scribbled down the information and called it in, and I texted my thanks to Sam and then texted Boyce: You okay?

Sam answered me: No problem.

Boyce didn't.

"*Jesus H. Christ.*" Sheriff Walker shot out of the velvet-upholstered parlor chair, his phone still pressed to his ear, and Mama and I stood with him. "Call Bobby over at San Patricio—we may need backup. I'll meet you at Wynn's." His mouth twisted in contrition, he turned back to us. "Well young lady, your ex is wanted in Nashville—assault and battery at the least, possibly attempted murder. He's armed and dangerous. Sounds like you were lucky today."

I didn't believe in luck, but in that moment, I wished I did. Mama crossed herself—which I'd never seen her do outside of church—and sat back down.

"Excuse me, I need a drink of water," I said. I walked to the kitchen, picked up my keys, passed through the mudroom and into the garage. The garage door was still up and the sheriff's car was parked in the drive behind Mama's car, not mine.

No one ran outside when I backed down the drive and turned onto the road. *Sorry, Mama*, I thought, switching the stereo off so I could consider my course of action. If anyone could talk Mitchell down, it was me. If I had to lie and say I would take him back or go with him, I would.

My phone rang— *Mama*. I turned the sound off, but it continued to light up impotently during the last mile. I parked on the street outside Boyce's place, behind the blue sedan with Tennessee plates. The doors to the garage were up and a car, hood raised, sat in one of the bays. I took a deep breath and listened for any sounds coming from inside the trailer—shouting, shots.

Nothing.

I was halfway across the yard when the front door of the small wood-framed house next door flew open. "Don't go in there, young lady!" the old lady called, huddled in her doorway. Mrs. Echols, Boyce's crabby neighbor. "C'mere now!" She waved a thin arm commandingly.

I wavered and she renewed her appeal, her arm circling like a windmill on speed. Her next words froze me in place.

"I heard a shot! The sheriff's on his way—I called him. That boy of yours wouldn't want you getting shot doing something *stupid*. Let the lawmen get shot at. That's their *job*, and they've got their own firearms to answer with."

Right on cue, the sheriff and a deputy arrived simultaneously from opposite directions and parked nose to nose. I expected them to cross the yard and burst through the door, but they crouched in the street behind one of the cars, discussing how to proceed.

Before I could process their lack of action, Randy pulled into his driveway, taking in the two law-enforcement personnel in the street, Mrs. Echols in her doorway, and me halfway between her door and Boyce's. He crossed the street, forehead creased. "What's going on, Pearl?"

I hadn't realized I was crying. "My ex is in there with Boyce, and Mrs. Echols heard a shot, and Mitchell is armed and wanted in Nashville for attempted murder—"

Mrs. Echols gasped and Randy muttered a harsh, "Goddamn." He shook his head at the two men on the other side of the squad cars, who didn't look as if they planned to storm the trailer anytime soon. "All right then. Fuck it." He pointed at me. "*Stay. Here.* I fucking mean it."

We heard an ambulance's siren in the distance. Randy took a deep breath, shook his arms as if he was shaking off excess nerves, and took off for the front door. The deputy noticed him just before he went inside. "Hey!" he called, poking his head up over the roof of the squad car.

Five seconds later, Randy threw the front door wide. "Officers! They're both down!"

I ran for the front door with the sheriff and deputy, guns drawn, right behind me.

"Pearl, honey, you don't want to—" Randy said.

I bolted around him.

Neither man appeared conscious. As my eyes adjusted to the dim interior, I saw that Mitchell—a gun on the floor beside him— looked as if he'd been run over by a truck. And then I saw the pool of blood around Boyce. Randy and I went to our knees beside him.

"Shirt," I said, and he stripped off his tee. I wadded it and pressed it to the still-flowing wound in Boyce's side. "Hold that—press hard."

Randy complied and I searched for a pulse. It was weak, but there.

"*Ohthankgod*. Boyce? Can you hear me?"

"Ambulance on its way," the deputy said, taking pics before bagging the gun and casing.

"I take it this one is your ex," the sheriff said, gesturing to Mitchell. I nodded. "Call for a second ambulance for that fucker," he told the deputy. "Let's get the homeowner seen to first."

The EMTs rushed inside seconds later, praised Randy for stemming the blood flow, and replaced the blood-soaked T-shirt with proper bandages while checking and recording vitals. Boyce didn't come to, not even when they lifted him onto a stretcher, but he jolted awake outside during the minute or so it took them to get the ambulance ready to receive him.

"Pearl?" he said, his voice gruff, pained.

I leaned above him to shade his face from the sun overhead, holding his cold hand between both of mine. "I'm here. Mitchell's in custody. I'm so sorry—"

He squeezed my hand weakly, his voice so soft I had to lean close to hear him. "S'okay, baby." He squinted one eye open, beautiful and bright green. "Guardian angel. Remember?"

A soft sob escaped me and I swallowed it back. "Yes. My guardian angel. Man I adore. Please don't leave me, Boyce."

"Sweetheart, if and when I leave you, it won't be by my choice. I'll love you straight on through eternity." He blinked groggily but, true to form, kept talking. "Would this be a good time to tell you I wanna marry you someday? I wanna give you babies and a home and lay you down and love you every night. If I live and that bullet didn't pierce anything essential to doing those things, that is."

I choked a laugh. "Boyce, you idiot. Your *man parts* are fine."

He closed his eyes and sighed tiredly, his grip on my hand weakening. "Thank Christ."

At the hospital, Randy identified me as Boyce's fiancée, his mouth turning up on one side when my brows shot up. "Next of kin," he mumbled. *Ah.*

I cleared my throat and smiled. "Yes, I'm Mr. Wynn's fiancée."

Hospital personnel gave me Boyce's wallet and boots—his clothes were evidence in the impending criminal charges against Mitchell. I filled out paperwork while waiting for news from the ER doctor, who emerged just as Thomas and Mama tore into the waiting room and attached themselves to opposite sides of me.

"He was hemodynamically stable on arrival," the admitting doctor told us, and I felt Thomas relax next to me. "The wounds were tangential—bullet went straight through—so we opted against laparotomy. We'll keep him here on watch for at least twenty-four hours, but assuming he holds steady and surgery remains unnecessary, he could be discharged tomorrow. He'll need assistance at home for a bit, of course, but his prognosis is excellent." He squeezed my shoulder, smiling. "Never hurts when they're young and healthy to start with."

"When can I see him?" I asked.

"Few minutes. The nurse will take you back."

"Thank you, doctor," Thomas said. His smile faded when he turned to me. "You scared us to death, Pearl! What were you thinking, driving over there ahead of the sheriff—what if you'd been shot?" His voice broke and he pulled me into his arms. "Dammit, little girl…"

He pulled Mama in too, and we stood in an emotional little

huddle in the middle of the waiting room.

"I'm sorry," I mumbled into his chest.

He sighed. "No, you're not."

We laughed and he held me tighter. He knew me too well.

· · · · · · · · · ·

Texas and Tennessee grappled with who would charge Mitchell with attempted murder first—first-degree in Texas and second-degree in Tennessee, where he'd nearly strangled a fellow student to death in a fit of rage the evening before he showed up at my door. The details were still emerging, but news reports said they'd gone out once or twice and he became enraged when she told him she wasn't interested in seeing him anymore. He'd gone to her apartment with a gun. They argued and he choked her until she lost consciousness. Her roommate—also a med-school student—hid in a closet until he ran out the door. She called 911 and did CPR until help arrived, saving her friend's life.

He'd come straight to Texas. Straight for me. I didn't even know he owned a gun. I didn't know if he'd had it on him when he came into the house—when Mama confronted him. I felt ill thinking how much uglier that situation could have been.

I sat next to Boyce, his hospital bed angled halfway between lying and sitting, as he told the sheriff what had transpired from the moment Mitchell stepped foot on the property to the last thing he remembered. He pulled at the thin hospital gown, and judging from the way it stretched across his chest and hid nothing of his defined arms, I assumed it resembled a long, split-down-the-back shirt.

"I knew the only chance I had was right after we went into the trailer. When it's sunny out, you're half-blind for a minute or two after going inside. Soon as he shut the door, I turned and tackled him. I heard the shot but honest to God, I didn't feel a thing. I grabbed his wrist and elbow and busted his forearm over my knee—"

"Boy howdy, you sure did—you snapped his damn ulna!" Sheriff Walker snorted a laugh.

"Huh. Well, then I just beat the shit out of him until I started feeling woozy, which was when I felt the bite of those bullet holes and saw the blood. I hit him one more time, and then I guess I passed out."

"You lost quite a bit of blood, son, but he wasn't going *nowhere* after the pounding you gave him. He looked like he fell down a long flight of concrete steps and landed on his face."

From the toothy grin and literal knee-slapping glee that followed, I guessed Sheriff Walker would have paid good money to see that fight.

The whole account made my stomach churn. The way Boyce had looked on that floor—pale and still and lying in a pool of blood—I couldn't think of it without tears stinging my eyes, and I couldn't *stop* thinking of it. If Sam hadn't texted me, if Randy hadn't been willing to run into that trailer, Boyce might have bled to death. He wouldn't be lying in that bed holding my cold hand.

As if he knew the direction of my thoughts, Boyce squeezed my hand and brought me back to the present. "I've got too much living to do to let a little bullet stop me." He smiled wearily at the sheriff, eyelids heavy. "I'm feeling dog-tired, Sheriff Walker. Is that all you need for now?"

"Yessir, that'll do it for now." He jumped up and gathered his things. "The DA is gonna want his shot atcha—sorry—wrong choice of words there, *heh-heh*. He'll be wanting statements from both of you. We'll be in touch."

After he'd hustled from the room, I asked, "Should I leave so you can sleep for a bit?"

"Hell, no." Boyce's mouth twisted into a roguish grin. "I want you up on this bed so I can claim my reward."

"I don't want to hurt you—"

"Then get that pretty mouth up here. This body denied a *bullet*, baby." He gestured to the body in question, both arms wide. "The only thing killing me right now is not touching you. Boyce Fucking Wynn has to live up to his middle name, and I can't do that without you."

"You and your *middle name* did just fine without me for a while."

He tugged my hand and winked. "Naw, baby, I just got by. I was saving the good stuff for you."

I laughed, settling gingerly onto his left side regardless of his claims of bulletproofness. "Oh, were you now."

Pulling me close, he held me against his shoulder, tipping my chin, fingers spreading to cradle my head, thumb caressing my face. "There was no one before you, and anyone in between was my sorry-assed attempt to ignore what I thought I couldn't have. You broke my heart every time I saw you, sweetheart."

"I'm sorry," I whispered, dragging my fingers over the planes of his face, watching him close those beautiful eyes that had never once lied to me and lean into my hand. "I'll never break it again."

Tugging me higher, his breath whispered over my mouth. "Do these lips belong to me?"

"Yes." I smiled and he pressed his lips to mine softly—a murmur of a kiss.

"And those dark eyes—I could sink and drown in those eyes—are they mine too?"

I nodded, lids falling closed as he touched feather-soft kisses across them. My fingers curled and slid to his neck.

He kissed me again—sweeping his tongue through my mouth as his callused hand skimmed down my arm to press our palms together. "And this hand that could lead me anywhere and I'd follow?" He threaded his fingers through mine and turned the back of my hand to his mouth for a kiss.

"Yes."

His left hand stroked over my hip and curved over my side. "This body," he whispered, trailing our joined hands down the center of my chest. "Will it surrender under my hands? If I swear to worship you from the top of your head to your toes and *everyfuckingthing* between?" At my nod, he left my hand low on my belly, his palm roaming back to cover my heart. "And this heart, above all else. Does this heart belong to me?"

"All yours," I said. "Always yours."

The realization that followed was like the sun surrounding his head the day I died and didn't die. That little boy, kneeling at my side, holding my hand, telling me to wake up—he didn't have a perfect life, but he hadn't been damaged yet. He hadn't been disappointed and misunderstood, neglected and battered. He hadn't suffered the loss that was coming for him.

He hadn't needed salvation that day—I had. He had saved me, and his love for me had somehow saved him. I felt no pride about that. Just gratitude and relief that I finally had my finger on the pulse of our shared heart. Not just Boyce's and mine, but everyone we knew and everyone we'd ever known. We were all parts of this interconnected life. We existed for it and because of it and sometimes in spite of it.

Life was part survival and part contentment, and in each other, we'd found both of those things. Whether that was miracle or fate or coincidence, I'd take it. I'd take it with both hands.

tammara webber

Epilogue

Nine months later

BOYCE

"I know this is where I'm supposed to say, 'If you don't want to do this, we can jump in my car and get the fuck outta here.' Sorry, Wynn. She's the best you'll ever do and we both know it." Maxfield chuckled, watching from the second-story window as guests arrived while I paced on the opposite side of the room. "When she's too good for you, man, you don't run. You thank your lucky stars and hold on tight."

"Thanks for the confidence booster, asshole," I grumbled, moving next to him to glance out the window at the cloudless blue sky. Pearl couldn't have ordered a day that looked more like a postcard. Dr. and Mrs. Frank had rented out the whole inn to house all the out-of-town guests, the courtyard for the ceremony, and the dining room for the reception.

Maxfield smirked and grasped my shoulder. "You don't need any more confidence, Wynn. You got *that girl*. All I can figure is you must be fucking amazing in ways I *do not* want to know."

Ray Maxfield knocked and stuck his head around the door. "You boys about ready?"

Maxfield held up a finger. His dad nodded and shut the door.

"In all seriousness, man. It shouldn't be me standing next to you today."

I frowned, confused, but then I knew—*Brent*.

"Since I never knew him, I've talked to a few people about Brent—Thompson and his mom, old Hendrickson, and of course, Arianna. He was a war hero when he died, but first and foremost he was a protective big brother. He was a good man. And he raised a good man." He clapped my shoulder. "He'd be so fucking proud of you."

Fuck. "Maxfield, don't make me lose my shit right now, for chrissakes." My voice shook.

"Almost done—just one more thing." He looked me in the eye. "I didn't have a brother growing up. You're as close as I ever got, and damn if you weren't exactly what I needed. I'm honored to stand up with you today." He jerked me in for a hug and I went easy because I needed a minute. "Don't forget what I said, man," he said. "Just hold on tight."

He slapped my back and I slapped his. We separated and shrugged our shoulders. Torn between the desire to punch him in the face or hug him again, I heaved a deep breath. "Sorry Dover will be standing across from you during the ceremony, by the way."

He shrugged. "This is Pearl's day, and I was over that shit a *long* time ago. My only concern is if she gets catty with Jacqueline, because she will find herself face-first on the ground and eating dirt."

"Oh man, what I'd give to see that. Just… not today." Melody Dover had been almost accepting since Pearl's and my engagement. I reckoned she'd assumed it wouldn't last, but here we were. She still bit my head off when the opportunity arose, and she'd cornered me for a convincing *Hurt my girl and I'll cut your nuts off* speech night before last, but I sorta respected her for that.

"I'll ask Jacqueline to hold off on any ass-kicking until *after* the reception."

"Deal. You got the ring?"

He pulled a small pouch from his pocket. "Got it. Randy outdid himself."

I'd gone to Thompson last fall and told him what I wanted. A ruby stone for her July birthday. A few small diamonds. A design with all the stones completely inset so she could slide lab gloves over it and whatever else she did for work or research without catching it on anything. The ideas he sketched out were cool, but they didn't do justice to the finished product.

When she was home for winter break, I brought her to my place on Christmas Eve. "I have one more gift for you," I said, leaving her standing in the middle of the living room with no lights on but the ones strung through the tree in the corner. "Stay right here."

The Christmas tree was the first one that trailer had seen since I was seven years old. I'd threaded white lights all over it and called it done, which was all manner of wrong according to Sam. "Jeez—lazy much? Where are the ornaments?" she'd said. "It looks dumb with just lights."

"I don't have any," I'd admitted. "I haven't had a tree since I was a kid."

She'd shown up with four boxes of shiny ornaments from Walmart the next day. "Merry Christmas from me and Dad. It's sorta lame to give you Christmas ornaments *for Christmas*, but I had no choice."

When I brought a kitchen chair out to the living room and sat Pearl in it, facing the tree, her expression was a blend of a worry, laughter, and total confusion. "Boyce...? We set gift limits—you made me promise not to go beyond them! What—"

I knelt in front of her and she sucked in a breath and fell silent.

I took her left hand, pretty sure we were both shaking. I just hoped to hell it wasn't all me. "Once upon a time, an undeserving boy pulled a little half-drowned, wannabe mermaid out of the ocean. He laid her on the sand, thinking his heart would break if she didn't wake up. The moment she opened her big dark eyes and looked up at him, his heart wasn't his anymore. After that moment, his life's quest wasn't a matter of searching for his other half, because he knew right where she was. His mission was waiting for her to know he'd left his heart in her hand that day on the beach and hoping that someday it would bring her back to him."

She raised her trembling right hand and covered her mouth. Glassy with tears, her eyes reflected the lights from the tree like handfuls of stars in a clear midnight sky.

I pulled the small, carved driftwood box Thompson had converted into a ring box from my front pocket and opened the lid. "Pearl Torres Frank, I want to have you and hold you and love you for as long as we both shall live. Will you let me do that, sweetheart?"

She nodded and burst into tears.

I'd waited five more months for her to come home. Five months for me to have that trailer hauled off and a little house erected in its place with help from Vega and Thompson and a few customers who were happy to barter construction services for car maintenance and repairs. Five months to develop the cold feet I never got. Maxfield had nothing to worry about on that score. I knew what I wanted, and I was about to stand under a flower-covered arch in front of half the town and get it.

Whether Pearl believed in luck or not didn't matter. I believed enough for the both of us.

SWEET

Pearl

This morning, I woke up in my bedroom for the last time. I was only moving ten minutes away—again—but for a happier reason. Mama brought me coffee to wake me up, but I'd been lying awake, thinking, for at least an hour. When she opened the door, I sat up and slid my glasses on. "Morning, Mama."

She perched on the edge of the bed, her dark hair damp from an early shower. She and Thomas liked to get up at dawn every day and watch the sunrise from the little terrace off their room, Tux on one lap or the other. They were in love, but they'd become best friends. Boyce and I were best friends who'd fallen in love. Our way to each other was more convoluted than theirs had been, but we'd come to the same good end, no matter the path.

"No second thoughts, *mija*?"

I took the mug from her and smiled. "None."

She cupped my face and kissed my nose. "Good."

· · · · · · · · · ·

Mel and I peered out the window. The courtyard was filled to the brim with flowers and people. I spotted Mr. and Mrs. Thompson next to Mrs. Echols, who'd started bringing Boyce cookies and casseroles after he was shot and hadn't ever stopped. Lucas's girl, Jacqueline, sat next to the Hellers—Carlie, Cindy, and Charles. They had given me the perfect grad-school home for the past nine months. Next to them were Ray and Arianna Maxfield, who'd shocked the entire town last October when they eloped to Houston for a shotgun justice-of-the-peace wedding before anyone even knew they were seeing each other. Their spontaneity became more obvious around Christmas when Arianna started showing. Lucas's little sister was due next month.

Sam wheeled down the aisle just ahead of her dad. In thanks for her assistance at Wynn's while he was recuperating, Boyce had helped Mr. Adams find a used, adapted truck for her seventeenth birthday last week. The girl who loved cars finally had her own. She'd driven herself and her dad here—Brit and I watched her taking five minutes to park it *exactly* between the lines in the lot.

"New drivers." Brit laughed. "Give her two weeks. She'll be lurching that thing into a spot inside five seconds, lines be damned."

Sam had also instructed me to aim for her with the bouquet. "It's not like I can lunge for it," she said. "I might run over somebody's toe."

I told her I'd do my best.

Mel told me to aim as far from her as possible. "I do *not* wanna hear it from my mother," she said. "If that thing comes my way, I swear I will spike it like a volleyball."

Mr. and Mrs. Dover were seated behind the seats reserved for my parents, who tolerated them the same way Boyce tolerated their daughter—with frequent asides.

Any minute Lucas and Boyce would take their places, Randy or Mateo would lead my mother to the front, and the wedding march would begin. The little Vega boys had been appointed to toss flower petals ahead of the wedding party. I didn't see Yvette, but she'd promised to personally send them down the aisle—on the other end of which their father would be stationed.

Shanice and Brit had gone downstairs to check that everything was in place.

"You do realize how bizarre it is that you've got *Brittney Loper* in your wedding party, right?" Mel said. "Even if she did plant the *get married* seed in both y'all's heads, the crazy bitch."

I smiled. "Yeah. It's weird—but she's one of the kindest people I've ever met. And she cried and squealed like a pageant winner when I showed her the ring Randy designed." I'd worn that engagement ring for almost five months. My hand felt naked without it.

"Your boy does have decent taste in jewelry. *There's* a shock."

"C'mon, admit he's grown on you."

She sighed with her entire body. "A little. But mostly since he stopped calling me Dover." When I pinned my lips together, she rolled her eyes. "To my *face*, at least."

Shanice and Brit came in the room then. "They're almost ready!" Brit said, joining us at the window. "Look, there's Boyce and Landon—Lucas—whatever he goes by now. *Rawr.* They look hot as a couple jalapeños."

Mel rolled her eyes and Shanice tried and failed to stifle a giggle, joining us.

"Wait! You aren't supposed to see him yet!" Brit said, taking me by the shoulders and walking me backward, away from the window.

"Pretty sure that rule is for the *groom*?" Mel said.

"Huh—maybe you're right, but I don't believe in taking any chances. Plus, he might look up and see her! No bad luck is happening to these nuptials on *my* watch." She reached to pull a few coils out of my updo, which Mel had spent an hour doing.

"Wh… what… *what* are you *doing*?" Mel sputtered.

Brit turned me toward the full-length mirror in the corner. A curl fell down the left side of my face and a few smaller strands fell down my back. "A man likes a girl to be a little bit disheveled. Kinda like a loose thread on a sweater. He just can't help but wanna *pull* it."

"This is her *wedding day*, not a *hoedown*!"

Brit was undeterred. "When a bride goes down the aisle toward her guy, she doesn't want him thinking about being shackled to perfection the rest of his natural born days. No man can live up to that. If she's smart"—she winked at me—"she wants him to ponder that little thread and how much he's going to enjoy pullin' it all the way loose later on."

"She looks gorgeous, Melody," Shanice said, giving my hand a covert squeeze. "You did a fabulous job on her hair and makeup. Brittney's tweak just adds that touch of *sexy* to the elegance."

A knock sounded on the door.

"Come in!" Brit called.

Thomas stuck his head in and smiled. I smoothed my hands over the embroidered bodice as Mel arranged my veil.

"Oh, Pearl, you look beautiful," he said, crossing the room and taking my hands in his. "You ready, little girl?"

"Aww," my bridesmaids said in unison—likely the first and last united opinion of the day for the three of them.

I nodded, suddenly nervous. Spotlights were not one of my favorite things.

"It'll be over soon," Thomas promised. "Grin and bear it."

I grimaced and he smiled. He'd given me the same advice before my valedictorian speech five years ago.

The ceremony was a blur. Boyce and I repeated vows, exchanged rings, kissed in front of everyone—and all I retained at the end of it all was the dark green of his eyes, steady on mine with every step I took and every word I said. Once Thomas put my hand in Boyce's, he never let go. His voice was calm and sure. It made all the buzzing anxiety go soft, like footfalls on a forest floor. Before I knew it, we were presented as Boyce and Pearl Wynn, and he leaned close.

"Now *that's* a Wynn-win," he said, and we laughed.

BOYCE

I carried my new wife up the steps and into our house. She hadn't been allowed to the top floor yet. A quarter of the footprint of the rest of the place, it was surrounded with a widow's walk wide enough for a couple of chairs, accessed by french doors. In the distance, the gulf was just visible—a sliver of water below a sky that ranged pale gray to bright blue, depending on the weather's mood. It wasn't the bay view her parents had, but she swore she didn't need that.

The bottom floor was a double carport—no more bedroom windows up against the side of the garage. The second-floor living quarters were brighter on cloudy days than that trailer had been in midsummer, and our bedroom had a bed like the one in that hotel in Houston. I was looking forward to performing my husbandly duties in that bed, but first I wanted to show her the top floor.

Instead of setting her down once we got inside, I walked straight to the winding staircase and put her over my shoulder because it was way too narrow to carry her up any other way. I probably didn't have to steady her with my hand on her ass, but hell—there was no reason *not* to.

"Boyce!" She laughed, holding on to the back of my shirt.

There was no door—the staircase emerged into the center of a blue room, windowed on all four sides. I'd installed a big L-shaped desk into one corner—the one facing the gulf—and a sectional sofa in the opposite corner. Above the windows and the doors to the widow's walk was a continuous shelf. On it were whelk shells I'd collected over the past few months—a couple hundred of them in just about every size. None were as big as that first one, which sat on her new desk.

I put her on her feet and watched her walk around, peeking out the windows, trailing her fingers over the reclaimed-wood desk, the upholstered desk chair, her diploma on the wall—space for the next one just over it. She touched the glued-together shell I'd given her when she was a pretty little fourteen-year-old who'd turned my world upside down with one kiss.

After walking around the room twice she returned, cuddled her hands on my chest and stared up at me. "This room is—?"

"Yours. You've got three or four more years of school, and though I'll welcome you in your sexy little glasses at the kitchen table anytime, I reckoned you needed a room all your own."

One tear and then another tumbled down her cheeks and her lower lip wobbled.

"Happy crying?" I said, winding that escaping curl around my finger, tucking it behind her ear.

Her hiccup of laughter made the rest of those tears spill, and her nodding smile was the clincher. "So happy. You?"

I slid my arms around her and pulled her close. "I'm the happiest son of a bitch in this whole damn state." One thin strap slipped off her shoulder, and that coil popped back out from behind her ear, and in our positions there was no hiding what would make me even happier.

She raised one brow and gave me a sharp look. "I think that sofa behind you needs some breaking in." She stretched on her toes and kissed my chin.

I lifted her just off the ground and strode backward, kissing her, until my calves hit that sofa, where I paused. "In your wedding dress?"

She pushed me down, lifted her skirt just enough to get it out of the way, and straddled me. Eyes shining, she bit her lip on that naughty grin she got sometimes. "Not like I'm planning to wear it again, right?"

I shook my head and wasn't sure where to start—the one million buttons down the back of that dress or the hundreds of hairpins in her hair. She reached up and started pulling pins out and tossing them to the floor. *Buttons it is.*

"Sweetheart," I said, kissing her while threading buttons the size of baby teeth through equally small holes, "I know you don't believe in luck, but you'll never convince me it doesn't exist. Because I know for a fact that I am one *lucky* man."

tammara webber

Acknowledgments

To every reader who takes a chance on me as a storyteller, who chooses to spend time with my characters and their stories, please accept my sincere gratitude. I couldn't do what I do without you. You cheer my heart and touch my soul every day with your support and love.

I would never say that an author can't write in a vacuum, but I'm grateful that I don't have to do so. Many thanks to the people who help make me a better writer: my critique partner, Tracey Garvis Graves; my beta readers, Colleen Hoover, Robin Deeslie, and Hannah Webber; and my new editor, Anne Victory, and her team of oops-catchers.

Thank you to my husband, Paul, for the miracle of over thirty years spent in love with you. You inspire every story in my heart and every moment of swoon in my imagination. Your voice shows through in every lead man I've written. Boyce owes getting a book of his own to your belief in him and the fact that *you* wanted his story before anyone else had a chance to.

Very special thanks to Cammie Hyatt of UTMSI, who is as passionate about marine biology as I am about writing. She provided great insight into the work of researchers who study the effects of everything from overfishing to protected habitats to disasters like crude-oil spills and the associated cleanup efforts. Thank you, Cammie, for the campus and lab tour and for spending your valuable time in person and through e-mail to help a nonscientific fiction writer understand her scientifically-minded character!

Thank you yet again to my amazing team at Dystel & Goderich. I feel so much support for what I do from everyone I've ever had the pleasure of dealing with there. Special thanks to my agent, Jane Dystel, and my foreign-rights agent, Lauren Abramo, who are tireless in their efforts on my behalf. You two are Wonder Women.

One of my favorite contemporary quotes is from author Stephen Chbosky: "We accept the love we think we deserve." (*The Perks of Being a Wallflower*, 1999.) Dear everyone who is accepting love that is less than you deserve: Let go *now*. Don't wait until circumstances align. Don't wait until you're less scared, less weak, less flawed. Be afraid. Be fragile. Be imperfect. Respect yourself as you are and demand that same level of esteem from those you choose to give your heart to, because you are worthy of it right now. Please don't be afraid to be alone, because you'll discover just how strong you really are and you'll fall in love with yourself again. Create a divine void that can be filled by the love you really do deserve and nothing less.

About the Author

I'm a hopeful romantic who adores novels with happy endings, because there are enough sad endings in real life. Before writing full time, I was an undergraduate academic advisor, economics tutor, planetarium office manager, radiology call center rep, and the palest person to ever work at a tanning salon. I married my high school sweetheart, and I'm Mom to three adult kids and four very immature cats.

TammaraWebber.com
Facebook.com/TammaraWebberAuthor
Twitter.com/TammaraWebber